One who knows the Mississippi will promptly aver—not aloud but to himself—that ten thousand River Commissions . . . cannot tame that lawless stream, cannot curb it, or confine it, cannot say to it, "Go here," or "Go there"; and cannot make it obey . . . cannot bar its path with an obstruction which it will not tear down, dance over, and laugh at.

Mark Twain, *Life on the Mississippi*, 1879

The Unusual Adoption

by
Mark R. Sneller

Published by Fresh Air Press

Visit Mark's website at
markrsneller.com

This edition was prepared for publication by
Ghost River Images
5350 East Fourth Street
Tucson, Arizona 85711
www.ghostriverimages.com

ISBN 979-8-9881588-4-4

Library of Congress Control Number: 2024903856

Published in the United States of America
July 2024

Other books Mark R. Sneller:

A Breath of Fresh Air

Greener Cleaner Indoor Air

Greener Cleaner Indoor Air – 2nd Edition

The Jeffrey Shenero Series

- *Toxic Exposure*
- *Dying to Read*
- *Rising To Eminence*

The Mars Virus Series

- *The Mars Virus*
- *The City Beneath the Earth*
- *Treasures*
- *Soap Opera*

Strange Adventures

Miners' Revenge

The Mongolian

The Persian Connection

PREFACE

Raj and his twin sister, Aruna, were second generation ragpickers, a term used universally for those who pick up trash for a living. Less than a year before, on their seventh birthday, their parents moved to the giant trash landfill outside Delhi, India, one of four major dumps surrounding the city, "landfill" being the operative word.

This one was different from the old dump site down in Mumbai short miles from the oily ship-dismantling yard. This one promised to bring in riches. Their father had paid good money to find out where the trucks dumped the countless tons of garbage that originated from the richer sections of the city. Waste had accumulated for well over a century. It was in a particular locale where the family set up their makeshift dwelling, among so many others on the less dense east side of the huge mound that measured some 200 feet tall at its peak with lower foothills on four sides. The dump site occupied some 300 acres. Housing, now such as it was, surrounded the hillocks to constitute another 1000 acres.

The four saw good fortune continue to go their way as they managed to find room atop a modern express train for the ride to Delhi; a ride that would last approximately 22 hours. Some 70,000 miles of rail system criss-crossed the country, a gift from Britain when India gained its independence in 1947. That system, along with the postal service and the English language, helped propel the subcontinent into a world powerhouse. The Singh family, however, could care less about the nation as a whole.

The instant the train stopped at the station, passengers streamed from the cars, or climbed down from the roof tops to be replaced by waiting throngs who scrabbled on; a swirling maelstrom of bodies each with its own purpose, many spitting red juice of the areca nut mixed with tobacco angering those who chanced to be in the line of fire.

The Singhs entered the large stationhouse to use the facilities and to find potable water. An electronic sign flashed 105° F or 41° C. The hour was too late for them to begin the ten mile trek to the dump site, so they found an unoccupied spot on the concrete outdoor platform to claim as their own to spend the night among other travelers of their ilk. At first light, the four would begin a new life.

Their possessions were meager. These consisted of some cookware, minimal clothing, a few bottles of water, some personal possessions, and a few rags to sleep on. Only the absolute essentials were taken. Once at the final stop, the family would rely on their skills as thieves to take what they needed from others in their community when those same others were at work. There would be tens of thousands climbing onto and picking apart the mountains and hillocks of trash, doing the recycling the city promised to do, but never delivered.

At dawn, the family ate a meager breakfast of cold lentils and shared six ounces of water buffalo milk purchased at the station; both food sources rich enough in nutrients to keep them going until dinner, which would consist of more lentils and some rice.

Their walk took them through the bustling city of Delhi into Old Delhi, through oppressive heat and eye-searing smog, wending their way through a gray pall that stank of diesel exhaust from double-decker buses and lorries, avoiding bullock carts, cow paddies and scooters, completely unnoticed among a city of 17 million.

At last, outlying city structures passed them behind and a looming mountain stood in the distance—their destination. The odor of the smog was replaced by a stink associated with the pile of cans, bottles, metals, clothing, discarded food, plastics, decomposing plant matter, broken furniture, and whatever people decided to discard, all of which constituted their destination.

The careful observer would notice several areas of smoldering trash, fueled by bacterial action and aided by the ever present methane. Experts had calculated that this site alone contributed thousands of metric tons of the gas to the atmosphere each day, equal to the exhaust of nearly half-million cars. Over 3000 of these sites were present throughout the country. Most were smaller, few more impressive. The four considered themselves to be fortunate enough to be working at the best of the best.

Reality dictated they establish a home site among the other pickers while also hunting for marketable items. Skill and experience allowed this to occur in short order and soon, plastic trash bags were filled with non-sharp items to be stacked in a square with a small opening in the front through which one could crawl. Sleep for the Singhs would be on pieces of cardboard spread on a floor of dirt, swept clean of insects on a daily basis by their industrious mother.

Long since experienced in such work, the children slung a bag over each shoulder, one for plastic bottles, the other for metals and other valuables. Once out of the hut they made their way through the maze of hundreds of makeshift dwellings and piles of sleeping rags. These dotted the terrain like errant leavings tossed about after a tornado had struck civilization. The parents ensured their own sandals were secured, and then headed in the same direction. This time they would climb as high as possible; climb to where no man has gone before, initially overstepping areas of toxic slush that could pool at any given area around the base where rats scurried.

India had legally outlawed the caste system decades before. This changed little over time because whiter skin was preferred over darker skin, caste system or no caste system. Many middle and upper class women used talc and other means to whiten their faces in order to appear more attractive. Not so on the trash heap. Nobody had time for such foolishness where everyone was equal. Collecting, trading, and selling to local waste buyers was the order of the day. Survival outranked prejudice.

The family of four possessed a pair of stout sticks each some 3' in length sharpened at one end which they shared to push trash aside for a closer look at what lay beneath the surface. This minimized the chances of getting stabbed by needles, or cut by shards of broken glass. It also gave the Singh family an advantage over most of the hundreds of thousands of ragpickers who scour the four waste sites of the city, playing a major role in the informal recycling workforce.

However, the real strength of the family lay in their secret—an exceptionally strong magnet recovered by the father years before. As valuable as gold, in its own way, the magnet was securely attached to the end of one of the wooden poles for the attraction of metals, which brought in more money than plastic bottles. The real treat came when a discarded cell phone would be recovered. These promised to be more numerous in the area in which the family now worked. Aruna held the pole with the magnet and it was Aruna who did recover a phone on their first outing in their new digs.

When she pulled up the pole and found the phone attached, she signaled her brother, who was some 50' above her. He worked his way down and she surreptitiously showed him what she had recovered, lest other children and pickers decide to make it their own. The wooden spiked poles would serve as a deterrent to that line of action, and both children were skilled at using them without hesitation and without remorse. They also served as effective defense against feral dogs that roamed the area, or to chase away the countless crows landing and pecking for food, no different than the humans in some regards.

This particular waste site was so old and huge that it had compacted into a mountain. It had become so dense, in fact, that bulldozers had formed switchback roads leading where a never ending stream of dump trucks could take the trash to the top. It was along one of these roads that the children hiked, working the base of the mountain behind where old spillage fell for easy pickings compared with the thousands of tons of compressed matter above it.

After the day's work and the family evaluated their finds, Raj would go to the local buyer and receive some value for their efforts. At home, the phone would be evaluated by the four. From a small change purse the mother had found years before and always kept on her person, she would pull out enough money for its repair. Sometimes a new screen would be required, sometimes a new battery. A charger would do them no good in the complete absence of electricity, but if one could be obtained, an occasional odyssey into an electrified area would prove rewarding. In the evening, the Singh's would huddle around it to watch part of a movie, or play some game, perhaps even make a phone call, until the battery ran out. Use it till it's gone. No saving for tomorrow. The mantra of basic evolution was alive and well.

The scene shifted to the reporter for CNN. She was dressed in sneakers, blue jeans, T-shirt and baseball cap with hair emerging from the opening at the back of the cap. A former beauty queen and runway model, most would call her black, others might say the witty Melanie Brown engaged the viewer as appearing to be a rich shade of dark oak. The fearless, tall, beloved, veteran reporter was highly personable. She had no desires to go into the movie business and had no desire to memorize lines. She began as a fledgling reporter who became top dog after ten years. At some point, she wanted to get into CNN management and would take the risks to do so.

Melanie stood in the early dawn hours of Delhi at the edge of a sea of cardboard makeshift homes and filled plastic bags that served as dwellings for the ragpickers. Many slept and cooked in the open air with the use of open fire pits, or charcoal in metal pots. A cacophony of background sounds split the air, comprised of arguments, the clanking of cans, dogs fighting, and the cawing of crows. Someone in the distance played a small wind instrument.

The reporter announced herself to the viewing audience; then she waved away a fly before stooping to speak with two emaciated very dark-skinned children, ostensibly seven years of age, dressed in dirty tatters. Each held a three-foot wooden staff, as though it were a spear. Indeed, one end had been sharpened to a point. Flies buzzed about her as knelt.

Before she spoke she said to the viewing audience, "Today's program is not for the faint of heart. The community of ragpickers has no health care, no salaries, and they work without gloves. Their hands are unwashed. They have no protection from the elements. They are subjected to countless diseases including HIV, worms, hepatitis, typhus, Dengue fever, tuberculosis, dysentery, skin lesions, and boils, to name a few, because those diseases are in the trash they pick at, or is rampant throughout the community. It is the rare person who lives life to its full life potential here."

Holding the microphone in front of the children, she asked, "Can you tell us your names? Do you speak English?"

"My name is Raj and this is Aruna," the boy announced proudly, in perfect English, more akin to British English than American English.

"Where are your parents?" the reporter asked.

"Mum died last week from coughing and bapu died last month from a landslide over there," Aruna offered, pointing.

Neither child seemed phased by the loss of their parents, apparently inured to the presence of death in the lives they led.

"Have you always lived here and don't you have any other family?" asked the reporter.

"We came here from Mumbai last year on the train," said Raj, without a trace of emotion, in the manner of saying, "That was a dumb question. What are we going to do, take a rickshaw?"

"We don't have a family?" Aruna added, as calmly as if she were enumerating the number of rats she had speared for fun.

A plane flew in low, coming from the southwest, possibly from Mumbai to land at Indira Gandhi International Airport. The reporter halted her questioning, as another came in from due east, possible from Kolkata or Bangkok. Finally free of jet noise, she switched to a different line of questioning. "What are those sticks for?"

"For digging and fighting," Raj announced proudly, twirling the stick like a staff, jabbing and poking front and back.

The camera came in for a close-up of the children. They were both handsome, yet terribly underweight by Western standards. Flies buzzed around open sores on their faces and the exposed portions of their lower legs.

A crowd had begun to gather, a regular occurrence whenever a news crew interviewed people. In this case, most of them were children, some trying to insert their faces into the camera.

Melanie laughed good-heartedly and tossed away a handful of wrapped pieces of candy she pulled from one pocket to momentarily scatter the group.

One of them remained; a sandaled, short, toothless gray-haired woman who was braless beneath her ragged brown sari. She took a drag off a stubby cigar she had found somewhere and asked the children in Hindi what was going on.

Their native tongue was Marathi, which they

only spoke to each other, but had picked up limited Hindi, out of a matter of survival since moving to their new location. Most Indians spoke two or more languages for the same reason, with more than 22 languages spoken in the country. It was as though one were in Europe traveling from one country to another, or, indeed, traveling from one state to another in the U.S. Aruna told the crone that this was for television, which broadened the grin of the visitor.

She asked if they could film her. Aruna translated for Melanie who watched the exchange with interest. Her love of native peoples was evident during her interviews.

Always ready to oblige, Melanie told Aruna to tell the woman they would love to film her, giving Brandon the nod. The old gal adjusted her sari, swept back her hair, and said a few words into the camera without a thought to the cigar held between first and second fingers.

Once she had given her short speech, she closed her fist and put her mouth to its end, drawing in smoke in that manner.

"What did she say?" Melanie asked.

Raj answered, "She said she can tell her friends she is a movie star."

Little did the woman know that a single picture of her would grace the cover of magazines around the world.

"Just a few more questions," Melanie continued, seeing the two children in front of her, eying the trash heap, anxious to get to work. "Do you like living here?"

Aruna shrugged, in a universal gesture of neutrality, "This is our home. What's to like or not to like?"

At that, she nudged her brother and both ran off. The twins were already late for work.

PART ONE

1

Hayden Lake is a suburb of Couer d'Alene located in northern Idaho with a population approximating 600. The lake itself is tree-lined with sandy beaches and ringed with homes. The lake brags various cold and warm-water fish, such as salmon, trout, northern pike, sunfish, perch, and bass. Until recently, the community was home to the Aryan Nations White Supremacy Organization, comprised of members of the KKK, skinheads, and anti-Semitic hate groups that had spread from Hayden to some 15 states.

Pale of skin, the blue-eyed, blond haired Arthur Tremont grew up in the Township of Hayden Lake. As he grew into adulthood, Tremont led rallies in a number of cities, but was never caught, nor convicted of a crime. No fingerprints remained on record.

Governmental charges, law suits, and wholesale imprisonment of members by state and federal authorities closed down the local chapter, although die-hard members continued to recruit while behind bars. The more educated factions began their own newsletter.

When he wasn't causing mayhem, Tremont's father, Jonathan, a die-hard racist, constructed homes, a trade he passed on to his son. The man had bragged that if it were over a century ago, he would be a plantation slave owner and contribute what he could to the Confederacy.

Smelling trouble in the wind, Jonathan pried loose a reluctant Arthur from a number of romantic entanglements, and sent him south to Arizona to make his escape and to start a new life. Researching construction companies in the Phoenix area, Arthur selected one named Adolph Construction. He found the company to be in need of licensed contractors, passed the interview, and was hired to find suppliers for building materials.

The job would require travel. After a number of years and having made numerous unreported return visits to his home state, the personable Tremont was repairing the interior of a home in Phoenix belonging to a widow named Christina Rossi, a well-maintained stalwart Italian woman who preferred to keep her graying hair dyed black through frequent visits to the beauty parlor. The two quickly found companionship in one another. The woman had been alone for so long, she believed the time had come to find a mate. Arthur immediately found himself in a large house by a lake in the northern portion of the city, a far cry from the single bedroom apartment he had been occupying. Over the years he maintained a cordial relationship with his wife's son and daughter in law, as long as politics were not discussed, a common avoidance among many, if not most, deeply divided American families. He was also introduced to Christina's son's next door neighbor, Hans Hobert, his wife, Klara, and their two boys, a mere half-hour drive from their residence.

Once Arthur found the couple was of German heritage, he demonstrated his knowledge of German history, proudly claiming that he, too, had German blood.

2

Anthony and Megan Rossi sat before the television, holding hands, transfixed by what they were watching unfold on the other side of the world. A drone flew over one of the largest waste dumps on the planet, some 200 feet in height and spreading out over 300 acres. Children and adults climbed over it like ants, picking select items of trash which they placed in various sized plastic bags for recycling.

Anthony Rossi previously held the position of General Manager of ReCyclo, one of the largest recycling companies in the country. Upon the sudden death of his father, owner of the company, he now moved up the ladder to oversee thirty employees, part of an industry that had grown to over $90 billion annually.

It took him time to adjust to civilian life after spending three years with the Army Rangers in two different theaters of war. His father, a former Sergeant in the army, insisted Tony join the military before he began in the business and left the choice of which branch to join to his son. Furthermore, after the service, he needed a degree in engineering to make him eligible through government mandate to run the company at some point.

Thus, after two years of college studying math, and not wanting to join an outfit that had little chance of action, he chose what he considered the best; the 75th Ranger Regiment.

He soon found himself in Georgia, USA, for two months of insanely intense training in both jungle and mountainous terrains, day and night torture, averaging 3-4 hours of sleep a night.

He'd be damned if he was going to be among the 50% that quit. The thought of getting mocked by his father drove him to complete the program. The military considered him prepared for action.

When he finally returned home, he took two months to decompress with lingering tendrils of war and bloodshed represented in dreams and changes in everyday behavioral patterns.

Furloughs between assignments had prevented total burnout. Finally, he went back to school to earn a degree in engineering. It was his strength, not his preference. He wanted to become a draftsman. However, not willing the break away from his father, he announced his readiness to accept the job, which lasted only two years. The sudden death of Anthony Rossi Sr. reorganized Tony's life.

Two years later he found himself congratulating his mother upon her remarriage; doubtless on the rebound and in need of companionship. He hoped she would be compatible with a man who asked her opinion rather than giving it to her. She did find acceptable companionship with Arthur Tremont, who now owned a home-remodeling business, but who never hired any people of color to work under him. Other than that, Tremont was secure and confident in himself. Tony considered him a smooth talking blond-haired pretty boy, but as long as he treated his mother right, what the heck.

Now, watching the TV special on India, Megan blurted, “Tony, I want those children.”

“It’s so sad,” he said, not getting the gist of her statement.

“No, Tony, I want *those* two children. Can you get them for us?”

Tony let go of her hand to stare hard at his wife, her blue eyes flashing, her Irish spirit giving no quarter, then returned to the television to learn more, at the same time digesting what she had said and, more importantly, the way she had said it.

Megan O’Reilly had come from a family of five children growing up in Fort Collins, Colorado. In close proximity to Denver to the south her parents insisted she attend the University of Colorado. Megan had other ideas. The year her parents pleaded with her to stay, a blizzard had rolled through. Typically, cold blasts and two feet of snow will last for short periods. This year, the temperature dropped to 20 below. Anybody who walked outdoors for five minutes could be legitimately called frosty the snowman.

"No, thanks, I've already been accepted to Arizona State University down in Phoenix. During the summers I'm going to feel like a duck roasting on a spit and love every minute of it," she told them.

She took her meager savings, along with a modest contribution from her parents, and headed south moving into a dorm. She soon found a job in the administrative offices of the school because she could type virtually error free at 60-70 words per minute. A few months after her arrival a co-worker sold her an old junk car her husband was trying to get rid of which gave her the mobility she missed.

During her junior year she met Tony, fresh back from the service who was trying to finish his engineering degree. After they were married he went to work for ReCyclo and she went into elementary school teaching.

Having lost two children during her pregnancies, she didn't want to go through the torment again and had her tubes tied, all while she continued to teach. She and Tony had discussed adoption on a number of occasions, but never made the move. Now she wanted *those* two children.

In contrast, Tony was a single child who

came from Italian-Greek blood, the Italian part from his father's side.

Megan's attention diverted from her husband to the famed reporter, who asked the children, sweetly and gently, "What were you doing in Mumbai?"

"We found things to sell, like now," answered Aruna.

"How did you get here?" inquired the reporter.

Raj replied, "We came on top of the train. Bapu said he found a special place for us."

"And is it special?" Melanie asked.

"Oh, yes, we are rich now," beamed Raj.

A voice could be heard in the background saying something in English. Melanie looked up at the camera from where the voice had originated, listened, then she returned to the children asking, mostly for the viewer's sake, "That's a whole day on top of a train."

"A day and a night," replied Aruna, proudly.

"Bapu said it was an express train," interjected Raj. Almost lamenting, he added, "On another train we could ride maybe two or three days."

"Can you show me where you live?" asked Melanie.

Tony and Megan stared at the screen, almost cringing at the thought of what they might see where these orphans called home.

Melanie stood and walked behind the two children followed by the camera. An occasional crying baby could be heard. She looked ahead to ensure she didn't trip on any landmines, occasionally glancing at the camera. She said, "The children came from Mumbai, which used to be called Bombay in my day. With a population of some 13 million, the city was built on a landfill. Here, in Delhi, there are 300,000 of these people they call ragpickers, almost half of whom are children. From what I'm told most of the children are illiterate.

"Until recently, India had no recycling industry. Even today, it is a fledgling industry. Without these workers and others like them who go door to door, or pick up trash from the streets, there would be no recycling whatsoever. Just as in Britain, or in the United States, as the economy grows, along with the population and manufacturing, so does the amount of trash. Experts tell us this country is similar to virtually all other countries. They can recycle as much as possible, but cannot come close to breaking even."

"Spot on," muttered Tony, fixated on the story.

Shortly, they came to a dwelling constructed of plastic trash bags filled with trash and tied off, securely stacked three high on four sides and covered over the top with rags. A small crawlspace had been constructed between the bags on one side through which the children crawled, followed by Melanie and the cameraman named Brandon.

Brandon was once a pale-skinned, blond-haired Brit whose years on the job had darkened his skin, but not his hair. Not viewed by the audience, he was dressed in blue jeans and dark blue polo shirt overhanging his pants.

He was a rugged looking, genial man, who insisted on always wearing work boots rather than sandals wherever his assignment took him. The boots were enough to attract the attention of virtually any Indian, as was the medium-size hand-held digital video recorder he operated. It was rigged with WiFi and assorted electronics, which replaced the old shoulder-mounted behemoth of old.

Within the trash-bag enclosed space, large pieces of cardboard covered the floor some fifty square feet. Compared with makeshift beds out in the open throughout the area, this dwelling was upscale.

Aruna pushed aside some rags to open the top and permit the morning sunlight to enter. "Where did you learn to speak English," Melanie finally asked.

Aruna replied, "Mum and bapu made us speak English here. They were school teachers."

Raj picked up the short tale. "Umma told us that people said our God was different than theirs and burned down our house. They made us all leave. I don't remember a lot."

Clearly confused, Melanie pushed onward, "Didn't they have family somewhere; anybody who could help?"

Raj said, "Bapu said we all lived together. Some got burned up in the fire. Everybody left."

Melanie looked around and said, "Where is your food?"

"We ate it," Aruna replied.

Receiving some unseen signal, Melanie said, "We have to go now. Thank you. We'll let you go to work."

Brandon, closest to the exit, scooted out to face a rising sun, followed by Melanie, followed by the children, who dashed off toward the mountain of trash, spears well in hand for a day's work.

3

Over-watched by his stern and overarching father, Anthony Rossi Junior began his career in the recycling industry by picking up aluminum cans and soda bottles turning them in for cash. He soon learned to scavenge the hot spots, such as trash cans in city parks, dumpsters, and whatever people threw into the garbage in their alleys. He soon found himself successful enough to hire other kids to work for him, paying them for each pound they delivered to him, which he weighed on a bathroom scale, making a good profit. The dirty and arduous business taught him invaluable lessons about turning a profit and managing workers.

Industrious and good with his hands, Tony worked his way through school while employed part time at his father's company. While in school, he fell in love with history and read every spare moment he could, even carrying with him in the service a copy of Sun Tsu's *The Art of War.*

Tony had a love-hate relationship with his Anthony Sr. He hated his authoritarian approach to those around him, but had always appreciated the man's work ethic. It was like proudly saying to a child at his or her birthday, "There, you got everything you wished for," when life dictated otherwise. You rarely got everything you wished for, so don't expect it.

Thanks to his upbringing, an occasionally embittered Tony stood on his own, and was the stronger for it. If, and when, he had children, he would pass on his own views on life, coupled with hard-ass dictates.

He also learned from his father that people talk while money shouts. If you make wise investments, your goals will be obtained sooner. Tony enjoyed the hard labor, picking and sorting, with new machines always entering the picture, from odor reducers in the workplace, to crushing machines, or mandated regulations to either help or hamstring their work—it was all about the challenges.

Tony pushed the pause button on the remote and said, "All right, Meg, what's going on? Talk to me."

Megan shrugged and said, "Oh, nothing. It's not that complicated. It's a calling. We were meant to see the program and we are meant to adopt those two children."

Tony had to smile when he asked, "Who are we going to get to help us with this task?"

Megan responded, "You are, dear. I will contact CNN while you contact immigration and whatever authorities and lawyers are necessary to make the arrangements. Then you and I are going to fly over there to pick them up."

"Oh, is that all. Tell you what. Here's a reasonable suggestion. Why don't we sleep on it?" Tony suggested.

"You sleep on it. I'm calling CNN now," Megan said, and pulled out her cell.

Tony shook his head. There was no stopping this girl. When she got a certain look about her, the world be damned, because here comes Megan. She placed the call to the local affiliate only to find the newsroom had closed for the day, but the hot tip line was open.

She said to the recording, "My name is Megan Rossi. My husband and I saw your broadcast on India this evening and we would like you to help us adopt those two children Melanie Brown interviewed. You can call this number any time day or night. Thank you." She gave the number knowing it was already recorded.

Tony looked at his wife, this time his countenance displayed no amusement. He said, "You are serious. Let's talk about this, shall we? We've discussed the issue of adoption and I gave my total approval. However, this instant decision on your part has me confused. Help me understand, would you dear?"

Megan shook her head slowly and looked off

to the side for a moment before commenting, "I can't explain it. It's like a magnetic pull."

"You mean like when you and I first saw each other?" Tony asked.

"Yes, exactly; that strong. And here we are," Megan said with finality, displaying cheery smile.

Tony scratched his head, having to accept the truth of her statement, while trying to evaluate the consequences. He knew his wife well enough and over the years had learned to pretend concession. "All right, we can give it a good try."

"No, sweetheart, this is not a try, it's a 'take no prisoners' full-on attack to accomplish our goal," Megan Rossi informed him, so bluntly that she connected with one of her husband's basic business philosophies he had learned from his father: "Once you decide to do something, do whatever it takes to make it happen."

Tony also remembered his mother saying, "Your father always got what he wanted. But it didn't always work out for the better."

He pushed the pause button again to watch the remainder of the broadcast. This consisted only of the two children running off to the mountain dominating the landscape.

Preparing for bed two hours later, the couple resolved to find time the next day, between her teaching duties, and his position at the plant, to work on her new project. Tony had every confidence his false promise to follow up on her the flash-in-the-pan impulsive move would disappear almost as fast as it had appeared.

However, the wheels had been set in motion when Megan's cell rang. She looked at the screen to see the same number she had called earlier. "It's CNN," she mouthed to Tony, as though the phone could hear before she picked up.

"Hello," she answered, cautiously.

"Yes, hello, I'm with Cable News Network. We received a call from this number from a Megan Rossi. My apologies if my call is in error."

"No, it's not. This is she," Megan answered, in a business-like manner, with a trace of expectancy thrown in.

"My name is Jimmy Smith. I handle the news tip department, late shift. Could you please reiterated what you said on your recording to us to ensure we are all on the same page?"

"Mr. Smith, I have a degree in journalism and shifted to elementary school teaching for my career where I've been working for a number years. My husband is Tony Rossi, owner and CEO of ReCyclo. We are childless. We saw Melanie Brown in India who interviewed those two children. My husband and I want to begin adoption proceedings."

Tony lay in bed speechless listening to events unfold. Smith was silent for so long Megan was about to ask if he was still there, when he said, "I was having a few words with my tech about this. Are you up for a Skype call on your computer, one that will be recorded?"

Megan pushed the mute button on the phone and looked over at Tony, telling him what Smith had proposed. He gave her a sheepish grin, shrugged, looked down at his pajamas, and held out his hands as if to say, "Whatever, but can I change first? You know, never mind me. I'm just along for the ride."

Megan nodded and said into the phone, "Mr. Smith . . . "

"It's Jimmy."

"Jimmy, give us about ten minutes to get organized. I'll give you our email addresses," Megan said.

"I'll need maybe a half hour or more to get set up on my end, if that's not too long," Smith said. "We like to move on a story before it becomes old news, you understand."

"We'll expect your call," Megan concluded, looking at the clock. It read 10:30 pm, 12:30 am in New York. They did work the late shift out there. By all indications, it would be a late shift for everyone involved.

The break gave the couple time to prepare. Reluctantly, Tony shaved, combed his hair and put on a short-sleeve button down. Megan changed into a non-obtrusive tan blouse and made adjustments to her hair. They ensured the books in the bookcase set against the wall behind her computer were orderly.

When the phone rang and the picture came

through on the computer 45 minutes later, both their faces appeared in a small square in the upper right corner of the screen. The majority of the screen revealed the face of a man in his late forties, clean-shaven, with a mop of curly, dark brown hair and ears that stuck out, somewhat. His face gave off-a business-as-usual appearance. The face of a full-bearded man appeared in another inset.

"Megan, it's Jimmy Smith again. You'll see our producer on your screen, who is also named Jimmy—no relation," he said, with some humor. The producer waved.

From his end, what Smith saw was a blue-eyed round-faced, not quite middle-aged woman with light brown hair swept back at the sides, but not overly styled. She wore the slightest amount of lipstick and a warm smile. Next to her sat a tall man with dark eyes with no facial hair, and black hair parted down one side and sideburns beginning to turn white. He, too, had a bright look about him. No negativity or super weird stuff here, other than the entire subject matter itself.

Smith said, "Mr. and Mrs. Rossi, Tony and Megan, we are going to record this entire conversation, with your permission, including the words I am saying to you now. We reserve the right to portion it into segments as our editors deem appropriate for production purposes, however I will tell you at the outset we will not put words in your mouth and hopefully, your words will not be taken out of context. If you find either is the case, you have the right to make a public correction. Are those terms agreeable?"

The Rossi's looked at each other in silent ESP mode followed by both of their nods with Megan saying, "We agree."

Smith said, "Great, take your time to relate to us why you called CNN so we can have a discussion. And Mr. Rossi, your wife mentioned that you are CEO of ReCyclo. We would also appreciate your input at some point in this interview. At the start, I will mention that we did a little quick research on your request and find you are facing a lot of obstacles."

"Of course, we realize that," Megan replied.

"Just to make certain you understand, according to the Central Adoption Authority of India, which follows The Hague Convention on Adoption Policies, the average time for adoption is 2-4 years at a cost of $30-40 thousand per child. Presumably, you are financially viable and will pass the fingerprinting and background checks. Obviously, you already meet the age requirements. You are aware of those facts, are you not?"

Megan squeezed Tony's hand hard out of shock, while Tony hoped Jimmy wouldn't catch the stutter in his voice. Accustomed to recovering from an adrenaline dump after getting hit with heavy artillery, he said, "Yes, we have made allowance for the money, although the time frame is a little disconcerting." (Tony thought, *Allowances, like taking out a second home loan, selling our investment stocks and wiping out our savings, while the two kids work on the trash heap for another few years. Other than those minor details, no worries.)*

At that, Megan began her story about growing up in a large family, reporting local news and teaching for many years. She wanted badly to adopt, after which Tony connected with the recycling theme, seeing two sides of the same coin, albeit on opposite sides of the world. More importantly, he wanted to join his wife in this venture, focusing on the children's welfare, not their own.

At the conclusion of his narrative, Smith asked, "You folks must have some vision about how to go about this. Is there a deeper calling?"

Tony felt stymied for the moment. This was Megan's deal. It seemed he was all in. He wanted to launch into some platitude about saving the planet, but believing the entire enterprise would soon fall flat, said "Who can explain how love works?"

Smith replied, "Got me there, Tony. Why don't we get back to the children? How exactly do you folks plan to make this adoption happen?"

"Jimmy, we don't have exact anything. This whole enterprise is only some three hours old.

We were hoping you could help us with this," Megan asserted, a note of determination in her voice.

Smith asked, "Not to throw cold water on your desires, but suppose all the hoops are jumped through and everybody signs off on it—I mean, it's hard enough to adopt here in the States—how would you physically obtain the children? Would you have somebody pick them up for you and bring them to . . . where? ReCyclo is in Phoenix, right?

"I can't imagine seeing those two children in proper clothing, let alone them getting on an airplane. You would have to spend time in India itself for all kinds of reasons I can think of."

Tony wasn't about to lose face. "Jimmy, we've traveled to a dozen countries, so we're no strangers of foreign cultures. I'm also a big contributor to Doctors across Borders and we also contribute to organizations that deal with providing sustenance for children in other nations.

"As for why we called CNN, we believe with your support and your push, the time frame might be reduced."

Smith leaned back in his seat. This call was not about spotting a fugitive, or a bomb blast, or a shooter gone berserk, or a building on fire, or a plane crash. This was totally off the charts; finally a positive story, which was badly needed, something they could cover, not as an in-and-out quickie, but something they might be able to follow for years.

Smith said, "All right, folks, you have my attention. I'll pass this up the chain of command and we'll see what they say. No guarantees. I'll let you know either way. When that will be, I don't know. I do thank you for your time. You have my number if anything else comes up regarding this situation."

The screen went blank.

Tony tugged on an ear, hoping loose change might fall out. He said, "Once this request reaches Indian ears and we fill out the application forms, they're going to want serious money up front. And good luck on getting it back if we change our minds. Do you honestly want this, because I'm having second thoughts; first thoughts, actually?"

"Honey, I've never wanted anything more in my life, except for you," she said with honest conviction.

Tony was torn. The old fight rose up in him. You don't spend years trolling endless miles of alleys and parks at night collecting cans and salable items from trash cans and dumpsters without running into stray dogs or other pickers.

At the age of 15, working an alley in the dawn hours before school, he spotted a newly installed dumpster that had joined its mate. Approaching the green monster, another youth came in from the opposite direction. Each claimed possession and the fight began. They kicked and clawed, each trying their special secret fighting tricks to no avail.

The fight continued for so long that the two slumped against the metal casing of the dumpster, totally exhausted, both bleeding, shins swollen, each with a bruised rib or two, and were forced to call it a draw. Tony suggested they work as a team, because two people can carry three times as much as one.

Light from a rising sun reminded Tony that this was a school day. After evaluating the face of his opponent with his deeply split lip, swollen eye, and deep bruise to his right cheekbone, Tony had no trouble equating that to his present appearance.

He still needed to run a couple of miles to get home, shower, change, and get to school on time, lest his father do worse to him. It if were up to his father, he would be sent to school as is. In matters such as these, his mother prevailed. She would have him hold a package of frozen vegetables against his face, while she wiped away the blood and placed a Band-Aid on the worst of the cuts. The darkening, swollen eye would stand alone to complete the visual testament to the fact that nobody fucks with a Rossi.

The two became close friends, until Billy Riggs got killed by a hit and run driver down the same alley they had worked when they had first met. With a shiver, Tony knew it could have just as easily been him, rather than his new friend.

At the present time, he had another negotiation to make with the chance of taking a beating if it went south. If he said "Absolutely not" to the deal, she'd hold it against him, unless they adopted locally, then she might put this misadventure in the false start category. If he agreed, they'd be scraping pennies for the foreseeable future, raising two children who would be teenagers in a half-dozen short years. He'd have to go back to dumpster diving. They just went from potential riches to guaranteed rags within the time span of a few hours.

The couple spent the remainder of the night conversing, interspersed with doses of tossing and turning, with an occasional insert of sleep to upset the pattern, until it was time to robotically slide out of bed and prepare for work.

Megan drove to her school, and Tony attended an executive meeting with his department managers. A breakdown of the newly acquired and expensive AI, which separated the seven classes of plastic bottles, required an input of manual labor that had to be pillaged from other areas of the workforce.

It wasn't until 4:00 pm, on her way home, that Megan received a call from the Phoenix affiliate of CNN saying they wanted to run with the story and had either she or her husband done anything today that would begin the adoption process. Or, before the story ran, had they changed their minds. She said she hadn't had a chance to do anything, but gave them Tony's number, concerned he hadn't done anything either.

For Tony's part, he had contacted his mother after the morning business meeting. To her, the idea was thoughtful, but impractical.

When Christina told Arthur about Megan's desire to adopt children from overseas, he merely shrugged, as if to say, "That's nice, hopefully it will be from Germany or Austria." It wasn't his problem, anyway. When Tony told his neighbor Hans, he agreed to make a few calls of his own.

By the time Tony received the CNN call, Hans had already spoken to an attorney experienced in international law and another in adoption proceedings. Connections and money helped speed up the process that might otherwise involve foot-dragging to the extent that the children might even be elderly ragpickers by the time they got the word.

Without giving any names, Tony explained the present status to the CNN affiliate rep on the phone and noted that on the morrow, he and his wife would be meeting with at least one attorney. After he hung up, he called Megan to inform her that she would need to call in for a day off. The dominoes were beginning to fall.

4

The adoption of a child from overseas requires contact with the U.S. Citizen and Immigration Services, (USCIS), contact with foreign country adoption agencies, along with a vetting of the adopting parents. The child (children) may be relocated to the United States before adoption, or may be adopted in their own country. Considering the radical nature of the cultural and lifestyle differences and time considerations, Tony and Megan opted to make the lengthy airborne journey of nearly a full day, or longer, depending on layovers, and adopt in India. Curiously, their travel time was comparable to the length of time the Singh's spent atop the train traveling from Mumbai to Delhi. Returning with two children could be a different matter entirely.

Prior to meeting with the immigration attorney, the couple went online to visit a number of adoption-related websites, some belonging to the USCIS. After the meeting, they responded to a request from CNN to visit their home.

Considered modest for a couple with a better than average income, the four bedroom 2200 square foot residence was located in Tempe, not far from the Arizona State University campus. The home possessed a well-watered lawn, presently being converted to desert landscaping, a medium-size backyard pool, separately fenced by a chain link, in a cedar fenced side yard and a double garage, home for an SUV and a Prius, the latter belonging to Megan. At the rear of the home lay an alley wide enough for city trucks to pass through, while it emptied trash containers behind each home. A six-foot cedar fence ran the length of the alley on both sides with a gate opposite each home.

The couple had requested to be interviewed by Melanie Brown. To their misfortune, she hadn't left India, yet. Advised that the Rossis had seen her story and of their intentions, she made plans to revisit the children to discuss the matter with them. First, though, CNN wanted to line up an Indian social worker in Delhi to accompany her.

Never slow to break a good story, especially one promising long-term benefits for their ratings, CNN broke the story the day after the visit to the Rossis' home. When the story aired, millions of viewers saw the contrast in lifestyles between the trash-laden home of the two children, and the upscale home of the potential parents. The news outlet became flooded with calls, many bemoaning the fact that the children, instead of being isolated to assist in their adaptation to their new life, would attract paparazzi, as if Raj and Aruna were the offspring of Princess Diana. This latter prospect scared the hell out of Rossis, who simply wanted to adopt without repercussions, with Tony lamenting his wife's spontaneous decision to call CNN for assistance and his own decision to go along with it.

As Tony Rossi Senior had been quoted to say, "The intensity of repercussions is directly related to the goal you seek, which is multiplied by the shortness of the time factor."

The morning after the story broke about the adoption, Arthur saw the broadcast. Putting the pieces together, he felt he had been suckered into playing a bad hand. He called Tony at the office and when Tony saw which phone line lit up, he moaned, "Oh, boy, here we go."

"Are you crazy?" Arthur bellowed when Tony picked up.

"Probably," Tony replied, leaving any further words hanging, expecting the call, toying, playing with the man, knowing what was coming, almost looking forward to it in a perverse way.

"Trying to adopt a couple of black kids into this family, are you nuts?" Arthur spat. "Why didn't you tell me to start with? Whose idea was it, yours or Megan's? Probably hers. You have more sense than that."

Tony was surprised by the attack and vitriol

behind it. He had smelled something wrong with Arthur from the start and that smell never left after many years, despite the man's seemingly too smooth demeanor. Hans also had shared his concern. He and Megan, along with the Hoberts, had discussed the issue of mixed families on an intellectual level, examining it from all angles. In today's world they were common. As long as love was supplied in abundance, virtually any problem would be overcome. Now he faced a problem with a family member.

He instantly recalled a story told to him by a Jewish business associate who had married a wife with a son, who, in turn, had a grandson out of wedlock. When the friend came home from work one day, the son was standing next to the now, four-year-old grandson. The young boy remarked, "Here comes the Jew boy."

He told them both to get out of his house.

The businessman was stuck between a rock and a hard place. If he incurred the wife's wrath as she sought to protect her progeny, he would be would be forced to file for divorce, after which the son and grandson would move into *his* house. The really bad news was that the wife died two years later of a lingering cancer. The really good news was that he never saw the son or grandson again.

Tony needed to ensure this particular issue with his own stepfather would be short lived. He knew Arthur despised the shortened version of his name, so he said, "Art, "I've never seen a black person, or a white person. Even with your pasty pale skin I wouldn't call you white. I would say the kids are a beautiful shade of dark mahogany; ebony, if you will. You should see them, you know, give them a big hug, then go home and take a good shower like a good little boy."

He could feel the heat of his stepfather's skin temperature through the phone line. It gave him a glowing sense of satisfaction. He tried hard, but not too hard, to suppress the urge to drive across town and beat the man's face to a bloody pulp.

Tony pointedly continued, with his own vitriol, "And Art, for what you said, I'm coming for you. Start being afraid for your life. Until we meet again, I have black children to adopt and raise."

"Is that a threat?" The fear was evident in his voice.

"No, a threat is a conditional term. This is an unconditional promise," Tony growled, and closed the call.

Tony leaned back in his chair, exhaling. He figured his stepfather would be pulling out a bottle of whiskey from somewhere and pouring himself a double shot. If he were a drinking man, he would do the same.

Tony never saw it coming, like a rabid dog that bites you to transfer its poison. The conversation rattled around in his mind, word for word, like a song one obsesses over. His day was ruined. His night was ruined. His mind schemed. Tony Rossi never forgot nor forgave. He knew he would never clean it out completely. He needed to hit the gym hard to keep his blood pressure in check.

Before the day was over, it would rise again.

Two hours later he received a second call. The ring tone told him his mother wanted to chat.

"Hello, mom, what a pleasant surprise," Tony chimed, waiting for the next words from her mouth.

"Did Arthur call you yet?" Christina asked.

"As a matter of fact we did have a short conversation," Tony answered, smugly.

"I'll bet. Don't worry about him. When he gets home, he and I are going to have an intense one-sided conversation," Christina said, pleasantly.

"Thanks, mom. I really do appreciate it," Tony said, not caring whether she did or not. He had set his mind.

"You're being kind. Why don't you tell me what you said to him," Christina requested, in her best motherly tone.

"You're not old enough," Tony told her.

"That bad?"

"That good."

Christina gave a deep throated laugh. He had

hit home. "Well, say 'hi' for me to your lovely Megan. And if you need anything, call me, not him, okay? Oh, and it might be best not to mention any of this to her."

"Will do, mom, thanks for the support. Love you."

"Love you too." Tony put his head in his hands. Would this day never end?

Thirty minutes later, he left the office, pulled into the garage, and entered the home to see Megan standing over the stove, preparing spaghetti and meatballs. The range-hood fan was in operation.

"How was your day, Hon?" Megan asked, giving her husband a peck on the lips.

Tony replied, "Fairly average, I would say." He made an effort to migrate to the bedroom, when she returned quickly, "Heck of a show last night. They do know how to produce visually captivating reports."

Tony knew his wife. She was going somewhere with this. Playing innocent, he said, "Sure thing, babe," trying again to leave.

"I wonder if your parents saw it too," she offered, looking at him, inching her head upward in a half-nod.

Tony felt trapped. "Probably," he replied. He about-faced and walked into the master bedroom. Time to relax. Time to put the day behind him. Time to change into something more comfortable. He sat on the edge of the bed. He heard the clang of a metal lid being placed on top of the kettle a little more heavily than necessary. He began a silent count . . . one, two, three . . .

Megan appeared at the doorway. She slowly walked over and sat next to him. She asked, "Did Arthur call you at work?"

"Uh, yeah, why?"

Megan challenged, "Why? I don't want to be a dentist pulling teeth. Did he talk about us and what did he say? Talk to me, because he called me too," she thrust, like a dagger, like throwing in a large chili pepper into a stew pot on the verge of boiling over.

Tony was surprised, no, enraged, that Arthur had the audacity to call Megan. Briefly considering the issue, he weighed the possibility that the kids might be raised by a single mother by the time he got finished with the man and the law caught up with him.

Reluctantly, Tony told her all that had occurred during the conversation between him and his stepfather and the subsequent conversation with his mother. Honesty is the best policy, he reminded himself.

Megan sat next to him and demanded sharply, "Is that what you think too? I want to know." She looked at the facial scars he had accumulated from his youth, not wanting to know what the other guys looked like.

Tony whipped his head around and accused, "How dare you say that of me, your husband.

How dare you," he repeated, fury in his voice, still smoldering from the earlier encounter. He didn't relish tonight's sleep.

Megan wilted and began to cry. She put her arm around him and said, "No, I don't know where that came from. I'm so sorry. I know how hard this is for you, sweetheart. You have this weight on your shoulders and you're trying to balance so many things at once. I love you for it. Let's keep together on this and we'll make it work. Okay?"

Tony was not so fast to fall into her wiles. The entire day, from beginning to end, had given him cause to wonder about a lot of things. He recovered enough to ask, "Everybody is suffering, but some people need to suffer more. Tell me what happened when Arthur called you. I was honest with you and, damn it, Megan, you be honest with me."

Megan's cries turned to deep sobs. Tears streamed. Through her pain she managed to say, in bits and pieces, "He told me they were, well, he called them niggers and wanted to know if they were queer too."

Arthur had crossed the line by a long way. Vengeance may be a dish best served cold, but satisfaction waits for no one. Tony's mind went wild with varied thoughts of retribution. Grimly, he placed a call to his mother, who listened patiently, trying to give him low-key assurances. This inferno did not need more fuel.

After a brief moment of deliberation, she said, “Okay, Tony, relax, trust me. I dealt with your stepfather.. Let me take care of a few things and get back with you. Afterwards, you can have your turn.”

5

Three people exited a taxi outside of Delhi city limits, releasing the driver to find an area distant from the mountain and to await their call for a return. He gladly did so.

The trio wended their way around garbage pickings strewn randomly about to approach the residence of the children. They were guided by the careful observations of Brandon, who had tracked their original progress through the maze of encampments. On this day, Melanie and her companion came at that early hour to duplicate their original success and to not take the chance of missing the youngsters.

They were accompanied by a Mrs. Indira Gunta-Rao, whose 30-plus years of experience had overseen the adoption of hundreds of children, none of whom, however, had originated from a family of ragpickers. She possessed an additional quality. She was born in the state of Maharashtra, with Mumbai as the capital, the same state in which the children were born. Because she also spoke that language, she might bond on that level as well.

This visit was a new experience for her. She had seen squalor aplenty, but had never walked among so many children working in one place, and so young. Rao was wise enough to understand that if she were to go to a number of other countries, she would see the same thing, where children worked in mines and tunnels until they died from overwork, disease, or malnutrition. At the moment, the stench and number of overflying carrion-eating birds and insects without number made her stomach turn.

Approaching the bags of trash that were the walls of the dwelling, Rao took it upon herself to say in the Marathi, the language spoken in Mumbai, "Raj, Aruna, are you there?"

Suddenly, the rag-roof covering the makeshift dwelling separated and Raj poked his head up, crying, "Umma, is that you?"

Abashed, Rao shrunk back, realizing she had made a terrible mistake. Melanie said, "Brandon, make sure you delete that segment."

Melanie said to Raj, "It's me, Melanie, remember me from the other day?"

The boy appeared confused for a moment. Aruna suddenly stood to show herself. Melanie said, "Aruna, Raj, I want you to meet my friend here. Her name is Indira. Can we all talk? We will give you money so you don't have to work today. Will that be all right? Maybe you want to come with us to get some food."

The information dump caused the two children to speak with one another for a moment. Rao had pulled out a 50 rupee note as did Melanie, the equivalent of several days of work for the children, totaling $1.25 in U.S. currency.

By this time, the usual crowd began to gather to watch the unusual event taking place. The crone was among them. On a hunch she would appear again, Melanie had instructed Brandon to make a print of the best frame he had of her, which he did. At her signal, he pulled out the 5" x 7" color photo and handed it to the woman.

The old gal didn't know what it was at first, until she looked at it and recognized herself. Nobody could guess when the last time was that she had seen herself, but her face beamed with delight in recognition, as she gawked at the photo. She kissed Brandon on the cheek and hobbled off with the picture to show it to her friends and neighbors, along with anybody she ran into.

"Looks like you made a friend today," Melanie beamed.

"Maybe she wants to go out with me," Brandon gibed, slyly.

"Let me know how it works out," Melanie teased.

Ready to get down to business, Rao asked the children, with all the charm she could muster, "Can we all come inside to talk?" She was not at all pleased with having to get on her hands and knees to crawl into the space surrounded by a circle of trash bags. For this visit, she had been advised by Melanie not to wear a traditional sari, but to dress in a Western manner. Now she could see why.

Within short moments, the tiny interior became crowded with three adults and the two children all seated on cardboard. A few dirty cups and dishes were packed in an open cardboard box Melanie had not noticed before. Perhaps one of the children had been seated in front of it.

Like Smith or Jones in the States, in India, if one said the name Rao, untold millions might respond. In the field of adoption, there was only one whose last name was Gunta-Rao, which was shortened to Rao among her colleagues.

Despite her matronly appearance with her long salt and pepper hair, Rao knew she had to be very careful here. This was new ground. From what she had been told by Melanie, the children had a terribly traumatic life thus far, from the early fire that killed household relatives to the deaths of their parents.

She guessed that if the mother died from a coughing disease, ostensibly it would have been from tuberculosis, a common disease among pickers, and other poorer classes in their country. In this present instance, there was absolutely no lineage of record and nobody to consult about their mental stability. This was not a case where parents chose an infant, where the child would never know the difference, unless told. This case was not about the separation of teens, each going to a different foster home, or any one of a number of other scenarios. This was about her flying totally blind, trusting to instinct and experience in order to introduce them and her to a new concept.

She took a deep breath and said, "Raj, Aruna, Melanie here tells me you don't have an umma or bapu anymore. Is that right?"

Raj said, "Yes. Umma died from coughing."

"And the mountain fell on bapu," chimed in Aruna.

Gunta-Rao observed carefully. She saw no remorse, only the acceptance of the hard cold facts of life. She continued, "Melanie and I know some people who want to be your new umma and bapu. Do you think that would be all right?"

A slight spark of excitement appeared in Aruna's black eyes when she asked, "Will they come to live with us here in our house?"

Melanie held back the impulse to laugh when she thought of the Rossis moving in with the children, perhaps going out to pick trash with them dressed in tatters. CNN could run a special series entitled From Riches to Rags and sell millions in advertising.

Swallowing her mirth, she said, calmly, "No, you would go to their house. They live far away.

They would come here to see you and then you would go on an airplane to where they live." Co-operatively, a plane passed overhead to which she pointed.

The children spoke to one another in Marathi for a few moments. Rao caught the concern in Raj's voice, but not in Aruna's. Raj said, "If we go, can we take our . . ." here he used a Marathi word for tool. Presumably he was referring to the sharpened sticks.

"No, but maybe you can get new ones," Melanie offered, "and, you won't have to work anymore."

Aruna's face shifted from upbeat to deep concern. "Then how will we eat or sleep?"

"Your new umma and bapu will give you food and you will go to school," Rao offered, hoping she hadn't pushed one of their hot buttons.

Before either could answer, the counselor offered, "Can I show you a picture of the people who want to be your new umma and bapu?"

Noncommittally, both children shrugged, but closely followed Rao's reach into her purse to unzip an inside pocket from which she pulled out a small folder. Opening the folder, the counselor pulled out a picture of Tony and Megan Rossi standing in front of their home in Tempe. She handed the picture to Raj who stared intently at the photo with his sister.

As she watched the two, Rao knew these were

special children, destined for a better life and capable of dealing with that life, if they could only escape their present circumstances. Even without the Rossis, a simple phone call could have these children removed and sheltered by the state. Instead, she wanted, no, needed, their consent. This would serve to speed up their emigration and their adjustment to a completely new world.

The conversation among the two children centered on the clothing worn by the smiling Rossis more than about other elements of the picture. Certainly, not all ragpickers dressed as they did, in fact, the pair would find an occasional shirt or a pair of pants of various lengths that could be worn until they disintegrated, only to be replaced by another. At the moment, however, they were in-between.

Raj whispered something in his sister's ear to be followed by a return whisper. This went several rounds back and forth until Raj finally turned to the watching adults and said, "Okay."

"Okay, what?" Rao asked.

"Okay, they can be our new umma and bapu," Aruna announced.

Melanie beamed. Even the camera went off-center for an instant.

6

Instead of feeling jubilation, their acceptance became an instant nightmare for Rao. In a flash she had gone from a pleasant motherly negotiator between foreign and local entities; a day's work totally within her data base, to feeling pressure thanks to Brandon's recording for the world to see. She must provide assistance to the children until their new parents arrived in-country, whenever that might be.

She had not been prepared for this eventuality. In her mind's eye, everybody would have a pleasant get-together chat for starters. Over time, numerous small crises would be resolved. Now with the two children committing to adoption, she had to ensure they received safe housing. She excused herself and crawled outside to make a call.

Initially, the news crew couldn't be happier. They dared not run the story without first getting approval from the Rossis after they viewed this clip. That would not bode well for the corporation as a whole, especially if the prospective parents backed out. However, once approval was obtained from them, CNN—read Melanie—could serialize the story. On the negative side, she was in deep shit if anything happened to the children before the Rossis took charge. She needed to impress upon her employer that, despite its time-worn hands-off philosophy, they must do everything in their power to expedite the adoption process.

New Delhi time was 12 hours ahead of Phoenix time. The parties in India had at least a day's work to do before contacting Tony and Megan. If the call were made at 6:00 or 7:00 the following morning, it would be received in early evening the same day, almost exactly half way around the world.

When Megan's phone rang the following evening, she and Tony had just completed putting away the dinner dishes. The CNN caller opened by reporting the very good news that the children both gave their consent for the adoption.

This news caused them to reflect for the nth time that the adoption would take several months to years. Aside from applications and endless forms to fill out, the children had to be clothed, vaccinated and screened for a variety of ailments before leaving the country. This process had to be repeated once they arrived in the states. In the meantime, Rao was making arrangements to house them in a youth hostel, where a number of health related tests could be conducted and could the Rossis come over here as soon as possible and stay for an indefinite period of time until all matters were settled?

This lengthy report led to another sleepless, but excited, night of planning, which required a list of things to do: obtain a boatload of money, packing for an extended period, perhaps selecting appropriate games for the children to play during their long travel, looking into the expense of flying coach vs. first class, making arrangements at work to be gone for one-to-three months, and fallback plans for the unexpected. As owner/CEO, this was not difficult for Tony because he could have daily meetings and conference calls via computer. Megan would be out of work and without income.

In truth, Tony was swamped. He had to deal with the Feds breathing down his neck about worker health regulations, software updates, worker complaints, new dumping regulations, and an endless stream of reports to write, phone calls, and left field events. If he had a preference, he often considering re-enlisting for combat duty.

Fortunately, the couple was well traveled and could keep their luggage to a minimum. The conversation regarding time spent in flight went something like this:

Tony: “In the northern hemisphere the Earth

rotates counter-clockwise. We will be flying clockwise for about 24 hours. Delhi is 12 hours ahead of us on the clock. Draw a direct line through the planet and connect us with the other side. If we leave on a Tuesday, what day of the week and what time of day will it be when we get there? Never mind the short stop in New York's JFK."

Megan: "Huh?"

Tony: "I looked at tickets. Round trip First Class will run you and me about $3500. Add about half-again $1750 for the kids, since they're going one way. Coach will be a heck of a lot less."

Megan: "Yes, taking other humans into your life can be expensive. I want us to go First Class."

"The kids won't know the difference."

Megan: "No, but we will. Sitting on my butt for a full day in coach will be challenging. In First Class, we get more personalized service, the seats will be bigger, we can pair up better with the kids, stretch out our legs, and we'll all have more room to sleep."

Tony: "From what I've seen, those two can sleep anywhere. I do see your point, though."

Megan: "Good. That's settled."

Tony: "Melanie said she expects donations to start coming in."

Megan: "We can't base our happiness on the action of other people."

Tony: "Huh?"

During the time of preparation for the journey, the Rossis received calls from their Phoenix affiliate advising them of progress made from the Indian side regarding the children, giving them a head's up before the broadcast of another episode. Reportedly, Raj and Aruna had been taken to a youth hostel thanks to Rao's efforts, bathed, given medical treatment, a haircut, clothing, and more food they could remember seeing at one time.

It would appear the authorities were going the extra mile, after learning they are under a magnifying glass. Indeed, millions were hooked on the series in both countries. Everybody in India wanted to be a film star. The Indians were not about to throw a monkey wrench into the machinery.

The kids were being introduced to other children, although, Aruna punched another child in the nose because he had called her brother Raj Mahal, as a takeoff on the world famous tourist site. So far, the children were fascinated by what they saw in the mirror, never having seen themselves before, an important step in accepting one's identity. The half-hour segment will be shown twice this evening on the CNN channel.

At 8:00 pm Phoenix time, Tony and Megan sat before the television, not having any idea how the producers would lay out the program, which they had dubbed, *The Unusual Adoption.*

The episode began with the first interview with the children. This soon morphed into the Rossis' proclamation that they wanted to adopt, followed by a second interview with the children when Rao was present. Neither Brandon's voice nor face ever appeared.

After recaps of earlier episodes, the present one began in a moving car. Within the car could be seen the driver, with Rao next to him and Melanie seated behind her. Melanie narrated as they traveled. Through the windshield, the now familiar 200' tall mountain of trash loomed in its dominance, surrounded by smaller foothills on all sides.

Turning her head to face the camera, Melanie said, "We have received approval to pick up the children and Mrs. Gunta-Rao will be with us to ensure they are safely in custody. We are running late today, due to a bus accident blocking the road, so we hope the kids are still at their home and not at work."

The camera zoomed in for a close-up of the mountain. The south side was on fire, gray-black smoke filled the air with the acrid smell of burning anything and everything in the dump. Anaerobic bacteria well beneath the surface had begun to digest what they needed for survival. Oxygen wasn't needed to generate enough heat to create a smoldering mess. The smoke blew over the top of the hillock to roll down the other side.

The driver took the car around to the side

where the children had set up their residence, hundreds of yards to the east of the nearest mound with the fire to the south and west of them. He waited until the others exited the vehicle to go in search for Raj and Aruna. Within minutes the trio had returned empty handed.

Melanie waved away tendrils of smoke blowing their way and said, “Indira, why don’t you stay here in the car with the driver and keep your cell handy while Brandon and I go look for the two. Brandon, can you use your zoom on high to see if you can find them?”

Countless viewers watched the real life drama unfold. Through the digital magic of the camera, they saw what Brandon saw: close-ups of thousands of humans climbing and digging through old shoes, or tin cans, or rooting through anything a person wanted to discard. All were enveloped by the smoke rolling down the hillside and being carried aloft to be seen miles away.

Brandon moved over to a different area the kids had pointed out earlier as their best hunting grounds. Atop this relatively small hillock two children with sticks were sifting through the debris, occasionally stabbing at something to pull it up for closer inspection with carrion eating birds circling, confused by the smoke and the errant air currents, inspecting, and occasionally landing to capture a rodent scurrying along the ground.

"There," Brandon said, pointing.

Melanie said to the driver, "Let's go."

The pair got back in the car and drove a short distance to the hillock. Melanie and Brandon got out and with camera rolling, crunched over gravel and plastic bottles, coughing, shuffling through debris all the way. Two feral dogs were engaged in a fight some distance away. Melanie said, "Let's climb."

Within 30 seconds the camera went askew followed by a grunt. The viewers saw the sky through gray and black currents of fire smoke, then a close-up of the piles of cans, bottles, pieces of wood, clothing, old bicycles, and rotting garbage

Before the camera became stabilized on the two children fifty yards up the hill,, a larger boy, perhaps 14 or 15 years of age, came up behind Raj. Locally, he was known a badamashee, or bully and snatched Raj's collection bag from his hand. Raj turned to face badamashee who stood some six inches taller than him only to receive a shove with both hands from the antagonist to send him sprawling on his back to slide several feet down the hill.

The bully grabbed Raj's stick and stood in place laughing, but failed to see Aruna behind him. With both hands she grabbed her own heavy stick and with the heavy magnet securely taped to one end, raised it high and brought it down on the bully's shoulder, severely cracking the bone. He screamed and fell to one knee, the broken shoulder dangling uselessly. She helped Raj to his feet and recovered his possessions.

Both children heard a cry from below and saw Melanie wave and call. Other pickers, both young and old, turned their attention to the odd climbers on the hill and were pleased to see bad-amashee finally receive some justice. The Singh twins were thieves, they weren't bullies. There is a clear distinction.

The children acknowledged Melanie's wave. They half-walked, half-slid down the pile to join her and Brandon, who had missed the entire episode lasting but seconds. If he had captured it, he could be certain Melanie would instruct him to delete it.

Next scene: Everyone climbs into the car. Trash bags are left outside as are the sticks. Raj strips magnet from the end of Aruna's stick and maintains control of it.

Next scene: Rao takes children into youth hostel operated by adoption agency. It is situated among a number of similar structures in a residential area off a main thoroughfare. Raj clutches the magnet. The two-story concrete building is relatively large, with a fenced in rear yard. It is set back from the roadway somewhat, but otherwise nondescript, aside from a single wooden sign neatly painted in black over the front door that reads DAO (Delhi Adoption Organization), one of a number of agencies specifically designated by the central government for the protection of children's rights.

Rao proclaimed, "Sorry, the camera crew is not permitted to enter."

Inside the car, Melanie faces the camera and announces, "Next time, we will see the children up close and personal to get a close look at how they are adapting to this new life before their new parents arrive." An inset appears in a corner of the screen to show a picture of the smiling Rossis waving.

Megan pushed the mute button on the remote. Turning to her husband she asked, "When *are* we going to see our babies?"

"Soon, enough, I hope. The wheels move slowly. Tomorrow will help," Tony offered, referring to the short upcoming broadcast interview that will be shown to the children, and to everyone else.

Coincident with the arrival of the CNN news truck that pulled into the Rossi's driveway late the following afternoon, neighbors thought it might be a good idea to get some fresh air and migrate to their front porches.

Initially, CNN wanted to tour the interior of the home to show the world and the kids what their new home would look like. Tony nixed the idea from a number of standpoints, in part based on home security. He didn't need everybody to know the layout of the home's interior, or see their possessions. Social medial critics were already coming out of the woodwork like freshly hatched fly larvae digesting their meaty surrounds.

The first initial airing of Megan's assertion that she and her husband wanted to adopt the children was met mostly with "Ah, shucks," comments. As the story didn't wither away, but instead continued, the comments became more numerous and obtuse, such as "I'll bet anything they haven't even tried to adopt American babies?"

"If they want Indian children, what's the matter with American Indian children? I guess they're second class to these rich people."

"What's the matter with adopting white kids?"

"The lady, what's her name, Megan, said she wanted to adopt them when she first saw them looking like the trash they live on. Isn't love wonderful?"

"Some people will do anything to get in the news."

Megan wondered why it always had to be good vs. evil. She had quit a short stab at journalism because, in her view, she saw the news for what it was: a vicious cutthroat business not much different than the business of selling drugs, each network in competition with the others. It was normal to occasionally lose sleep over one's employ. Certainly, it is one's civic duty to pay attention to activities relating to local events.

She had an aha moment when she saw herself becoming overly attentive to national and international events. She would lie in bed while various stories and political scenarios played through her mind. It sucked the energy out of her. It made her feel insecure. It made her look at life with a negative view. This wasn't her.

She quit watching and listening to the political news, the war news, the problems within other countries, the problems within her own country, the volcanic explosions, who said what about whom, government overthrows, the rapine and plunder, the earthquakes, threats, counter threats, retaliation, and always the inevitable end of the earth scenario coupled with what we have to sacrifice to save the entire planet. Social media didn't help with everybody throwing in their opinion. She called the news cycle a whirlpool—get too close and get sucked in.

Ignoring the overload of tragedy, she slept better. Soon, her creative mojo returned. If, after having gone cold turkey for a period of time, she backslid to check on what she had missed, she found she had not missed a thing. However, she would be hooked once again on sensationalism, drawing her back into the never ending cycle of news-drug addiction, and of course, the complementary (or primary) business of selling ads.

In addition to not wanting to have the camera crew walk through the house, the Rossis felt they didn't want the children overwhelmed too early. There would be enough of that soon enough starting with the initial meeting, getting to know one another, visiting with them in what must be a splendorous hotel room, and at some point, taking a long plane ride home.

On this occasion, the male host and cameraman brought along a tripod to support and stabilize a slightly larger camera along with a lighting source, which was also set on a tripod. The couple sat on the sofa. The male host made slight adjustments to their hair and clothing. Then the cameraman ran a light meter over them, adjusting the light source to his satisfaction.

Once the minor setup routine had been completed, the host said, "Tony, Megan, I'm going to ask you a few simple questions. There won't be any tricky stuff. We all want this to come across as natural as possible. It's good for everyone that way. If you make a mistake, we can reshoot. This isn't live. We'll edit it back at the station, anyway. I want you to look at me over to this side when you answer the questions, which won't take long. Then I want you both to look into the camera so you will be speaking directly to Raj and Aruna, all right?"

Megan grasped Tony's hand. The host and the cameraman nodded to one another and the host asked, "Tony, Megan, your request to adopt these two children has gone viral, not only here in the States, but internationally, especially in

India. How are you feeling now and how are things progressing at your end?"

Megan replied, "We're overwhelmed by the attention. We had no idea our request would blow up to this extent, so we try our best not to get caught up in others' opinions. We are trying to stay focused on getting the necessary documents for our travel to Delhi."

Tony said, "In that regard, we are expecting a clearance from our immigration department and once we get that and a few other details taken care of, we will make the trip."

The host nodded approvingly, giving them encouragement. So far, so good. He inquired, "A lot of people want to know why you chose those two over so many other children needing adoption. Can you help us understand why those two in particular?"

Megan replied, staunchly, "Because when I first saw them on your own program, I knew they belonged to us. It might have a little to do with Tony in the business of recycling like the kids are, in their own way, but you'd have to ask a psychologist about that part. All we knew was that we were childless and, call it a psychic connection, or something that was meant to be, but we had to make it happen."

The host gave a smile and another encouraging nod. He said, "Thank you both for your honesty. I'm certain our viewers appreciate your feelings and a lot of us can identify with them.

Now, is there anything you would like to say to those two children you are fighting so hard to adopt?" He pointed to the camera for them to shift their gaze toward, which they did.

Megan said, in a short speech she had rehearsed a hundred times, "Raj, Aruna, this is your new umma and bapu. We are trying very hard to come there and to bring you both back with us. We love you."

Tony added, "We want you to have good happy lives. I know that the four of us will make a nice family. We'll see you soon." He wanted to say how smart he knew they were, but he'd be slammed for choosing children based on their intelligence. If he had mentioned their poverty, he would get criticized for being rich, whatever that meant. He played safe and kept it neutral.

Those interviewed always wanted to know when their segment would be aired, so as he and his teammate were packing up, the host said, "To keep up interest, we're going to air today's recording occasionally, even before the next episode is shown. Besides, we need to get it over to the children as soon as possible. Thank you again for allowing us into your home."

Within sixty seconds, the news crew had gone and the neighbors left their front porches to return indoors.

7

Part of the deal Tony had negotiated with CNN was that the company would be permitted to follow his and Megan's movements in exchange for them occasionally noting the expenses the family was incurring as a gentle manner of generating donations without being overt.

On the plane, aside from assundry phone calls made during a short layover in JFK, and another look at the video of the children, the couple turned off their phones in a desperate need to escape the outside world.

The kids didn't look quite as gaunt as the first time they had appeared on TV, especially when wearing decent clothing, which was that of the typical school child's dress. This consisted of a short-sleeve khaki button down shirt and khaki shorts. Half-broken shirt buttons was a glaring indication the worn clothing had been pounded onto rocks for cleaning purposes, commonly seen among even the middle and sometimes upper class. Citizens. (Pounding and hand scrubbing shirts on rocks employs a lot of people.) They also wore new sandals. At some point, the pair would have to be introduced to proper footwear. Both were learning to play soccer in a short segment of the piece.

When the plane touched down at Indira Gandhi International Airport at 3:15 pm carrying 226 passengers on a not-so-sunny smog-filled day, CNN was there, specifically Melanie and Brandon, to film the deplaning of Tony and Megan Rossi. By design, they had otherwise left their itinerary a secret. For the moment, at least, the hound-dog-oriented paparazzi could go chase somebody else.

By the time the couple had arrived at the Crown Royal Hotel, their bodies and minds demanded they get into a little exercise. Their biological clocks required resetting. While doing so, Tony's mind reeled with possible schemes to grease the skids.

During their side-by-side treadmill runs, Megan remembered to turn on her phone. Once she did, she punched the Emergency Stop button. Her phone had become overloaded with texts and messages. Tony, too, stopped his machine out of concern for her abrupt movement. She held her phone up for him to read the string of texts, all alluding to the fact that the city had taken the children from the protection of the adoption agency into their own "direct care." Rao's fingerprints were all over the missives.

When Tony did read the texts, he exclaimed, "Shit."

Other exercise enthusiasts looked over, quickly linking his declaration and linguistic attributes to a speech pattern most common to Americans. Admittedly, their usage of the word was as commonplace as the American display of the middle finger, along with a number of their colorful and descriptive words and phrases beginning with the letter "f."

Heading back to their room, Tony punched buttons on his phone. In a short while, the flood of emails emerged. Apparently, in light of the international attention afforded this particular adoption, some do-gooder in the Ministry of the Interior had decided to have the children moved to a more "secure" location—this occurred while the Rossis were in-flight.

Rao had reasoned their lack of response to her calls and texts were due to in-flight circumstances. She had taken it upon herself to surreptitiously contact the Rossis' Delhi lawyer, whom the family had retained to handle the case. If asked, Rao would sheepishly say she didn't know how the attorney had found out about the transfer.

The attorney had told her he would call his brother, who worked with the state agency in question, namely, the Children's Rights Foundation, and with whom he had spoken about the case. The foundation was located in the R.K.

Puram residential section of Delhi, where multiple-storied apartments for government workers and high-rise buildings were also situated.

Tony, Megan, their attorney, and Rao pulled into a lot fronting the state agency with the attorney at the wheel of a Mercedes S-Class Sedan. Following in a second car was Melanie and Brandon, playing low-key and whose vehicle lacked brand advertisement. This particular agency held some 200 children, ranging in age from four to fourteen. Numerous other agencies located elsewhere in the city covered the earlier or later years.

The interior of the four story building was impressive. Satellite dishes dotted the top. The viewer saw stock footage of classrooms with TVs, rows of sleeping mats in rooms segregated by age and sex, a dining hall large enough to feed everyone at one sitting, kitchens, staff offices, a small soccer field, a basketball court, and two swing sets.

Soap operas were a huge industry in India, as they were elsewhere in the world. In this reality show, nobody wanted to step on anybody's toes. The sooner the transactions could be completed, the sooner the Rossis could take custody and let CNN take it from there.

At this point, the Rossis had yet to meet Raj and Aruna. That was about to change.

8

The elderly gray-haired receptionist at the front desk wore a colorful red sari interwoven with silver threads. Over the years, she had seen the calm transfer of children to their new parents interspersed with emotional melt-downs on either side, primarily by the new parents, but occasionally by a rebellious child.

But the agency had never encountered the show of force entering her domain that day, especially when one of the three men identified himself as attorney for the now famous Rossis, who accompanied him. These three were followed by none other than Melanie Brown, her cameraman, and Gunta-Rao. The attorney politely requested they be permitted to visit with Raj and Aruna. At the moment, the camera was off, unless, of course, somebody would like to make a statement.

The receptionist made a quick phone call and a moment later, a tall gray-bearded and turbaned man, emerged from a side office. He was dressed smartly in black slacks, white shirt, and red tie to match the color of his turban. The door was open long enough for Tony to see that his walls were decorated with pictures of a soccer team. In many, a taller man stood in the middle holding a trophy.

The man announced, "Ah, yes, my superior told me to expect you. My name is Pradeep Vishaswami."

The attorney introduced himself and the others, beginning with the Rossis and pointing out that CNN was represented.

"So you are the famous Tony and Megan Rossi," returned Vishaswami, jovially. "I almost feel as though I should ask for your autographs.

" And Ms. Melanie Brown, I am honored. I so do appreciate your newscasts and hope you look upon us favorably."

"No worries, sir," returned Melanie. "We have heard nothing but good reports about your establishment."

Tony took over and said, just as politely, "Sir, we will be happy to supply you with our autographs. First, though, at this time, we would like to see the children, if you don't mind."

The pre-advised Vishaswami chimed smoothly, in the sing-song manner of Indian-speak, heavily rolling the Rs. "Not at all, Mr. Tony. Hmm, at the moment they are napping, Just, I am getting them. For the visit, I am suggesting a lounge area inside that door," he pointed. "Although, I must request that Mrs. Gunta-Rao and you, sir, remain here," speaking to the attorney.

Grinning broadly, he added, "The press, I am informed, will be permitted to film the occasion. And Ms. Melanie, if you wish a statement from me afterward, I will be pleased to provide one."

Vishaswami hesitated for a moment to look at the prospective parents, and said, "Um, Mr. and Mrs., Rossi, if you don't mind, please visit with me in my office for a moment."

The couple accompanied the man him into his office to take the proffered seats across the desk from him, while the others migrated to the designated lounge area, a separate room with comfortable chairs, a few pleasant pictures of lakes and streams, another soccer picture, and a wall TV that was off at the moment.

Vishaswami's face turned from delightfully cordial to deadly serious. Looking from one to the other he began, "I must tell you that the boy has some problems. They weren't evident under the watchful eye of my colleague, Mrs. Gunta-Rao, but they are manifest here."

Megan and Tony looked at each other in shock. Turning back to their host, Megan uttered, "What are you talking about? What kind of problems? Is it his heart? What?"

Vishaswami continued, "It is far too early to make a true professional diagnosis. I am not a medical specialist, nor a trained mental expert, but after some 30 years in this field, I see evidence he is bipolar, the new term for what we used to call manic. Depression or anger can be triggered by a list of factors including reaction to certain foods, changes in barometric pressure, lack of sleep, missing meals, and arguments around him, or those he might be engaged in. The key word is 'stress', which, as I understand, causes the release of certain hormones. In his case, stress can be induced internally and externally.

"Today, this condition can be managed with medication. Our medical staff is equipped to handle such issues, which they do on a regular basis. Raj is currently on a common stress-relieving medication, which should help, although I would caution the actual condition will have to be defined. This means you will have to keep thorough records for proper evaluation by medical professionals. Raj's condition is unusual in that it is occurring at so young an age. In my experience, one doesn't see mood swings like this until more mature years. I fully believe Raj will become a useful citizen as he grows."

A useful citizen? For a moment both parents looked as though they would be in need of anger management and depression therapy. Tony glared at Vishaswami, as though he were the cause of the boy's reputed problems. He was about to speak when Megan asked, "How is the girl?"

Vishaswami gave the slightest of smiles and

said, "Aruna appears to be fine. This is something she has lived with and is used to it. When we asked about her brother, she shrugged it off.

"That's Raj," she said.

"What happened to make you think Raj has mental problems?" Tony asked.

"He doesn't have mental problems. I prefer to say he has physical problems that affect his mind," Vishaswami corrected.

He continued. "It's hereditary. He could have gotten the defective gene or genes from one of his parents or grandparents. As to what happened, he got into a little altercation on the soccer field and tore into the other boy verbally. He was about to strike the other boy. When the pair was separated, Raj grabbed his head. It looked like he had a migraine. We kept him in the dark for several hours until the headache eased enough for him to try and function. Even then, he stared into space for several hours. When he came around he didn't remember what had happened and was normal from that point on."

Megan quickly glanced at Tony and, almost frightened, implored, "Please don't mention this to another person outside this establishment."

"You have my word on that," Vishaswami said, with all sincerity.

Tony took a deep breath, trying to calm himself. He didn't need this. Megan didn't need this. He asked, "Can we see them now, please/"

"Of course." Vishaswami slid back his desk

chair, followed by the others. He opened the door for his guests. Like zombies they passed the four others who gave them curious glances about the private meeting assuming the matter revolved around legal matters. He led them to a visitor's room and disappeared. Melanie and Brandon followed, as per agreement.

Within a short while, Vishaswami opened the door to usher in the children; then he gently closed it and departed. Melanie and Brandon had found a seat in the corner of the 15' x 20' room, recording the moment.

Not surprisingly, objectively watching a video played on a cell phone differs from one subjectively becoming part of that event in real life. When the brother and sister stood with their backs to the closed door, it was as though a shock wave had passed through the room.

Rao, and later the DAO, had performed the miraculous. Both children's hair had been trimmed and obviously was freshly wet and combed, their faces washed and free of open sores. Their scrubbed and washed dark mahogany-hued skins reflected the lights of the room. Their shirts and shorts were freshly pressed.

Too aghast to speak, all remained petrified for the moment until it was Raj who spoke first. Ignoring Melanie, he said, smiling, "You are our new umma and bapu," at which time he and Aruna came over to the couple for hugs. It was the adults who cried openly. The camera wavered again.

Tony was the first adult to speak. Raj was closest to him so he chanced placing a hand on his shoulder, trusting he wouldn't receive a punch in the nose for a trade. Searching for any words to offer, he said, "You both look great. How do you feel? Are they treating you all right here?"

"Oh, yes, this is so much fun, bapu," Aruna replied.

"You can call me dad, if you want. Bapu is okay, too," he said. If this adoption doesn't go through, I'm going to shoot myself, he thought.

"I like dad. It's new," Raj said.

"What's fun about being here?" Megan asked to both of the children, glowing, starting to relax. The kids would pick up on bad vibes. There were none to offer.

"We get to play a lot and sleep and eat a lot and watch funny things on the big phone screen," Aruna replied.

"You mean the television, like that one there?" Megan asked, pointing to a large wall-mounted unit.

Both kids nodded.

The four spoke of superficial topics for several minutes, feeling out each other. Tony and Megan had decided to learn from the children about their past, how they collected what they collected, and the tricks they employed, topics which opened the floodgates. The prospective parents talked straight to the twins without baby talk, trying to earn their respect and teaching them complex linguistic skills early on.

A light knock at the door caused Tony to flinch. He got the message, and said, "Kids, we have to go now, but we want to come back tomorrow. Will that be all right with you? After we visit more times, maybe the people here will let you go out with us."

Both children nodded. Megan gave them both a great bear hug, which they accepted and returned in kind. Of a sudden, Megan said, "Melanie, I know we have to go, but do you mind terribly if we spend a couple of minutes alone with them?"

Melanie consented; they had more than enough footage and motioned for Brandon to exit with her. She walked over to the door, slowly opening it. Instantly, Vishaswami appeared. He had been watching the clock with the other guests. Melanie said a word to him and the door closed, leaving the parents alone with the children.

Megan said, "Now it's just us. We will have fun together and we'll get some nice books for you to read."

Aruna replied, "But mum, we don't know how to read."

"Then we'll teach you and have fun doing it. We'll teach you numbers too," Tony said.

"Oh, we know numbers," Raj answered.

"You do? What's eight times four?" asked Megan.

"Thirty-two." answered Raj.

She tried something more difficult. "One point six times eight?"

"Twelve point eight"

This is nuts. Tony asked, "Twelve times thirteen divided by four?"

"Thirty-nine," giggled Raj.

Megan laughed, "How do you know numbers?"

Raj looked at her as though she were daft. "We have to know so we don't get cheated when we turn in our stuff for sale and they weigh it. We get paid by the kilo."

Tony considered saying to Megan, "I don't care what their reason is, seven year olds aren't this sharp," when another knock interrupted them. Megan went to the door to face Vishaswami. Megan asked him, "Can we come back tomorrow?"

"Absolutely," he replied, looking over at the children, who looked to be laughing at something Tony said.

Tony looked up and asked, "How long before we can take them with us for part of the day?"

Vishaswami said, "It's fine with me, Mr. Tony, but it's up to others, not up to me. I would have to ask for permission."

Raj spoke up and cried, "But we want to go with them."

"Yeah, we want to go," said Aruna.

"We'll see what I can do," Vishaswami replied, looking around, only to find that Rao and the attorney had been standing behind him.

Out of camera shot, Tony slipped Vishaswami a signed slip of note paper with each of their autographs, including that of Melanie Brown, to his great delight.

For her part, Melanie was in hog's heaven knee deep in slop. She had taken notes during the interview, handiwork she considered to be promissory notes, which promised to keep her on this special case. Brandon's shooting of the visit streamed the video live to CNN in India, where a team of editors were already working on it.

After showing Brandon's recording, standing before the DAO building, Melanie would say the following words, never mind mixing fact with fiction, "The governments of two countries are trying desperately to deliver these children to the adoptive parents, but political forces are in disagreement as to protocol. You have seen the footage and you have seen what DAO has done to revive the lives of these two babies, with the thankful assistance of Indira Gunta-Rao, and especially, Predeep Vishaswami. Do we want to wait four years for the transfer to occur?

"We want your opinion; yes, you the viewer. Should Raj and Aruna remain here for years, or should the Rossis be permitted to take them off-site, and even, yes, take them home with them after all the sacrifices they have made. Or should political forces separate the loving parents from the children, who—you heard it with your own ears—state clearly, want to live with them. Our lines are open. And any donations received will be applied to this cause."

CNN producers were quick to edit. When the next long-awaited episode aired the following day, phone calls jammed their circuits, as well as those who oversaw immigration and adoption agencies in both countries. Social media was ripe with voices of the people expressing their opinion, not all of which were positive. To Melanie and CNN, the opinions didn't matter. The number of responders did, which included advertisers who knew a good thing when they saw it.

Only two mornings had lapsed before the Rossis received a call granting them permission to take the children with them for the day.

9

The day after the initial visit and the day (evening) when the episode aired, the Rossis were unable to visit the children, spending virtually every minute in legalities, meeting with officials, attorneys, and bankers, transferring funds and signing documents. They were followed by the news agency to highlight their struggles, armed with enough material for another episode. Forced to call in their apologies and regrets to DAO, insisting they speak directly with Raj and Aruna, the exhausted couple spent the remaining hours of the day shopping toy stores.

When Tony and Megan brought the children to the hotel room, CNN was not invited. The young boy and girl walked into a room in which they found a stock of Chinese puzzle rings, Tetris pieces for shape creations, Rubic's cubes, jigsaw puzzles, and host of mind bending challenges. Curiously, the children paid little attention to their ostentatious surrounds, devoting their time to game playing. To Megan's delight, the kids took to her teaching them the written numbers, which they considered to be in the same vein as puzzle playing, and, like mathematics, had endless possibilities.

"These kids are too damn smart" Megan whispered to Tony, watching the children challenge each other, waiting for the next shoe to fall from Raj, the one that might spell the end of the games.

Tony answered, "They're unusually talented. I'm thinking of home schooling, if you're up to it."

Megan nodded and acknowledged, "I'm more than up to it. We certainly can't send them to public school at this stage. There must be a settling in for some length of time. Besides, the way I'm told to teach and what to teach in public school turns my stomach. It's like the administrators want every child to be as stupid as possible."

"Hey, maybe the children you teach will become administrators someday. Joking aside, the kids will need interaction with other children at some point in time, though," Tony offered.

"Absolutely. Let's get them home first," Megan concluded. In truth, she was inwardly delighted to get away from public instruction. She was witness to it going downhill in the years since she began teaching and now she had the perfect opportunity to express her teaching talents to their full potential, something she had been yearning to do since forever. She would soon have the *tabula rasa,* not exactly the blank slate philosopher John Locke envisioned, but close enough. She would have children whose minds and experiences were limited, ripe to be imprinted.

Cleared for takeoff, the Dreamliner increased its speed until it was airborne. On either side of the plane, a child occupied a window seat, wearing headsets and holding a Nintendo Gameboy Console. Megan thought that if the plane ever hit turbulence, controlling the kids would be like trying to contain a dog during 4th of July fireworks. First Grade reading books were packed beneath the seats.

The first stop would be Paris to be followed by another in New York City and Immigration. An overnight layover would be followed by a change of planes to Sky Harbor International in Phoenix where CNN would greet the family with open arms to begin the real adventure.

The Rossis counted themselves fortunate in the sense that their home site was not located in portions of the country subjected to dramatic changes in weather. Hopefully, the stability would assist in Raj's pace of adjustment.

PART TWO

1

CNN filmed the plane landing and the passengers entering the concourse, paying close attention to four of them, two adults and two children. This was followed by a few seconds of filming the migration of passengers to baggage claim, the Rossis' recovery of their goods, and the SUV pulling out of the long-term parking area. The family would get its privacy, at least until the news team paid another visit to the home.

During the short 20 minute drive home from the airport, Megan pulled out the phone and made a call to the Hoberts. "Klara, it's me. We're on our way back and should be home in a few minutes."

She listened a moment and said, "No, we're not movie stars; we're just four very tired people coming home from a long trip. Anyway, thanks for watching the house. If you don't hear from me in a couple of weeks, it's because the dust needs time to settle. Call me if you want to chat.

Say 'hi' to Hans and the boys and thanks again. We'll get together soon. Love you too, bye."

Tony then punched a button on the steering wheel and requested the car make a similar call to his mother.

Tony pulled into the drive of the home. He got out, disengaged the alarm system, pushed the DOOR OPEN button, got back in the car, and drove in. Megan instructed Raj and Aruna to assist in carrying the packages into the home through the laundry room, past the kitchen, and into the dining room, where they could place everything on the table for the moment. Tony closed the garage door and followed them in. Thus far, to their delight, the kids followed instructions well, especially from those superior to them.

Prior to leaving for the long journey, Tony had ensured all small items of value were put away in the floor safe in the master bedroom to join the Glock 9mm and ammo, the same weapon he had used when in the service. The neighbors had been notified of their pending absence. Perhaps months might elapse before they returned. The neighbors watched TV, too, and wished the Rossis good luck, sometimes said in a facetious manner, as in "Good luck with that, ha ha."

"Let's show you the house," Megan said, turning on the lights. Twilight had begun.

"Where is everybody else," asked Aruna,

looking around.

"What do you mean?" Tony said.

"Where are all the other people?" Aruna said, throwing her arms out wide.

"There are no other people," Tony replied.

"They're playing hide and seek with us, Raji. Come on, you go that way and I'll go this way," Aruna proclaimed, as each child ran off in a different direction to explore the rooms. Tony and Megan looked at each other, smiled and shrugged until the children returned, puzzled.

Raj confessed, "We can't find anybody. Where are they hiding?"

Megan said, "Sweetie, there is nobody else. It's only us here."

"Only us in this house?" Aruna cried, spreading her arms wide, with great exaggeration.

"You had only four in your house, didn't you?" Tony asked, attempting logic.

"Yeah, but . . ." Raj began.

"Come on, Raji, let's go outside," Aruna proclaimed, heading out the back door, only to find it locked. Tony unbolted it and, in an instant, the children were liberated into the outdoors like dust motes in a wind storm.

Aruna stopped to look at the pool, the greatest body of water she had ever seen, while Raj headed for the back gate. He unlatched it, heading out into the alley, with three other dust motes in his wake. Looking around, he asked, "What are those?" pointing at the blue trash barrels behind each home down both sides of the alley.

"That's where people throw out what they don't want," Megan explained.

"Really, we never saw that happen," said Aruna, excitedly, as though she were watching the birth of a baby seal, or the hatching of turtle eggs. She took a few steps to the large barrel behind their home and tried to lift the lid, but she was not tall enough to get it opened enough to peer inside.

"Raji, give me a boost," she directed.

With rapt fascination, Tony and Megan watched Raj kneel at the base of the bin. He folded both hands together as an aid for his sister. He boosted the girl high enough for her to toss open the lid. In an instant, her top half disappeared, only to emerge a moment later holding an empty plastic container that once held vinegar.

"Wow, that's great," Raj declared. "We can use it for water."

"I can get more of those for you, all you want," Megan said.

"That okay, umma, we can get our own," Raj replied.

Tony said, "You can call her mom. She needs help making dinner. Will you help her, Aruna? Raj, can you please help me put away what we brought in our suitcases and find a place for all your toys."

"Put them in the fourth bedroom," Megan suggested. Then she added, "Pretty soon, I'll show you your own bedroom."

"What's a bedroom?" Raj asked.

"It's a place where people sleep," said Tony.

"That makes no sense. When we were in DAO we slept with maybe 100 boys in one room and the girls had another room. Are those bedrooms?"

"Yes, they are. A bedroom can also be a place where one person can sleep," Megan explained, patiently.

Two houses down, a man walked out his back gate holding a shepherd on a lease preparing for a daily walk. When the kids saw the dog coming their way they screamed and ran through the gate of their own home. Tony raised a hand as a hello to the neighbor and turned to follow Megan who had followed the kids. He had better things to do than to chat with Curious George.

Meeting with Megan in the yard, Tony asked, "What do you think set them off?"

Megan said, "Remember the CNN videos of their camp? Remember those scrawny, emaciated dogs we saw. Well, if those mangy feral animals didn't have rabies, they had distemper, or a bad attitude. The kids might be deathly afraid of dogs."

Tony nodded, and replied, "That makes sense. Sometime we'll have a long talk with them about it."

Enwrapped by the enormity of the new life she had created for herself and her husband and, well, the world, really, Megan had given no thought about their first dinner. With no ready food at hand, she dug into the freezer and the pantry to identify the following: A two pound pot roast, three T-bone steaks, four hamburgers, four packages of stir fry, frozen corn, peas, and mixed vegetable, two chicken breasts frozen so hard they could be used in a construction project, a package of chicken thighs, and a couple of plastic-wrapped packages she failed to label. She removed the package of thighs and put it in the microwave, punching the button for fast defrost, then she turned on two electric stove burners to the shock of her new daughter. "What's that?" she asked, staring at the glows, backing away.

"It's electricity and it's very hot. Can you promise me to never turn these knobs without me or your dad here?" Megan asserted.

"I promise," replied the girl, her eyes riveted on the two glowing burners. Megan had her doubts as to the whether her request, or the subsequent promise, even registered with the girl.

More often than not, simple is the best. Requesting the girl to assist, she created a stir-fry vegi dish with rice along with several orders of mac and cheese. Both were simple and quick to prepare, suited to all but the most discriminating taste. Including the chicken defrosted and fried, dinner would be ready in a half-hour. The teacher in her wanted to prepare a meal which would require use of utensils.

Directing Aruna to set the table, Megan multi-tasked, giving directions and cooking, aware that unforeseen catastrophes might occur. If that were to occur, game over, life over.

Discovering she was totally out of milk, she asked Tony to make a quick run to the store. He quickly decided against taking Raj to a supermarket on his first outing lest he incur a dog in the market, or overwhelm the boy with sights of so much available food, and drove by himself, returning in 20 minutes with two gallons.

At last, Megan set food on the table and declared, "All right, time to wash your hands." The Indian method of eating with the right hand only would find its end in this household.

"Why?" asked Aruna.

"So they will be clean," she said.

"Why?" asked Aruna.

"Because dirt has germs," Tony said.

"What are germs?"

"They are invisible animals that can make you sick."

"How can you get sick if you can't see them? Oh, I know. They're like bad spirits," Aruna concluded.

Dual sinks in the master bath ensured each parent supervised a single child in an elaborate handwashing ritual that far exceeded their own. Handwashing and hand drying completed, the family returned to the table where Tony began the formal lesson. With the left hand he stuck a piece of thigh with the fork to hold it in place and used the serrated butter knife to cut. He sliced off a piece, switched hands, stuck the piece, and placed it in his mouth.

Raj held the knife as though it were the handle of King Arthur's sword, managed to slice off a piece, stuck it with a fork, and got it half-way to his mouth before the piece fell to the plate. He stabbed at it so hard with the fork it might have been a snake crawling across his plate. With the others watching the show, Tony gently assisted his son to correctly manage the piece onto the fork.

"Why can't we eat with our hands, if we washed them?" Aruna asked.

Megan contributed, "Because we like to develop good habits, although there are a lot of foods we can eat without utensils like fruits and vegetables and hot dogs . . ."

"What is a hot dog? What is a utensil? Why do you want to eat a dog anyway?" Raj asked.

Tony looked over at Megan for assistance. His eyes held a message of pleading. Grinning she said, "It's a name of a food somebody brought over from Europe a long time ago." She didn't get a chance to launch into the subject of German immigrants and their sausages at this time, because Aruna asked, "What's Europe?"

"Tell you what. Let's all try the mac and cheese. Bet you guys will like it," Tony deflected.

"Bet?" asked Raj.

"I think you guys will like it," he corrected.

A showing of the kids' room followed a carefully instructed post-dinner cleanup in which the entire family participated. The room consisted of a 3-drawer nightstand, a gooseneck lamp, and two beds, each with a blue bedspread. Megan regretted not decorating the room, but with so much uncertainty prior to their leaving, she had decided to deal with it when the time came. The time had arrived.

Neither Tony nor Megan looked forward to properly training the kids to use a Western commode and toilet paper, which different significantly from porcelain-lined (or not) squat toilets and a can of water. When the time came, the sexes would unite in the training program. Hopefully, the children would be fast learners; otherwise unnecessary mistakes might make for colorful stories.

The children appeared emotionally neutral about the bedroom and accepted Tony's offer to watch cartoons on TV. He and Megan were hanging on by a thread. Within the first half-hour, the entire family nodded off. The sun had set some time ago. With considerable effort, Megan pushed herself up from the armchair and offered to help the children get into pajamas she had purchased. This introduced the youngsters to another novel idea, the concept of changing into something in order to go to sleep. It made no sense. Just lie down and go to sleep. What's the big deal? They followed orders well and did as they were bade, which was followed by another crazy idea, that of brushing teeth. Why not simply poke your teeth with a small twig?

Before she tucked them into bed, the twins stared at the beds and the positions of the pillow, moving the pillows to the opposite end. Megan allowed this without question, gave them each a kiss, and departed the room, leaving the door open with the hall light on. Barely able to stand by herself, she crawled into her own bed.

Hearing their new parents settle in, Aruna whispered in Marathi, "Hey, Raj."

"What?" he whispered back.

"What do you think about them so far?" she asked.

"They're all right, I guess. They're trying pretty hard to make us happy with all the neat toys."

"I like them," Aruna said.

Raj wanted to keep speaking in their native tongue. His umma had told him that if you want to keep secrets, then speak very fast in English, because none of the other kids will know it. He hoped he wouldn't forget his Marathi because he and his sister would lose the ability to keep secrets. Life was moving too fast.

Only a short while ago everything was fine, even after umma and bapu died. It is what it is.

Every kid and every family had their personal stories to tell, theirs was different only in that death had reared its ugly head. Curiously, their deaths did not bring them fear, not like the terror that gripped them on the airplane ride, keeping their heads buried in the games, afraid to appear as cowards. But he did feel guilt. All he had ever known was work. Wasn't it supposed to be like that? Yet, here he lay in luxury beyond belief while his friends—and not friends—toiled at the mountain on the other side of the world. It would be morning there; time to go to work, and here he slept.

The big question remained: Why were they chosen among the thousands young and old, some years younger than they had been, others, like the crone, were skeletonized so much that the age of their bodies could not be discerned, unless radiocarbon dating were employed.

Raj saw the in-between world of the orphanages, not rich, not poor, just kids hanging out, not working, waiting for nothing to happen, or, for the rare occurrence that somebody might come along and take them for better or worse. He had touched this base, to get spring-boarded to a place called America to be the son of incredibly wealthy people, not having to work. It was all wrong. There could be no good future for him and his sister. Shut up, Raj, he told himself. You are promised enough food for each day. What else do you need?

"Right now I'm lonely. It's too quiet," Raj complained. He tried not to feel stress because he knew what would occur when that happened. At least his new umma had ensured he got his pill. He hoped it worked all the time. He hated it when he went all wongo.

"We're lonely," Aruna yelled, hoping her entreaties would keep her brother from going into a meltdown.

Megan found that Tony had beaten her to the children's room. Taking a guess, she supposed that perhaps the lack of background noise in a large house vacant of people might be problem. Tony retrieved a small stereo and took into the bedroom along with a number of CDs. He tried a variety of music types until he hit on one by Ravi Shankar his wife had purchased and had doted on years before.

"I like that," Aruna declared.

"So do I," Raj repeated.

Tony kissed them goodnight and left the room. He made one last check on them three hours later to find that both had migrated off their beds and were sleeping soundly on the carpeted floor. He left them where they lay, recalling with amusement *Tobacco Road,* an Erskine Caldwell novel he had read in high school. It was about a small town in rural America where one family member was so lazy that if she tripped over a tree root and fell to the ground, she took advantage of the accident by remaining in place and going to sleep.

Tony arose at 6:30 ahead of Megan. He planned to make a quick stop at work to announce his presence before returning home, planning to spend increasing amounts of time each day at work in order to enable the children to adapt to their parents' schedule. Plus, he had to earn a living.

When he did amble into their room, he found them gone. Pajamas were on the floor, their khaki uniforms missing. He instantly panicked, quickly toured the other two bedrooms, one of which was their personal office, the other to be converted to a game room. With no evidence of his new children, he returned to the master bedroom. Sitting on the edge of the bed he gently shook his wife and said, "Honey, the kids are gone. Wake up."

After several attempts, the zombie-like creature opened her eyes and croaked, froggily, "What?"

Tony repeated the words until Megan's baggy eyes flew open and she cried, "Get off the bed. Let me get up."

She made her way to the master bath and closed the door, soon emerging wearing a robe, slippers, and headscarf over her morning friz. "Let's go," she ordered.

The couple made another search of the home, checked the front door to find it bolted, and hurried to the back door to find it unlocked. "The pool," Megan shrieked. Her heart dropped to her stomach when she envisioned a double drowning and its aftermath. Soon finding no bodies in the pool, Tony noticed the back gate partially open.

"They're out back," he announced, loudly.

Quickly hurrying to the alley, Tony spotted them several houses down, with Aruna dumpster diving as before, her legs dangling, her head submerged. Raj held two plastic bags filled with select items they had retrieved from the neighbors' discards.

"Thank God," Megan uttered, leading her husband toward the budding entrepreneurs. Comedy relief in a tragedy.

Seeing the adults approach, Raj announced, proudly, "Hi umma, dad, look what we got. We're rich." He held the bags nearly full of cans, bottles, and damaged discarded toys.

What is the next step in the guidance protocol? The manual forgot to cover this particular issue. Tony said, ad-libbing, "Good find, you guys. Why don't you bring your treasures back home? We'll empty the bags in the back yard and look at your great collection together while umma gets dressed and starts breakfast."

Ignoring Tony's request, Aruna cried, "See what the guy with the dog just threw out?" She fished in one of her collection bags to retrieve several empty pint bottles labeled Southern Comfort and an old VHS tape. She handed the latter to Megan who read the title: *Desiree Meets Linda, Episodes 1-10.*

Megan said not a word. Smiling, she made a quick turn-around sighing with relief as she headed back to the house. Another crisis averted.

2

Megan had planned to set the timer for 25 minutes. With a child on either side of her, each with a pad, paper, and pencil, she would begin with a single number, then progress to double digit numbers. Using a first grade book on arithmetic, she would start the lessons by showing the four different signs and how they worked. At the dinging of the timer, everyone would get up for a walk-around and a stretch.

However, 15 minutes into the first lesson, Aruna cried, “I’m lonely.”

“Me too,” repeated Raj.

Megan gave thought to the words repeated from the night before. The quiet in the giant house must be deafening to them. Growing up around hundreds and thousands of people 24/7, there was no escape from noise, whatever its guise. The cawing of birds, the barking of dogs, arguments, banal chatter, bargaining, nighttime conversation with parents, the midnight crying of hungry babies, traveling on the top of a train;

throughout it all, humans had surrounded them like flies on meat. Now thrust into a twilight zone of dead silence and loneliness, her children had only one person with whom to speak—herself.

An idea came to her. She had an app on her phone that acquired music from virtually every corner of the earth. She said, "Raj, Aruna, I want you to help me with something. I'm going to search for music in different countries. We'll start with India. Let me know when you like something."

On an impulse, Megan searched for a station that played music from popular Indian films and immediately hit pay dirt, when they both cried, "We like that."

Bollywood was alive and well in the Rossi household. Its music had permeated down to the lowest classes of society, to provide a small measure of joy in an otherwise tortured existence.

With phone plugged in and the music on low, Megan repeated these sessions two more times. She directed the fourth session of the morning to verbal math skills, again stopping at the ding of the timer.

Time for a swim. Unfortunately, she had not purchased bathing suits. Dare she take the children shopping? Would she be able to control them in Walmart? She decided to wait for Tony to get home shortly. He could take over the reading lessons while she went shopping, which could take some time based on the growing list of items she needed. When she thought of Walmart, she automatically thought of big box stores. How many of them had closed because Amazon offered competitive, if not lower prices combined with home delivery. In her view, this was fair in that the big boxes had caused the closure of countless small businesses. What monster would rise up to take down Amazon?

Indeed, at that moment, the sound of the garage door opening halted the lesson. "Bapu's here," cried Aruna.

"It's dad," corrected Raj.

Both children ran to the door to grab Tony by the legs while he tried to maintain control of the bag of groceries he had purchased. "No complaints. Works for me," he said to Megan, with a toothy smile.

"What did you get, Hon?" she asked.

"Lots of food. There's more in the car," Tony said.

Megan said, "Good, after we put this away it's my turn to shop." She explained about the music and what she had covered in the morning lessons. Tony agreed to take over the reading lessons while she was gone. He would make lunch if she wasn't back and after she picked up bathing suits for the kids, they would all go in the pool. Then it was nap time. This time sleeping would be, not on the floor, but, if not under the covers, at least on top of the bed. Raj rarely slept during this time; in fact, he rarely slept at all except in broken spurts at night and occasional short naps during the day. He always made the complaint his brain wouldn't shut up.

Megan was an experienced elementary school teacher. She knew the benefits of one-on-one teaching, short attention spans, the benefits of arts and crafts, and the need to encourage every child, assisting whenever she got the chance. She also knew about the latest styles in children's clothing and their sizes.

When she arrived home with her own packages, Tony said, "These kids are hungry."

"Okay, I'll get lunch going in a minute," Megan said.

"No, I mean they're hungry to learn. When I show them something once, they get it," Tony replied.

"For all the years I've taught, I've never seen anything like it," Megan said. "By the way, at some point, we're going have to take them out to buy sneakers."

"What did you get, mom?" Aruna asked, excitedly.

"Help me carry in the other bags and I'll show you," Megan answered, leading the way to her car. She showed the two how to pop open the rear gate, each of them grabbing a light-weight bag of clothing, a few items of which were for herself. *Can't pass up a good sale.*

The sofa soon became littered with swim wear, T-shirts, blue jeans, shirts, blouses, and underwear. Few girls in Megan's class wore dresses, so she opted to let Aruna make that decision for herself at a later date. Her main concern was money. They had never relied on credit cards before and it hurt her to do so now. She knew Tony felt the same way. It looked like Povertyville from here on out. Darkly projecting the worst case scenario, she envisioned them selling their home in order to downsize.

"Let's have you try on the clothes, then we'll all go swimming," Megan announced, happily. When she saw the frown on the children's faces she realized they may never have seen a body of water as large as their own swimming pool, or had never worn long pants. More challenges.

The children were putting on weight. Daily swimming lessons were progressing nicely, tantrums were minimal, and the adult Rossis neared the edge of sanity listening to Indian film songs all day and all night to the point of dreaming some of the most popular.

Tony wanted to take the children to a nearby park surrounding a lake inhabited by a score of ducks, and had purchased a couple of small balsa wood airplanes and a soccer ball. Their major concern was the reaction of the children to any dogs at the park, leashed or otherwise, but decided the issued needed to be confronted.

The senior Rossis had a long discussion with the children about wild vs. domestic dogs. This went a long way toward alleviating their fear, especially when the adults pointed out that many Indians also had dogs as pets. The ones the kids had seen lurking around the trash heaps were sick and hungry. Like any animal, humans included, dogs would stop at nothing to get food, or to protect their young. Once pets were well fed and loved, all was well.

This simplistic view proved its worth when the family encountered numerous contacts with dogs at the park. The twins were delightfully surprised when a Cocker licked their faces. This occurrence was akin to their utter fascination when Megan prepared microwave popcorn for their Friday night cartoon session. New emotions were coming out, each of which related to happiness and good times.

On the flip side, Tony dearly wanted to watch a good sporting event, if not at the ballpark, then on TV. He was successful in his high school football playing days when he learned about camaraderie, loyalty, bonding, and devotion. Over time, his sense of duty in the military translated into his duty to the children. He uncomfortably rationalized that giving up what he loved might evolve into something new to be loved.

A knock at the door caused Megan to look at the clock above the stove. She announced, “It’s your mother, right on time. I hope she’s alone.”

Reflexively clenching a fist, Tony said, “If she’s not, she soon will be.”

"Who is that?" chimed Aruna from another room.

"It's my mother; your grandmother. Go let her in," Tony told her.

The twins ran to the front door and yanked it open to reveal see a beaming Christina standing in front of them. She squatted down and put an arm around each child to give them a big squeeze just as Tony arrived. "Let's see, you must be Aruna and you must be Raj. Or is it the other way?" she guessed.

"You're silly, grandma," Raj said.

"Welcome home, mom," Tony said.

Christina slowly unwound herself from the children and raised up an aching body. "Ready, willing, and disabled," she declared. "Knees giving out."

"Come on in mom, Dinner's almost ready," Tony said.

Christina announced, "Dinner can wait. I want my babies to show me where they play all their games. I can't wait to see. I also have some bubble gum for them after dinner."

"What's bubble gum?" Aruna asked,

Tony turned away mumbling "Freaking, bubble gum, great!"

Like two dogs pulling a human, the children fearlessly grabbed a hand each and hauled her to their special room. In a gesture of complete happiness, Christina permitted her grandchildren to manhandle her until reaching their destination.

3

The west portion of the rear yard contained a fenced-in pool and a covered patio where a barbecue, picnic table, and outdoor chairs were situated. A graveled walkway led from the west of the patio out the back gate. Just beyond the patio, in clear view of the sliding door to the outdoors, lay a rocky birdbath with three wells, one beneath the other.

Tony considered the pond, as he called it, a royal pain to keep clean and he would have to drain and scrub it to remove the algal growth that would take over quickly in the desert sun. Typically, the water attracted doves, quail, hummingbirds, finches, jays, Tanagers, and a wide variety of other species. The remainder of the yard was grass, which Tony wanted to have removed for water conservation purposes. A large sycamore tree stood proudly in the center of the lawn, shading the home.

Finally, a four-foot gap lay between the east and west side of the home and the cedar fence separating the home from the nearest neighbors.

One evening at dinner, Tony explained to his family, "I have some ideas for the back yard. The first thing I want to do is to buy a swing set. The delivery van can bring the boxes down the alley and through the rear gate. Raj, Aruna, and I will put it together."

"Does it have a lot of pieces?" Aruna asked.

"Hundreds, with screws, nuts, bolts, seats, chains; all kinds of parts," Tony said.

Completely dismissing the words he didn't understand, Raj reacted to words he did know and exclaimed, "Wow, hundreds, when are you going to get it?"

Tony said, "I don't know yet. Pretty soon, I hope. Other things I want to do is to get us into bird watching, start a meshed-in vegetable garden, and set up horseshoe game pits on the side of the house. Also, I want to build you a tree house."

By the time he had finished explaining his ideas, defining terms, and answering questions from a couple of very sharp seven year olds, Megan had begun dishing out servings of chocolate ice cream for dessert.

Tony's mind was all over the place, flagrant thoughts replacing a brain he'd prefer to keep in neutral at the moment. The kids and Megan had gone to bed and he tried not to feel guilty about enjoying himself by watching a rerun of a ball game that had been played days before. Instead, he caught one of the best players espousing his political view during a game, which sent a wave of madness through him because this self-possessed person tainted the game in general.

Tony shook off the flagrant thoughts. He tried to stem the surge of anger-inspired adrenalin that had sped his heartbeat. He called it a day, brushed his teeth, softly crawled into bed, got the pillow adjusted, and listened to Linda Jones playing on the stereo in the kids' room as an experimental change to the playlist.

"Is it too much too soon? Megan asked, softly.

Caught off-guard, he thought about what she asked and replied, "It can't be helped. We can't keep them isolated. Life has to go on. I'd like to flood them with sensory experiences. I'm so confident they'll embrace comfort over poverty, I'm thinking about us going to the movie theater in a couple of weeks. A box of buttered popcorn can add to the treat."

"Sounds yummy," Megan said.

"And you look yummy," Tony said, turning toward her, thankful for a positive diversion

"Put up or shut up," she ordered, trusting love to conquer all.

During the fourth week, a knock on the door interrupted the reading lessons. Megan opened it to find Hans and Klara Hobert and their two children standing on their door stoop. The two tow-haired boys were eight and ten years of age. Tony was due home any minute.

Klara began, "Megan, we hope we're not intruding and appreciate what you're doing. We wanted to leave you alone, but our sons keep nagging us about visiting with your children, uh, Raj and Aruna, isn't it?"

At the mention of their names, the Rossi children appeared at the door. The contrast couldn't have been greater between the larger, paler Hobert boys and the dark, thinner, albeit growing, Rossi twins. The children stared at each other, taking measure of the other.

Where's my spear in case I need it," Aruna thought, knowing her brother would throw down with both of the boys at once, if it came to open warfare.

For their part, the Hobert boys wondered why their parents had insisted they be brought over here to meet the skinny little runts. And no, they hadn't nagged their parents to visit; it was the other way around.

"Karl, Billy, I want you to meet Raj and Aruna," Klara said. "Now shake hands."

Karl took a half-step forward and reluctantly held out his right hand, followed by Billy. They did as instructed.

The Rossi children stood in place, not knowing what to do, until Megan said, "Do what they do. Put out your hand and grab theirs."

She demonstrated by holding out her own hand to Mrs. Hobert to shake with her. The women glanced at each other, amused by the learning lesson. Shaking hands was not practiced socially on the debris field of a dump site.

"Introduce yourselves when you shake," Hans instructed. He and the Rossis had been neighbors for a number of years, since before their children were born and had gone out to dinner together several times. Each was frequently invited to the others' barbecues.

The Hoberts were large folks. Hans the same height as Tony, but weighing 20 pounds more, similar to Klara vs. Megan. From German stock, their children promised to be high school football players the way they were growing. As a CPA, Hans began his career approving construction loans, then became a licensed contractor, then morphed into operating a financial advisory service. He preferred to maintain an office rather than working from home, where there were too many distractions, although, in these post-Covid years, homework had become the norm. Megan looked to the side to see an approaching SUV and said, "Here comes Tony."

The group watched Tony pull into the drive. He parked in front of the garage without opening the door. He emerged, went to the rear of the vehicle, and pulled out a large flat box. Carrying the box, he came over to the group and announced, "If I knew we were going to have a party, I would have bought two pizzas."

Klara said, "Well, if it's a party you want, we've got some left over ribs, potato salad, and corn on the cob we can share. We'd love to hear your story."

Megan inquired, "How much time do you have?"

Raj grabbed the younger of the Hobert sons and said, with his accented English, "Come on, I'll show you my Rubic's Cube. I bet I can beat you."

Megan explained, "We converted the fourth bedroom into a playroom. Hopefully, they'll get along."

"Kids usually do," said Hans.

Klara said, "Come on, Hans. Meg, we'll be right back." At that Klara and Hans departed for their home next door to return shortly with armloads of food.

Two hours later, the adults were thankful only one mishap occurred, which was when Raj and Aruna looked at the ears of corn on the cob and asked how to eat them. This struck the Hobert children as funny and they both laughed, at which time a near fight ensured with the Rossi twins on the offensive, Raj picking up a fork in a threatening fashion.

"You can laugh with them, never at them," Klara advised her boys.

"Yes, ma'am," said the boys in unison.

"We're sorry," they both said to the twins.

Whether they were truly sorry was doubtful.

At the conclusion of dinner, the four children went to the bedroom to play what they will and the Rossis recounted their tale. At the end, Klara asked, "You're not working, right, Meg?"

"No, we're getting ready to sell off a few things, in all honesty," Megan replied.

"Like what?" asked Hans.

"Like just about everything," Tony replied. He went through the list of sales and refinances they were preparing to make.

Hans and Klara exchanged glances. Hans said, "I'm curious. Don't either of you watch television? I mean, you're joking, of course."

Tony was mystified. He gave a quick glance at Megan and with a straight face said, "Joking about what, our finances? You asked a question and we answered it. And no we don't watch TV, unless Donald Duck counts."

Seeing his friend of many years was absolutely serious, Hans said, "Tony, you guys are multi-millionaires. It's all over CNN. They're releasing the donations received on your behalf to you." Grinning, Hans added, "If you need a new accountant, I'll volunteer."

Tony shook his head. "No thanks. What kind of money are we talking about, anyway?"

Klara answered, "CNN has this rolling wheel, you know, like when they show the population increase of the earth, or the national debt. There's one for your family called Rossi Donations. Last night it rolled past the 20 million dollar mark, more coming in each time an episode is aired."

Tony laughed. "Yeah, right. Nobody told us anything. In fact, I'm happy to be left alone. As my father would say, what you're telling me is 'if-come' and 'will-come', not income. Come on, you know how these things go. CNN doesn't owe us a damn penny."

Megan said, "Tony's right. They helped us enormously in getting these children adopted and if they keep all the money, we won't hold it against them, whether they say it's coming to us or not. I see it as promo to bring in more for them. Call it the skeptic in me."

Tony said, "Wait a minute. Meg, you weren't skeptical when you wanted our children. Where is the skepticism coming from all of a sudden?"

Megan had a sudden blush of embarrassment. The financial bind she had put them in ate at her. She said, "You're right. It was a foolish thing to say. What I should have said was that I'm pleased we didn't hear any fights break out from the game room."

Hans said, "Not to belabor the point, but CNN will get ten times the revenue by giving you the money from the donations. Watch their evening World News program tonight at 9:00 and you'll see what we're talking about."

At that, Klara made a motion to stand and said, "Well, it's been a lovely evening with good friends. We're glad you shared with us. Anything we talked about tonight will remain between us. Oh, we never told our sons about your fame. As far as they know, you did adopt from overseas, but they never saw the TV specials. They were in bed when the features came on."

Tony mused, "When your sons tell their story at school about visiting with us today, somebody is going to make the association."

Reverting to Elizabethan English, Hans mused, "Fame and glory dost hast tendrils."

4

After the departure of the Hoberts, Megan asked the children about how they got along with the Hobert boys. Their responses were non-committal. The kids went to bed having received a light lecture about how it is proper for people to sleep in a bed and not on a floor.

With great skepticism, Tony and Megan remembered to watch the CNN station at 9:00 pm. Under the heading of *News You Can Use*, one reporter attended a national holiday in South Korea where the government paraded its armaments. In a curiously coincidental manner, on the same date, North Korea declared a new national holiday, parading their own armament in a demonstration of "Mine is bigger than yours" show. At least this ravaged impoverished country had enough money to make nukes and sell arms to Russia, bless their soul. Hey, a buck's a buck.

Following this useful news, a reporter in Australia filmed a 16' python crawling from the roof of a home onto a tree to slither down into the trap set by a well-meaning environmentalist, who got entangled by the 250 pound snake to his immediate regret.

Melanie Brown reported from London and presented more useful news about the royal family. This was followed a spinning wheel, measuring over 20 million dollars down to the pennies.

The caption at the top of the wheel read: ROSSI DONATIONS. The camera cut to Melanie again, who said, "We are nearing the one month mark of the adoption date. Stay with us when we visit the home and interview each of the family members. I can't wait to talk to Raj and Aruna and I know you'll want to watch when we do." She concluded by giving several numbers to which contributors could call or mail their contributions.

Tony hit the remote to turn off the TV. Megan said, "It was nice of them to keep us in the loop, don't you think?"

Tony said, sarcastically, "You must have been sleeping when some guy in a suit came by the other day and told us to get ready for an impromptu visit from CNN."

Megan quipped, humorously, "You know how much I always hated getting humiliated in public."

Tony said, "What the heck. What else do you have going on? At least it breaks up your day."

Two mornings later Megan did receive a phone call from the local CNN affiliate who wanted to set up a date for the one-month anniversary visit. She wasn't surprised at the call. It did introduce a level great gut-wrenching fear. Her joke about public humiliation was no longer a matter of mirth. The butterflies in her stomach gave testimony to her fears. Damnation; what any of them said during the interview would be seen and remembered. She needed to talk with Tony about possible questions to expect and to prepare all four of them for the event.

The tall CNN reporter hugged the four Rossis like long lost family members. She carried a flat briefcase on a strap over one shoulder.

"Melanie," the kids screamed, grabbing her legs and making it impossible for her to walk for a few moments. She leaned into Tony and Megan to confess, "I swear, I'm getting saddle sores from flying so much."

A six-foot-long well-worn faux leather sofa sat some 10 feet back from the 65" TV screen. It was balanced on either side by two recliners. A table with a reading lamp stood at either end of the sofa between the chairs, all on dark brown Berber carpeting. Nothing ornate. People on welfare who played the system, had more material goods than they did, living in homes screaming poverty on the outside with a new Cadillac or Camaro in the drive, a TV in every room, phones and laptops for each of the numerous family members, full health coverage, and food stamps for everyone.

Then there's their gun collection: an AR-15, an over-under shotgun, handguns of all makes, spare magazines, lots of ammo, everything loaded and ready to go for the Big Shootout. Wait, mother did go out and clean houses to make ends meet.

"Kids, go on and play. We'll call you in a few minutes. The grown-ups want to talk for a while," Tony directed, ignoring the camera and the man covering the get-together.

Melanie motioned for him to stop recording while the adults talked.

Megan told the story of the kids getting lost and then found raiding the neighbors' trash cans.

Tony told of their nightly dinner games when he set up a scoreboard to see which child would win the evening contest: "Which of you will have the least amount of food on the front of your shirt when dinner was over?" On one occasion he had purposely been the looser, on another occasion he had accidentally dropped an entire meatball with sauce onto himself, an event which set the others into a round of laughter and finger pointing.

Melanie laughed at the stories until tears rolled down her cheeks. Conscious she would soon face the camera, she pulled a tissue from a small makeup clutch she carried and daubed the tears away.

Megan said, "I will confess they do throw tantrums, mostly about loneliness and lack of people around them. We think it's a little early to take them to the supermarket because, frankly, it's an effort to keep them from stealing—don't you dare say anything about it on your show. We had anything of value locked up, just for general purposes, but a few days after they got here, I couldn't find my phone anywhere, and asked Tony to call it from his. It rang from under Raj's pillow." She left out the part about dosing Raj on occasion with anti-depressants. If he had another episode, she would find a professional therapist to help them, another item on her long list of to-do items.

In response to Melanie's question, Megan said, "They're reading at a second grade level, and math skills are well beyond their years."

Tony told about meeting the Hobert boys and began other tales, until Melanie held up a hand and said, "Guys, you know I love you, but we need to get in some footage or my producers will ship me off to do a series on Siberia."

Melanie excused herself and went into the hall bath to put her face back on. When she returned, she nodded to the cameraman. The camera light went on to show the reporter announcing, "Well, Megan, you should know about your children's skills after all the years you've spent in the school district. To remind those watching, it's only been a month since the seven-year-olds were brought home to the States. Do you think our viewers would like to see the progress they've made, I mean, from not reading at all to actually reading anything?"

Show time. The children sat on the sofa, feet dangling. Both wore blue jeans with white T-shirts, each with the logo of the Philadelphia Union, the No, 1 ranked US soccer team. Somehow, Hans had found the shirts and contributed them for the occasion.

Melanie announced, "On this episode of *The Unusual Adoption* we are going to interview Raj and Aruna. We'll start with Raj." She held the microphone next to him and said, "Can you tell us how you like living here so far. What do you like and what don't you like?"

Tony and Megan cringed. They squeezed hands. It's all or nothing. Would the producers cut a segment if either of the kids said the wrong thing? On the surface both trusted the children, but didn't know them well enough to know what was in their hearts. Even so, rehearsal was one thing, reality quite another. Kids can say the darndest things.

Raj replied, "I like all the food, especially corn on the cob."

"Me too, especially with butter on it," Aruna chimed.

"We like to read and do numbers with umma. Dad is always asking us number questions," Raj inserted.

Melanie said, "Can you add and subtract?"

Raj said, "Sure, and divide and multiply too."

Melanie asked them simple math questions, which progressed to more difficult questions. Receiving correct answers in all instances she reinforced what the audience could see, that these two were unique. She turned to reading, handing them a second grade book Megan was currently working with, and easily made it through a small paragraph with few stumbles..

"We like to play with a Rubic's Cube too," Raj inserted.

"Yeah, I'll show you," Aruna got up and ran to the game room. She emerged a moment later with the cube, which she handed to Melanie.

The reporter confessed, "To tell the truth, I've never played with one. You show me," She'd tried it a number of times with no success, finally giving up deciding her skills were elsewhere.

"Let me do it," Aruna said, taking it from Melanie and twisting it until all six sides matched."

"I'm faster than she is," Raj proclaimed.

Melanie asked, "Can we all see your game room" She had a sudden vision of her young cousin's bedroom where hundreds, if not thousands, of plastic pieces littered the floor in no organized manner. A boxful of more toys stood in the corner of the room. The vision made her think the parents might want to donate the pieces to the war effort for use as land mines against the enemy. If her sister and husband hadn't encountered the weapons while padding through the home at night in their bare feet, they had missed out on a treat.

Instead, the camera captured a full three-tiered bookcase, a building under construction made from an erector set, a kit for the making of scores of electronic components to create an assortment of bells and whistles, along with puzzles of all sizes and shapes, suitable for small hands. She saw a Monopoly set, a game of Clue, and another of Battleship. Two small desks and two chairs adorned the room. Clothes were hung neatly in the closet. Melanie shook her head. There was no end to surprises. She asked the kids, "I can see what you like and what you're good at. What don't you like?"

"We didn't like sleeping on beds," Aruna declared.

"Yeah, but umma . . . mom tucks us in every night. It's pretty neat," Raj said

Doubtless, CNN would flash to a scene showing the children's original home when the footage was edited for maximum effect. Tens of millions would see the contrast.

"What else don't you like?" Melanie asked.

"We don't like to wear shoes," Raj said.

"Being alone. It's too quiet," Aruna confessed. "After mom started tucking us in, it made a big difference."

"Dad plays music for us," Raj contributed.

"What kind of music do you like?" Melanie inquired.

"We like Indian film songs. We also like Ravi Shankar, Nora Jones and Linda Ronstadt and Elvis Presley and maybe some soft Jazz sometimes," Aruna said.

"Thank you both. I'm going to talk to your mom and dad for a minute, so you can go and play if you want," Melanie said.

"Do you want to see our game room some more? Mom got it all neat before you came," Raj said.

The camera panned to Megan, who threw her hands to her face in embarrassment. Melanie liked the gesture. It was good for the human interest angle.

"Thank you for the offer, but not right now," Melanie told the kids.

She and the camera turned to the parents, who had been standing to the side during the interview. She said, "Well, it looks like you've done a very good job with the children. We'd like to follow them as they grow and find out how their lives shape out."

"We can only do the best we can," Tony said. "Every day is a new challenge for all of us."

"From what I understand it must have cost you a lot for the entire enterprise," Melanie said.

"You'll never know. We're deeply in debt, but we'd do it again. This is worth every cent,"

Tony confessed.

"I have it from good sources you don't watch television, not even our own channel. Shame on you," Melanie laughed.

"We all watch cartoons Friday night," Tony responded, eyebrows giving a quick jerk up and down. His face told the audience he spoke the truth.

Melanie turned to the camera and said, "Now we come to the highlight of this episode." She opened up the flat case she carried and pulled out some papers. Selecting one of them, she showed it to the audience; then she handed it to the Rossis. "I now present you with a check for $ 22,687,232,11. This is made out to Anthony and Megan Rossi. These are the proceeds we have received thus far in your name."

Tony took the check, stared at it, and his mouth flew open. Megan stared hard at the number and the printed numerical words beneath it. With jaw slack, unfocused, she looked up at Melanie and down at the check again. She began to sob, flopping down on the sofa. She looked up teary-eyed, dazed, the camera capturing every precious second. Again, both hands went to her face, fingers covering the eyes. Still, the tears flowed through.

Hearing the sobs of their mother, something they had not encountered before, the children ran from the game room to come to her, one on each side, to put their arms around her. In the most poignant moment of the crazy interview, the two asked, "What's the matter Umma? Are you sad?"

To which Megan looked up and gave them each a kiss and said, "No, I'm very happy."

"That's a funny way to be happy," Aruna said.

"You should laugh," Raj contributed.

Melanie shook her head from side to side wondering why everyone was crying on this day of happiness, herself included. She asked, "I know this is premature to ask, but do you have any idea what you will do with the money?"

Megan was incapable of speech. Tony replied, his voice cracking with emotion, "I can tell you we will surely donate a large portion of it to adoption agencies. We will invest some of it for the children's future. I can't believe your viewers care this much. Thank you all from the bottoms our hearts. We had no idea. We will try find to find a way to return it in as many ways as we can."

Tony wasn't at all certain why he had made the statement. He appeared to have great trust in an uncertain future, a future that would change in ways he could never have envisioned, and he would have a hand in it.

5

Melanie smiled, basking in the feeling of bringing joy to this family of international stars, not to mention her own rising status. Her own eyes clouding, she said, "And thank you, Tony and Megan, for your efforts. Our viewers will be anxious to follow the progress of your children. We are all part of your family. At this point it is fair to say that we have all adopted them."

The camera turned from capturing the three adults to the face of the reporter who announced, "This is Melanie Brown with CNN signing off and wishing you all a good day"

At the close of the session and with the cameraman packing up his gear, Melanie pulled out a number of legal documents and disclaimers the Rossis needed to sign before taking possession of the check. She went over them in detail until, after the signatures, she said goodbye to the children, promising to keep in touch.

Megan began crying anew at her departure, recovered, waited several minutes, deliberated, to finally decide to call Klara. She needed to share the news and have a little fun doing it. "Klara, what are you doing?"

"I'm in the back yard pruning our rose bushes trying to decide what to do for dinner. Why? Need a shoulder to cry on?" Klara asked.

"Yes. If you come over with the boys, I'll have Tony call in a large order of Chinese. I'll have to break the bank to do it, but what the heck," Megan said as a tease, knowing the show wouldn't air for several days. It would seem Klara hadn't noticed the CNN vehicle. She forced herself to hold down the laughter, which could flip to tears in an instant.

"Want me to loan you some money?" Klara asked, in all seriousness. She understood the financial difficulties the family faced.

"Nah, we're okay for the moment. Tony said he could shift around some money," Megan said.

"On second thought," Klara added, "I've got enough wienershnitzel and kraut to make it work. Do you want to try that? It will save you some money."

Megan paused for effect before declining the offer, "Thanks, but no. Your food is all right with Tony and me. You know that. We're trying to ease the kids into our diet after the poor guys grew up on rice and whatever. Chinese is a good tweener meal. Besides, if all else fails, they can settle for the rice that always comes with the Chinese."

"I'll show your kids how to use chop sticks," Klara offered.

Megan said, "Great. Tell your boys not to laugh while you do it. Otherwise, I can't guarantee their safety. One or both of them might get stabbed."

"You got it, lady. See you in a few," Klara said.

Megan checked the time and believed Hans should be home by now and said, "Bring Hans too. Tony might need some financial advice."

Karl and Billy were getting beaten badly playing Monopoly on the floor of the game room. Raj had quickly learned to pay attention to who was short of cash or needed money to get out of jail. He would offer to buy their properties at a discounted price or loan them money to get out of jail with interest attached to the loan. If a token landed on a good property, but the player didn't have enough money to buy it, if Raj had enough, he would loan them the difference and take a percentage of the rent each time another player landed on it.

Aruna quickly followed suit. Out of mercy, Raj suggested they team up, with him partnering with Karl and Aruna with Billy. The game became more competitive with Karl and Billy soon learning the art of fighting back through cut-throat negotiations.

This, while Hans discussed finances with

Tony and Megan. "Take a photo of the check. If anything goes south, you can always paste the picture up on your wall with the collection of free credit cards you get every day," Hans suggested, after they had all happily toasted the great news.

"Maybe I should give it to you for safe keeping," Tony gibed.

"Good idea, Tony, sign it over to me and I'll make sure nobody will steal the money," Hans laughed.

Megan said, "Seriously, it is a problem. We could use your professional advice."

Hans said, "Absolutely. Standard rates will apply. Doing business with you two will be a pleasure. It will add to my resume and attract more expensive clientele."

The following day, Tony ensured his attorney made plans to contribute designated amounts to the two adoption agents in India that assisted them in acquiring the children, including private checks to Gunta-Rao and Vishaswami. The latter earned the equivalent of $50 daily.

Both were upper-middle class, although, as a woman, Gunta-Rao received a lesser salary. It gave him great pleasure to think about each of them receiving a year's worth of money in a single check. The rest of the donations would have to wait until he and his wife got their bearings. His mother would be overjoyed to hear the news, but Arthur would be pissed if he had to find out about the money from watching the show on TV. No, let his mother tell him.

In the morning he called his mother. When he told her the news she laughed.

"What's so funny?" Tony asked.

"That should humble the old man," Christina replied. "You now have more than six times what we're worth. The way Arthur thinks, those terrible misbegotten kids of yours are suddenly a good investment. He might even want to come over for a visit."

As is usually the case, a large sum of money that befalls a person or a family can be a curse and a blessing. Attention has to be diverted toward protecting their interests. The elephant of financial difficulty had been replaced by the weight of having to manage the weight of overabundance. Like lottery winners, their brains totally flipped in their perspectives toward life, some could cope, others shot themselves.

Shortly after the show aired, Megan's cell blew up with congratulatory calls from her parents and all four siblings all wishing them the best and thoughtfully offering to help in any way they could.

To muddy the waters further, one month later they received a check for another $5 million and miscellaneous hundreds of thousands from the latest donations, which flooded in despite the amount the viewers had seen the Rossis receive. Instead of backing off the donations, from what anyone could fathom, the viewers saw the Rossis as a go-between—an honest agency they could trust to forward their moneys to other honest agencies, whatever that might mean; or damn it, just because they felt like giving money to the kids, and, all right, because Melanie Brown said so.

A voluminous amount of mail overflowed their curbside mail box, most of it credit card offers, donation requests from domestic and foreign causes, and an occasional nice letter. Tony had their mail forwarded to a P.O. box, hired a secretary who could pick up the mail, and toss all but the most relevant. He needed to reorganize his life. He still had a business to run.

Megan's story was different. She would be despised eternally and probably excommunicated from her family, if she didn't give them something. She made up her mind to give each $50 thousand and her parents getting twice that amount. She would declare the gift to be a one-time only present.

Would Tony approve? Would a fight occur between them? There was nothing in the documents they had signed to indicate money couldn't be given to whomever, only the admonition that if the public found out the couple had purchased a luxury yacht and an upscale home, the world as they knew it would come to an end. In a way the money represented entrapment. Any vacation that smacked of over-expense would be minutely examined by the public at large. These decisions occupied her mind during the day and trying to quiet a restless mind at night, while trying to sleep next to a husband who rolled about in his own sleeplessness.

"He does what?" Tony asked, incredulously.

"He wants to meet his grandchildren," Christina said.

"It wouldn't have anything to do with you lecturing him on moral decency or the fact that we came into a few dollars, would it?" Tony asserted.

Christina ensured the phone wasn't on SPEAKER and replied, "They probably won't remember meeting him and I want to have some fun before I file for divorce."

"You, divorce? I thought you were a staunch believer in eternal vows," Tony threw out.

"I changed my mind. At first, I believed Arthur had softened. However, his callous objectivity and his insults to your children were far overboard. I finally have grandchildren and Arthur would not accept them. Therefore, I will not accept him. I am at the end of my rope with him. You know as well as I do his obstinacy and lack of respect for others has gotten worse over the years. I didn't want to tell you, but he was rough on me. We've had our blowups and our half-way measures toward reconciliation. I refuse to tolerate another minute of his denial of my own grandchildren."

"Does he know you're going to divorce him?" Megan asked, taken aback at the bombshell news.

"You're damn right he does. Did you ever do something you wish you'd done years before? I looked into his past, something I never asked him about in detail," Christina said.

"Wait a minute, with everything going on between yours and my words to him, he still wants to see the kids?" Tony asked, confused.

"I told him that if he shakes hands with them, I might reconsider," Christina said.

"You will?" Tony asked,

"Not a chance," Christina laughed.

"Mom, you know our house is yours, too. Please keep us informed and come over anytime. Your grandchildren need you."

Two days later, Arthur got a ride to the airport to fly off on another week-long business trip. With well-planned and impeccable timing, Christina hired a company to move Arthur's possessions and his car into storage. Then she filed for divorce, changed the locks, and upgraded the home security system. She followed this by informing the neighbors and the local police substation of her activities and to keep an eye on the house.

For the moment, Arthur Tremont had disappeared from their lives.

Tremont had been indoctrinated to the depths. Whenever he thought about it, he felt a quaking fear such as he had never known. He began to sweat hoping his parents and associates would not find that his stepson was connected with . . . well, colored people, and the lot were rich beyond belief because of that adoption. What absolute inanity. Some of those people back home must have watched one or more of the CNN specials and if the word *ReCyclo* was mentioned, somebody might connect the dots. If so, his accidental death insurance policy might need to be upgraded. He had to stay distant from the adoption and hoped he didn't receive a call from his father anytime soon. You don't explain away those things. He thought, *Wait, I can always say I divorced her and left the family as soon as I found out. That should work, shouldn't it?*

6

"He told me his parents were dead," Tony said.

"And that's what you told me," Megan said to him.

Christina said, "He told everyone the same thing. His parents were supposed to have died in a car accident in Idaho shortly before we met."

"What else?" Tony asked.

"What else?" Christina answered, handing him a report. "It's a document from *Private Investigations, Inc.—We dig to the Depths*. This is a top quality locally-based private agency. These guys have former FBI people working for them. I hired them after I closed the door on him. I wanted to know why he lied about their deaths."

"Mom, it must have cost you a fortune," Tony exclaimed.

"Depends on how you want to look it at. I took all of our joint savings and unless he has a hidden stash, he's broke. Plus, I have more than enough money I got from your father's life insurance policy to last me."

"Mom, you sure play rough," Tony mused, delighted to see his mother take positive action.

Christina replied, "Your father was a rough man, fair, but rough. Whenever he sensed a threat, he went right for the jugular. Look, the document here says there is no record of the deaths of an Alice and Albert Tremont in Idaho, or anywhere else. It does say that those two are alive and well in Hayden Lake, Idaho and are tied to the Aryan Nations extremist cult."

"What!" Megan exclaimed, her face turning crimson.

Christina said, "I got suspicious when I looked at his cell numbers when he was taking a shower one day, getting ready to go on another one of his lengthy business trips. I copied down two numbers that kept coming from Idaho and going to Idaho, at least as far as the area code. I figured he had a girlfriend up there. I gave those numbers to the investigating agency. That's when they linked the numbers to his parents and to a Wilma Peterson, a married woman with children, probably his. That's why his travel itinerary included Idaho as part of the route. He always said it was to visit an old aunt and uncle in Boise."

"That's why he lied about his parents being dead," Tony concluded.

Christina said, "Any police records are sealed for his juvenile records, not so his school records. Even in that hotbed of racial tension, he got sent to the principal's office frequently for beating up black kids. Probably a chip off the old blockhead."

The horror of the scene played out as Tony and Megan saw what fury their adoption must have roiled within Arthur Tremont.

"Mom, what do you suggest we do?" Megan asked. Her wits were lost in the jumble of information.

Christina said, "I'm willing to bet that since he's gone independent several years ago, he hasn't hired a single Muslim, Jew, or person of color. He keeps a file of all the applications he received for work with his company. I now have that file. The federal EEO needs to know about it. He'll be so busy paying lawyers and fines he'll forget about all of us."

Megan needed to laugh hard, so she did.

Christina said, "But wait, there's more," at which time Tony began to laugh. His mother did not.

In a serious tone, she said, "If the world finds him guilty of hatred against these two famed children, we all should prepare for consequences. We'll keep that information as our Ace in the hole."

Megan said, "Can you imagine CNN showing up cold at this other woman's house for an interview? She would be the talk of the neighborhood."

Christina added, "It sounds like great fun, but we'd best leave it to his imagination, which should carry him to very dark unexplored depths. Your children have a life. They don't need this dirt."

"Mom, I knew your marriage to Arthur was rough for you. It was rough for all of us. Why didn't you divorce him a long time ago?" Tony inquired, gently.

"Call me old school. I believed marriage was sacred. I still believe it is, except for when it applies to me," she laughed.

Arthur Tremont returned to Idaho penniless with prosecutors dogging his every step. This occurred after investigators received ample documentation from an anonymous source presenting strong evidence. Close to one hundred persons, who had submitted job applications to Arthur Tremont for employ were rejected. Close to a hundred of them were non-white or Jewish.

7

The first Christmas took a twist. The neighborhood in which the Rossis lived had been high profile for years. It was one of those neighborhoods where the decoration of homes in a six-square-block area was reputed to be a sightseer's dream. Neighbor competed against neighbor to put on the best show. Countless lights of all colors were strung up and flashed, either sequentially, or in some kind of cadence, nativity scenes were lit, Santas and reindeers dominated roofs, and mechanical dwarfs sang carols.

Twinkling colored plastic icicles hung from eaves, not quite matching what nature had in mind. Cars came from miles away to make the tour. Orange cones placed in the street curbside served as gentle reminders to the public of No Parking regulations during a near two week time period from December 20th until January 2nd.

Holiday décor could be found on all but two homes, one of which belonged to a non-Christian family and the other belonged to the Rossis.

By choice, the couple had never participated in the tradition. They hosted their share of holiday parties and had gone to a number of others; they purchased and wrapped presents and had received gifts. They just didn't decorate. Some in the neighborhood called them cheapskates, others quietly celebrated their courage, enabling them to save a lot of money and time by not getting involved in the whole process each year.

Klara Hobert was heard to moan. "We could go on a cruise to the South Pacific for what we're spending this year. I mean, like I need another fruitcake in my house."

Megan pointed out, "You know, the lights have been on for a couple of days. The kids just got into bed. We should all take a close look at what others have done. There must be a dozens of cars out there cruising our street."

With impeccable timing, the instant Tony sat down to watch the game he recorded, Megan had made her statement. He popped up like a Jack in the Box and without saying a word, walked into the bedroom to rouse the children. He found both of them in pajamas. Aruna lay in bed under the covers and Raj stood at the window, blinds open, staring at the decorated homes across the street.

"Hey guys, do you want to go with me and mom outside to take a close look at those lights?" Tony offered.

Raj turned to stare at him a moment, realizing he was being handed a gift. "Sure, let's go," he said, with Aruna watching the exchange.

Soon, the four walked along the sidewalk. The air was clear, but cold. The smell of fireplace smoke filled the air. Megan was sorely tempted to borrow Raj's headphones. If she heard Jingle Bells or Silent Night one more time she would scream. The worst part was the children hadn't heard the songs before and wanted them played at bedtime. She wouldn't permit it.

At each home they came to, Raj stopped to stare in a daze at details of the lighting arrangements, until someone had to pull him along. At one point, Aruna spoke to him quietly in Marathi, "Raj, what are you staring at?"

He glanced briefly at her and replied, with all honesty, "I don't know. I can't figure it out."

"What is there to figure out?"

"A lot."

Eight months into the adoption, Megan and the kids had the routine down, a crucial factor for adaptation to a new environment and maximizing the learning process. Each mini session concentrated on a different topic, such as learning to read and write in the printed word and in cursive, mathematical skills, and explorations into a wide variety of subject areas. She felt sick at hearing news about many American high schools not requiring the need to read, compose an essay, add, or subtract, to graduate. When she mentioned the news to Tony, he commented, sourly, "Maybe one of them will become president someday."

During that period, Tony would take over spending weekends with them bird watching, overseeing their play on the swing set and swimming activities; even taking them out shopping. He and Megan were fully aware that, at some point, the two would need interaction with other children besides the Hobert boys.

Raj had complained of occasional mild headaches, but it wasn't until well into the eighth month when he had two consecutive sleepless nights. He was irritable during the day and unable to concentrate. Aruna discovered the cause of the problem. She pulled up a phone app and said, "Look, mom."

As parents, Tony and Megan were adamant the children should not have cell phones of their own until the age of 13 or 14. Megan, especially, believed the devices were destructive to young minds from a number of aspects, none of which were related to electrical activity or vibrations. Use of the calculator was one such subtraction from mental competency. On one occasion, when the four had gone to a restaurant, Raj observed more than half the patrons reading their phones and not conversing. He asked in his own manner, "Is this something people have to do?"

"Yes, to many people it is a bad habit. It has to be managed," Megan replied, simplistically, in lieu of using the words "addictive narcotic."

She and Tony did permit the children to use their personal phones on occasion to allow them to become familiar with the outside world via various apps. Aruna had been intrigued with wind currents around the world, especially those offshore. It was during one such occasion when she made her discovery.

The weather-radar app revealed a storm coming up from Mexico. It would be upon them in two days. The forecast called for several inches of rain to fall on the community. Megan remembered what Vishaswami had told her about weather triggering headaches, but with Raj, it was more than that. Her own research had found that weather sensitive people began to react even before the barometric pressure began drop and continued to suffer days after the storm had passed. Furthermore, a precipitous drop in barometric pressure was expected, followed by high winds. As Vishaswami had alluded, Raj might have additional underlying conditions.

His migraine began in earnest the third night. For the next several days, Megan devoted periods of time in his newly blacked-out bedroom, rubbing his temples, neck and shoulders, all of which helped lessen the pain, while the storm raged about them. She cursed herself for not tending to it sooner. The headache finally subsided, but the boy had become irritable, rude, and unable to concentrate. He ate little and had lost weight. Megan forced him to drink water and juices despite his claims of not wanting to ingest anything.

When Tony arrived at this office, he placed a call to Hans, who would also be in his own office. He discussed the matter with his friend, who replied, "Tony, I have just the man for you. His name is Peter Franklin. He's a medical doctor and a psychiatrist. He specializes in children. His wife, Linda, is a neuropsychiatrist. Don't ask me the difference. They met in graduate school and have three children in college somewhere. They've been clients of mine for a several years.

"Linda has an office, but Peter runs his business out of their home in Scottsdale. How they got a business license in a residential neighborhood I don't know. I went over there once and was afraid to scratch my head. I got paranoid and thought maybe the two of them would psychoanalyze me to the point where I would need counseling.

"Anyway, if you want, I'll call him when we finish talking and run interference for you. When you do call, he'll already have the background. Got a pencil? Here's his info."

Tony called Megan to tell her about the conversation and said he would call Franklin after lunch. When he did call, a female voice chimed, "Doctor Franklin's office. This is Eva."

Tony said, "Yes, this is Tony Rossi. A friend of mine named Hans Hobert might have called this morning . . ."

"You are *the* Tony Rossi. Yes, he did call," she said.

"I don't know about the *the* part. I would like to speak with Dr. Franklin, please," Tony told her. Fame dost hath tendrils.

"Of course, one moment please," Eva politely requested.

Shortly, another voice said, "Hello, this is Dr. Franklin."

"Doctor, my name is Anthony Rossi. My neighbor, Hans Hobert, suggested I contact you."

"You can call me Peter. Hans and I did speak at some length this morning about your situation. I understand you have a daughter the same age, as well. How is the boy now?" Franklin asked.

Tony frowned, in a sign of helplessness and responded, "Depressed, withdrawn, angry, tired, and confused. He's frequently moody. His sister says he's always been that way. Other than those issues, I guess he's fine."

"If it's all right with you, I'd like to see him at your earliest convenience. Is that a possibility?" Franklin asked. His voice was relaxed, but with clinical concern.

"I'll cater to your wishes. We're seeking professional help," Tony replied. He could not hide his own anxiety.

To Franklin, every case possessed its challenges. From what Hans had revealed, this one might be more so, especially since he had seen the TV specials on them, although he had heard nothing of any medical problems confronting the boy. He suggested, "This is Tuesday. Hang on a second."

A moment later he came back and said, "I'd like to visit with your entire family, your daughter included. I have an open slot this Friday from 9:00 am to 11:00 am. You can check with Eva, my secretary, regarding my fee schedule. We have a room here with various toys where children can interact. With your permission, I'd like to video the time they're in the room without being obtrusive about it. I'll need to review the video. The time I spend doing that will be added to the fees.

"Oh, I'd like my wife to be present. She's in the field, as well. She's the brains of the outfit. No charge for her. Will that work for you, Tony?" Franklin attempted to interject a note of levity into the conversation in order to relax the concerned caller and for him to be prepared for a very unusual case.

"Like I said, we need professional help and we'll go with Hans's recommendation to work with you," Tony returned.

Franklin added, "From what you're telling me, I have a feeling there is a lot more than migraine going on here. If he's not under a doctor's care at the present time, the medication you're using may be over the counter. It works for some cases, but change may be indicated. I won't know which type to use until I do the evaluations. Bring what you have with you, please."

"We'll look forward to seeing you Friday," Tony said. He waited to be transferred to the secretary. Breathing a sigh of relief, he knew his son stood a good chance of receiving help. Who knows, the entire family might finally get some sleep.

Raj did not receive the information well. He had no problem about seeing a doctor to fix his headaches and whatever else might be wrong with him; he did have problem about being exposed to the bright outdoors.

The hour of departure approached. Raj remained in his pajamas. Tony did not sit on the edge of Raj's bed to negotiate. He stood over his son. He had an urge to shame the boy into submission, but quickly thought better of it.

It wasn't as though the boy were petulant and required strong arm tactics to bring him to face reality; he did have a true medical condition.

Tony put an arm on his shoulder to give him encouragement and presented, gently, "Raj, I'm proud of you. How about if you and me and mom and Aruna team up together to make a good try at getting you fixed? Here's a mask your mother sometimes uses to cover her eyes at night so she can sleep."

With considerable effort, Raj grinned up at his father with painful eyes, and simply nodded, taking the mask and putting it on.

Tony pushed the button to open the garage door to lead the family into the glare of a sun where hydrogen is turned into helium in a fusion reaction 93 million miles away. The red of pre-dawn glow had quickly disappeared to provide life-giving yellow-white light and warmth to a planet some believed was unique among worlds. No others might ever be found like Earth, nor ever would be reached if they were found. After evaluating all the years of accumulated data, even NASA gave up on believing in UFOs (UAPs).

What kind of country was he training his children to live in? In Phoenix, Tony saw hundreds of tents lining the roadways and under bridges downtown. How could he and Megan prepare their children for this worsening situation, to teach them to have a direction in this new country of theirs spiraling downward? Indeed, he had to admit virtually every nation faced its overwhelming difficulties from what snippets of news he caught. It seemed no problem existed when he didn't know about it.

The morning rush hour was still rushing when, using his GPS and following traffic alerts, Tony took back streets to arrive on time at the Franklin residence. The sign above the front door of a relatively nondescript home in a well-manicured neighborhood read: PETER FRANKLIN, M.D., Psy.D.

The woman answering the knock stood a short 5’3”. A little on the chubby side. A slight amount of rouge highlighted her cheeks. Her short hair was black and spiked in keeping with the times. Greeting the visitors, she said, “Good morning. My name is Eva. I spoke with you on the phone.” She looked down at the boy and girl, saying, “And you must be Raj and Aruna. Please come in. Peter is in his office with Linda.” They were all family now.

Tony’s earlier call about Raj’s migraine had forewarned the Franklins to close the blinds and pull the curtains to darken the home. The family entered the home and Eva gently closed the door behind them. She put a light hand on Raj’s shoulder and said, “Raj, you can take off your eye covering. It will be all right.”

She led them to a large bedroom that had been converted into a comfortable office with enough expensive leather chairs to accommodate a half-dozen people. A woman rose from a seat in front of a desk where a man sat behind it. He stood as well. Eva introduced the family to the doctors by name. The woman said, “How pleased to meet you all.”

Linda Franklin was thin and well proportioned. Her movements were lithe, suggestive of a person who spent more time in the gym than reading a cell phone. She had a healthy glow about her face and twinkling green eyes framed by short and styled brunette hair.

Eva departed, closing the door behind her.

Peter Franklin did not look like his deeper phone voice sounded. When he stood, the man was some two inches shorter than his wife, with a good head of hazel hair to match his friendly eyes. He came around the front of the desk to shake hands and invited his guests to take a seat, then he returned to his own seat.

Tony asked, to no one particular, "What's the difference between a psychiatrist and a neuro-psychiatrist?"

Peter said, "I've been asked that before. To put it simply, a psychiatrist, or mental health therapist, will look at how the external world is affecting your behavior and personality. A neuropsychiatrist will look 'within', often examining your neurological networks and the brain's chemical makeup. But let's not get caught up in minutiae. We're here today to meet you and to play games; that is, if Raj and Aruna enjoy games."

"Yeah, we do," reported Raj. Aruna nodded vigorously, each trying to understand what the hell the man just said. "Great, so do we," Peter remarked brightly. "After we talk for a while, Linda will take your kids to the Playroom. Before we go further, what is their exact age?"

Megan answered, "In truth, we only know their age was seven-something when the adoption process began. The first counselor, a Mrs. Gunta-Rao, made a note of this when she transferred them to DAO. It was some time in the early fall. The date of September 1 had been arbitrarily chosen by her and all official documents reflect this date, so they recently turned eight.

Linda pointed out a room next door where a window had been installed in the connecting wall. She said to the children, "I'm ready to play some games. You can choose some and I will choose some." She arose and led the children to the adjoining room while Franklin spoke with Tony and Megan until the time expired. Raj replaced his mask and Eva held his hand to lead the family to the front door.

Several days passed before Raj's headache had dissipated, although he remained petulant. Franklin himself called to invite the family for a return visit, which Tony absolutely needed to attend, although he was facing a crisis at work. One of his workers, a man by the name of Rick Froman, had been secretly meeting with an outside influencer, who was trying to get the entire staff unionized, despite the absence of grumblings about hours, pay, or benefits. He did not need a union sticking its nose into his business.

While Linda visited with the children, Franklin passed a report across the desk to Tony, who quickly read it and gave it to Megan.

Franklin said, "It's too early to tell for certain. From our viewpoint, Raj is suffering from a combination of Asperger syndrome, bipolar disorder, and some aspects of environmental sensitivity. Nothing in there is clear cut. Also, we have another factor to consider."

The doctor pointed out the left window of his office to expose the toy room where Aruna appeared to be following Raj's instructions, while Linda sat on the floor with them. Raj had configured a number of plastic interlocking pieces into a building with legs that had mobile joints. From all indications, he was directing his assistants to find more batteries. Evidently, his concentration on a specific task overrode his ailments. The recording would note the record time it took the twins to assemble a 250 piece jigsaw puzzle.

Franklin drew their attention back when he said, "He is the most intelligent child we have ever tested, and those tests were conducted when he was ill. My wife and I are thinking about co-authoring a paper about him for *The American Journal of Psychiatry*. He will be called Patient X."

Megan said, "I agree he's smart with a lot of genetic disorders, two qualities which, in my experience, frequently partner with one another.. You just described a lot of people."

Franklin shook his head and replied, "Not this young and not this aware. His brilliance is quite shocking. The girl, too, is very bright."

"So where do we go from here?" Tony inquired, wondering how the heck one properly educates brilliant children.

Franklin said, "I need to spend one-on-one time with Raj. We can schedule those meetings. For now, though, I'm going to prescribe a new oral medication. It should stabilize his moodiness and lessen the intensity of anxiety peaks when they occur. It must be taken twice daily. Read the directions carefully, especially the part about side effects. Let me know of any of those occur."

"Is it like lithium?" Tony asked.

Franklin said, "Yes, it is in some ways. With lithium, though, we worry about loss of memory and potential kidney damage, something I'm not fond of, with special dangers for his age group. This new medication will assist in suppression of manic symptoms such as aggression, extreme hyperactivity, and anger, without lithium's side effects. Linda and I will take careful notes and I want you to do the same. Also, I want to start him on probiotics. Their effect on adults is questionable, but for his age we have evidence they will help him better manage stress and anxiety because the population of various microbes in our gut are known to affect our attitudes. We need microbial balance to provide the proper nutrients for good physical and mental stability. With his past diet overseas, those microbial life forms are lacking and will take time to repopulate. Once they do, he should stabilize even more.

"Start a log book. Like I said, we can make

him a case study, which will go a long way toward treating other children." Franklin pulled out a prescription pad from a desk drawer, wrote something on it, tore off a sheet, and handed it over to Tony.

Glancing up at a wall clock, Franklin said, "It looks like we're about out of time for now. Eva will set up your next appointments. Tony, Megan, I look forward to continuing more work with your lovely family."

The sessions at the doctor's office appeared to have done Raj some good. On the drive home, he remarked, "The lady was really nice. I like her."

"Me too," chimed Aruna.

"She kept asking us stuff that mom already taught us like all kinds of simple number games and reading things," Raj said.

"Except when we couldn't do it anymore. It got too hard," Aruna confessed.

Tony laughed and said, "Kids, the way you're going, what you can't do today, you will do tomorrow."

"Promise?" asked Raj.

"It's a promise," said Tony, glancing at his wife who was leaning back in her seat, eyes closed, with a smile on her lips. At least, events were moving in a positive direction. He dropped off the family at home and drove to the plant.

The first thing he did was to pull Rick Froman's file. He was the field boss who oversaw the arrival and departure of the waste trucks to the yard. Rick was a good man, He also had two teenage children and, according to rumor, had a wife who was running up medical bills. He decided to double up Rick's duties by also putting him in charge of overseeing the dumping of trash into the conveyor belt and give him a good pay raise. That should shut him up. The man already in charge of the chute would be moved to the interior of the building. Problem solved.

8

Three years passed. The routine of training and teaching became as predictable and dependable as a wound clock. Because the children had been born and bred into routine, the teacher had two choices: she could break or maintain the routine. She chose the latter.

Her two charges came to know what to expect and at what time to expect it five days a week and a half-day on Saturday. Sundays belonged to the children to play, create and read as they pleased. Tony set aside one Sunday a month to chase store-bought balsawood planes in the park, spending hours at the Phoenix zoo, visiting all manner of museums, boating at a lake, fishing, or having a barbecue. Those were times of adventure for the children and for the parents. During those early training years, neither child was diffident; their quick learning gave them over self-confidence. As a result, Megan came to trust them to fulfill their study assignments and to turn them in completed on schedule. She didn't want them to compete against another, because, if one was a consistent winner, the other might quit the contest. Instead, she offered a small cash reward at the end of each week when all assignments were turned in on time.

Sociologists would later submit that, given a lack of familial background, their curiosity and drive was purely genetic presenting strong evidence to show one's genetic code is physically changed through intense experiences by parents and grandparents. Indeed, the new science of epigenetics had found this to be true.

Others would present that the "simple" flip-flop of lives combined with proper education helped bring them forth. Moderates accept both viewpoints to be manifest. To this date, the debate still rages.

Megan's gifts to her brothers and sisters did not go well in all cases, something she feared might happen. One married brother with children enjoyed an occasional visit to a local casino. In four months he had gambled away all the money she had given him and had maxed out three credit cards. His wife took the children and moved to another state.

In a second instance, a sister invested her money into the pharmaceutical industry, in particular the branch specializing in cocaine usage. She spent months in rehab.

In a third instance, a brother got a hot tip on a

stock, invested his fortune, only to find the company went bankrupt the following month. The friend who gave him the hot tip ceased being a friend.

The fourth sibling, a younger sister, purchased several acres of vacant land as a future investment.

As for her parents, they paid off the mortgage on their home and had enough left to add to their retirement fund.

Over those three years, Aruna had grown from a below average 45 pounds to the normal of 71 pounds, and stood taller than Raj by an inch. He had grown accordingly in weight. In another two years both would pass their high school GEDs.

To be sure, 100 years ago elementary school students from Middle America knew more about this country and had more reading and math skills than today's college entrant. By any measure, however, the twins were exceptional, especially their math skills. Both possessed a strong grasp of algebra and trigonometry. Numbers seem to be their calling. Both understood mathematical shortcuts. Their reading skills were at the level of college students some forty years ago.

In terms of their interests, Raj became drawn to the biological sciences, especially those dealing with human health. Aruna, too, followed biology with her interests leaning toward nature in general.

Raj's monthly visits to the doctor became quarterly until they became semi-annual. Medications were adjusted, IQ tests administered when he was healthy to find the score had climbed, and logs were maintained by his parents. Climate and stress were the two factors deemed to be at the heart of his reactions, aside from underlying genetic deficiencies which served as the basis for his mood swings. The genetic deficiencies could be controlled, not so the weather sensitivity, which science had yet to get a good handle on, other than to note the presence of an elevated level of serotonin. The hormone was well known to affect moods, some more than others. Depending on the person, the mood can be depressive or excited. To Raj, the clinical terminology translated to a single word: pain.

9

Peter and Linda Franklin considered all the variables when they co-published that Patient X, was his own worst enemy. He was self-driven in a way even his sister couldn't explain. Although she had tested with a very high IQ, it was nothing close to her brother's, which measured at the highest end of the genius range. When one got scores as elevated as his, the old measuring system broke down.

As is frequently the case, experts noted little correlation between extreme intelligence and success in life. This was because other social factors overrode the intelligence, with "success" being the operative word. Criminal masterminds, along with brilliant individuals in all walks of life, found their own brand of success. The challenge became a matter of learning how to teach the boy various ways in which he could regulate his creative impulses to minimize the frequency of the mood swings. These were held in check by medication. As he grew, he would come to appreciate the efforts made to keep him from self-destruction. This proved to be a difficult undertaking in that the more the boy learned the more he wanted to learn.

Megan faced an ongoing problem of time. The huge metropolitan area of Phoenix often necessitated a one-way travel time of 45 minutes, or longer, to reach a given activity, unless it were local. Thus, she would spend hours driving and then waiting for the activity to be completed, something she refused to do. She believed in the philosophy of "diamonds in your own back yard," so she sought more regional enterprises.

In addition to home schooling, Megan had arranged for them to play in local sports leagues, with soccer as the primary sport. At the six week mark, another boy deliberately tripped Raj and he punched the offender in the nose. This impulsive action got him kicked off the team, his parents lectured to, and triggered a migraine to lay him up for the remainder of the week. Upon hearing the news, Aruna quit her team, as well. If her brother couldn't play, then neither would she.

Following this effort, Megan got the twins involved in a youth-oriented local playhouse. Their excellent memories enabled the twins to recite long lines with Raj excelling in his roles as antagonist. They found great fun in the challenge, until the playhouse burned down.

Tony commiserated with her and had the idea

to stop by a local Walmart to pick up a box containing three games: chess, checkers, and Chinese checkers. Introducing them to the family turned out to be a good decision. His skill at any of the games was quite unremarkable, although at one time he had enjoyed chess and checkers during junior high school.

The family frequently played the games after dinner, with the children's skills soon far outstripping those of the parents. Of the three games, both kids enjoyed chess the most.

After a full month had passed, Tony stopped at a game store. He spoke with the sales clerk about his situation and the clerk pointed out a number of electronic chess sets. Tony purchased one that was portable, battery operated, and had ten different computer skill levels guaranteed to challenge the best minds. One could play against another person or play against the machine. The salesman told him, "There are 600 million chess players in the world and the United States alone has some 85 thousand registered championship players. How can you go wrong?"

Tony became an instant hero at home. Before too many days had passed, he was forced to purchase a second unit to avoid arguments between the children, who didn't always want to play against one another, or worse, to beat up on their parents.

Aruna became a devotee of surfing the web, trying to separate fact from fiction. The bulk of her online time, though, was spent researching the endless forms of life on earth, all of which must be preserved.

To Raj, the gift of the chess game was a Godsend. It permitted him to put his mind into a wondrous slot where he could look into the future, predict, calculate, strategize, defend, and even go on the attack. From this point forward, he could be lost in space, exactly where he preferred to be.

CNN continued to do annual updates on their progress, always sending proceeds back to the family. At this point, the contributions were minor. The major flap had ended. Melanie had been taken off assignments and got hired to oversee the Asian desk for the corporation.

The only real minutes Tony and Megan had conversing in private was when they went to bed, with soft music coming from each of the bedrooms, having converted the game room into Aruna's room.

Tony said, "We need to challenge them more. I agree with my mother. We have two genies in a bottle. How we set them free under controlled conditions is up to us."

Megan said, "I'll get them enrolled in online courses of their choosing, with guidance, of course. They'd be bored in nothing flat by attending lectures in a classroom and would draw more unwanted attention because of their age.

They appreciate straight talk from us. If we sit them down and explain how they can shortcut basic courses by testing out, it should strike a nerve.

"You have to understand the age we're dealing with. Both are pre-puberty. Raj wants to be accepted and stand out at the same time while showing his independence. He needs affection because of a lot of uncertainties and conflicts in his mind."

Tony felt guilty. Megan knew so much more about his own children than he did. Part of his guilt stemmed from his work ethic. He would have to sacrifice time at a job he struggled to keep afloat in order to spend time with his children. "What can I do to help?" he asked, wondering whether he actually could help when she told him.

Megan said, "Spend more time talking to your son. I'll talk to Aruna. Take him to a book store. He needs hands-on experience, you know, building, creating, using his imagination. Maybe you can ask him if he wants to join an engineering club, maybe hook up with a bunch of nerds. Tempe has a school here for gifted children. It may be what both of them need. Encourage Raj to go for something that gets him excited. Express interest in the same thing. He's a good person. He'll work it out. I'll do the same with Aruna. What concerns me is this violent streak she has. We need to get a handle on it before she gets into trouble."

"Violent streak? Aruna?"

Megan passed up a sudden urge to wrap her knuckles against her husband's head. She said, "Yes, our Aruna is looking for trouble to get into. Raj is more covert. She is more patient. Academically, she's leaning toward the biological sciences. Only yesterday, I bought her a book on coral reefs and other books relating to general ecology. It looks like she's leaning toward environmental issues. I also bought him a picture book on the muscular and nervous system of the human body.

"At this age, her coordination is increasing and her voice may change. In addition, she will begin to grow breasts and start her periods. She needs female friends with whom she can identify and compare notes."

Tony said, "At least the Hobert boys are sticking with them, and vice versa. I wonder how long that will last. By the way, tomorrow is Saturday. I was thinking about taking the four of them to see Avatar in High Def. Want to make it a six-some?"

Megan smiled, giving a soft grunt in reply.

Tony paused a few moments, thinking, then he said, "Good night, dear."

His received a gentle snore for a reply.

The movie experience did not go well. Taking the SUV, the six arrived at the beginning of the trailers, all armed with boxes of buttered popcorn and drinks. Raj wore a T-shirt that read on the back:

JU-JITSU IS THE ART OF FOLDING CLOTHES WITH PEOPLE STILL INSIDE THEM.

KARATE IS THE ART OF FOLDING PEOPLE STILL INSIDE THEIR CLOTHES

Unfortunately, his temporary sense of bravado was short lived. Five minutes into the explosive action of the previews with the Dolby Surround Sound pounding out its drumbeats, Raj grabbed his head in pain.

"Oh, boy," Megan said, putting her arm around him.

"I'll take him home," Tony said.

The Hobert boys turned to look at Raj, totally at a loss as to what might be happening to their neighbor hoping with all their might they wouldn't miss the movie.

"We only have one car," Megan said. "I'll take him home and stay there. You can call for an Uber after the movie."

Tony agreed. He explained the plan to the remaining three children. They could care less. If he had gone with Megan for a short time and returned and any trouble occurred during his short absence, he felt certain Aruna would try to stab any child molester in the eye with a soda straw. For Raj, this particular headache offered a new experience in pain coupled with the addition of multiple colors. In the past, if color were present, his closed eyes saw a red glow. This time it was as though his father had turned a corner in the car and had run into a roadblock with a score of emergency vehicles flashing red, yellow, and blue lights. The colors came from the edges to the middle, filling the dome like stars in a night sky. Sometimes the colors were dots of light. Sometimes they morphed into shifting splotches.

This occurrence was different in another way. Numbers and mathematical symbols came and went, as though he were playing three dimensional chess with him on the inside watching the figures come and go around him to combine and separate. Some portion of his brain had been tapped, which added a sense of curiosity to the painful experience, as though he struggled to solve some kind of mystery.

Megan gave him two baby aspirins along with doses of medication she always carried on her person for just such an occasion. The colors had been replaced by the standard migraine that Raj almost welcomed as an old friend.

Megan needn't have worried about Aruna. She appeared to have her life under control. The first week of soccer practice, weeks before she left the team, she met a girl named Marie Koraskova. The attractive brunette was two years older, an inch taller, and much more physically mature than Aruna. The girls bonded immediately through some undefined chemical reaction. She attended a private school, and like her fifteen year-old brother who attended the same school, was picked up from and delivered home by a private school bus. A second older brother attended college. Marie's father was a surgeon. Her mother wanted to cut back to part-time nursing, but with a serious shortage of nurses, she found herself working long hours.

Freshly degreed and certified, the parents had met while working the same hospital in Odessa, Ukraine. Each saw a bleak future for their country and made arrangements to fly to America with a fair amount of money transferred to a major bank in the States.

If you wanted to go anywhere in your career, you spoke English, which the young married couple did. Their families in the Ukraine were already entrenched in both the medical and political arenas and assisted the couple with their move.

The United States needed good doctors and nurses, especially those experienced in gunshot wounds. Plastic surgeons qualified. The skids were self-greased. Within a year, both had passed requisite medical examinations and quickly became certified in the State of Arizona, where they began work at the Mayo Clinic in Scottsdale.

The timing couldn't have been better in a period when the number of doctors skilled in surgery had declined, while the number of shootings had increased. In a sense, the young couple had crossed the world only to find they had returned home.

The evenings belonged to the couple, so, while Raj constructed moving remote-controlled cars that turned into moving remote-controlled buildings, Aruna read all about the anatomy of a whale in Melville's *Moby Dick.*

She got caught up in the universe of sea life, until she got caught up in the study of life on land, which intertwined with life in the air, until she returned to the sea. One night, while Tony made the rounds to receive his mini-education from each of the children, Aruna asked, "Dad, can we see Marie sometime? You remember, she's my friend from when I played soccer. Ever since you got us phones, she's the one I talk to all the time. She already asked her parents and they said it was all right."

To protect his family, Tony needed to know what kind of problem they might be heading into. He asked, cautiously, "Did you tell her about, well, our whole adoption deal?"

"Dad, I'm not a self-possessed person who loves to bring attention to myself. Of course, not," Aruna retorted. "Besides, I don't think she would care."

Tony backed off and replied, "If you go, Raj

might want to go along too."

"I guess that would be okay. She says she has two older brothers, one is fifteen and the other is eighteen," Aruna responded.

Tony had to think about this. Other than going over to visit the Hoberts and seeing his mother and Megan's parents during holidays, the kids hadn't visited other homes. He'd want to talk it over with Raj and Megan. If Raj was adamant he didn't want to go, Raj and Megan would stay here for a couple hours while he and Aruna visited.

He saw no reason why there would be a blowup. His gut told him everything would be fine. He'd have to talk with Marie's parents. Why was he stressing about this, anyway?

In the end, it was Megan who spoke with Marie's mother and Megan who took Aruna over for the introductory visit—something about a woman taking a girl. It would appear less officious. Tony didn't get it, but he was very pleased with the way the situation worked out. He would have to stay home and forced to watch a football game, darn it.

The red-brick red-shingled single-story Scottsdale home was situated in a gated community. The majority of occupants were engaged in the legal, medical, and real estate businesses. A large well-manicured lawn fronted the property lined with rose bushes in front of a red brick wall with two thornless mesquite trees side-by-side, so large, their branches intertwined.

The directions given to Megan by Mrs. Koraskova were explicit and at 7:30 pm sharp, Megan rang the doorbell. A camera above the door oversaw the front of the home and another was associated with the doorbell itself.

A pause occurred, ostensibly because the occupants were checking the screen on the wall next to the door, or on their phone, to identify the caller.

A moment later, a young girl opened the door and shouted "Aruna, you came." She wore baggy jeans with pre-cut holes in the knees (extra charge for designer clothing) and a plain gray sweatshirt.

Behind Marie stood a woman, not wearing a nurse's uniform, but a short blue shift, tied at the waist by a red sash. She wore blue flats and maintained her light brown hair flipped in the back with only a slight amount of lipstick and a trace of blush at the cheekbones. She looked like an older version of her daughter. She spoke with only the slightest of accents. "You are Megan and Aruna. My name is Olena. Please come in."

The couple entered the large living room fashioned in tasteful Western motif to meet another member of the family, Anton, the 15year old son. He looked clean, stood of average height, possessed a shock of curly yellow hair, and wore blue jeans, sneakers, and an Arizona

Cardinals T-shirt. Approaching the pair, he extended his hand, smiling, with all courtesy, and said, "Mrs. Rossi and Aruna, welcome to our home." His voice had long since changed from the cracking young voice that sought to bridge the gap between pre-puberty to puberty.

"Come on, Aruna, let's show you what we're working on," Marie said, grabbing her friend's hand and hauling her off, followed by Anton.

Olena said, "Megan, come. Ivan is in the kitchen preparing some snacks."

Ivan looked more like a chef than a surgeon wearing an apron around his neck over a brown polo shirt. His own curly yellow hairline had receded and a bald pate was emerging.

He pulled a tray of cookies from the oven and set them on the counter. Closing the oven door he turned to the women and confessed, "You caught me at my real passion."

"Hello, Ivan. It's a pleasure to meet you," Megan said. "I'm curious. What kind of surgeon are you; heart, brain, hand and feet?"

"Plastic," Ivan remarked, removing his apron and hanging it on a small hook. "Even in Odessa"—he pronounced it Adyessa— "people want face lifts. I also help with fire and shooting victims, although I have my preferences."

I understand you are schooling your children at home," he added. "Marie seems to be impressed with your daughter. We saw your history on TV, the children didn't. Why muddy the waters, as they say?"

Plastic surgeon. To Megan, the word permeated everything from the very top of the tallest mountains to the bottom of the oceans, to the bodies of life forms themselves, to consumer goods, and, of course, to doctors' titles. She replied, "We're fortunate in that both our children are fast learners. How is private school working out for your kids?"

This time Olena answered. "It's so much better than public school. Those are so terribly disappointing."

While the adults chatted, the three children visited Anton's room. In addition to the bed, the furnishings consisted of a desk with a neat stack of manila folders, a computer, a roll away chair on a plastic floor mat, a book case filled with books on sea life and political science. According to Marie, if you met Anton, you also met the older brother, with the younger emulating the older.

Both Aruna and Marie had rebellious tendencies, driven to change the world in some way. Passionate Marie was unstoppable and invincible.

Aruna wanted to save life in the seas as much as others wanted to protect dogs, crayfish, and frogs gone astray. Marie knew a lot about the world of water and sent links to Aruna's computer to educate her new friend about how humans were decimating absolutely everything.

"And we're doing it on purpose," she would note with finality.

Anton pointed to a 2' x 4' laminated colored poster on his wall which depicted a wide variety of sea creatures. These included whales, dolphins, fishes, sea turtles, and seagulls. A number tag on each creature corresponded to its name listed at the bottom of the poster.

Anton said, "Each year we dump 8 million tons of plastics into the oceans. There are at least 14 million tons of plastic on the ocean floor. On the surface, it swirls around in great masses. Fish eat it, get tangled in it—it's absolutely *everywhere.*"

Aruna watched carefully. Anton had given the lecture before. In fact, he had a plan to bring more awareness to the problem and force people in charge to bring a halt to their abuses. The plan was fraught with danger. It would take time and planning. Was Aruna in or out?

"Absolutely, I'm in," Aruna cried, her heart throbbing with excitement.

"There are several of us," Marie explained.

Anton said, in a more quiet voice, lest he be overheard, "We are gathering members to execute our great plan and we need people we can trust."

"You can trust me," Aruna declared, unabashedly.

"Good. We'll count you in," Marie declared, taking pride in having obtained another recruit for their grand cause.

"You have a brother don't you? What about him?" Marie asked, excitedly.

"Raj? Nah, forget him. He's lost in space somewhere," Aruna said, truthfully. She thought about recruiting the Hobert boys, but dismissed the impulse to mention them. They were too much into themselves and could care less about saving what's left of the world. She felt certain she would see its end during her lifetime.

The timing couldn't be better for Aruna. Megan wanted to start them on a heavy dose of biology to include a CD series on *Life on Planet Earth.* Biology had been Megan's major in college through a Master's Degree before transitioning into teaching. Now that the kids were better disciplined, she could spend more time with them on something she personally loved.

Constantly on the lookout for new ways to impart knowledge to her bright children, she had found a source for programmed learning books of all types, in which one sentence leads to the next to the next and so on, each time adding a piece of knowledge until the subject had been covered. They had worked well for her and she had no doubt the kids would relish learning their favorite subjects at their own pace.

At the least they would stay out of trouble.

10

Raj couldn't concentrate. His mind jumped from one topic to another. For one thing, his sister was up to something over at Marie's and it didn't smell good. Every time she got involved with some new pet project, it proved to be a bad idea and she never saw it through.

First, she wanted to collect stamps that had pictures of animals until she found out it would require either money to purchase them online, or travel to stamp stores when she lacked the means to travel. Then she began her coin collection with the buffalo head nickel and a koala bear coin from Australia until she ran into the same problem of acquiring more.

He'd have to ask her what was going on. He thought about going next door to play some games with Karl and Billy. No, to be honest, he really wanted to play with Alex, their five-year-old German Shepherd. The dog loved to romp with him and slobber all over his face.

He pulled out his phone to inspect the calculus app he'd downloaded. He knew his dad promised to take him to a spate of used bookstores so he could buy more math books, but he found the app useful, especially when he had to stand in line with his mom at the pharmacy to pick up some prescription.

Talk about learning; summer would be here soon enough and so would a full schedule of laboratory courses at the university. He signed up for Chemistry I and Physics I. If he completed the college level courses successfully, he would not only complete the lecture requirements for high school, he wouldn't have to take those two classes in college and could go to the next levels.

Because of his youth, he'd be stared at a lot and maybe even made fun of. The thought made him smile in anticipation. He had no doubts, no fears, no expectations. Lack of faith in himself never entered the picture.

Successfully completing those lab courses would be as automatic as walking across the street, not because of an ego issue, but because he saw it as his destiny. Understanding theory was one thing, putting it to use was another. The hands-on challenge of lab work made his heart beat faster. He pulled out a large picture book of the human body and began leafing through it again.

He had overheard his mother tell Klara he had loner tendencies. Klara said she thought it meant a person was anti-social. His mother explained that a loner is a person who prefers to be alone, but can also mix with others, which fit him perfectly.

The sound of the garage door opening pulled him away from his thoughts. The time had come to find out what kind of mischief his sister was getting into.

Raj put down his phone, pivoting his chair to face the door when he heard a knock. The door opened and Aruna stepped in, Her eyes were bright with excitement. She proceeded to tell him all she had learned and that their dad was a hero. This was news to Raj.

"How so?" he asked.

"Because he tries to keep plastics from getting into the oceans," she replied.

Raj knew the work his father did, yet he never looked at it from the other side. He turned down his mouth in a show of appreciation, something he had seen Tony do.

Aruna went on, "There's a bunch of them, well, me too now. We want to make a statement, you know, make the world aware of the problem."

Raj shook his head and said, "I'm sure the world already knows."

"Well, we're going to make sure they know better. Do you want to join us?" she concluded.

"Join you to do what?" he asked.

"To make changes," she stated.

"That's stupid. You want me to join you and some other kids to do something you don't even know what it is?" he said.

"As soon as I find out, I'll tell you," she said. "It probably won't be until after our birthday."

Aruna left for her own room to email Marie and Anton to report she had told Raj and he seemed interested, while Raj rolled his eyes after she left, picked up his phone, and returned to the calculus app, thinking, *I'm sure glad I don't have any hang-ups like she does.*

In the ninth month of the year, the kids turned 11 years old—9/11 for those keeping track. Aruna could tell you about anything a person might want to know about the oceans. She could describe the direction of the deep currents, El Niño, La Niña, the changing temperatures of the water over time, and about the migratory patterns of whales and dolphins. She could tell you that over 700 species of life in the seas are known to ingest plastic. You name it, they ate it. Plastic sheets, bags and packaging cause the greatest number of deaths. Hard plastics cause the most deaths of sea birds, especially hard rubber and fishing debris. Turtles and whales swallow the plastic, which affects their ability to navigate away from approaching boats. Check any fish you catch and odds are it will have plastic in its gut. Check any human and odds are you will find the same thing—ditto soil and food stuffs, salt deposits, and high altitude air currents.

She also understood her impotence. Was there nothing she could do to help? To her great chagrin, her dear brother wanted nothing to do with taking action. What she didn't understand, or didn't want to understand, was the worldwide efforts already afoot to control the problem through technology, local regulatory actions, and governmental decrees.

When you grow up a certain way, anyway, that way seems normal, with nothing in your experience with which to compare it. The twins did have the comparison and were forced to adjust to a new norm.

Their initial complaint of loneliness referred to lack of childhood companions. Basically locked into Megan's teaching-learning regime, she ensured those human companions were replaced by books and their stories, whether they be adventure on the high seas, great inventors, or Ali Baba and the Forty Thieves.

Raj, in particular, would much rather challenge his mind than to associate with others. Spending time with them cost him precious lost hours of investigation; hours in which he could spend examining abstract concepts. He was happy in himself.

Aruna sought out the components of her personality. She read books on the great philosophers and bios about bold men and women, trying to extract what she could in order to mold her own philosophy of life. What are the thoughts and actions of a good person? Benjamin Franklin created a check list for himself for rules of life to follow. These rules helped him become one of the greatest statesmen and inventors in American history. He had invented the bifocal lens and had started the nation's first lending library and was appointed by congress as the first Postmaster General to begin a US postal service.

On the other hand, the man also suffered from gout, the affliction of the wealthy, of those who ate too much red meat, too many organs like liver, and drank too much red wine. He had one illegitimate child. He must have known about the cause of gout. Didn't he care? Didn't he have any will power? Aruna dissected these factors, seeking hidden truths. Is everybody the same, whether they are rich or poor, statesmen, or ditch diggers? What's the matter with people, anyway?

For their eleventh birthday, Tony and Megan had invited the Hoberts, the Koraskova family, and grandmother Christina, for a pot luck pool party. Karl and Billy brought over several card tables, which were set up indoors and in the back yard, while Tony provided the folding chairs he had stacked in the garage.

The get-together proved to be successful in that Hans Hobert obtained two new clients in the Koraskovas and all the educated and well-traveled adults had ample material about which they conversed. For the children, however, Raj wound up swimming and playing horseshoes with the Hobert boys, while Aruna, Marie, and Anton huddled together speaking about topics related to sea life.

Presents for the children included movie passes, Walmart and Amazon vouchers, and two blue-toothed CD player with headsets.

Tony happened upon Aruna's secret project quite by accident when he visited Aruna in her room after the guests had departed. She was lying on her bed texting when he walked in. He asked, smilingly, "I never saw you so engaged in conversation before. Is this the new you?"

Aruna hit the send button and set down her phone. "Oh, dad, it's so interesting. Anton is so into political science like his older brother and he's educating us on how to make a statement."

"What does that mean, go on TV and talk about whales?" Tony asked, confused.

"No, dad, it means we're going to take action, spray paint, carry signs," she told him, explicitly, as though it was a first time ever event.

Maintaining a straight face, Tony asked, "I see; who's heading the project? Is it you?"

"No, it's Marie's older brother, Stephan. He's done this before," she said, authoritatively.

Tony nodded. He completely understood. Without criticism, he asked, "I can appreciate your commitment to a cause. If whatever you do, you get on TV and you're featured, do you think it will reflect on the rest of your family? Considering everything we've gone through together, do you think it will be good or bad?"

She replied, "I never thought about it like that; probably bad, but I can handle it. I do think a lot about how we're killing the life in the oceans."

Suddenly, Tony had an idea. He said, "Tell you what. If Marie is a true friend and she isn't being nice just to recruit you, tell her you got a better offer—and no, you can't do both. Tell her you are going to work for me."

Aruna opened her mouth, but nothing came out. Tony filled in the gaps. "I can't pay you to work. That would be against child labor laws. But I can let you work for free and pay you a weekly allowance."

Aruna pondered the offer. One or the other. "What about Raj?" she asked.

"I will make him the offer to work, as well. It can get pretty noisy in there. I've got a pair of noise cancellation head phones he can use to keep down his stress level. You'll both have your own money to do with what you please, up to a certain point based on common sense, of course. Both of you are so good with numbers, it's time you can manage your own finances. Let's say you work four hours a day. We'll work around classes and your study schedule.

This way, you'll be doing some good instead of talking about it.

"And," he added, "to sweeten the deal, you can take over a large room we have in the basement of the plant you can call your own, where you can study, or research, or experiment."

Aruna glanced at her phone, as though she wanted to make a quick call. "Can I think about it?" she asked, hesitantly. She didn't want to sound too eager, even though she wanted to jump up and kiss him.

"Sure. Let me know by tomorrow." Tony said, bending over and kissing her forehead.

Aruna waited another five minutes after she heard Tony leave Raj's room, then she went across the hall to compare notes. She knocked three times and opened the door to find her brother staring at the screen on his laptop.

"What are you looking at?" she asked.

"I think this is advanced physical chemistry," he replied.

"Do you know what it means? All I see is a bunch of chicken scratches and symbols," she said.

"Right. I'm trying to figure out what they mean," he told her.

"Why don't you start at the beginning and work your way up," she suggested.

'Why do that when you can go directly to the end and figure it all out from there," Raj told her.

Aruna let it go and returned to the reason why she had visited him. "What are you going to do about dad's offer," she asked.

Raj snorted, "Are you kidding? Take the job. I need the money and I'm tired of asking them to buy things for me. It has nothing to do with them having all the money in the world. I want to learn the trade. Getting paid to learn is better than paying to learn."

The thought of having the basement to themselves excited him more than anything he'd heard in a long time. For the last couple of years, he had this dream of having a place where he could begin experimenting. The more he learned the more the idea seemed it could come to fruition.

This was different than classwork, this was real hand's on for him, for them, for everybody. Aruna left the room. She flopped onto her bed and thought it through for another half-hour before calling Marie. A warm personal rejection is so much better than a cold email or a dismissive text. She didn't have to go into details, only that she had a chance to work for her dad and couldn't spend any more time with Marie's project.

Marie didn't take it well. She argued, "We have you paired with the 'Man' himself. Aruna, listen to me, with your reputation, we can all proclaim that the youth of the world stands together in our struggle."

There it was. Her dad was right. Marie had shown her true colors. Aruna felt an ancient anger rise up. She wouldn't let it go until she had said her piece, "Marie, thanks for being a false friend. You showed your true colors. This friendship is over. And honestly, I don't care whether you have a nice day or not."

Aruna closed the connection, smiling, having quoted the lines she had heard on TV the other night, which fit the occasion perfectly. Damn, it felt good to shove a sharp stick into somebody's mind.

PART THREE

1

Both children had grown up basically isolated from the world of their peers. They didn't attend normal classrooms, where peer interaction occurred on a daily basis, which included interaction with members of the opposite sex. This was in direct conflict with society's plan for them to be invited to parties, or for them to invite others to their home. It did not help Aruna, who wanted to be asked out, nor did it help Raj, who wanted to ask a girl out on a date—location, transportation, and girl to be determined.

Social interaction is at least as important as education for mature development to occur. Millions of people around the world dealt with fame, however its guise. Yet circumstances surrounding the admixture of the twins into this society took a different form.

Tony offered, "Maybe we should ask them what they want?"

Megan replied, "Maybe they don't know what they want."

Tony repeated, “Maybe we should ask them what they want.”

Tony and Megan Rossi understood it was time for the routine to change. If the children approved without rebelling, classroom attendance would replace home schooling. Once the online courses had been completed, real life interaction would add to their growth. The four-hour-a-day work schedule would remain in place until the time came for them to leave home.

During their 15th years of age, Raj and Aruna were slated to be awarded their Bachelor’s Degree in Biology pending completion of several 3-hour laboratory courses. The same held true for Raj in order for him to obtain another degree in engineering. The pair had been working for their father for some years. Aruna presently had rotated to the bundling section and Raj worked the sorting section. As Tony had promised, each had sufficient spending money, which went a long way toward them learning money-management skills.

Two days before the school semester began, brother and sister visited the labs together. The basic engineering lab was shared with the basic physics lab. Here was constructed a miniature roller-coaster with a marble at the top. At each dip and curve a different equation was pinned at that inflection point; there, balls hung from a pendulum awaiting a trigger that would enable them to strike one another, losing energy at each touch; a four-propeller drone stood alone atop a miniature hillock awaiting a command from its master to fly with a robotic eye on its underbelly; a model of a human eye was affixed to a white piece of cardboard with a small telescope to its right and a small microscope to its left.

A timeline followed the discoveries that came from the use of each instrument—atoms in one case, distant galaxies in another. On and on; endless equations, knowledge, and imagination for those who wanted to imagine. At each new view his mind spun and made calculations. He ached to see it all in motion.

From there, the pair walked into the biology building to find the scents to be over whelming. They smelled death in the form of formaldehyde-soaked frogs, lizards, and fish.

A three-foot-long intestine of a mouse was strung out on a board, pinned like the crawling insects and butterflies on boards next to it. Everything was labeled as to genus and species. An actual human skeleton hung from a hook, with each bone labeled; a life-size laminated colored chart was framed against wall with organs, muscles, and blood vessels colorfully depicted. At this chart Raj spent some time. He already knew the names. Still, a knowledge base opened to him, like a man who had been given a book to read, which he traded for an encyclopedia.

Aruna became attracted to the large 50-gallon saltwater aquarium where colorful species of fish swam in small groups including clown fish, angel fish, and yellow watchman gobies. Sea anemones waved their tentacles. She became mesmerized by a small octopus that moved out of a red castle to feel about the gravel bottom, and by a sea cucumber that lay in a corner where a miniature rocky shoal had been constructed.

She wondered how fish knew which group they belonged to if they couldn't see their own color. She concluded it must be a hormone thing. A chart on the wall depicted each species within the tank with a notation about it, which she read and instantly memorized.

There was one class Raj absolutely had to take in person. It was called Materials Sciences. The class was held first thing in the morning Monday, Wednesdays, and Fridays, which did not conflict with the lab courses on Tuesdays and Thursdays.

Early on Monday, Raj paid the Uber driver and began the walk across campus toward the engineering buildings. The bright Arizona sun welcomed the arriving students in the early morning hours, many headed toward a coffee shop of their own preference to join friends on this first day of classes.

This is not a small-town private school. Arizona State University is the largest university in the country, just ahead of Ohio State in terms of attendance. The main campus occupies some

2000 acres with ca. 56,000 students. Add teachers, administrators, buildings and grounds, security, medical staff, cooks, and assorted support personnel and you had a good-size city.

Of all the engineering disciplines available, Raj's discovery of a Materials Sciences program grabbed him more than any other. For some unexplainable reason, he fell in love with the concept of studying about how to make materials interact with one another, critical in today's world. It involved a number of disciplines he excelled at. Most of all, it offered room for his expansive mind to flower. Although he didn't see it in those terms, he only knew he absolutely had to take the first course hoping to merge it with what he could learn about the human body. Those reviewing such matters accepted the youth into the class. The boy's grades and on-line course records spoke to his potential.

Class began at 8:00 am and ran for 90 minutes on Monday, Wednesday and Friday for the 13 week quarter. The class was accelerated and would be intense with a lot of study time. Word had it pop quizzes would take place with tests every two weeks plus a mid-term plus a final.

Raj arrived at the school early to find a seat at a coffee depot near his intended building. The well-windowed building was relatively small with a capacity to hold 30 students. It served only the bare minimum such as juices, coffee, tea, jelly rolls, and prepared sandwiches. Raj set down his heavy backpack and paid for a coffee and donut. Bringing the small meal back to his table, he pulled out the heavy textbooks. He had already thumbed through them, but began anew. Both his parents thought the textbook business had become a racket and that anything a person wanted to learn was available online and could be printed out for less than the cost of the $200+ worth of books now in front of the youth.

In general, they were correct. In particular, they were not. These books had been written by the professor who taught the class and no used copies were available, nor could they be downloaded. Apparently the books were keepers. His teacher, Donald Richards, Ph.D. and author, was Professor Emeritus. He had amassed scores of patents during his previous life with DuPont Chemical Company working in their science and technology division. Word had it the tall gray-haired scientist was an absolute detail freak. After hearing the rumors, Raj smiled at the information. That was the way he preferred to be taught. He didn't care about competition; he'd stand on his own merits.

The classroom held some 50 seats in a tiered arrangement. For this class, Raj counted 24 attendees, only five of whom were women. Within two weeks, the number would be down considerably. Unquestionably, Raj was by far the youngest in the class. A moment later, a woman who appeared to be in her early twenties sat to his right, a younger man sat to his left.

Richards strode in carrying his books. He set them on the long counter in front of him. A large white board was attached to the wall behind him. He took a moment to look over the class, one by one, assessing. His eyes lingered on Raj a little longer than on the others, then went over the names aloud, reading them one-by-one, requesting an appropriate reply from each person. Richards spent the next 20 minutes telling everyone how difficult the course would be and why it would be so.

In Raj's eyes, he was trying to trim the herd down to those who could fend for themselves.

Richards spent the remainder of the class time going over the books. He requested that each student do the same on their own, page by page, to fully understand the depth of the course. The first book related to the sciences involved in materials engineering, and the second related to applications of the knowledge in the creation of new products and the improvement of existing products.

At the conclusion of the lecture, the woman to Raj's right said, "Did you get all that?"

Raj replied by saying, "Yeah, I think so."

"I'm Janice," she said, holding out a hand.

"I'm Raj," he replied, shaking hers. She was small, clean, wearing Bermudas--common wear for the clime, green-eyed, a matching green blouse, with short hair, almost butch cut. *Easy*

Raj, you're a little young for her and she's way too old for you. But she might make a good study partner, he thought. "Want to get some coffee?" she suddenly asked.

Wondering if she recognized him, he replied, "I already had some, but thanks anyway. I have to go to work."

"Where?" she asked.

"ReCyclo," he said.

"I've heard of them. Well, see you next time," Janice said. She picked up her books and walked down a couple of tiered steps to the door.

Raj turned his thought to what his dad had said about getting the best grades with minimal effort, albeit it was only in high school, 1) Read ahead so you're already familiar with the topic of the day, 2) Condense and highlight your notes, which should be short-handed in your own code to prevent copying from others, 3) Don't study the night before an exam unless you find something you totally missed, 4) Pretend you are the teacher asking the questions, 5) Answer the easiest questions first, 6) Don't change any answers unless you find a mathematical error.

Raj quickly read the next chapter to be covered, highlighted his notes, copied over the highlighted points, and called Uber for a ride to his place of employment.

When the pop quiz was given at the start of the next class session, two days later, everyone moaned, including Janice, especially when Raj scored top grade in the class.

"How did you score that high?" she asked.

"Just lucky, I guess," he confessed.

"Come on, Raj, help me out. I'm just a poor graduate student trying to survive," she complained.

Raj chuckled. What the heck. He said, "Okay, come in a few minutes early next time and I'll teach you some tricks."

"Can I ask you how old you are, if you don't mind?" Janice said.

"I'm fifteen. Why?"

"That's a joke, right?" she said,

Raj threw his hands up and said, "Honest truth. Why?"

"No reason," she answered, trying hard not entertain illegal thoughts.

By the start of the third week six students had dropped out. Raj continued to dominate a class of intelligent people using organization coupled with smarts. There were no Cs or Bs. These were all A students. Each was an island to himself or herself, self-invested, trying to survive, rarely sharing insights with one another, each locked into the evolutionary pathway demarked Survival of the Fittest. If parties occurred, he was never invited. So much the better. He would have to politely refuse, anyway. What was the gain? Janice became more objective toward Raj and stayed that way throughout the remainder of the course. He had hoped for an alternative outcome.

Before the final exam, Professor Richards requested each remaining student to stop by during his office hours the following week to go over their exams with him. When Raj appeared, Richards handed him the final and chuckled, "Congratulations, sir. At least you were consistent. You made high score."

Richards sorted through the remaining stack of exams stacked neatly on one corner of his otherwise vacant desk. Computer and landline stood on a second table behind him. He found Raj's test handed it to him, checked an enrollment sheet, and said, "I see you are signed up for the more advanced course. It is more mathematically oriented. Do you think that will be a problem for you?"

The student replied, almost lazily—medication tended to minimize his level of excitement--"No, sir, I should be okay with that."

Richards paused a moment, then added, "I notice you always use ink when you answer the questions. I've never had anyone do that before. It's pretty dicey when math equations are involved, don't you think?"

"Yes, sir. My preference is a fine-tip gel pen," Raj replied, casually objectively, without the slightest indication this might be an issue.

Richards took a long hard look at this kid, wondering what kind of freakazoid had infiltrated his class.

Both Aruna and Raj proved be adept at lab work in biology. When Raj told her about the woman next to him in Materials Sciences who wasn't too friendly after learning his age, she reported a similar circumstance in the bio lab with members of the opposite sex, except several men who didn't care if she was underage for a lot of things they had in mind. Raj confessed to her whenever he put on a lab coat it made him feel gloriously important.

Aruna followed her heart to specialize in ecology in general and recycling of plastics in particular. Her heart-felt desire was to attend the noted Woods Hole Oceanographic Institution in Massachusetts, the world's leading non-profit organization dedicated to oceanographic research. If that was not to be the case, she would see if she could make something work here. She counted the days until her 18th birthday, when she could find her own place to live. Then she might live with the once-scorned Marie.

They had talked about it afterward. Marie's close call with the law had scared her back to the straight and narrow. She was happy to remain in high school. The alternative could have been juvenile hall. When she had called Aruna, a month after the misadventure, she confessed she had made a bad error in judgment.

At that time, Aruna had seen the caller ID and reluctantly answered the call. Marie had said, "Aruna, I need to talk to you in person. No text, no phone, no email. I don't trust them."

"I don't have a car and you don't either, so I guess we'll have to wait until there is some kind of family get-together," Aruna replied, coldly, leaving out the part about always taking an Uber whenever she went somewhere, without having to rely on her parents.

"Can we meet at the Scottsdale mall on Saturday to go shopping?" Marie asked.

"I'm busy on Saturday," Aruna replied, quickly deciding she had better things to do.

"Sunday, then, at noon at the food court." Before Aruna could comment, she quickly added, "My brother Stephan got picked up by the cops. He's facing federal charges. My parents are losing it. Two men from the FBI came over and Stephan doesn't even live here. Please, I need to talk to someone," Marie beseeched.

This was heavy news. Intrigued by the information, Aruna wanted to know more about what had happened. More importantly, she wanted to understand how circumstances had prevailed to rescue her from possibly making a very bad decision. Her destiny was hidden somewhere in the cards. She needed to read them carefully. She had almost gone out with them, but had chosen to work for her father, instead. Worse, she would have to relinquish a perverse sense she had been harboring: doing something important without including her brother. As a small saving grace, she would retain another ten dollar bill she had stolen from her mother's purse for emergency purposes.

Agreeing to meet with Marie, Aruna got the okay from her mom to go shopping with her friend. Meeting at the food court, just as the adjacent movie theater let out, the two old friends wandered the isles for several minutes, feeling the moment, until Aruna finally asked, "Why are we here, Marie? What's this all about?"

Marie told the tale. "Anton and I snuck out the window and got picked up at 1:00 am by Stephan in his car. We were supposed to meet some others in front of the federal building, but nobody else showed up. It was only three miles from the house. Stephan had spray paint in the car, so we painted the building in red *Save the Whales* then Stephan went to the trunk to pull out some bricks and a bottle filled with gasoline. He wanted us to throw the bricks through one of the windows and he would light the rag he had stuffed into the bottle and throw it into the building afterward. It was stupid and juvenile.

"Anton and I got scared when we saw what he was going to do. That's not what we signed up for. When we said we're not going to do it, he threw the brick through the window himself. Anton and I spotted a patrol car turn the corner down the street and Anton yelled 'cops'. The two of us ran like hell and turned the corner before the cops saw us, but apparently Stephan had lit the fuse and the cops saw it and saw him. He was dead in the water. He never got the throw it into the building, but he threw it into a storm drain instead, according to what we heard. It didn't matter, because he had more bottles in the trunk of the car.

"We ran all the way home, snuck back in and shivered in fear all night and for the next few days. We tried to act normal in front of our parents, which was the hardest thing we'd ever done. We heard and read on the news the same morning that a Stephan Koraskova had been arrested and booked. He will be charged with domestic terrorism along with a dozen other local, state, and federal crimes. He'll be an old man by the time he gets out of prison. His life is over. You're the only real friend I ever had and I want you back."

"Holy shit," Aruna mumbled, thinking about how far she would have had to run the make it back to her own home. "You have such nice parents, too. They'll never be the same after this."

Marie said, "I'm sure we're under surveillance. It wasn't my fault, was it? Or was it Anton's?"

"No, it's not your fault. If Stephan hadn't been caught, he would have continued to do it. There must be something wrong with him. You need to support your parents as much as possible. I'll make sure we visit you more often and vice versa. And to your next question, yes,

I want you back in my life. Now give me a big hug," Aruna concluded. She had her own ruminating to do.

Although she had the great feeling of going it alone, had she told Raj about the enterprise, he might have gone with her to ensure her safety. What would the press do to their family if either one or both of them had been caught?

The years they were to miss college cost them a number of life's experiences: No joining of fraternities or sororities, no drunken orgies, no clandestine weed-smoking before a speaker came to speak of government overthrow or anti-Semitism, no cheerleading tryouts, or rallies for their football team, or cheering in the stands, no running for student government, or, alternatively, meshing with the masses to get swept along in the tide with an eye toward the boredom of graduation ceremonies; and finally, with rare exceptions, no spending endless hours learning nothing that will apply to becoming successful. Instead, they did it the way one of countless side streams of life dictated. For the most part, it meant going through these years alone, until maturation gave them independent thought and when free will overrode years of isolation.

That aside, their lives were far from boring. Working for their father not only provided the kids with money, it opened up another avenue of exploration in addition to academia. Reluctant at first, Aruna got talked into using the basement to help her brother develop an idea he had been harboring for some time. The gift changed Raj from a traditionless person to one given a tradition with a cause. He wanted to make housing for the ragpickers in India out of recycled plastic bottles.

2

Raj supervised an AI machine that struggled to separate seven grades of plastic bottles from tin cans, paper and cardboard, Styrofoam, cellophane, plastic wrap, miscellaneous unidentifiable objects, countless used diapers (non-biodegradable diapers take 500 years to degrade in a landfill, biodegradable diapers take 50 years to decompose), tree and shrubs parts, batteries, old computers, computer hard-drives, paperback and hard cover books, and any miscellaneous garbage that people had thrown into their recycling bins. Most solid objects flowing along the big conveyor belt would find their way into landfills, or get incinerated.

At the end of his shift, he removed his earphones and ambled to the rear of the huge 50,000 square foot 8 acre recycling plant out into the half-acre hard-packed gravel rear to check in with the yard boss. A line of city waste trucks came and went via three ingress and egress points, dumping their loads, each of the green-marked machines carrying a recycling logo on its side. The hole that constituted the actual dumping point was found to the west side of the structure.

A large fenced-in area for forklifts, generators, and a small shed that held seldom-used hand tools had been set up immediately behind the building. A number of trucks of various dimensions held the fort at the rear of the yard, which included side and rear-loaders similar to those used by the city. The desert lay beyond with scrub oak, lots of spiny prickly pear, cholla cactus, scrub grass, and tumbleweed. A series of low hills in the distance were noteworthy for their differing shades of brown.

The yard boss, a heavy-set bearded man, pointed to one of the side-loaders lying in wait, filled with crushed non-recyclable debris. Each truck was filled with compressed loads of unusable waste from the plant, destined for disposal. Raj watched the city trucks open their rears and dump the loads, where workers would assist the trash heaps down in the hole where the conveyor belt originated. You had to stay ahead in this game with a thousand tons a day going through this facility alone, close to 300 million annually for the U.S., and over 2 billion annually around the world. The United States consistently took the world's grand prize for the most plastic used and the most trash created per capita.

Raj hauled his growing frame into the cab

where the truck sat under an awning next to single diesel fuel gas pump. He started the engine, sweat already soaking his shirt from the short walk. He'd be back to the plant within a couple of hours to retrieve his car, drive home for a shower, meet Aruna, and figure out what to do for dinner. After dinner, they would go back to the shop to play in the basement room his father had given them years before; thenceforth, a room Raj had designated The Workshop.

On the way to the landfill, Raj placed a call to Aruna. He suspected she would pass him on the road driving another company truck on her own return trip. In her instance, it would be from one of the giant incinerators located farther out in the desert. The only incinerator close to theirs in size belonged to the DEA. Not surprisingly, RVs and campers parked downwind from the burnings, hoping for a downdraft.

"Usual schedule tonight?" Raj asked.

Aruna replied, "I'm on my way back. After I scrub down, I'd like to pick up some Chinese."

Raj paused before answering, "Works for me. Make sure you bring chop sticks. Better keep the coffee pot hot. Are you prepared for tomorrow's telecast?"

"Couldn't be CNN, could it?" Aruna grumbled.

"The one and only. Don't complain. They got us where we are today, you know, driving dump trucks," Raj returned. He was having a bad day.

Aruna shot, "Don't start your whining with me, Rajish. I am sick and tired of it. You are so impatient you make me crazy sometimes. You play like you're in a happy place, but I know it's the opposite with you. I see you always putting on a show for mom and dad. If you're so unhappy, why don't you quit your job and move out? Quit the Workshop project, too, because that room will be gone when you leave. Go out on your own and see how far it gets you. Hell, Raj, I know of a great dump site that will be happy to have an experienced ragpicker like you. Don't expect me to follow. That's all."

A long pause ensued, until Aruna said, "Did you hear a word I said? Are you here?"

"Yeah, I'm here," Raj mumbled. "As far as a career, after my fourth course with prof Richards, he said to contact him and he'd set me up in any one of a half-dozen well-paying jobs anywhere in the world. He also introduced me to a professor in the astronomy department. They're always looking for numbers freaks. The astronomer guy was funny. He said, 'We have an opening for a Master's in Astrophysics in Nice, France, for someone specializing in galactic archaeology focusing on retrograde metal-rich stars in the Milky Way'. I should have taken him up on it."

"Then why are you driving a dump truck instead of taking one of them up on their offers?" Aruna shot.

"Because I want to accomplish something by myself, not do it working for others," Raj retorted.

Aruna wanted to say "Who said you can't do both?" but instead, she commiserated. "I think a lot about mum and bapu. They worked so hard to take care of us. We need to make them proud."

She had no qualms about mentioning her birth parents except over time, the memory of them was like sharp rocks getting rounded to smoother stones over time. She wondered, *Maybe the mind protects itself from getting overloaded with trivia. No, I remember details of all kinds of garbage I read. I'm confused. Do dogs and cats remember? How does memory work?*

"We owe a lot of people," Raj said. "Anyway, I'm sorry for being a jerk."

Aruna instantly cleared her mind, responding, "Right, everybody is sorry after they get ripped out a new one. Trouble is, you'll be back to square one tomorrow. Start thinking about what you're going to say when CNN comes over tomorrow and it better be good. They want a show. For tonight, let's get the job done. We're getting close, I can feel it."

When CNN did come shortly after their arrival home from work the following day, the focus was on interaction with their new parents. Their mathematical skills and photographic memories were kept a secret, like superheroes in hiding. This had a spin-off effect in that the international viewers could see how personal attention given to learning skills paid dividends. The first year had been the roughest. Megan had quit teaching, devoting all her time to raising the children, guiding them toward everything of value, minimizing the amount of television they watched, and concentrating on language and math skills, the two most important factors that contribute to success in life.

Both were angry at their birth country—infuriated would be a better word to describe Raj's sense of rage—for not prioritizing the trash problem, leaving millions of children to find their calling as trash pickers. The vast majority of them were completely uneducated.

As the twins grew to understand the larger issue in that technology was indeed addressing the same issue of recycling on a more massive scale. Technology was fine, policy decisions were slow in coming. The problem came down to the same common denominator: You can recycle plastic all you want and make what you will of it, but it will end up where it has always ended up. You can't make computers and cell phones out of compressed corn stalk leaves.

While Aruna got the coffee pot going and opened up the boxes of Chinese for what could be another weekend of late-nighters. Raj put on his freshly washed and ironed lab coat, which he didn't need at all, except for its questionable statement that its wearer is a scientist, and opened a fresh bag of lime. If all went well tonight, the samples would come out off-white in color, each weighing only ounces.

The 1000 square foot room of walled-in slump-block had been personalized, the fork lifts long ago moved through the double doors out to the yard. The room bragged its own bath, small fridge, and recliner. It also had an exhaust fan to remove errant vapors. On one table stood several electric blenders next to a balance. A few smoothies were in the offing this evening, none for drinking.

Two microscopes stood on a separate table with which the couple could measure particle sizes, one scope a geologist's, the other of higher magnifications. Raj preferred his plastic beads to be roughly 2 mm or BB sized, called micro-plastic in technical terms. The ionic charges on the surface of the smaller beads created a much better bonding surface than those larger. He had determined this size to work the best after countless attempts to bond larger particles. In a single experiment, the would-be scientist ruled out the fragmented chipboard model.

All he had to do was to add a calculated amount of lime, plastic particles, and water to a blender, like preparing a mud-straw-petroleum mixture for the making of adobe blocks.

Aruna had changed from work boots, cargo-Bermuda shorts and blue tank top, to sneakers, cargo-Bermuda shorts, and red tank top. Aruna preferred to maintain her hair very long, which she dealt with in any manner she could devise. She found it to be a time-consuming pain, promising herself she would cut it short one day.

She placed a disc of Mozart into the CD player and turned it on. This could be the final experiment—well, maybe another final experiment. She hoped to play a disc of intense Tchaikovsky concertos to grace the airways should they be granted success this night.

She turned on the blender for a slow churn. Too fast a mix would grind the particles unevenly and the final binding process would fail. Likewise, melting the plastic into a liquid form might work to extrude into fibers, but wouldn't work here because it wouldn't mix with the other ingredients. It would be like trying to mix oil and water.

Now they would wait an hour for the slow mix to even out. This was fine with Raj, who took out his trustworthy chess set, toggled it up to level 10, and bucked heads with a computer that had learned to learn his moves, while Aruna picked up a collection of stories on sea adventures.

The temperature of an incubator had been preset. Both investigators had learned enough about history to understand how easy it is to pursue a dream, and in the end, die without bringing the dream to fruition. They also had visions of the opposite. What their youth had yet to comprehend was that inventing a workable product had nothing to do with its manufacture, its marketing, or its acceptance.

3

Raj turned off the mixers. He looked closely at the solutions, while Aruna removed several clean glass dishes of various sizes from a lined box and placed them on the table next to the mixers. Using a level of ensure the table was not on a tilt, Raj poured the thick grayish contents of the blender into the forms, some of which were simply shallow baking dishes, only a half-inch in depth, others the size that might hold a gold bar weighing but a few ounces rather than 32 pounds.

Aruna placed all six samples into the incubator already preset to 85° F. Neither of them was at all certain the temperature needed to be at any degree of warmth. They could have left the forms on the table, or out in the sun, but it lent an air of exactitude to their work and served to protect the product from unknown contaminants, or more likely, human clumsiness.

Their work completed for the evening, the couple returned home. Tomorrow might see a different routine when they returned to view the results of their handiwork after the interview.

Aruna arose at 6:30 am, showered, applied an ice pack to her face to reduce the size of the imagined bags under her eyes, ate a breakfast of oatmeal and strawberries, and drove with Raj over to ReCyclo. Neither student had classes at the moment. After work, she would normally continue writing her own Master's thesis. Her course work had been completed. Once the thesis was accepted by her graduate committee, she would be awarded a degree and be on a par with her brother to celebrate another proud day for the family.

The family spent some time creating a neat, homey atmosphere. Since the old days, new carpeting, a new sofa and two new armchairs had been purchased. With Hans Hobert's assistance, mom and dad had invested the money into tech stocks and real estate, after making their own deep contributions.

Melanie Brown's appearance at the door came as a shock. It was her request that CNN keep her visit to the Rossis a secret from them. When she did appear, the stunned family broke into joyful laughs, as though she were a long-lost, beloved, family member come to visit, which she was. Her hair had grayed considerably, which she liked to keep natural in appearance. She wore gold bangle earrings and a small, red heart-shaped pendant over a white blouse. "I am so, happy to be here," she cried. "I have thought about you all these years and these jerks at my agency kept me on the move so much I couldn't break free."

"Come in, please," Tony offered. He had gained a few pounds over the years, as had Megan. No surprise there. Busy schedules focusing attention on others tended to do that.

At the door, Melanie introduced the Indian cameraman by the name of Sanjay Kumar. He served as the company's war-zone-behind-the-scenes recorder of uprisings in India and Africa. He, too, had grown up in poverty spending his days sitting at bus stops selling bangles and, if the circumstances permitted, drugs, to other national and foreign tourists, trying to escape the violent murder and atrocities which were part of his youth. In his case, it was Hindu vs. Muslim riots in the area of Calcutta, now known as Kolkata.

Kumar struggled for years to crawl and gouge his way to the top, using the only skills that began from begging, to negotiating, to displaying his meager drawings of faces, and learning to speak openly. His artistic talent directed him to photography.

Over time, Kumar worked up the chain to radio, then as a successful TV broadcaster where CNN found and hired him. Now in his late forties, when he was offered the opportunity to join the famous Melanie Brown to cover a number of stories in the United States, a country to which he had never visited, he slathered at the thought. When she teasingly told him one of the interviews would be with the Rossis, especially, with the internationally famous Raj and Aruna, Kumar thanked her profusely. Once he entered the home to see the children and they saw them, a bond was created without a word spoken.

Melanie took a proffered seat, relaxing, courteously declining the offer for a glass of water. She had wanted for so long to follow this family that she now savored the moment because yearly updates were given to others of her ilk. Taking her time, she told Kumar to forget the camera and visit with the children while she spoke with Tony and Megan.

Kumar felt overjoyed to join the pair, finding a seat at the kitchen counter, jabbering, excitedly trading war stories about their home country. He spoke of his successes and failures, putting up with occasional interjections by his two listeners.

With subtle excitement, Kumar leaned toward his audience to reveal he had another motive for coming to the States; his brother, Sunil, had moved here years before and worked for a major custom home builder. Although they had communicated regularly, neither had seen one another for many years; that is, until earlier in this tour.

He trusted his listeners so much that he quietly revealed his and his brother having been temporarily lured into the darker side years ago in the field of porn, something he had never told CNN.

The Singh/Rossi children promised to keep it a secret while surreptitiously exchanging email addresses with him. In trade, they revealed their own secret efforts to save the world from an overabundance of trash. "Don't tell a soul," they admonished.

Melanie sat on the sofa between the Rossis telling of her own varied assignments, many of which threatened her and those around her, although, theirs was the standout experience in her life, by far.

In turn, the Rossi's shared their personal views about raising the twin ragpickers, They told her about the stresses of integrating what might be considered to be aliens, into the lifestyle of Earth inhabitants, trusting what they said would not be aired. ("We give a world of credit to their birth parents, who taught them well, despite the struggles everyone faced.")

The Rossis told the reporter of Aruna's occasional theft of money from Megan's purse. Nothing the Rossis revealed alluded to the intellectual gifts of the children. In their view, people are permitted to keep secrets to the grave. However, their educational development was an open record.

At last Melanie said gently, "This visit was wonderful. We'll keep in touch. I'll give you my direct contact number. We'd better get into the interview, if you don't mind."

She stood and motioned for Kumar to begin the video. She ensured the Rossis sat together holding hands before she began. "We are live here today with Tony and Megan Rossi on the 10th anniversary of their adoption of the famous twins. In a moment we'll get to visit with them. First, I'll ask Megan a few questions. She was the one who home-schooled them from the beginning."

The camera left Melanie to settle on Megan, who maintained a neutral visage. "Megan, can you give us a brief description of what it's been like to raise these children over the past ten years?"

Megan said, "For a long time I had to teach them without them knowing they were being taught. Both loved puzzles and games, so I guided them through games that led to knowledge about different subjects. I worked on their English at the same time, until their concentration improved to the point where I could teach them to read.

"Raj had more concentration and is goal oriented. Aruna was more patient and acted out more—petulant would be a good word. She has a bent toward artistic design."

Tony said, "I thought getting them to the dentist for a checkup would be a nightmare, but we found one who specialized in children and after a few easy visits, he established a good relationship with them. They use him today."

Melanie asked, "When we spoke earlier before the show you told me about their daily routine. Can you describe this to our viewers?"

Tony replied, "In the old days, Megan gave them short lessons and long breaks. That changed to longer lessons with shorter breaks. Once they came into their own, both took online courses. It's safe to say their rate of learning shocked us. Today, they both attend or take on-line classes from Arizona State University and work for me at ReCyclo, a recycling facility here in the Phoenix area."

Megan offered, "As far as their personalities, Raj is more the recluse, Aruna is the socialite destined to be a heart breaker. I do believe they want to change the world for the good in some way, but don't we all?"

Melanie laughed at the comment, faced the camera, and said, with animation, "You heard from the parents, folks. Now the moment we've all been waiting for. Let's hear from their adopted son and daughter."

The cameraman walked over to the kitchen counter. It focused on a stunningly beautiful woman and her handsome brother. Good genes all the way down the line. Focusing on the woman, Melanie asked, sweetly, "Aruna, we hear good things about you and your brother."

Aruna said, "Don't believe a thing our parents say. We're headstrong." Nice short statement to bring mirth into the personal touch.

Raj laughed, "Don't believe a word she says, either. They've been wonderful to us and leave us to find our own destiny." A little philosophical thought from a wise young man never hurt.

"Seriously, guys, you'll turn eighteen on your next birthday. What are your plans for the future?"

Raj answered, "To move out and probably continue working for dad. We're already shopping around for apartments."

"Will you continue with your education?" Melanie asked.

Aruna said, "Education comes in a lot of forms. For me, as for formal education, absolutely."

The camera flashed over to the parents on the sofa who shook their heads in unison, looking downtrodden, as if wordlessly saying, "None of our lives will be the same once they leave."

The camera turned to Melanie who smiled into the camera and declared, "You saw it first here first. It's fair to say we will all wait to see what these two come up with and we wish them the best. This is Melanie Brown with CNN. Have a nice day."

4

Time is absolute, depending on perception. Patience is a human condition, subject to interpretation. When Aruna had first told her brother it couldn't be done, his first perception was that it could be. *Everybody* was wrong about a lot of things. They said you had to separate plastics, because some were made with various additives, or were harder or softer than others. In fact, even when recycled, their separation only delayed their entrance into the landfill, a universally accepted fact.

But what if it could be done? What if, say, the damnable seven grades of plastic bottles could be ground together into a workable size, and formed into bricks used for long lasting waterproof walls and ceilings to build into homes, where light could penetrate, thus saving on electricity and reduce the amount of coal and oil required to produce that electricity. Wouldn't the carbon footprint be reduced? Yes, electricity had to be produced somehow. Wind farms, solar, and hydroelectric only went so far. Yes, he could go in the direction of corn stalk leaves or banana tree leaves. He could do a lot of things to make structures. None of them would permit light to pass though like his home design, but in the end, the carbon footprint would be the same. Everything takes energy to make.

Initially, the frightening part of Raj's early vision to Aruna sounded too good to be true. Her brother was in fantasyland. A psychiatrist would testify under oath that the young man dreamed of a fictional future. Indeed, no earth-shattering changes would occur, no matter how the pie was cut. Fortunately, Raj might need a psychiatrist, but he wasn't one.

Upon learning of his children's aspirations to build housing, Tony advised "Explore all avenues. Don't hesitate to think outside the box. If you think inside the box, you will remain trapped there. And always watch your backs."

"But why?" they had asked, almost in unison.

"Because unknown forces will eat you alive," Tony replied.

After awakening the day after the interview, Raj spent the day carefully going over their notes, reviewing years of records, allowing his brain to process the inputting data points. He wanted to find success this evening when they pulled the samples from the incubator. They had wanted success for the past years, ever since he completed the second course with Professor

Richards. Why would tonight be any different?

"Never have any expectations," his father had advised. Like a coach advising a team, or a career scientist advising a student, "When you try for excellence, have a goal in mind. Have no expectations. There will be enough disappointments without having to shatter your immediate dreams."

All that went by the wayside when the pair pulled the samples from the incubator and carefully placed them onto a long folding table. This batch looked different. No oil floated on the top, the samples didn't stick to the glass, nor did the samples come out looking like a layered cake. These were all uniform in consistency, like hardened glass, somewhat duller than their Pyrex baking dish containers. Each slid out of its respective container, whatever its shape, as easily as eggs slide out of a non-stick frying pan.

Starting with the 1/4" thick samples, Raj picked one up held it up to the overhead neon and found it to be rigid. The ingot shaped units weighed ounces each, as expected, according a cooking balance Raj had acquired from a thrift store, a small fraction the weight of a standard brick. Neither was under any false impressions. At the start of the project, their dad had explained: "An apparent victory can be a defeat in disguise, but the opposite might be true. By learning from mistakes, it pulls the end closer."

Impatiently, Raj said, "I need to call *Plas-*

tiques in the morning. They're east coast. They'll be open then."

"Why that company?"Aruna asked.

"Beads," he said.

At 7:13 am, he did call. "Plastiques," came the reply by a pleasant female voice.

"Yes, I'm trying to reach the shift foreman. I'm calling from ReCyclo," Raj offered.

"One moment please," she said.

Shortly, a male voice came on the line, "This is George Harrington. You say you're from ReCyclo?"

"Yes, sir. My name is Raj Rossi and I'm calling on behalf of a client of ours."

"Rossi. You're Tony's son, right? *The* Raj Rossi?"

"Yes, sir."

"Well, say hello to your dad for me will you? Tell him next time he's in Connecticut I owe him a beer."

"Will do. Like I say, I'm calling on behalf of a client of ours who wanted some information. I thought he could get a better deal if I called instead of him." Raj chuckled slightly.

Harrington chuckled in return. "All right, what's the request?"

"You make 5 mm pellets for recycling. He wants 2 mm pellets."

"What for?" Harrington queried at the odd request.

Raj was prepared for the question. "He didn't

say and I didn't ask."

"Plain old recycled bottle stuff, right?" Harrington asked.

"He wanted a mixture of colored and plain," Raj added.

Harringtonn exclaimed, "That's BS, man. We don't do types #3 and #6, or #7. Stick with PET (polyethylene terephthalate). It's strong, lightweight, clear and 100% recyclable. If you melt down those bad boys, you've serious toxin issues, not to mention headaches you'll run into with OSHA."

Raj laughed out loud, "That's what I told him too, but I promised I'd ask anyway. Sometimes clients can be a little funny. He said to tell you he won't do any melting down."

Raj could hear Harrington exhale as a show of impatience, before he said, "Give me a few minutes."

"Take your time. There is no emergency," Raj threw out, nonchalantly.

Harrington went silent for some time. At last he asked, "You there?"

"I'm here," Raj replied.

"Okay, here's the deal. We'd have to do a little retooling. The least we can sell you is a ton and it won't be 2s, just like the 5s aren't fives. They're between 4.5 and 5.5. Yours would be 1.5 to 2.5. Okay so far?"

"Go ahead," Raj said, encouraged by the answer. That would give him at least four times the surface area to volume ratio of the 5s, exactly what he wanted and what was presently working for them. He dearly hoped he wouldn't be stuck with a ton of beads he couldn't use. If all else failed, he might be able to sell them for pennies on the dollars for use with plastic straws as a peashooter.

Harrington said, "Give us about three weeks to get it all done. It'll run your client about three grand plus shipping, most of the cost is in the labor. We'll invoice you for the job order. Normally, we want a deposit for this, but if you're Tony's son, that's good enough for me."

Raj closed by saying, "Sir, I appreciate that. I'll pass along the information. Thank you and have a nice day."

Something Harrington said had hit Raj hard. It wasn't the money part. What was it? Leaving the conversation aside, he ruminated further. Once he got the pellets he would get a used cement mixer and find some outdoor place where he and Aruna could work in peace. As for the money, he wouldn't have to come up with it for at least a month after he placed the order, say six to eight weeks to make good on the promise. He ran a quick calculation. How much diesel fuel would be used in the cement mixture to make, say, 100,000 of his houses? At some point, a do-gooder would make the calculation and slam him for it. The do-gooder was likely to be his environmentalist sister.

"There is always a trade-off," Tony had said. Raj had read that one of the largest toy manufacturers in the world had spent over a billion dollars trying to turn recycled plastic bottles into toys, but pulled the plug on the project when the company found the carbon footprint to be excessive, a conclusion Raj had come to. It took too much energy to make the toys using old bottles compared with the old way of using butadiene and related plastic-making materials. In Raj's case, he cared about the carbon footprint, but he cared more about housing for the poor and he cared about reducing the amount of accumulated trash.

He told his sister, "We need money. Here's an idea. You're currently working in bailing with five others, and I work in sorting along with ten others, even after AI and the electromagnet do their part. At the present time, we each work 8-hour shifts five days a week. But the company is in desperate need of truck drivers, like everybody else in the country. Well, we occasionally drive the trucks. Full-time drivers make good money. How about if we both propose to dad that he let us off our current jobs and we work 10-hour-a-day shifts six-days a week driving the trucks. That would put us in the overtime pay as well. Our combined income would multiply several-fold."

"It's worth a try," she said, suitably impressed by his idea. "Although, knowing dad, I suspect we'll need some wiggle room."

When they did make the proposal to Tony at home, he replied, "I'll say one thing, you guys have great timing. A while ago, I got the word. China just passed the National Sword Act. As of right now, they won't take trash from any country, with few exceptions, which means North American, Europe and Japan are in deep trouble. The U.S. alone sold millions of tons of trash to them each year.

"In particular, cardboard and plastics will flood the market, which means companies like ReCyclo will struggle because we don't get any money from the sale.

"In short, we're not in the business of making products, we ship out materials for others to use in their manufacture of hundreds of goods. With the market soon to be flooded, we make less and for us, pretty soon, even recycling won't pay. We expect two other countries that take our stuff will soon follow suit. They're Malaysia and Thailand.

"So, for your proposal to work the trucks, the answer is yes, for a while. I'll give you five days a week, 8 hours a day. No overtime, but your hourly pay will be two-and-a-half times what you get now. If I need you for overtime work, I'll let you know. You'll need a couple of days off for exercise and to rest your butt muscles. Make sure you get out of the truck a few minutes and walk around after each trip."

"When do we start?" Aruna inquired, hoping for a week to get organized, or maybe do a little more treadmill walking.

"Tomorrow morning at 6:00 am," Tony said.

Raj arrived at his destination, dumped his load, stretched, took a ten minute break, and began the return trip. A niggling thought worked on him. He replayed the conversation with Harrington until it came to him. Nobody recycles several categories of plastic bottles because of toxins in the plastic. Fine. He could stick with good old #1s. There are only a few hundred billion of those around. But categories weren't the problem per se. It was the heat issue. No city or fire department would approve the construction of a home made out of plastic, would they? He had no idea. He literally began to feel sick.

Forced to have a talk with himself, Raj thought, *Are we really dead in the water? First, I blindly believe my idea will work and then blindly believe it won't. Relax. How many dreamers have gotten this far and stopped? Every step is going to be a fight.*

The ring tone on Raj's cell identified his caller.

"Our father?" Aruna asked the obvious.

"Yep." Raj set down the papers in his hand and answered, "Hey, dad."

"How's the new job going?" Tony asked.

"Almost two weeks now," Raj replied. "We

have it worked out where we go to alternate sites on alternate days. That way we don't have to drive the same boring route four times a day. All we have to do is to remember what day of the week it is."

The kids were too young to obtain a standard driving license. However, under the old Farming Exceptions Act, family members under the age of 18 may be permitted to drive a car or truck when it is directly related to family or "corporate" interests, as long as the standard testing procedures are followed, as per state mandated motor vehicle department regulations. This did not include 18-wheelers.

Tony grinned, "Good thinking. How are you holding up?"

Raj's suspicions began to rise. He answered by telling his father they were following his advice by stretching and walking after every trip.

There was a pause before Tony said, somewhat demurely, "Raj, we are presently in worse shape than we were. Malaysia is shutting down."

Raj's mind raced. Their deepest fear had come to light. "Starting when, the first of the year?" he asked, hoping for the best.

"As of this morning their time," Tony said, coldly.

"What about the ships and barges in transit?" Raj asked.

"They get to turn around. The environmental groups are screaming bloody murder. Thailand will be next. Everybody is following China's action. There are a few other places that take the stuff, but the cost to us will be enormous, and I don't just mean monetarily. We'll remain profitable with glass and heavy metals, not with plastics."

Raj began to see a glimmer of what his father was going to suggest. He wouldn't call him at this late hour just to give him this bit of information, important as it might be. His suspicions were confirmed when Tony asked, "What are you doing tomorrow?"

"Saturday? Probably working on the project," Raj replied.

"Everybody is in panic mode. I need you both to haul," Tony said, flatly.

How do you say no to a request/order like that? It's what they both wanted from the start, but now, after two weeks, they were both looking forward to going back to their routine jobs. On the other hand, here was a chance to make money they desperately needed. According to legal documents, they'd get family money at the age of 21, another three years plus several months away. He refused to put his life on hold until then.

Raj relayed the information to Aruna, who was hoping for a free weekend. "When does he want us to start?" she asked, keeping her fingers crossed, a Western habit. (An Indian habit she remembered and followed was sleeping with the head to the south if one were in the northern hemisphere. It had something to do with the magnetic poles of the earth. She refused to do it the other way, fearful of the consequences. Raj also followed the rule. He also didn't cut his hair or nails on Saturday, which would bring bad luck.)

"He wants us to start tomorrow morning at 6:00 am," Raj told her, knowing she would probably blame the bad news on something she had done wrong in life.

That night he had another return of the eternal dream, fading somewhat in frequency, but not in intensity; never to go away. He was back on the trash heap, collecting with his sister, returning to their home, such as it was, sometimes with his birth mother and bapu, sometimes in a new version, this time with his new mom and dad. Regardless of the company, he felt cloaked in warmth, security and dominance over his surroundings.

After he awoke, he was reluctant to leave the dream, basking in the feeling, hoping the dream would reappear. The dream represented reality, the life he lived at the present was the dream. Maybe sometime soon he would awaken for real and find himself back home. His sister told him she had the same dream the same nights he did.

5

Raj said, "Dad, I already checked on patents. There are several similar to mine. If I apply for a modification of an existing patent, I won't have to reveal details of the manufacturing process."

"Did you check on the price of a patent attorney?" Tony asked, expecting 'no' for an answer.

Instead, Aruna replied, "I did. Hourly rates for quality patent attorneys average about $500 an hour. In order to get a flat fee quote, we would have to let him know all the particulars. In short, we'd better get ready to pay thousands. The filing fees alone range from $200 to $800. I suspect that would be for big corporate stuff, not for backyard inventors like us. Frankly, from what I've read, we should be able to do the whole thing ourselves and claim 'Patent Applied For' for a fraction of the cost."

"You said you researched the others. How does yours compare?" Tony inquired.

"I don't know how they're manufactured, but I can see the ingredients," Raj said. "After messing with chips, I got the idea to look at the patents that had been issued and saw some did use chips with different additives. I don't think they'll get very far. At least I never heard about them. One that attracted me used the 5 mm pellets." He explained about contacting *Plastiques* for smaller spheres.

Tony had to give his children credit. They were thorough. He looked at the enthusiastic young couple and offered, "You mentioned you didn't think the other patented bricks wouldn't go far. Maybe they do what they're supposed to do and somebody bought their patents from them, never to be seen again."

In another month, the couple found that using the slurry itself as mortar worked much better as a bonding agent than did lime and it cut down on weight. They were becoming familiar with building regulations and quickly came to the conclusion more money and political backing was needed if their grand scheme were to succeed. Production had to be ramped up to manufacture the bricks on a large scale. In their minds, construction of a miniature shelter would have to be accomplished at some point.

Raj's concerns ate at him, until, in an instant, they vanished when he saw an article about how plastic mini-homes were being created by 3-D printing. Other startup companies used plastic sheeting to make small structures by other means with hopes to build larger dwellings. The issue of fire never came up because the plastic they used, whether it was from bottles with PET Level 1 and next levels up, were non-flammable, in fact were self-extinguishing. The cost was $40-$60 thousand to construct a mini home; more for larger structures. Additional costs included ground setting and ties to power and water.

Between the two industrious youths, somewhere between 80 and 100 trips to the dump and the incinerator had been made, depending on when one began the counting process. The pair had become so robotic in their routines that when Tony informed them they could return to their normal duties, the two were almost disappointed.

Aruna conceived the idea of building on their own property. The fenced-in area at the rear of the building, where forklifts and other equipment were stored, still had ample space for other purposes.

With limited resources, Raj ordered the ton of pellets from *Plastiques*. For less than $200, he purchased a small electrically powered cement mixer and moved it into the fenced-in area where he would also store the numerous bags of pellets when they arrived.

Raj had a bad feeling he was on the wrong track. For one thing, he was an engineer-biologist, not a builder. He had a concept, not a product. He needed to hire someone.

Driven to succeed, the couple worked the

6:00 am to 2:00 pm shift, each went home for a short break, then began answering some questions.

With the use of instrumentation, Raj was able to show conclusively that the bricks made with the smaller beads transmitted 75% less heat and cold than did the older original bricks with the larger beads. The advantages of ease of transport and construction, combined with light penetration over conventional construction materials were profound. If a cost savings could be shown as well, so much the better.

6

Aruna looked over her brother's shoulder as he typed:

Dear Sanjay, the last time you emailed, you and Melanie were in California covering the earthquake and planned to pay your brother another visit before going back overseas. We wish you a safe journey. For ReCyclo, we project our own tsunami to be coming soon in terms of trash inflow. If you ever need another job, say, driving a dump truck, we have contacts and can make it happen (ha ha).

We have completed an important phase of our research and we're very satisfied with the end product. Let me know where you'll be and we'll mail you a plastic brick. Along those lines, we are in need of a person who can give us advice, or otherwise assist us in the construction of a house or other structures made of our bricks. We have tons of data on all kinds of tests we've performed on them and ours have passed code, as far as county requirements, without having to reveal details about how they are made. Anyway, you mentioned your brother is in the construction business and, as that is the only contact we have, we would like to ask him a few questions and get some guidance. We can always get a local contractor, but I'd rather keep this low key for now---you know, keep it in the family—until we reach a state where we can go into mass production. There a lot of directions we can take this and we don't know enough yet. Stay in touch and don't buy too many plastic bottles.

Warmest, Raj and Aruna.

The couple read it over purposely leaving out any mention of money. After making a couple of text adjustments, Raj hit SEND.

Hoping to hear back from Sanjay by the next day, they were shocked to receive a return missive within the hour; not from Sanjay, but from his brother, Vijay.

Dear Raj and Aruna: Sanjay forwarded me your email. He wanted me to tell you he'd get in touch later when he can relax for a nice chat. He told me a lot about you and said you are smart and we are all brothers and sisters in this cause. (To Aruna, it sounded like the old rhetoric she got from the leftist ecological extremists, when she got attracted to their dogma). He asked me to give you anything you need and to work with you. I own a custom home construction company here in Southern California, so it's not too far for either of us to visit.

I am excited to hear about the progress you've made and would like you to send me a video of your product(s). I have two children about your age and when I said their uncle knew you two and after they saw the special on TV recently, you have some new fans, myself included.

Let me know your thoughts.

Warmest, Vijay

After the siblings discussed the letter at some length, Raj returned:

Dear Vijay, thank you for your kind words. If you send us a physical address, we will be happy to mail you a variety of different samples and technical data, as per our tests, for your consideration.

Best R &A

Raj suggested, "Dad said to explore all avenues, so this is a new avenue."

Aruna said, "And to watch our backs. We'll ship Vijay small sheets ranging from 1/8" to 2" and some bricks of different sizes."

"We should be all right as long as he doesn't get the formulation," Raj concluded. "Before we do anything, let's go online and look up *Homes by Vijay,"* Aruna suggested.

Seconds later the website popped up with pictures of million dollar plus homes of varying designs. The text read:

HOMES BY VIJAY. UNIQUELY DESIGNED LUXURY HOMES AT AFFORDABLE PRICES FOR THOSE WHO WANT COMFORT AND CONVENIENCE. SPACE EFFICIENT, ECO-FRIENDLY. SEVERAL FLOOR PLANS AVAILABLE, OR WE WILL HELP YOU DESIGN YOUR OWN LAYOUT.

A smiling picture of Vijay Kumar was inset at one corner. He appeared older than his brother, but the resemblance couldn't be denied. Both had the same head of pitch black hair neatly combed, ears flat against the head, deep-set dark eyes, and medium lips with a strong nose. A woman stood at his side along with two males in their late teens. The ratings of Kumar's company were five star.

Once the large package had been sent by UPS, Raj and Aruna returned to their daily work and research routine. Two days later, UPS informed them the parcel had been delivered. The couple was not so naive as to wait for Vijay to come along for assistance. "Never wait for, or rely on other people for your happiness," Tony had told them, repeatedly.

While Raj, The Impetuous, raced ahead, Aruna saw the real problem lay in a lack of direction. Their visions fit into their fantasies, but didn't necessarily fit into reality. She saw their early years affecting him more than her. She knew his thinking. Live for the moment. Survive one day at a time. None of this "Haste makes Waste' crap. The faster you work, the more garbage you collect; ergo, you trade junk for cash to buy enough food to eat for a day or two. What did "planning for the future" mean to him? For Raj, it was doing it for the *now*. The future would take care of itself. It was she who, as a child, had found a hiding place for their magnet. It was she who saw the real vision, the one who had come close to spending time behind bars for her visions.

Vijay's new email gave the couple something else to think about.

Dear R & A: I apologize for this late response. When I received your samples, I gave them to my engineers and planners for further study. They were impressed by the thorough work you've done so far and the product itself. I believe we may be able to use your product(s) in the future and I'm willing to offer you $10,000 for the patent rights. It's a generous offer and I invite you to accept it forthwith. Please call me if you have any questions.

Regards, Vijay Aruna broke out in laughter. "Wow, there it is. Standard Offer 101. That's good news, Raj. The offer tells us they are excited with our samples and either see a bright future for themselves, or better yet, keep it out of our hands."

Raj agreed. "I could politely tell him we thank him for his offer, but we're not selling the patent under any circumstances and he can either work with us or we'll go it alone."

"Maybe we should ask mom and dad for a discussion session," Aruna suggested.

"Sometimes fools rush in to get the best seats," Raj philosophized.

"Or get trampled," Aruna returned.

At the dinner table, Megan advised, "Do nothing. Sit on it."

"I agree," said Tony. "Now you know your product has value. Shop it around. Prepare more samples and get ready for mass shipping to other construction companies. It may take years, but at some point, either our government or a foreign government may be interested; India, itself, for example. Start thinking big."

7

Over the next few weeks, the entrepreneurs found that the plastic would hold screw hinges, which worked better than nails. Even with minor advances, Raj couldn't shake the nagging feeling that something was very wrong.

During this time, Raj followed his mother's advice and contacted Vijay thanking him for his offer, wishing him the best and concluded by saying the patent is not for sale.

A revelation came to Aruna when she announced, "There is nothing wrong with our product. It's our marketing that sucks."

"How so?" Raj queried.

"Our cover letter talks about the bottle problem, but doesn't focus on it. The problem is second place. The bricks are in first place. One thing I learned from people I used to associate with is to go directly for the jugular."

Raj laughed, "You mean convince people to stop making plastic bottles?"

"Of course not, but we need to focus on the

superiority of our product," she replied.

Raj saw the truth in her view, yet it didn't strike pay dirt with him. Until he did get it. "I'm thinking," he said. "How much does an empty water bottle weigh?"

"It varies from, say, 7 to 14 grams," she replied.

"Right. Call it 10 grams. There's 454 grams per pound . . . "

"I see where you're going. Our original plastic brick weighs a pound with only 10% of that is additive, so we're using maybe 45 bottles per brick," she said.

"Correct, except we say it's a hundred," he said, beaming. "Let somebody prove us wrong. The point is to emphasize what we are trying to accomplish."

"Why isn't it a hundred?" she asked.

"Why don't we double the amount of beads and forget the bricks. We go to ¼" sheets. Here, let me draw what I have in mind."

After she had completed the sketch, she said, "We need a place to work and a lot of forms."

"We'll ask dad if he has any ideas," Raj contributed.

At that, Raj went to work and made up the same slurry with double the weight of the fine beads. To their great surprise, the brick weighed less than the original by 40% and had greater tensile strength with more light penetration.

Raj said, "Now we make two small model

homes and check the energy differences in terms of lighting, heating and cooling, construction, etc., make a video and send it along with a new write-up along with new specs."

Their 18th birthday rapidly approached. The older Hobert boys had already passed the milestone. Karl, the oldest, had grown to his father's height. He began college. He spent a year as a math major, then he switched to accounting. His goal was to integrate with the family business.

On the other hand, Billy couldn't decide whether to join the military or go to college. His parents would ensure he didn't start working full time as a supermarket checkout clerk. Hans knew of Tony's military background and asked him to talk to the boy.

He called to invite himself over one evening and brought the young man with him. He turned out to be more adventurous than his older and larger brother and hearing stories from his own father about Tony's war experiences, looked forward to the conversation. Would Tony advise the military or college for him?

Tony advised, "Sign up for the military for four years. You take an aptitude test. Based on your scores they will steer you in a particular direction, such as diesel mechanic, or airplane/helo, or something in the medical field. The list is long. You'll learn a valuable trade. You won't have to kill people. Plus, you'll be able to take college courses while you're serving and maybe travel. When you get out, you'll have the GI bill under which you can go to college for a further education in your specialty field and have health benefits thrown in."

Hans asked, "You didn't do that, though. Why not?"

Tony said, "I felt pressured to get into a tough outfit. I saw a lot of action. Truth be told, I don't know whether I'm better off for it. If that pressure hadn't been there, I might have gone the route I suggested to Billy."

Billy stuck out his hand and said, "Thank you for the suggestion, sir. I am definitely going to look into what you suggested.

Thirty days later Billy signed up for the air force.

Turning 18 is a big deal in both India and the United States. A person can vote, get a driver's license, and join the armed forces. This birthday was special in other ways. The comparative data were presented in an introductory pamphlet. The data, unarguably, demonstrated the superiority of the product line. The writeups followed professional writing formats. Even Megan and Tony had been kept in the dark as to their creative endeavors. The pair worked 40 hour work weeks and Aruna earned another college degree, taking occasional time off from work to attend required laboratory sessions.

The prospect of losing the children had weighed on the Rossis for some time. As Megan fluffed up her pillow, not ready to give up the day, she said softly, "Aruna told me she wants to move out as soon as she has enough money."

"Yes, the world calls. At least you can go back to teaching to fill up your days," Tony said.

"And come home to what?" she replied, wistfully.

Tony chuckled, "Do you know how many guys at work have hit on Aruna? She hasn't even been out on a date. Not Raj, either."

Megan said, "Maybe that's our fault. My guess is each will find their own apartment. Maybe after they move we can have a regular thing here, like one certain night of the week at mom and dad's place for dinner. Set the rule in stone."

Tony said, "That's a great idea. They can even bring a friend. Everybody will look forward to say, Wednesday, or Thursday night. We wouldn't want to tie up their weekends.

"Okay, we'll talk to them about it once we get past tomorrow," Megan concluded.

"You mean today, don't you?" Tony said, glancing at the clock.

8

The wooden box outside the basement door was addressed to Raj and Aruna Rossi, ReCyclo Industries, 2500 E. American Way, Phoenix AZ, 85003. The return read: Exotic Pets for Everyone, 693 San Houston Blvd, San Antonio, TX, 78023.

Aruna unlocked the door to their private laboratory and Raj hefted the lightweight crate into the room. The small crate measured two feet square. Raj evaluated the face of the plastic enwrapped cover sheet securely attached to the top of the wooden box and to the stamps accompanying the plastic sheet. Markings on the container indicated This Side Up. Bending over to read the label, he saw the parcel wasn't sent through the U.S. Postal Service. It came via FedEx, which has similar, but not identical, rules for mailing. These include more exactitude as to tracking and arrival times.

The table was full of experimental equipment, so he left the small crate on the floor. He looked at his sister, both wondering what kind of exotic pet someone would send to them and what the heck an exotic pet was, anyway. Even as a well-meaning present, you don't send a Myna Bird or a cockatoo in a crate. Could it a collection of lizards?

Raj retrieved a heavy screwdriver and worked loose what appeared to be a lid. When he got the lid off, it became obvious that somebody had not paid attention to which side was the top because a blue plastic container inside clearly lay on its side. The container was large enough to hold a 12-pack of beer.

Raj flipped the entire box on its side so the lid of the plastic container could be opened, which he assumed would now be the top. Velcro straps held the lid closed. "You want the honors?" Raj said, as his cell rang. It was his father.

"We got it. Thanks, Dad," he said, light heartedly. "Who know? Maybe it's champagne on dry ice and you can have it for dinner. She's opening it now."

Aruna shrieked. Three large rattlesnakes squirmed out of the container, swimming across the concrete floor, one of which had bitten her on the ankle.

"Rattlesnakes, Dad, fucking snakes. Aruna got bit," he screamed into the phone.

Tony shouted, "What. Where did she get bit?"

Raj shouted, "Lower ankle."

Shell-shocked, Tony managed to instantly revert to type and he exclaimed, "Cut it now and bleed her. Tie her off below the knee. I'll call 911. I'll be right down."

Raj danced around the snakes squirming randomly across the lab floor trying to gain traction as he desperately tried to reach his sister only yards away.

Aruna said, through extreme pain, "Cut me Raji, now, cross-cut the bite. Let it bleed. Sit me up, keep the wound below my heart level," Aruna shrieked. Sweat began to beat on her brow. She began to pant.

Raj kept a wary eye out for the snakes distancing themselves from the turmoil, relieved to be free from days of captivity. With no other sharp tool at hand, Raj pulled out a small pocket knife and sliced her as she directed, squeezing the wound, allowing it to bleed freely. He pulled her to her feet and sat her on a chair, not knowing what else to do.

Within sixty seconds, Tony appeared, his long-ago training for various snake toxins and their field treatments ramming his mind from all sides. His daughter faced neurotoxins and hemorrhagic toxin. On auto-pilot, he instantly evaluated the situation, looked around to find soap and water, which he used to wash the wound. He noted the time. "What's in the fridge?" he asked Raj.

"Not much, just a jug of cold water and a

couple of Cokes," Raj told him.

Tony pulled out a cold can of Coke and held it against Aruna's head. He heard the dim sound of sirens and said, "How are you doing, honey?"

"I guess I'm just scared, daddy," she cried.

"We are on top of this, baby. You will be absolutely fine. Hang in there and you'll be home before you know it. Let me get back upstairs and get the medics down here. Raj, keep her fever down. Ensure the leg is tied off. Keep as little of the poison from going to the heart and the central nervous system as possible. I'm going to call your mom now. Keep your phone line to me open."

Tony was shouting as he ran out the door. He ascended a single flight of stairs to the surface where he met the ambulance team he had directed to come to the rear of the building. Another siren could be heard. This near of the city it could be police, fire, rescue, or dog catcher for all he knew.

Within seconds, the paramedics arrived, a man and a woman, forewarned about the dangerous environment they were about to enter. Tony quickly explained the situated, first grabbing an umbrella he had parked next to each of the exit doors, at his wife's insistence, as protection against the maybe five days of rain the city got each year, leading them down the stairs.

Tony opened the door and instantly went after the only snake he could see with the head of the umbrella, while the paramedics injected Aruna with antivenin, a not unusual carry-along in the Desert Southwest and another dozen states. The snake stopped its escape, turned and coiled, raising some eight inches, hissing at Tony and rattling. That was a mistake. Tony swung the handle just as the snake shot forward in an attempt to bite him. He hit the creature hard enough to fell it. He clubbed it again and stomped its head with the heel of his boot enough times to ensure the snake would enter the afterlife.

Before Raj and the two paramedics assisted Aruna to a waiting ambulance, Tony photographed the open container, the snake, and the addresses on the labels, in case everything should mysteriously disappear. Ready to leave, he heard the second ambulance arrive—animal control.

Running up the stairs again, he repeated the explanation and led them to where Raj thought the other two snakes had taken cover. Then he and Raj hurried to the car to chase after the ambulance toward the Mayo Clinic, only blocks away. Shortly,Aruna's throat would begin to swell and she would have difficulty swallowing. Hopefully, her good health and the quick application of antivenin would lessen the toll.

"Why, who, dad?" Raj demanded during the drive.

"We'll find out. It could be anyone in the world. Even rock stars get death threats," Tony said, truthfully. Yet, the occurrence was too obtuse; so random as to butt against his trained instincts.

"Dad, threats are different than somebody trying to kill them," Raj rejoined.

Tony pulled into the emergency area parking lot and raced after the attendants who had pulled under the covered space reserved for emergency vehicles. Two paramedics carted Aruna into urgent care, where car crash victims and attempted suicides were normally brought in.

Tony signed in at reception and filled out necessary forms while Raj paced in waiting with other people huddled together awaiting news of their own loved ones. Megan arrived shortly. Finding a private corner, the two men animatedly described to her the circumstances, while staring into the look of incredulity on her face.

Once Megan had dissected what she would out of the tale, Tony pulled out his cell and retrieved the photos of the box, the interior container, the label, and photos of the snakes, all three-to-four feet in length and all with the classic diamondback pattern. The size didn't matter. Tony had eaten smaller ones. Even the smallest were poisonous, although their venom glands were smaller and their bite less harmful, despite common misconception to the contrary. The size of the snakes was meant to intimidate and to kill. Instead he had done the killing with use of the umbrella handle and his foot. He passed around the phone for each to view the pictures.

Tony Googled Exotic Pets Inc. in San Antonio to find it was a legitimate business with a website. He went to the site and found a list of animals and pets, most of which were not so exotic. They also sold snakes, but the kind that were used for rodent control like kings, or to put into old fish tanks like garters and crickets.

Exotic Pets had closed for the day. The business would not open until 9:00 am. Tomorrow would come soon enough. He called his mother and had a short conversation, promising to keep her up on developments.

A nurse entered the waiting room through swinging doors to call the name of Rossi. The three arose and followed her into a lit corridor where a white coated doctor introduced himself and said, "Aruna is stable. We'd like to keep her overnight for observation. She's fortunate in that the type of bite was immediately identified and you administered first aid quickly. You probably saved her life. She should be ready to go home by noon tomorrow."

Megan said, "I'll stay with her tonight. You two go back and find out who did this. We'll keep in touch. I'll be okay. I know this hospital and they have a great cafeteria and a good magazine stand." She tried to sound cheery, but she was unable to hide the fear and anger in her voice.

"Can we see her?" Tony asked the doctor.

The doctor motioned for the nurse to lead them to her room and he departed.

Aruna lay propped up and appeared to be somewhat sedated. She beamed as her family entered the room and pointed to her throat, indicating that she couldn't talk. Nobody ventured to discuss the details of the occurrence leaving that to Megan if she so chose.

"Dad, I'd like to stay over with you tonight," Raj requested.

"Of course. We have a call or two to make in the morning." Tony drove Raj back to ReCyclo where he retrieved his car and met his father at home to await the morning.

Tony paced impatiently for the 8:00 am hour to arrive. San Antonio was an hour ahead of Phoenix and the business was open from 9:00 am to 5:00 pm, six days a week. With Raj next to him and the phone on SPEAKER he made the call at 8:05. A cheerful woman calling herself Mary answered.

"Yes, Mary. This is Anthony Rossi. I'm calling from Arizona."

"And how can I help you, sir?" Mary chimed.

"We received a parcel yesterday from your business that was sent to Raj and Aruna Rossi."

"Absolutely. How are they enjoying their new pet?"

"I'm confused. Do you normally send rattlesnakes?"

"Oh, my, no. If this is a joke, I don't have time for this. Have a nice day," Mary said.

"Wait, don't hang up. I need your help," Tony said, trying anything to keep her on the line. "Listen, somebody sent us snakes with your address."

Mary said, "Now I'm confused. I boxed it myself. We have a P.O. for one *Gopherus agassizii.* That's your Sonoran Desert Tortoise. We sent you a cute five pound guy, maybe six years old. They're fun little pets. They'll follow you around and all they need is some vegetables like a head of lettuce and a little water. I enclosed a booklet for you. They hibernate during the winter even in your desert yard. All you have to do is to find them a cool place to dig . . . "

"Mary, we received rattlesnakes," Tony shot, angrily, losing patience.

"Well, Mr. Rossi, I boxed the tortoise myself and sent it FedEx as per the purchase order. We don't sell rattlers, cottonmouths, kraits, cobras, water moccasins, boas, or any kind of poisonous or dangerous snake. That's a fact. Maybe you're getting us confused with somebody else."

"One of my kids got bitten," Tony shot. "I can even send you a photo of the box."

"Please do. You sound serious. This is awful. It doesn't make any sense," Mary said, joining his concern.

"Tell me about it." Tony replied. "Where did the purchase order come from?" he asked.

Tony heard paper shuffling a moment before Mary said, "Baton Rouge, Louisiana, three days ago."

"How did they pay?"

"By bank transfer. We do it all the time," she said.

"How did the parcel get picked up?"

"The FedEx guy came by after we called in for a pickup. We're in a mall and these guys come and go all the time."

"Did he sign for it?"

"Yes."

"Can you take a picture of the signature, the P.O. and other relevant documents and send them to my phone?" Tony requested, looking at Raj who was listening, locked onto the conversation.

"I can't send you routing or account numbers, but I don't have any trouble with the rest of it," Mary offered.

"Thanks, Mary. I'd appreciate it if you don't mention this conversation to anyone other than police, or federal agents, should they appear. It has nothing to do with you, of course, but everything to do with the sender." And maybe a FedEx guy, he didn't add.

Tony had just hung up his phone when it dinged. Three photos appeared. One was a purchase order from a person in Baton Rouge, a second was the bank name and the name of the account holder, which matched with the address and P.O. with the routing and account numbers covered up; and the third was a signature from the FedEx guy. He forwarded the pictures he had taken.

Tony then received a call from Megan who said she'd be bringing Aruna back by noon. He called his mother and filled her in with all the details. She said, "Anthony, it sounds like we may need to get my private investigating company a call. I like their reports. More folksy than clinical, no bullet points, not too wordy. And they give you straight talk when you call them back."

"I was hoping you'd say that, mom."

"What's your time frame on this, as if I didn't already know?" she said.

"Yesterday," Tony responded, bitterly.

"Got it. Why don't you send me what you have and I'll get things started," Christina offered. "I expect they'll be calling you."

Tony followed this call by another one to Hans, informing him of the details. He knew Klara would soon be called and probably come over to help Megan take care of Aruna, soon after they arrived. Aruna had a great fondness for the matronly Klara. In another life she might have been the face on a can of Old Fashion Chicken Noodle Soup.

Too many things were happening too fast. Tony decided to forego work, at least until his daughter got home. Indeed, before he could get his thoughts organized, he did receive a call from Private Investigations, Inc. He went over details again to ensure they had received the info he had send to his mother. Details and timeline of events that occurred before, during, and after the biting incident were requested and recorded. Photos were requested, along with exact wording of conversations. It was done. He could only wait. Meanwhile, Raj was busy on his father's computer in the home office and called out, "Hey, Dad, look at this."

Tony came over and looked at the screen. "What do you have there?" he asked.

"I went to Google Maps and looked up the address of this Charles Cragmore in Louisiana, who ordered the tortoise. This is his house. They don't say how old the picture is, though. I might be able to get into county records if we think it's important."

Tony stared hard at the image while Raj scanned the area around the residence. "You have to be kidding me. You can't make it up," he muttered.

"I double checked. This is what they're giving me," Raj said, leaning back in his chair, exhaling, hands behind his head, a habit he'd picked up from Tony.

"How does a guy like that even know about us and where you and your sister work and decide to order you a goddamn turtle?" Tony exclaimed, staring at a single-wide trailer in the middle of a row of trailers.

"Somebody should go down there and find out," Raj said, knowing his father was much more suited to the task than he was.

"Our agency friends are getting paid good money to open this guy's past like a worn book. Your grandmother told me they play dirty. I like that, especially because they're on our side. One way or the other, Mr. Cragmore's life will take a turn for the worse. He may soon find himself deeply involved in a federal crime."

Raj wondered how Aruna would philosophize about people on our side playing dirty vs. those on the other side. Should both sides play clean, or should both sides play dirty. Who sets the rules? He decided to have some fun and ask her to differentiates the two words.

Aruna arrived home at 10:30 am. Megan pulled into the driveway, opened the garage door, but left it open to assist Aruna into a wheelchair, which she removed from the trunk of her car. Wheeling the patient into the kitchen through the garage, she ignored pleas by the patient that she could walk on her own. Her left ankle remained bandaged. Megan parked her on the sofa in front of the TV and retrieved a handful of books for her daughter to read, placing the remote within easy reach. "Your choice," she said, just as Klara entered through the open garage.

Megan reported, "She'll limp around for a while. The doctor said to keep an eye out for soreness in her kidneys and blood in the urine."

Several evenings later, Tony received a certified hand-delivered relatively thin manila envelope, for which he signed. The return address was from Private Investigations, Inc, Scottsdale. Aruna had returned to her own apartment, as had Raj.

"Who was that, Hon?" Megan asked.

He showed her the envelope. Megan wiped her hands on her apron and stood next to him at the kitchen counter. "When your mom said this company works fast, she meant it," she remarked, watching him slowly and carefully slice open the envelope, lest he damage the contents. He pulled out several sheets. The first was a cover letter. The other four sheets were photos of the trailer, the neighborhood and of a man standing at a door. Another piece was a letter—more like a notice of sorts. Tony read the cover sheet:

Dear Mr. and Mrs. Rossi:

Enclosed you will find a picture of Mr. Charles Cragmore at the door of his residence. (The photo was taken from a distance and enlarged.) The man standing in front of him with his back turned to the camera is our representative.

Mr. Cragmore is 70 years of age and has been unemployed for several years, living on social security. He once taught physics at Louisiana State University, but was fired for his atheistic views, which he openly espoused to his students (see enclosure). He recently purchased a new truck (picture enclosed) for which a third party paid for in cash.

We were unable to obtain any email texts from his phone. As you can understand, charges will have to be filed against him before authorities can obtain those records, however, in our estimation, there is sufficient cause to file a number of charges against him. Only two of these include interstate conspiracy to commit fraud and conspiracy to commit attempted murder.

Mr. Cragmore admitted openly that he ordered the purchase of the desert tortoise because he thought your son and daughter might like a present. In his words to our investigator, he saw them on television.

A log of his phone records, which we did have access to, reveals a long history of calls to and from area code 208. This area code corresponds to Hayden Lake, Idaho. A cluster of those phone calls occurs before the date of the attack in question. We told him we are monitoring his phone calls and he is under observation. Neither is true, but it should keep him at bay until his associates are apprehended. He asked why this discussion was taking place because all he did was "to buy a stupid turtle for someone."

A review of family history records finds

that Mr. Cragmore is related to Alice and Albert Tremont, parents of Arthur Tremont, about whom we have researched previously, as per Mrs. Christina Rossi Tremont. Albert Tremont is a descendant of the founder of Aryan Nations. In our opinion, he changed his name from to Tremont in order to escape the name, but not the ideology.

The phone calls themselves are tied to two phone lines; one is associated with Albert Tremont, the other to Arthur Tremont.

We are presently tracing the origin of the money used to purchase the truck and the identity of the FedEx driver, whom we believe, was paid well to exchange one tortoise for the three snakes. We will inform you of further developments.

One final note: Mr. Cragmore's claim to fame locally is that he is a long-time president of the local atheist's society. Enclosed is a copy of one his short treatises on the subject of God, which is available locally. It is identical to one we obtained from the college archives where he once taught.

In summary, we believe serious crimes have been committed by a number of persons on a number of fronts regarding the subject you employed us to investigate. We will continue putting this package together for you, unless you ask us to cease our efforts.

Signed, Gerald Johnstone, President USMC

(Ret.) FBI (Ret)

Megan put the page down on the counter. She said, "Why am I not surprised? What do you want to do?"

Tony grunted. "There's no difference between what I want to do and what I will do, both involve going up to Idaho, wait for one them to come out of his house alone, and have words with him behind the barn."

"Words?"

"Figure of speech. We'll see what else our investigative friends come up with. For starters, I'll ask them to present their evidence to the FBI branch in New Orleans."

"How do you think the FedEx guy pulled the switcheroo," Megan inquired. "I can't figure out how that would work, I mean get the right guy there at the right time?"

"Don't know. Somebody had to think this through and make plans," Tony said. "These routes are automated for the most efficiency, but somebody has to oversee the hired help. Some person on the outside had to have their own guy in there in case they tried to bribe and report the attempted bribe to queer the gig."

Megan sighed, "Well, my dear, I guess it's back to business as usual."

"Thankfully," Tony replied. "Hold on. I'm curious about this anti-religious piece Cragmore wrote way back when. The agency must have thought it interesting enough to include in the package. I'll give you the honors." He handed her the letter and she began to read out loud.

THE ABSENCE OF GOD

"There is no god and there never will be. God is a construct of the human mind, necessary to explain pain and suffering, survival, winning, losing, success, failure, hatreds, loves, and most of all, death and the unexplainable.

"A superstition is a widely held, but unjustified strongly held belief in supernatural causation leading to certain consequences of an action or event, or a practice based on such a belief. Each society has its superstitions. This definition also fits and applies to religion, which implies the need to believe in God. Therefore, religion is another superstition, but one held in common by every society on earth.

"Along with mortal diseases, nature has built into humans the need to have a god as a means of population control. Consider the flu pandemic of 1918, the black plague, cholera, and many disease outbreaks, all of which have reduced and will reduce populations by countless millions.

"So it is with religious fervor expressed through wars that have decimated equal numbers of humans. Why is one religion better than another? Why is one subdivision worse than another? Why is there a god that permeates our money (In God we Trust) and our constitution, as in separation of church and state? We are stuck with it. Humans have worshipped everything from rocks, to sea and air creatures, from lightning bolts to seasonal change and the invisible God within us and the sky above. Yet the best anyone can do is to conjecture and make it up as we go along.

"And where there is no God there are no angels, no Devil, or Satan, no sin or sinners, no heaven or hell, or purgatory, religious cults, Kingdom of Heaven, Second Coming, nuns, fathers, priests, churches or prayer rugs. There is no more 'God help me', or 'I swear to God', or 'Go to the Devil'" or 'Damn you to Hell' or "Thank the Lord."

"There will be no more gospel singing or religious holidays anywhere or holy wars or Crusades or missionaries. There will be no more tithing to pay for church-sanctioned child molesters. There will be no more prayers before or after meals or before bedtime.

"The sooner we give up this notion and accept the absence of any God, the sooner we can stand as men."

When Megan finished reading, she had the strong urge to wash her hands. The letter made her feel terribly naked and hollow. It also brought to light the huge part religion played in her life. She considered herself a good Christian. Just because she didn't go to church didn't make her evil, did it? Her birth family had never been regular church-goers, except when Christmas and Easter came around. She thought about her adopted children, whom she had never taken to a service. She had asked herself the same question many times over the years to come up empty of answers each time.

Tony had told her that the Hindu religion alone, if the kids were Hindu—funny, she had never thought to ask, as if they might know—had over 30 major gods and goddesses, reaching back 4000 years. Add another couple of thousand *sub-deities* and the complexity of a many religious cultures integrated into a single functional society boggled the imagination. Tell them all there is nothing pray or worship to and see what happens, bringing the discussion back to Cragmore's thesis.

After his wife finished reading, Tony shook his head from side-to-side sadly, and noted, "I believe Cragmore wasn't fired from his teaching position because of his beliefs; he was fired because he was so good at recruiting. To top it off, the guy is a hypocrite, if I ever heard one. After all his ranting, he has his own fantasy god he has always worshipped and tried to belong to a group of people who believe in the same fantasy god. It's called the god of white supremacy and unfounded racial bigotry. Hate everybody except yourself.

"The problem for him was the people he attaches himself to are God loving, church-going law-abiding citizens who work in every walk of life from ditch diggers to congressmen and congresswomen. I'm guessing he was ostracized by the people with whom he wanted to identify because of his atheistic beliefs.

"These guys live and breathe white supremacy. The belief consumes them. It shapes their lives. Ten-to-one Cragmore wears a tattoo instead of some religious symbol hanging from a chain around his neck. By his logic, the belief in white supremacy should be lumped in with pestilence, because some 40 million died during WWII, a war initiated by a man of their ilk, and it also initiated the slave trade. Witness the Crusades of the Middle Ages and arguably, the history of white missionaries and their entourages going into almost every corner of the world.

"White supremacy is also part of caste systems around the world. From what Aruna told me, darker women in her home country use a lot of white talc on their faces. It works well, until they sweat or cry."

Megan did wash her hands, not believing Cragmore's thesis, but got caught up in his rant. It wouldn't be so easy to wash the words in the letter from her mind and the fact his words held certain uncomfortable truths, and, at the same time, had the contradictory effect of reaffirming her faith in God. Her head spun. "I don't think the children need to see this," she said, resolutely, turning to face her husband.

Tony shook his head and said, "I disagree. They are the ones who got attacked. Besides, it's healthy for them to better understand the world we live in."

Megan forced a smile, deep in thought. "Raj would take it as a data point. Aruna would say that if God were eliminated from mankind's thinking (an impossible scenario) humans would feel too alone. She'd agree with you in that we are already alone; therefore, she would say that perhaps belief in God is critical to our sanity to avoid the feeling of loneness. To her, Man will go to any length to avoid that reality."

Tony offered, "Let's stick with Tremont and not get into Cragmore's beliefs. They're not relevant to what we should talk to the kids about. Think about what we want to say and have an honest talk with the kids tomorrow."

After dinner the following day, Tony called for a family meeting at the kitchen counter where everyone could face one another. He and Megan patiently described the world as a place divided in many ways, especially geologically and ethnically. Tony said, "I'm sure you know all of this intuitively, so forgive me for stating the obvious. It is the nature of life to be around others of your kind. This means your language, your family history, your educational status, religion, and your skin color. Because groups stay together, it is their nature not to like others outside their group. Okay so far?"

Tony said, "Your fame and your skin color has caused a number of people to hate you and to hate us. You may be in danger."

Those words got their attention.

Tony continued, "Why? Because you are obviously different than your mother and I and they are different from all of us."

"Come on, dad, spit it out," Raj announced, abruptly. Tony sounded like a man talking to four-year olds.

Tony said, "Your grandmother was married to a man who belongs to a hate group. He hates you and he hates us for adopting you. We're pretty certain he's the one who sent you the snakes."

Aruna looked as though she had been pole-axed. The frozen look on her face lasted but a second when she blurted, "That's crazy, dad. I mean, how do you know? We never even met the guy. How is grandma dealing with this creep?"

A look of surprise came over Raj's face before it returned to a placid look.

Megan answered this time. Calmly and rationally she replied, "She's dealing with it in her own way. Don't worry about her. It's all of us we have to worry about. We hired a private investigating firm to find out more about him. The point is, on the surface he is a nice guy, sociable; he has his quirks like we all do. It's what's inside his head that's so intriguing."

Tony said, "As you go through life you will

meet all kinds of people. Don't take anybody at face value. Be careful what you tell them. They may appear to be friends, but they can turn on you. You can get cheated in business or stolen from by someone you trust. Defend yourselves at all times. There are a lot of ways to find happiness. A lot of people like to keep it simple, for others the driving forces are money and power. True friends are a rare find. Hang onto them. The Hobert family is one example of solid folks."

Raj mumbled, "Money and Power. Life is like a Monopoly game. I know Monopoly."

Tony caught his words and said, "Except Monopoly has rules. Real life has two: your conscience and the law, both of which are flexible.

"One more thing," Tony added. "There is a saying, 'The grass is always greener on the other side of the fence'. Be careful to evaluate, because frequently, the fence is made of barbed wire and the grass will be brown by the time you get there. In other words, don't be impetuous about decisions."

The word "impetuous" stung Raj. It described him perfectly.

Two days later, Raj presented his parents with drawings of three model homes the sizes of doll houses, yet to be constructed—one of miniature brick and mortar, one of framed-in drywall, and one with their Plasti-Brik, no rooms included in any of the three.

Comparable data were presented, which detailed the expected numbers: heating and cooling units, available lighting, per annum energy savings; on and on. Granted, things change when size changes. New variables will always occur, yet, he could find no glaring flaw in their presentation.

At night preparing for bed, Megan said, "At least it looks good on paper. I've been thinking. These kids are idealists. Soon enough they'll be coming into real money, but money can't buy a true idealist. Raj is the dreamer, Aruna is the pragmatist. Before you make any deals with them, how about we call them in for an interview to find out what their vision is for the future."

Tony said, "Let's invite Hans over when we have the conversation. If anybody in our circle knows about the rise and fall of businesses, it's Hans. He'll probably want to bring Karl with him for the experience. I want to do this before other people get the information and come back with a skilled negotiator, one who doesn't know how to say 'no' and offers them something so solid they can't turn it down."

"Then let us be those 'other people'," Megan asserted.

9

Reaching the age of 18 had changed the twins mentally and emotionally. It had transformed their thinking from juvenile to adult, almost overnight. A barred gate in the distant future had lifted, a gate they had been programmed to look forward to since adoption.

The seven sat outside casually dressed in the cool evening air. Karl sat next to his mother looking uncomfortable, as though he was sitting in judgmental superiority of his friends when he was only there as an observer. Billy was in the army sitting in a classroom.

Two bug zappers occasionally sparked, sometimes singly, sometimes in clustered events.

Tony said, "I invited everyone here because I want us all to have a discussion of where you would like to go with your idea of a plastic home. There are a number of other products on the market similar to yours, some of which have done nicely. You want to join them, I take it."

"Not join them, be apart from them," Raj

said,"Sorry, wrong choice of words. But do you want to sell your product, or your ideas? I'm not certain yet, which it is," Hans said.

"Both, with a greatly improved product line directed specifically toward a huge world-wide need," Raj replied. His mind had leap frogged from his original brick-like home through many progressive designs to end up with a much more efficient structure constructed of thin paneling. It had yet to be constructed. He obsessed about finding a place where he could tear into the work.

"Improvement is one thing; selling is everything. Just saying," Hans argued. "I'm impressed by your thorough testing, but nobody is going to live in a doll house. You want this for cheap housing, yet I see no cost of analysis, no comparative cost of materials, cost of transportation, actual size of the final product, and the big one, cost of labor to construct—how many? Don't you think it's important to note those factors?"

The youngsters appeared to take the questions in stride, as though they were expected.

"We did no cost analysis. In fact, we're certain we don't have a final product," Raj answered, truthfully.

Aruna opened a leather folder she had in her hand and withdrew some drawings, handing them to Hans who looked at them, then passed them around to make the complete circuit.

Raj said, "We use every grade of plastic bead

for our bricks and mortar, not just a couple of grades, but *all* seven classes. Most companies you are referring to make their products from one or two grades of plastic bottles. The shoes, too, are our own design."

"Sir, we are not about making more water bottles. Our technology allows for recycling of all types of plastic containers regardless of the type of the recycling logo, or its absence, and eliminates the need for AI to do the separation," Aruna stated, flatly.

Hans said, "Big deal. Nobody cares how many grades you use. What they do care about is how much money will come out of their pocket and I don't care whose name recognition is attached to it; yours, CNN's, or Santa Claus. If it can't be afforded, end of story."

Karl cringed at the harsh words and looked down. Klara watched the scene play out, the main actors confident in their roles. Megan spoke first by saying to Hans, "They do star in CNN world-wide specials. Even today, they have a large following. Melanie Brown absolutely adores them."

Tony asked, "Let's talk about this. We need a game plan and the final product. I see the marketing potential. It's way too early to go there. Personally, I want to see a final product. What is it you want?"

"A billion dollars for starters," Raj replied.

Aruna gaped. This was a new one on her.

Before anyone could say a word, Raj went on, “The pundits got it partly right. They blamed global warming on CO2 emissions, which began to increase along with the industrial age. They blamed it on automobiles, smokestacks, and burning of fields and forest fires. They left out methane. A molecule of methane traps more heat than 80 molecules of CO2.

“Methane is produced from agriculture and waste products, such as discarded food, along with degradation of paper and cardboard. Degradation occurs in landfills. Billions of tons of methane are released each year from dumps around the world. We’re only scratching the surface in understanding how much is released. It could account for as much as 25-40% of the global warming. Why? Because virtually all the landfills are out in the open and not buried. The amount of open air trash is proportional to the rate of global warming since the start of the industrial age. I want this trash buried. To accomplish my goal, I will need a fortune.

“Not from you. I’ll make my own way. You did ask me what I wanted.”

Tony stared hard at his son. Did he and Megan create this man with monster ambitions, or was he naturally born with monster genes? He considered several options, but decided to let the actor play out the scene. Which he did.

“In direct answer to your question, We keep the patent. We continue to work for you, dad, because we enjoy the work, but for only 20 hours a week. If you need us to drive trucks, we'll do that. Then we want to each get paid consultant wages for another 40 hours a week. Eventually, we want to build houses, not full size homes, but smaller homes made out of Plasti-Brik. For that we'll need to work with a builder on some vacant land. You fund all of that. We'll put our own money into whatever aspect of the project we deem necessary. If everything looks good and we get the kinks out, we contact CNN, once mass production is in place—all under the aegis of ReCyclo."

Caught up in her brother's presentation and seeing where he wanted to go with it, she added, "As a small aside, we want to negotiate with India, maybe even go back there, to see if we can make a deal to create housing. Mind you, this is all with the use of recycled plastic bottles.

"That's a lot of ask," Tony said, glancing at Hans, who gave one of those, "Hey, he's yours, not mine," looks. Karl avoided looking at anyone.

Hans chuckled, not out of derision, but to lighten the mood. He said, "This isn't Shark Tank where we play one against the other and force the budding entrepreneur to come up with a 'yes' or a 'no'. Let the people with business experience discuss this over the next couple of days and get back with you. Just hold off making any commitments until we can sort this out.

Is that fair enough?"

Raj and Aruna looked at one another to send mental signals. Raj said, "Fair enough."

The twins stood, preparing to leave, when Aruna said to her mother, quoting:

Whoever you are holding me now in hand,
Without one thing all will be useless,
I give you fair warning before you attempt me further,
I am not what you supposed, but far different.

Megan threw a hand to her mouth and declared. "Whitman. You remembered."

"Of course, mom, why wouldn't I?" Aruna answered, succinctly.

Karl felt the element of discomfort, which forced him to contribute, boldly, "I like your ideas. You guys look great. I haven't seen you in a long time. You've put on a few inches."

Aruna quipped, "Back at you. From what I hear those Monopoly games we used to play paid off for you, I mean, with your accounting background and working with father and all." She glanced at Hans, who sat immovable.

Karl laughed, unabashedly, "Getting beaten every time must have done me some good."

Raj reached across the table and stuck out his hand for a shake, remembering back when, not too long ago, the twins first met Karl and Billy and had to be told about the custom.

Raj moved impassively through it all, seeing the world perceived by his senses as necessary obstructions to a goal, driven by some passion he could neither define, nor control. He did not want to come up with new mathematical models about the operation of the universe, or accumulate wealth as an end game. He wanted to change the world in the manner of an obsessive-compulsive person, which is what he was.

He accepted his talents as easily as any person accepts theirs. For him, though, the intense nature of his drive gave him the view that everything and everyone around him served as tools toward that end. He could be personable when he had to be. A sociopath he was not. As time went on, his focus became sharper, which increased the intensity of his drive to make changes in the world at large.

Three days later saw the visit repeated on a more informal basis inside the house. Coffee and desert were served first. The group of six sat randomly around the dining room table chatting idly, sipping drinks, nibbling at slices of pies, until tony raised his hand for silence to address his children.

"Raj, Aruna, there are troublesome aspects of your offer. Here is our counter proposal: First, we don't need your physical labor, we need your minds and your work ethic. We don't want you working at the plant. We will, however pay you each . . ." he presented a figure—"to work as full-time consultants for ReCyclo. You will have use of a company car. If you want to buy or rent another one, that's up to you."

Hans took over and said, "My family owns a number of acres of vacant land about an hour south of here. We will earmark one-half acre for your experiments and we'll provide the builder. We'll give you six months to make something work, then you're off the consulting gig and back to regular wages at the plant, or you're free to find another job." He looked over at Tony when he made the statement. Tony nodded. It was as they had agreed.

Hans continued, "You two are the only ones who care about what grade of plastic the houses are made of. It's cost per unit and profit margin that run the business of selling. You'll have to come up with something else that will resonate."

Aruna sighed. She and her brother had already been schooled in Business 101, which included a section on learning from one's mistakes early on for preventive purposes.

For the first time in her life she felt embarrassed and angry at her brother, always pushing, never patient, while she, always the compliant follower. Pragmatism was her wheelhouse. Why hadn't she seen it? Maybe they needed to go their separate ways. They were adults. What was she supposed to do, live her entire life alongside her brother? If they took the deal, each would have enough money to live independently, maybe she could even date. No problem finding men, that's for sure. The entire thought scared and excited her at the same time.

"I'm in," Aruna said.

Raj looked at her in surprise.

"I'm in," she repeated, this time looking at him directly.

"Don't you think we should talk about this?" Raj asked her.

"No. Do what you want. If they want one of us, or if they want neither, so be it. The house is your idea, anyway. So are the shoes. Actually, you don't need me." she told him in a display of womanhood and independence, in an about face in front of witnesses.

Eyebrows raised and eyeballs flitted around the table almost randomly, sending and receiving messages. There was mutiny in the house.

Raj said to Hans and his parents, "Uh, I guess I'm okay with the offer too."

Anticipating another outburst from Aruna, Tony said, "Good, I'll write it up."

Raj looked thoughtful for a brief moment, glanced at Aruna, and stated, "Excuse us. We have some business to discuss."

Smiling teeth emerged at random points around the table. "We understand" the teeth declared, watching the negotiators exit the rear of the home to permit them to figure out life.

Raj slid the door closed behind him and stepped to the side, not taking at seat in one of the patio chairs. He asked, "Why did you say you don't need me?"

"Because you may need me to be your servant, but I don't need to follow your whims anymore. This whole thing is your dream. How many more years should I tag along behind you? Tell me, how many? One, five, ten, a lifetime? I need money, yes. So I took the deal before you maybe screwed it up."

Raj shook his head, and said, "It was only a negotiation."

"For your project, not mine," she shot.

"I thought it was ours," he said, sadly, hanging his head. At that, he looked to the nearest chair, a sturdy wooden lawn chair, and sat down heavily, pressing the heels of both hands against his temples. "Oh, shit, this is embarrassing," he said.

"What," Aruna took his words to refer to her challenging him, until she understood the stress had triggered a migraine.

"Where are your pills?" she said.

"Left hand pocket," he managed to say.

"I can't reach them. You're sitting. Stretch out," she ordered.

He did so. She had to negotiate her hands between the arm of the chair and the seat itself to get to his pocket. She pulled out the flat plastic container with two colors of pills. The whites were the twice-daily mood meds, the pinks were the bad boys, the pills he takes for preventative attacks, when he knows heavy stress is about to befall him. She tapped out a pink one and said, "Back in a sec."

Aruna ran into the house, said not a word, grabbed the nearest glass of water she could find on the table and brought it outside. Hans and Klara knew of Raj's affliction. Karl didn't. Klara stood and announced, "Come on guys, we need to go home. Leave these people alone."

Karl knew better than say anything at that moment. Within 15 seconds, the three swept out the front door like leaves caught in a sudden breeze.

10

A man by the name of Sam picked up the twins at the plant where they had consolidated everything required to build the simple houses they had in mind. Loaded into the back of the small U-Hall were the cement mixer, bags of beads, lime and sand for making of mortar for the standard brick house, and various tools used for the creation of the bricks. Also loaded were enough forms to make panels for Raj's latest vision.

Sam informed them he had already been to the job site on a number of occasions, at the direction of Hans. He had brought down a power generator and fuel to service a water well already on the land.

Sam looked to be a weathered sixty years of age, a happy, hardened gray-haired man who wore a wedding ring, denims, work boots, and button down. He stood a 5'10, three inches below Raj's lanky frame.

"I've known Hans for more than twenty

years. I started my own construction company about the time he began to buy real estate. I could tell you stories, but he'd kill me if he ever found out."

"Oh, come on, don't say that and not tell us," Aruna said, sitting between the two on the drive down.

Sam laughed. "We'll have plenty of time for that. For now let's talk about where we're going. It's an old brick church built over 100 years ago on tribal land. I know, go figure. Anyway, the story goes that a fire mysteriously gutted the place and the interior got cleared out leaving the shell. Apparently, the original builders planned to get it back up and running again, but it never happened. Hans bought the church, along with another 50 acres around it, back when land was dirt cheap. He made payments for years, but he looked to the future, which is now. The land is worth a fortune because it's outside a rapidly growing city halfway between Phoenix and Tucson.

"The three of us are going to be working inside the church to build your model homes, running every kind of test on them we can think of. I heard you guys never went to school and you're not too bright either, so just follow directions."

The comment set off a round of laughter. A bond had been created.

ReCyclo was situated in the city of Gilbert,

toward the southern portion of the greater Phoenix metro area and south of the huge airport. The dump and DEA burn facility were situated miles down the road in the direction of the church. Coming in overhead, a plane descended, which attracted Raj's eye.

"What are you thinking?" Aruna asked, already knowing the answer.

"You know, when we were kids back home and we'd see the planes coming into Delhi," he said.

"Are you feeling nostalgic?" she asked.

"Remembering, no big deal," Raj said.

Sam drove in the right lane, only 10 mph above the speed limit to keep up with traffic. He said, "Man, that was crazy. I saw the CNN specials. I can't imagine what is must have been like."

"You saw them?" Aruna asked.

"Hell, everybody did. What a life, trying to survive one day a time," Sam said.

"A lot of people are like that here too," Raj said.

Sam laughed, "Really? Look around you. Forget the homeless for a moment. I see people living in shelters with water and electricity. I don't see them climbing on a mountain-high trash heap to pick up a scrap to trade in. Say, you drove somewhere south of here to a dump site didn't you?"

"We both did for weeks" Aruna said.

"Then you're familiar with the drive. After today, we'll each take our own cars and set up meeting times. I still have a company to run so you'll be on your own a lot of the time. Here's an extra key to the church. You might want to have a couple of duplicates made." Sam reached into a pocket and handed Aruna the key.

ReCyclo ensured each employee got paid weekly. Employees had the option of buying shares in the company, the price of which had fallen considerably since the decision made by several nations not to take trash belonging to other nations. It was a good time to buy, which Raj and Aruna opted to do, having faith their endeavors would eventually reverse that trend and pay back their parents for their years of sacrifice as a "thank you."

A dirt road once ran westward to Casa Grande 100 years ago, when the community had a population of less than 1000. Numerous Indian nations and Indian communities occupied the entire Southwestern portion of the country, with the early Casa Grande area one of them and where national monuments still testify to their presence.

Today, the dirt road of old is replaced by a four lane highway connecting I-10, which doglegs northward from Tucson to a westward turnoff south of Phoenix. The turnoff runs through Casa Grande, presently registered with a population nearing 60 thousand.

Not far from the turnoff to Casa Grande and some 50 yards off the road to the north stood the church owned by Hans Hobert. Flat desert surrounded the edifice on all four sides with low hills to the west demarked by Picacho Peak State Park some miles away. Night blooming Cereus, desert scrub grass, and occasional small cacti dominate the hard desert landscape with occasional creosote and salt bush filling the gaps.

Vertebrates included lizards, horned toads, and the occasional Gila monster. Birds of prey cruised the edges of rising hot air bubbles looked for anything that scurried.

During his previous visits, Sam had ensured the water well and small WC inside the church were operational. When necessary, electricity would be supplied by a diesel generator Sam kept locked indoors when not in use. Upper windows shattered by pellet guns and rifle fire would permit ample sunlight—and rainfall—to enter the premises.

Pigeons had also found entry to the building conveniently easy where they were able to spend years cooing, fluttering, pooping, reproducing, and shedding feathers to their little hearts' delight. Mice and insects had also found sanctity there during all times of the year. Yet, the adobe block structure remained intact, as did the concrete flooring.

Part of the unloaded implements and supplies included a push broom, dust pans, trash bags, and scrub brushes. When Sam unlocked the chain that held the two portions of the front door in place, the twins stared at their new workplace. Sam had considered cleaning it before their arrival, but quickly came to the conclusion that two hands were better than one and handed them each an implement while he put them to work.

Excusing himself, Sam took the U-Haul several miles to the west into the city of Casa Grande where his work crew was in the final stages of constructing a large apartment building the government had hired him for, on rush status, in order to house some 200 illegal immigrants, ensuring the kitchen was large enough to accommodate the serving of that many people for three meals a day. A swimming pool was included in the deal, all paid for by the generosity of the American people.

When he returned, he found the double doors open and two slaves hard at work. Leaning against the truck, with arms akimbo, he studied them; totally focused on their work, he hadn't been noticed. If he were Raj and had gone through what the youth had gone through, he would have said to his prospective wife, "Don't ever ask me to take out the trash."

If he were Aruna, he (she) would have married a wealthy man to inform him at the outset that he will have to hire household maids, because his newfound love will never, ever, touch a piece of dirt again.

He worried about the two, watching sweat running down their faces, not stopping for a drink of water. She still limped a bit. Hans said she had improved tremendously since the snakebite, yet through it all she had been stalwart, never complaining. Did the strength come from their early years, he wondered. Granted he was down the chain of information, he still wondered if either of them knew of a person outside the family either one could call a personal confidant.

Sam and Hans were of like mind. They were riddled with doubts. Hans had told him he had agreed to hire the kids to keep the peace with his neighbor. Yes, they were intelligent and educated, but, in his book, clever and wise beats intelligent every time. Hans and Klara gave them credit for being good, decent human beings, inventive and creative.

Beyond that, they were naïve kids playing with Tinker Toys. The time had come for them to put or shut up. Sam had said he would help as much as he could. It turned out to be very little. The Feds had put him under great pressure to finish the apartment building in Casa Grande.

Raj wanted forms into which he and Aruna could pour their mixture. Ten would be fine. Sam took the specs to an adobe block yard in Casa Grande. For an extra charge, he could pick them up 48 hours later. By that time, Raj was driving a company car and Aruna had put a down payment on a very used Toyota Corolla. Still living at home, each searched for a place to live in their spare time.

Raj had hit on the simplest idea he could think of: The home would be six feet on a side and four feet in height. For the very first model, he would lay down a sheet of recycled polyester measuring 4' x 6'. Onto the poly would be mortared six 2' square pieces of plastic ¼" inch in thickness, to give three across and two high with a small gap between them to enable foldability. Once folded, each side would measure close to 3/4" in thickness and would weigh less than a pound to make the entire home portable. The top of each side would be looped over posts at either end. Three sides would be made similarly.

For the front entry, only the top two rows of panels would have three horizontals. The bottom row would consist of a half-panel on each end leaving a full two feet-wide piece of poly to serve as the ingress-egress point. The very top of the structure would be another sheet of poly with loops at each corner to hook over the posts. If the posts were 6' in height, an additional 2' x 3' panel could be easily added to each side.

The base would consist of foldable panels three on a side. If the application were to be used by pickers in, say, Colombia or Mozambique, palm fronds would be used for the roof.

Nobody wanted to think about how mass

production of the structure might occur.

"Why don't you just go into the tent-making business?" Tony asked, when Raj related their progress.

Raj said, "Because a tent is a prism. We're constructing a cube. The volume of a cube is more than twice that of a prism of the same height."

Tony asked, "Do you think these people will be able to figure out how to put your pieces together?"

Raj looked at him with quizzical expression to respond, "Excuse me, dad; these people may at the bottom of the economic scale, in the lowest caste of society possible, and uneducated, but there is nothing wrong with their analytical abilities."

"Amen to that," Aruna declared, resisting an urge to pat her brother on the back.

"I stand corrected," Tony apologized, deeply chagrined, instantly grasping the idiocy of what he had said and to whom he had said it.

11

Aruna found herself the center of attention at the apartment swimming pool, which was surrounded by a number of white metal tables and chairs stationed between a variety of well-manicured flowering shrubs. In the large pool, her excellence in the basic strokes paid off after years of being taught by her adoptive mother, i.e., mid-day-break lessons sandwiched between studying sessions.

Reaching her age of maturity, her mother had schooled her on the facts of life, yet kept both her charges isolated, perhaps more than she should have. Now at 18 and out on her own, personal fantasies aside, she had never been on a date, never been kissed on the lips or felt a loving man's touch; nor had she experienced the chance to say no; or, for that matter, to say, yes.

When she looked in the mirror, she liked what she saw, with and without her two-piece bathing suit. Apparently, the men around the pool did too. Her dark skin, large black eyes and length of straight black hair demarked her of Indian heritage, yet her speech lacked an accent. She didn't speak in today's slang short cut lingo, but spoke gently in a sophisticated, educated manner. She was not for the every man, which isn't to say that every man didn't make a try for her.

Her mother had taught the budding teenager a variety of rebuffing techniques, beginning with the various forms of polite refusal leading to the "Stop, or I'll call the police" threat. Her throbbing heart had longed to practice the rebuffs, several of which she used since moving out on her own.

One man did interest her, the only one who had no idea of her background, until the rumor mill brought it to his attention. Even then, he did not speak a word to her about her past life, only about her present interests.

His name was Clay Charles, a sophomore at the university with money, who shunned the dorms to find a studio apartment more to his liking. He belonged to family of lawyers who pushed him in that direction, but he confessed to her one evening, that he found saving the planet a direction he might like to pursue. Smelling a setup, Aruna discussed several ways in which he might do that without telling him of her own interests.

Charles was a blond-haired, handsome man, who stood a tall 6'3" and who frequently spoke of baseball, and casually mentioned he was on the college team. Noticing that Aruna had not tried to engage him further on the topic and who showed no interest, he left the subject and went on to other generalities about life, mostly about the wealth of his family and how much he hated money. When Aruna looked up the players on the Arizona State team, she found him to be the starting pitcher, nationally rated.

Among the women at the complex with whom she enjoyed casual evenings was her best friend Marie, who was now 20 years of age. She had moved into the complex two years before. One reason why she enjoyed the company of Marie was that the woman was honest, as she described her own flaws and her efforts to overcome them, one of which was that she talked about her flaws too much.

Very attractive in her own right, Marie had found a job working the phones at a busy Porsche dealership in Scottsdale, sandwiched between Mercedes and Rolls Royce dealerships.

As a single woman—not that marital status or age mattered in the setting—she had great experience in the category of cat and mouse. "Once you say 'yes' to somebody where you work, you're dead meat and your life will never be the same," she advised the budding dilettante. "And most likely, it will not for the better," she threw in for added emphasis.

Marie asked her if she and Charles had a thing going. When Aruna adamantly denied it, her friend cautioned her to watch out for him because he was making the rounds. If Aruna wasn't careful, she would be another strikeout for him, and guaranteed, the entire baseball team would know about it the next day. Marie spoke from personal experience, having turned down a number of his efforts, not so according to other women in the complex who had fallen prey to his slimy wiles.

Those comments annoyed Aruna so much she gave up her night fantasies about having an affair with Charles, not wanting to be a discarded piece of once-used trash soon to be recycled. She felt conflicted. She wanted her first time to be with him, but she didn't want Charles to be like he was.

Upon leaving for her own apartment after the dinner with Marie, she returned with a copy of Edward Abby's *The Monkey Wrench Gang.* A fast reader, she soon found herself deeply immersed in the antics of the anti-establishment group, likening their mission to her own, like small frogs croaking in a big pond trying to make waves.

From then on, she spent less time at poolside and more time reading alone in her apartment accompanied by a CD player and shelves full of technical books. These were mixed with American, European, and Indian classical authors. Her deeper and more entertaining thoughts were filled with what might have been.

12

The project was not going well at all. Sam had disappeared and two model houses had to be constructed using bricks, wood, drywall, and plaster, skills that Sam alone held. Aruna mused that if he never returned, she and Raj would never hear the stories about him and Hans, as promised.

For a while, Aruna had slacked off, finding that sleeping in occasionally did not affect the non-advancement of their endeavors, until Raj reminded her they were on a salary and it would be nice if she took it seriously. His words stung because she saw a bleak future. She suspected her driven, altruistic, self-absorbed brother felt the same way.

The more Raj learned about the recycling industry as a whole, the more he appreciated the extent of its great depth. Recycled paper saved countless trees, but didn't save the ones cut down by the billions annually to be used locally, or shipped by countless tons to developing nations. Missing trees don't absorb atmospheric carbon dioxide. He saw the tremendous progress the recycling industry was making in almost all aspects of life, but the percentage of waste kept increasing.

He felt a pang of guilt for having led his sister down a garden path where no flowers bloomed. Have faith, Raj told himself. Nobody can take that away from you, can they? What would we do in two more months? Admit defeat, return as humble servants, having taken a juvenile shot at the big league and going back to being another cog in the wheel.

Brother and sister were frugal. Their only expenses were fuel, a little for food, rent, and incidentals. Aruna had a car payment. That was about it. How long would their savings last if they were on their own?

Raj said, "We can't run final tests until we have a final product and all we have is this one plastic home. It means the other model homes aren't completed to run our comparative tests. It means we are dead in the water and will have to own up to it. It means . ."

"It means you're giving up," she summarized.

"Sort of," he said.

"Rajish Singh Rossi. How dare you," she accused. "You're giving up before the finish line."

Raj was taken aback at her expostulation. "It is what it is," he announced in the manner of a true philosopher. “Prepare for the future.”

“What makes you think I haven’t?” She asked.

“What does that mean?” Raj inquired. His sister was independent and not compliant by any means; agreeable, but not complaint. Now she presented a different front. After their blow up and his recovery, she told him she was going on her own at the end of the six month period. She had her college degrees, damn it, and she had her sights on certain careers.

“It means, for one thing, why do you need comparative data when you can go with the absolute? It also means I hired a retired general contractor who could use the money. We negotiated an hourly rate and he’ll charge us for travel time, work time, and report preparation. I showed him the plans for the two mini-homes Sam had drawn up and he said it was a no-brainer. I told him we had almost all the materials we needed and to bill us for what else he needed to buy in order to complete the job. You can split the costs with me.

“I told him we were having problems with the plastic house and he said he’d help.”

Raj said, “Did he ask you what this was about?”

“I said it was for a graduate school project and he bought it,” she said.

“Where the heck did you meet this guy?” Raj asked, floored by the revelations.

She said, "We'd seen each other around the apartment complex and waved, but never got around to talking about it until last night. He's pretty much a loner. Fortunately, he didn't know me from TV, or if he did, he never mentioned it. I told him I'd give him $250 for starters, if and when he shows up tomorrow morning at 8:00 am. Expect him then.

"Two more things. He goes by the name of Frankie and he has a hook arm as a replacement for the one he lost in the war. I didn't ask him which war. This country has so many."

Raj took the information at face value, he said, thoughtfully, "That could give us a different perspective."

Amused by her brother's response, Aruna came back with, "Let me write that down."

Aruna shooed away a hummingbird that had entered the building, thinking her red shirt a flower, and suggested, "Getting back to the topic at hand, I have some thoughts about contingency plans. You must have some too. As dad says, 'For good or bad, let's have a discussion'."

In Tony's office at the ReCyclo plant, Hans and Tony politely accepted the bound offering from his two guests. Leaning back in his chair he began to page through it, studying the drawings, the photographs, and the pages filled with columns of numbers. He set it down on his desk. An instant later, he picked it up again and turned to a certain page, studied it at some length, and set down the manuscript again. It could have been a Master's thesis.

Hans asked, "Was Sam was of any help?"

Raj said, "Initially, though we understand he had his own obligations. We took it upon ourselves to complete the work."

The work had been done on their own and their thorough job impressed Tony. He said, "The insulating qualities are quite astounding and you're saying a person can put up a large storage shed of this design for only $500 dollars out of pocket in less than a day." It was a statement rather than a question. He added, "That's maybe 20-25% the current price for a wood shed."

His guests nodded in unison. "Where's the profit margin?"

"That's not our department," Raj replied.

"What is your department, selling storage sheds?" Hans asked, somewhat callously, teasing, poking, testing the waters.

Aruna answered him by using a linguistic skill she had picked up since moving into the apartment complex, "No, sir, our department is concerned with recycling every goddamn piece of plastic we can get our hands on."

Tony stared hard at the beautiful woman. The mouth should not belong to her. Raj, he could understand, not her. She needed a wake-up call. She still didn't get it.

Tony asked, "What's this section on plastic shoes? In today's world, we make literally hundreds of different items from recycled bottles and other plastics, including shoes. Go look up a company called Adidas to see what I'm talking about. A couple of companies make shoes from plastic bags, clothing too."

"But I'll bet they're not made out of all the different kinds of plastic bottles" Raj argued, suddenly chagrined at the realization that neither he nor Aruna had taken the time to research manufacturers already making what they designed. He blamed himself for forcing the idea on her; Raj the Impetuous, she called him.

Tony said, "Young lady and young man, I applaud your diligence and your efforts. I truly do. You impress me. That said, we may yet be able to salvage something from your efforts, but the fact is that a large part of the recycling industry is quickly becoming a sham. The concept is great for a limited number of items, but overall, it is not cost effective. The cost of labor and energy used to recycle just about anything exceeds the amount of product produced. Here is one example. The vehicular exhaust pollutants from the thousands of trucks earmarked for hauling our recycled goods pollute the air more than the garbage they collect which are turned into goods.

"I can't speak for other nations, I can only speak for us. Landfills are wonderful, as long as they're underground and are not used for dumping radioactive materials. The most successful recycling to date is that of car batteries. Of the 100 million car batteries produced each year, some 90% are recycled.

"Back on point, some reports tell us at least one garbage truck of scrap finds its way into the ocean each minute. With a landfill, you dig a hole in the ground and add garbage until it's filled. It gets compressed, add some fill dirt, and build homes and shopping centers onto it. You want to save India and it's 3000 piles of garbage that look like small rolling hills, start a movement to dig big holes in the ground and tell them to bury it. Guess what, a lot of people will be unemployed now because they can't pick up recyclable materials. There is always, I repeat always, a trade-off.

"Americans have been programmed for decades into believing that recycling is the cure-all. Why? Because it sells, like vitamins, and skin cream, and hot news stories, along with guns, cigarettes and stand-up comedy. They're all businesses and they sell. The product? Save Planet Earth.

"I accept the fact that we will always be alone. We need to take care of ourselves. If that's the case, quit making plastic fishing lines and hundreds of billions of plastic bags and drinking bottles: How come everybody is so thirsty all of a sudden? What a damnable business. But no, we won't stop. Then you come along and have it all figured out.

"Yes, we can recycle things we never could before. That's technology. We can make just about anything today out of used materials. Up until recently, the industry was stymied because we didn't know how to recycle all those plastics when they fouled the machinery? So we improved the machinery.

"Today, we process them to make clothing. There's only one problem. While we are recycling tens millions of items a year, a hundred times that number are being produced. A number which is projected to increase several-fold over the next ten years.

"Frankly, there aren't too many other countries that care a rat's ass. We are the world's number one polluter. Recycling is a business, which doesn't means it is making a difference.

"Yes, the industry, my own included, employs a lot of people who may or may not believe in what they're doing. For a majority of them, it's only a job; they go home, maybe throw a tin can or a bottle into a separate container and hope it goes to the plant to be turned into diapers, or baby bottles, or plastic flower arrangements, when most of the time it goes to the landfill, or it's piled onto a mountain. In the end, maybe 5-10% of plastic bottles are recycled. Then you come to me with these ideas, but you fail to understand the larger picture."

Raj frowned at the lengthy monologue his father had presented. He'd never heard it all at once, only in bits and pieces over the years. He said, "Dad, you know I am going to ask you the obvious question."

Tony smiled and said, "I'll answer the question for you. At one time I believed in this as much as you do. Times have changed. We're at the break-even point. In a short time, ReCyclo will be losing money. We may have to close up shop like a lot of other recycling companies. The costs of operating this plant are enormous; the returns are becoming less and less with each passing year."

Aruna groaned, "And yet you paid us to follow through on something you don't believe in. Why?"

Tony rejoined, "I didn't say I didn't believe in recycling. What I said was that it is not making any measurable difference in our lives, to our economy, or to the planet. Are we saving natural resources by recycling? Absolutely, yes. Will it make a difference in the long run? Absolutely, no. Even as I speak, genetically modified bacteria and fungi are being developed tailor made to digest plastic. Fine unto itself. We need to stop trying to use more to make more, which is not going to happen. Most of the world doesn't have a pot to piss in. Wait until they want their fair share. Then start lecturing to them about saving the planet and see how far you get.

"Consider the pollutant gases, toxins, and carbon dioxide released from all the fires that occur around the world each year. More than 300 of them ongoing in Canada alone, as we speak. You get one of those volcanic events and it is a matter of record that human life around the planet will be reorganized. And you sit here telling me that recycling is the truth to the universe. And I tell you no matter what you or anybody else does, the planet is going to get hotter and the dominoes are going to fall."

Tony saw the crestfallen look on his visitor's faces and tried to put a smile on. "Hey, it's not all bad, just mostly. This is a nascent industry. We are tied to mega-corporations that are doing their honest best to turn waste into useful products, but, in my view, the industry is too far behind. We're taking one step forward and two steps back. Technology alone can't solve the problem. A solution requires good political choices. Our problem is that we're humans and humans always want more and politicians make the big decisions which favor the people who elected them. As somebody once said, 'There's the rub."

"Shakespeare used that term in Hamlet," Aruna said.

Tony gave a quick shake of his head, either to scare away a fly, or to shake off her comment. He'd have to speak to his wife about teaching these kids too much. Behind him stood a large bookcase filled with hardbound books. They included such titles as *Petroleum and Plastics, The Origin of the Plastic Industry, Plastic Products made in Asia, Future Technology in the Plastic Industry, Foreign Recycling Programs, A Listing of Recycling Companies in the United States, Substitutes for Plastics,* and *A Plastic Planet: Microplastics and our Destiny, The Deadly Microplastic Loop: Land, Sea, and Air.*

Aruna had read the last two. She found them to be total hormone pumps. They read like well-written adventure novels, although too pricey and data driven for the average reader. They were well documented, replete with colored satellite photographs, underwater pictures and airborne particle counts.

The volume on microplastics totally blew her mind. The authors' introduction was a little too doomsdayish for her. The husband and wife team maintained that the number of the micro-particles, already found everywhere, is projected to increase some 10,000-fold, if not more, by the end of the century and could spell the end of anything that swam. In an attempt to relate to the public, the authors compared the increase in the tiny particles, however many they may be, can be multiplied by a million. They compared it to a living room carpet made of synthetics that is placed in the ocean. Picture, they say, the same carpet disintegrating fiber-by-fiber when exposed to warmth and UV light. Then the individual fibers themselves decompose into microfibers, and so forth. In the case of plastics, the particles become the tiniest of spherules which can easily pass through the blood-brain barrier when inhaled or ingested by fish, man, or beast.

She had shuddered upon reading both books and swore to herself she would pursue a career in oceanography. The problem was, she is presently sitting with her brother and her father talking about making more plastic structures.

She had previously spoken with her mother about her situation and sought advice. Megan had listened patiently and said, "Do what you want to do, not what is expected. You have only one life. Live yours, not one belonging to another. Ensure you have enough adventures to tell your grandchildren about. What is it you want to do, get a different job? What?"

"Mom, do you have any idea of how many scholarship offers I've received? I mean the whole thing. Fly me there, room and board and monthly pay? All I have to do is to research with them," Aruna reported.

"And?"

"I can't make up my mind," Aruna tossed back.

"Why not?"

"I don't know why not. Don't get philosophical on me."

Megan laughed and said, "When the time is right, it will come to you."

An instant later, Aruna came back with. "I do know. I want to be a researcher and make great discoveries, not an inventor like Raj. I want to be in a laboratory on a ship, not a white-coated researcher at a university pouring one test tube into another. I want to stop a mass extinction of fish— no whales."

"Are whales dying of diseases?" Megan inquired, frowning, not understanding.

"Well, uh, not really. Plastics are killing them, I know?" Aruna said, confidently.

"So it comes down to you trying to keep them from eating plastics, is that it?"

"I want to go out on a good boat at see for myself. Yes, go to school, too, so I can learn everything I can. I'm certain of my goals."

"Good. You're thinking it through. Only you can make it happen," Megan encouraged.

Listening to her father, Aruna sighed, very pissed off at herself for not saying what was on her mind. She was done with the project, the toy house, with Raj's dreams, with their father's directions and admonitions and lectures. She wanted a life. Why hadn't she spoken up? Did she secretly want to keep working on her brother's fantasy, or did she lack enough courage to stand up for herself? *Damn it, girl, do something,* she flayed herself for the nth time. Worse, both of them had just had been schooled in higher education.

Watching his daughter think, out of the blue,

Tony managed to say, "Sometimes, when you try to do the right thing, you only make the situation worse."

Raj shook his head not understanding.

Tony continued, "I can give you a lot of real life examples, but I'll tell you a little story instead. Years ago I visited a lecture by a die hard environmentalist who told about one time when she walked along a beach. She came upon a huge number of starfish who lay dead on the sand. Upon closer inspection she found one still alive. Thinking she was saving a life, she picked it up and threw it back into the ocean. She announced this proudly and the audience oohed and ahhed at her bravery and strength of character, feeling overjoyed knowing they had come to right place, gaining courage from her. Then I stepped to the microphone set up for questions and asked, 'How do you know the group of starfish didn't have a terrible infection and they came there to die in order to save the rest of their colony, a common occurrence in nature, but instead, you poisoned the remaining healthy ones by throwing the single one back'?"

"What did she say?" the guests asked in unison.

I replied, "She was obviously blindsided. The only thing she could think of to say was that it is human nature to save lives, which, by the way, is open to discussion. Her answer did not completely mollify the audience based on their murmurs."

The whine of a plane gaining altitude came through the closed window. Tony asked, "What am I do with you two? What I need is for you to find a way to inject new blood into this company. I need your original thinking; fortunately your naïveté is evolving nicely into pragmatism. You can continue doing what you've been doing, that is, using your imagination to think big. I'll give you another six months. I want monthly reports. If, by four months, you have nothing, then it's over. Incidental expenses come out of your pocket. I have a lot going on and I don't want to play babysitter. Any questions?"

13

While Aruna struggled to shy away potential suitors, who yearned to suit, if only for a single night, Raj could be described as a typical rough-edged man who had good and bad memories. He moved into his own apartment complex some miles from his sister's, preferring to remain low key when surrounded by strangers. He possessed an air of confidence strangely mixed with a trace of insecurity. Both were attributed to his knowledge base with the latter associated with his lack of human contact outside the family.

Thus, he exhibited shyness during his initial meeting of others. Further contact with him revealed an exceptionally bright person with unusual analytical abilities and a good depth of knowledge about a wide range of subjects. His strange mix of youthful innocence, exceptional language base, depth of knowledge, and sophistication attracted members of the opposite sex.

The woman who he had "permitted" to conquer him was Susan (Sue) Gardner, a petite little thing, maybe 5'2", 19 years of age, with blond hair and blue eyes. Most men found her attractive. She had worked in her parents' meat and potatoes restaurant since she could walk. Her effervescence attracted many customers to the 15-seat always crowded restaurant where only breakfast and lunch were served (hours 7:00 am-1:00 pm).

After high school she worked full time with her family, cooking, cleaning, waiting, and balancing the books when called upon to do so. Her natural effervescence attracted customers, as did the pies she baked and sold.

Like the Rossi twins, upon reaching the age of 18, she moved into her own apartment, which turned out to be the same complex in which Raj lived. Like most complexes in the area, this one also had a pool. This is where the two met and began to chat. Raj sought no tan, but enjoyed the pool environment because it gave him a feeling of being at his parents' home. He preferred a single bedroom already furnished into which he moved his boxes of books. He lined them up in the living room college style: pine boards stacked onto slump block. When he did watch TV, he avoided the news based on his mother's cautions. News reports are intended to bring stress into the lives of the viewers. The news beast must be fed regularly with fresh food, she said. Otherwise, he enjoyed a good football or basketball game. His father would be proud.

Sue had a great interest in higher education and educated people, just no interest in college for herself. Why do something else when you're perfectly happy where you are? She found herself becoming bonded to this unusual man who was sensitive, undemanding, compassionate, and weak on the intimate level. Both possessed an inner drive and a conquer-the-mountain attitude. Thus, they found an attraction in one another.

One Saturday evening—her days off were Sunday and Monday—she invited him to sit on the flat roof over the office building of the complex. She had discovered a way to get up there and invited her new friend to join her. "We can look at the washed out stars," she told him, pointing to the brightness of the moon. The background glow of city lights was evident.

The couple leaned against a parapet wall to enjoy a not so dark night sky in the cool, clear air of the desert evening. He told her about astronomy and what his father had said about being alone and what we must do our best to ensure our longevity. He told her he had grown up poor in India and was adopted, leaving out the details. She felt warmth in knowing Raj trusted her enough to share his feelings. Where there is no trust, there is no relationship.

College didn't teach about life, the customers at her restaurant did. Sue became skilled at teasing out details relating to their conquests and sorrows, their list of things they wished could have been done over again. She commiserated with them about their deepest regrets without sharing her own. She spoke with soldiers who were trying to readjust, and housewives who were trying to readjust to their soldiers' homecoming. Patrons frequented the restaurant to share their feelings with Sue. She enjoyed drawing out Raj, casting no value judgments, only listening to this unusual man whose aspirations and imagination soared to its own stratospheric heights.

When she asked what, if anything, he wanted to do to ensure mankind's survival, he went into detail about his current project and the deadline placed upon him and his sister. She asked a question that had burned at her from the start. "If you don't mind talking about it, can you describe your first year or two when you came here with your new parents? I can't imagine how difficult it must have been. You don't have to tell me if you don't want to."

Raj felt comfortable sitting alongside this woman whom he had come to trust. He replied, "No, it's all right," he began. Lost deep in memories, he wistfully orated, "I don't think I could have done it without my sister. We put on a good face and pretended a lot, but, honestly, it took years to appreciate what our new parents sacrificed for us. We stole a lot from them over the years because we grew up stealing, yet we were never chastised for it. Perhaps we should have been.

"At first, we had frequent nightmares in vivid color interspersed among lots of random dreams. One would wake the other. A moment later, mom or dad would be there. It got so bad for me I was afraid to go to sleep. Over time the dreams faded in frequency and intensity. A lot of times, Aruna and I would have the same dream."

Pulled into the tale, Sue placed a gentle hand on Raj's leg, as reassurance to continue.

"We were kept pretty much isolated for the first couple of years, while she and I tried to make the adjustment from living on scrap heaps to living in a huge home. We could have easily put twenty or more of our co-workers into theirs—ours. Our new parents, too, struggled to raise children they never had; foreign, no less. If we hadn't already spoken English, the entire venture would have been impossibly difficult for everyone.

"Once we got to Phoenix, it took a good three days for everybody to readjust their biological clocks. Tony went back to work for short periods and Megan began instructing us. We had numerous toys awaiting us and we were permitted to play with them a lot initially, but to her best ability, she taught us in her special way. We looked forward to Friday nights when we were permitted to watch a cartoon channel. That was fun. We learned the rules of various sports we got to watch occasionally with dad during the four seasons as we grew.

"For the first three or four years, Aruna and I shared the same bedroom until we got separated. We cried a lot by ourselves, although Tony and Megan were always alert and came to our bedsides to soothe us."

"Can I ask you something?" she inquired, gently.

"Sure."

"Did either of you rebel?"

Raj gave a slight chuckle in the manner of one who wishes he could take back something he felt badly about, "A lot. We always respected elders, except for when we stole from them, but once the initial shock of the new home hit us, we had our screaming tantrums; our refusals to do what we should do, not what she asked us to do. They might have other descriptions for what we did."

"Do you ever miss India?"

"India, or my old living conditions?" he asked.

"Well, either," Sue replied, gently.

"They were one and the same to us. The first time I think we were inside any real building for the first seven years of our lives was when the city took us in after they said somebody wanted to adopt us. India was just a name then. To answer your question about missing India, no, I didn't. You could call it Bucktooth, for all we knew. It was a name only. I'm more educated now. I've studied the history of the country extensively from thousands of years back to independence from Britain in 1947 to present day circumstances. Back then, I didn't miss it. I mean, if you grow up in middle-class America and you got shipped off to a communist nation, or you get sent to work as a child laborer in a mine, or to pick up pieces of discarded trash, then, yes, you miss it. Not the other way around."

Raj paused a moment, forming his next thought. Since the snake attack, he had become more cautious and leery of people in general, yet he found himself getting pulled into a subject he considered private and didn't want to talk about, like a suspect getting prompted into a confession by a skilled detective.

Reluctantly, he yielded to the superior force, continuing, "You can't help thinking about where you spent 100% of your life up to that point, but once we were at the Rossis' residence, whenever I reflected on our past, I honestly thought there might have been some mistake and we'd be trundled back to the dirt pile on any given day. If that were the case, we could accept it. At least we could tell our children we visited America. We'd be heroes."

"Would you ever want to go back? If you do go, take me with you." Sue made the statement in such an honest manner that Raj had to suppress a laugh. He wasn't sure why, but something in her statement struck him as funny. "The answer is definitely yes to the first part. Aruna and I are making plans to do so." He didn't address the second part.

Sue considered everything Raj had said and shook her head in disbelief. The entire tale smacked of surreality. She suspected there was a lot more to the story, wondering if and when any dark side to Raj Rossi would show itself.

As was her habit, she prodded further. The night had begun to cool, the moon had risen. The signs were there. "Raj, what else? Do you believe I would think less of you if you told me about your life, or maybe I'd sell the information? Talk to me."

So, coaxed by a professional coaxer, Raj gave in, finally telling her most of the story, about how he and his sister were discovered, and to her amazement, told of the years-long coverage by CNN. He left out any mention of money, or his education, lest she be attracted to inert objects, or scared by his intelligence. He told his life to a new person, one he hoped he could trust, a waitress, no less. Then he did a stupid thing, at least in his eyes. He blurted, "Some people hated who we were and tried to kill us."

As soon as he said the words, he regretted them. Doubtless, she would see him as a sad little boy who had such a struggle and who should be pitied. His parents had warned them there are people who pretend to be your friend, but are after more than friendship.

Now she's going to want details. Good job, Raj, he chastised himself.

Instead of pouncing on his statement, Sue sensed the moment, waited for the breeze to ruffle their hair to take the heat out of the words, to carry them far and away. After a long pause, she offered, "Even if this is our last meeting, I will never ever tell another soul about it. But, Raj, you needed to tell someone. Thank you for letting me be that someone."

Raj looked at her in the dark, embarrassed by the surge of blood to his groin, which he hoped she wouldn't notice, placed his hand over hers, perhaps to keep it from moving further, and told of the rattlesnakes and the black-haters. He finished by quoting, verbatim, Cragmore's letter the investigative agency had uncovered and had sent to his parents.

Silent minutes passed. The craziness in this man's life, so far, made her head swim, like hearing tales from a soldier recently back from a war, only this time on a domestic scale. Sue needed to digest a big meal. Had she bitten off more than she could chew? She sat next to a magnet. He wasn't a bad luck magnet. In her life, they dotted the landscape. He was an adventure magnet.

Thinking it best to change subjects, she had to ask, "That was pretty heavy. What do you think?"

"About what he said in the letter?"

"Yes."

Like everybody, Raj's future was questionable. He had nothing to lose, so he opined, "First, he said nothing original. Literally a hundred philosophers, from almost every country have decried the existence of God beginning with Lucretius a hundred years before the birth of Christ to modern day revolutionaries. I think whether or not God exists is irrelevant. Evolution is a force built into humans as a survival mechanism. How we use it or abuse it is up to us. At first I thought the deity concept was a leftover vestigial organ; you know, something needed for early man to survive, but lost its function over time. Now I'm revising my opinion."

"I see your point. In other words, we're embracing a vestigial concept because we're meant to do it."

"Amen to that," Raj grunted, surprised at her insight."

Sue asked, "Did anything happen to the people who did this to you and Aruna? You never went into detail about it. Do you care to tell me?"

Raj shrugged off her relentless picking and related the entire story in detail. He did his best to keep a perverse sense of satisfaction out of his voice. Unemotionally, he told her about hikers who had found the fully clothed body of Arthur Tremont in a forested area near a stream some miles from his home in Idaho. The battered and broken body was identified by dental records, not by facial recognition. The police report stated the beating had taken place over a period of time. No clues were found as to the identity of the assailant. Authorities found his wallet and traced his ID to Tremont's wife, Christina, Raj's own grandmother. As it turns out, she was quite ill at the time and was tended to by her son, who took time off from the office to care for her.

Furthermore, shortly after the reported death of Tremont, James Cragmore of Baton Rouge, Louisiana, had disappeared, according to the investigative agency. Neighbors reported he had become extremely paranoid almost overnight, packed up his belongings and drove away for parts unknown.

Sue shook her head in disbelief at the tale of woe as Raj said the poor woman was absolutely grief stricken at the news. Everybody loved Arthur. Police assumed he might have been hanging out with a rough crowd back home and may have owed a considerable amount of money.

Raj did not mention that his father had left his mother's side to take a short business trip the time of Tremont's demise, nor did the police have any reason to check on the validity their story.

Using his vernacular and without any display of emotion, Raj honestly admitted he had no skin in the game, not knowing the man. He might as well as have read about some bum on the street. Besides, everybody dies. Without saying it, the beating threw him back to the old days every time he thought about it. The family never spoke of it again except for Christina, who wanted to celebrate the death of Arthur Tremont annually, but was voted down.

"Holy cow, what a mess. I'm so sorry," Sue sympathized.

"Wait there's more," Raj ventured to his captive audience. "My dad got another letter from the investigators. The letter said the woman who ran the pet store had been in on the scheme. Somebody contacted her in person and offered her a cashier's check made out for $10 thousand. She only had to call FedEx to pick up a parcel. She told the truth there. She did mail a turtle and she did call the company.

"FedEx wouldn't tell the investigators the address where the parcel was sent to or the name on it. However, they did report it was shipped to Hayden Lake, Idaho. A little creative relabeling on their part and the parcel was reshipped to us. And yes, her return address was still on the parcel. Our friends up there said they worked for Exotic Pets, Inc. and were on vacation, so the return label remained the same. She is presently spending her life savings on attorneys to keep from doing time."

Sue leaned closer to him and said, "Raj, with you working with your father all these years and your mother home-schooling you both, did you—and I don't mean to be indelicate,but did you ever have time for a formal education?"

Caught by surprise by the question, Raj could only scratch the back of his head with the hand not clutching hers, and spun out a sticky web, "I always had trouble with time management. I squeaked in a little here and there whenever I could."

Raj expected her to pry more. Instead, she leaned forward and said, "Raj, I'm getting cold. Could you put your arm around me, please?"

Raj's heart skipped a beat. He had no choice. He wrapped a long arm around the small woman and she snuggled in close to him. They sat together for some time until Sue took a deep breath, pulled away, stood, and took his hand to help him stand. "Come on Raj, let's go," she directed. Sue could totally fall for a smart, gentle, self-made man.

That night the couple stayed at her apartment, she in a trance-like state, glowing with a feeling she had never had before, introducing him to sex. Shy and embarrassed at first, her gentle, patient approach worked its magic on the youth. The couple dozed and touched, cooed and stroked, until morning when they showered. She made a breakfast of waffles, eggs, and strong coffee, accepting his invitation to go with him to the old church.

In his own trance-like state, Raj opened the

doors to the church an hour later. Almost immediately a pair of Inca doves flew past them into freedom. At his arm sweep, Sue entered before Raj to examine the three structures, no bigger than large doll houses, especially the one made of plastic.

Sue entered the opaque home. She could see Raj move without clarity. She assumed the same would occur from his point of view. She crawled out the front flap and stood, taking a step back to take another look.

Raj apologized, "That's the best we could come up with so far. The whole thing breaks down and is portable. We need to set it up outside because it's not meant to be used on a concrete floor. My sister and I are thinking hard about coming up with another project altogether. We're getting a lot of negatives about this one."

Sue cooed, "Honey, I think it's marvelous, but even if you get this perfected, how will you market it?" she asked.

Honey? Raj felt a jolt of surprise at the word. He felt a little uncomfortable for a moment, like all of a sudden they were an item. However, considering the previous hours he'd spent with the woman, this was light weight stuff. "I have some ideas. We're trying to come up with something huge to save my father's company."

Sue offered, "Maybe you need to redefine your goals. What are they? Is there room for change? My mother encouraged me to never stop seeking innovations to improve my pies, even when you think they're perfect." With those words, she laughed and uttered the words, somewhat poetically, "Your perfection is your perception."

He reflected on her statement and was about to come up with a counter truism, when she said, "I would like to meet your family, sometime."

"When the time is right, I guess," Raj said, simply, evaluating this woman. She appeared to have some depth, with an interest in him and his work. She couldn't be making a lot of money and he wouldn't have any real money for another three years. Maybe she wanted to latch onto somebody who might offer her a future, and, well, maybe she was actually attracted to him. Nothing complicated, right?

"Getting back to this house," Sue continued, nodding her head at the off-white cube, "when I started making pies way back when, it was my mother who taught me. You're starting from scratch, which is more difficult. My pies came out okay, but they were created mechanically by a machine named Susan. The more I worked at it, the more I liked what I saw and the more we sold, until I still can't make enough. In fact, a local market wanted to carry my pies."

"What did you do?" Raj asked.

"I turned them down. After their markup and looking at my net profit, I would be working twice as hard to make the same as I normally do."

"Your point being?" Raj asked.

"I could have given up on the pies and gone to cookies or cakes after my first series of defeats. Instead of caving, I worked at it so hard that other people wanted to buy what I had," she responded. "Remember, a product can be excellent, but under normal circumstances, it won't sell itself."

"Yep, one more cog in the wheel. You're saying we shouldn't give up on the house or change directions to work on another project," Raj said.

Sue chuckled, "You're quite up on the vernacular, aren't you?"

Raj replied, smiled in return, "One of my percs."

Sue walked off to look at the room-less minihomes. Raj followed closely behind. Suddenly, he asked, "What do you want to do with your life? Make better pies? Travel? What?"

Sue retorted, "Simple. I want to create something that will help as many people as possible. In my view, you will need a lot of money for all kinds of things which affect success."

Sue rose up on her tip-toes and pulled him down to her to give him a hard kiss on the mouth, then said softly, "I really do like you, Raj Rossi."

Aside from the present moment, Raj had not experienced a blush. If he had, it would have occurred during their sexual encounter only hours before, and that would have been invisible in the blackness of the night. This time there was no hiding it. The heat signature in his face gave it away. Deliciously aroused, he returned the kiss, even more passionately than hers. Raj was in love.

14

The diagnosis of cancer in Megan caused the world to stop, at least among those in her immediate surrounds. After an absence of more than a decade of teaching, she had returned to full-time work, feeling the need to be surrounded by children after her own had left the home to begin their own adult lives.

She had been feeling ill for some time, even before her children moved out. Her headaches were becoming more frequent until they morphed into a constant condition. She and Tony discussed the matter frequently and attributed the problem to the stress of not looking forward to an empty nest, or jokingly, something she had caught from Raj. No, the damnable Chinese were spreading another virus. Gallows humor aside, both came to believe her teaching duties should alleviate the problem.

Tony got the call from the doctor's office, while he was at work and Megan slept at home. The doctor had been the family physician for years and had treated Anthony Rossi Senior. Christina-Rossi-Tremont, Arthur Tremont, as well as Raj and Aruna; the latter through the children's various episodes of ailments. Fortunately, the twins' immune system was top tier, having spent their early years in an environment where biblical diseases still ran rampant.

Tony was seated in one of the half dozen small rooms comprising Dr. Wright's practice; offices into which people rotated like rounds in a semi-automatic weapon, fed by a magazine called the waiting room—one out and one in.

Wright walked in, stethoscope in his lab coat pocket, gray hair always neatly combed. He always looked so fresh Tony thought he must stop in the rest room occasionally to preen himself throughout the day. Wright was a gum-chewer, nothing crazy, just enough Juicy Fruit or cinnamon flavor, to cancel errant oral fragrances. Wright looked as though he had gained in weight. *Doctor, heal thyself*, Tony thought. Tony stood, held out his hand and said, "Warren."

Wright took the proffered hand and replied, "Tony, sit down please." Wright sat his heavy frame onto a rolling stool in front of a computer screen and hit the keyboard, fiddled with it a few moments and presented, "Megan has a small tumor in the occipital lobe of the brain—here."

Wright stood and pointed to a picture of the brain on the wall with the various lobes. The occipital lay at the rear portion of the brain. He took his seat again and continued, "This lobe is the visual processing hub of the brain. It works cooperatively with many other brain areas, as do they all. It plays a crucial role in language and reading, storing memories, recognizing familiar places and faces, and more. Did you notice any symptoms such as the ones I mentioned and when did you start noticing them?"

Tony thought a moment and confessed, "Well, yes, especially when the headaches became more constant. At first, we noticed small deviations, but we both had our problems when we knew the kids would be leaving the house. As far as specifics, I can't say for sure. Megan's speech and memory seemed to be a little off, but hell, so is mine." He and the doctor knew he was blowing smoke, avoiding the truth.

Wright said. "Tony, this tumor could be aggressive, which means things could go south real fast."

Wright rotated the screen toward Tony, who slid his chair closer. Wright pointed with his finger. "This point is the tumor. It will grow. Before you ask, it is operable and should pose no threat. These are not uncommon. I am not a brain surgeon, but I'll give you a referral. The sooner, the better."

Tony left Wright's office crestfallen. His first concern was how to tell Megan. Now outside the pressure of the doctor's office, he did recall a number of instances in which she had forgotten some past events that had come up for discussion when she complained about losing concentration quickly while reading. They both ascribed these to the idiosyncrasies of life and let it go, until the headaches began in earnest.

He began to prepare a way in which he would tell her the news. After he told her, his mother and the kids absolutely needed to know. The family needed to pull together.

Tony drove into the garage, pushed the remote in his car to close the door, and came into the adjoining laundry room off the kitchen, where he found his wife folding clothes. She asked, "What are you doing home? Is everything all right? Did you forget something?"

"Nope, I went to see the doctor about you. When I checked in with you, you still were sleeping, so I went alone," he said.

"What about me?" she asked.

"Let's go sit down," he said.

Megan said nothing, following him into the living room.

Short minutes later, she knew all Tony knew about her pending surgery, other than making an appointment with the referral Wright had provided. "Let's tell the kids," Megan sighed.

Tony hit a speed dial that connected with Aruna only to get a message saying she was unavailable and to leave a call back number. He hit the next speed dial. Raj's phone was on Vibrate mode. Susan was speaking to him when he picked up. "Hello, dad," he said, seeing the home number.

"Who's that I hear? Where are you?" Tony asked.

"I'm at the old church showing a friend around," Raj said.

"Oh, what's her name?" Tony asked, getting the light banter out of the way before dropping the bombshell, painfully holding off as long as possible.

"Susan. She goes by Sue," Raj replied.

"What does she do?"

"She's a waitress."

Pause. "Oh, uh, look . . ." Tony began.

"Coward," Raj heard his mother announce in the background, taking the phone from her husband. "Raj, I have brain cancer and they're going to have to operate. It's just a small tumor. We're going to set an appointment to see the surgeon. We wanted you and Aruna to know right away. She doesn't answer now. Maybe you can get in touch with her. No hurry and no worries. It's all good."

"There," she said, with finality, handing the phone back to Tony.

"Mom," Raj began.

"It's me again. We'll call you after we see the surgeon. And good luck with your waitress," Tony said, closing the call.

Megan said, "Waitress?"

"He's showing her the ropes at the church,"

Tony teased.

"I'll bet he is, which gives me an idea I think you'll like. Come with me, dear," Megan teased in her own way, while grabbing her husband's hand, leading him into the bedroom.

15

Sue saw the downcast look on Raj's face when he closed the call. He was looking at the ground when she asked, "Can you tell me, or is it too personal?"

"Both," he replied."My mom has a brain tumor. They're going to operate on her pretty soon." He refrained from telling her what was really on his mind. He wanted to tell her about the slow death of his birth mother over a period of a painful years, when one year of a child is equal to five or ten of an adult, when he and his sister and bapu had watched over her during her slow decline, when she had remained steadfast in her home duties, cooking, cleaning, even stealing when she had the strength, while her cough got worse.

He couldn't and wouldn't tell Sue his worst nightmare was coming true, that he was revisiting his mother's death again. She was a teacher, too. Then his father died and now it's happening all over again. He remembered the old adage about thinking about something hard enough you will bring it to pass.

His head began to ache. He refrained from reaching into his pocket for the pill container. Instead, he closed his eyes and took slow deep breaths, as he had been taught.

"I'm so sorry, Raj. I'll be there if you need me. What are you going to do?" Susan asked.

Raj put on his grim face and said, "To use the vernacular, I have to quit dicking around and start using my brain. Where the hell is my sister?" he groused.

Aruna's social network was small, despite the men clamoring for her attention. As a consequence, she rarely made cell phone calls and maintained her phone on Vibrate so her reading wouldn't be interrupted—not that it jumped off the hook, so to speak—to the great annoyance of those who did try to reach her. Enough with blowing up her email with discount sales for Viagra or home-buys. This was a Sunday, for Pete's sake. Nothing happens on a Sunday.

Besides, she had a hangover and had left the cursed phone at home. She disliked the naked feeling of having to fend for herself without her protective phone, and she cursed herself for allowing Marie to introduce her to red wine the night before. She awoke, thoroughly dehydrated, and drank the sports drink her friend had supplied to assist in recovery. Now, she felt like a dead man walking, lumbering down the aisles lost in space pretending she was having fun looking for a new wardrobe, which she had no use for. Nobody saw her anyway, because all she did was work with her stupid brother hidden away in some old dusty church trying to spin yarn into gold.

When she did return to her apartment in the mid-afternoon she found she had missed one call from her father and three from Raj. Damn, what a time to leave it at home. Raj had called the most so she punched in his speed dial. He answered on the first ring.

"Mom has cancer," he said, without preamble.

"What, how . . . "

Raj explained, letting her know what he and their father knew. Aruna felt like dirt, not being there when she was needed.

"We have to go into high gear, if we're going to make this a success, I want to make sure mom is around to see it," Raj said.

"Why wouldn't she be?" Aruna cried, loudly enough to attract the attention of Marie and the other patrons in the dress store. Looking up, Aruna saw she had gathered unwanted attention and migrated outside the store into the mall concourse, followed by a concerned friend.

"Just saying," Raj concluded, somberly, using one of Hans' favorite statements.

Aruna's blood boiled at his words. Not caring whether Marie was listening or whether passers-by heard her reply, she strongly and loudly said into the phone, "You know, Raj, I am so sick and tired of you dictating my life to me. Do your own thing. I'm dropping out. Keep in touch, I love you, but count me out of your idealistic dreams. I have a life to live and you're taking it from me; no, correction, I'm taking it from me."

She took a deep breath, then called her father and apologized for having forgotten her phone at home and said she'd be there whenever she was needed.

There. It all turned out fine. If it had been a true emergency, she wouldn't have forgiven herself. She'd have to think about whether there might be a life lesson buried in the event, such as never drink, never have a phone, and never go shopping.

On Tuesday nights she began attending public speaking classes with Marie. Her friend insisted, "If you're ever going to be somebody in life, you have to know how to speak in public."

The classes were held in an old building where a small theater group performed. On Tuesdays, the place belonged to the speakers. Some fifteen people attended from all walks of life who presented in a classroom off the main auditorium. When a certain level of confidence had been achieved, the individual would perform solo on the stage.

Leery of the enterprise at first, Aruna came to enjoy the company of other people in the same boat. Most were terrified of public speaking. The senior woman instructor pointed out they all spoke in public when in parties and at group gatherings, so why should this be any different. Consider everyone to be your friend and it will be so easy.

Aruna let herself go, looking forward to the class each week until she ended up doing solo recitations. Her photographic memory made her a natural, once she learned proper expressions and emotions to go with the words. The best part was that the time to do what she wanted was hers alone, a rare treat.

Raj lay back on his pillow and tried to relax. *When all else fails, use your brains*, he thought, bemused. Sue had suggested he redefine his goals, which, of course, would change the end structure. Shift one domino and they all fall in sequence. What was the ultimate goal? Foremost was to ease the life of as many ragpickers as he could. India wasn't going to dig deep landfills. That wasn't their style.

India's recycling industry consisted of human ants scouring the trash. If they weren't given incentives to work harder, whatever that meant, at least they should have more comfortable living conditions. Another fact: ReCyclo needed new life. Where to go from here?

Raj wanted to discuss his thoughts with Aruna, but she had taken herself out of the game for the time being. That left Sue. He made the call.

"Hi, Raj," Sue said, definitely pleased to hear from him. He wasn't a caller kind of guy.

"Can we talk about my project? Aruna blew me off," he confessed.

"Sure, give me as second to get organized," she said.

Raj heard some rustling, and thankfully, no other man's voice could be heard, or doors closing, as if somebody were leaving.

A few moments later, she came back and said, "Okay, I'm nice and comfy. First, how's your mother?"

"She's still in the hospital under observation," Raj said. He added, "They had to cut off all her hair for sanitary purposes. My dad said he liked the space-age look and she should keep it that way."

"I can only guess what she said to him," Sue threw in, amused.

"I'd tell you, but you're not old enough," Raj teased, trying to squeeze out a drop of humor from a sad situation.

"Cute. I want you to know I wish her the best. What's up with the call?"

He explained his thoughts on the housing issue, as per her recommendation to work with what he had, and the ideas he had on the subject.

She said, "I love the base you have. It's the

same design as the sides."

"Thanks for that," he said. "I'll get four telescoping poles of the right length. They would have to be secured into the ground. I ran the numbers again. The entire structure will weigh between six and eight pounds. I'll keep the loops on the corners of the top what go over the poles. I can work the packaging aspect."

"What package?" she asked.

"I'm not sure yet. I need to think. Later," he said, closing the connection.

And you're falling in love with this Brainiac? What are you thinking, girl?" Susan asked herself.

Two things happened to Raj the following day. They were both women. First, when he drove to the front of the church, he saw Sue's car. Then he noticed her casually sitting on the steps of the porch. She saw him and remained in place. He got out and asked the obvious question, to which she replied, cheerfully, "I took the morning off. I can do what I want. It's my family's business. People take off occasionally for events in real life, you know. If you want me to leave, I will."

Delighted to see her, he couldn't help but show his pleasure. He gave her a hand up, put his arm around her, and gave her a short kiss on the lips. "Come on in and I'll show you what I've done so far."

The moment he unlocked the door, another

car arrived. Aruna stepped out. Raj was almost disappointed. He had begun to enjoy his solitude and now had mixed feelings. He had no choice but to accept his sister and introduce the two women. Contrary to his initial concerns, Aruna and Sue began to chatter like old friends meeting at a theater to see a long–awaited feature, which caused him to feel like an on-stage actor pressured to perform well. The audience had arrived.

The trio walked into the church. For Sue's benefit, Raj remarked, pointing to the rows of forms surrounding their contents, "They're not fully dry yet."

He pulled gently on one form and it slid off nicely from its contents, which had melded with the polyester backing. With a pair of scissors, he cut the poly backing after the third tile and picked up the entire section of three, which he carefully folded it upon itself accordion like. A moment later, he held a piece only 3/4" in thickness.

Raj handed the scissors to Aruna who cut the next section, permitting Sue to cut the one after that. He said, "We'll have to pour more forms today. I'm going to take these outside in the desert sun for a faster dry. Aruna, why don't you get the generator started and the mixer going?" he directed.

"I'll help if I can," Sue offered, helping Aruna roll the generator from the safety of the interior of the church to the outdoors. Raj grabbed the accordion-folds along with four telescoping poles and headed outdoors to the side of the structure. He found an area next to the church free from what little vegetation there was, after first picking up a desert horned toad and moving it to another location close to a small ant hill where it could eat to its heart's content.

Sue assisted Aruna in measuring products for the mixer, like adding the proper ingredients to make a pie, simple stuff. During the process, Sue asked, "Aruna, tell me about your brother. We already talked a lot. He seems pretty educated. I got the idea he was hit and miss in school."

Thirty seconds later, Sue stood frozen like a sculptured human ice block, stunned after Aruna quickly summarized their educational achievements. She left out any mention of the money she and her brother would be given.

Was Aruna trying to scare her off? Sue had the sudden urge to cut and run, yelling behind her about being late for work. She felt confused and used, wondering how little ole' Susan Gardner fit into his life. This man had a lifetime of experience in a few years and pretended to be naive in the ways of love. Henceforth, she would proceed with caution, wondering again whether she was being played for the fool. The man would shortly have a Doctorate in Engineering with human physiology close behind.

Their parents wanted all degrees to be framed

and hung on a special wall, but the kids rebelled. They argued it would appear to be a competition to which child had the most framed items. Megan compromised by inserting all certificates, awards, and degrees into a picture book she had been maintaining over the years.

Unlike Aruna and her parents, who felt great pride for each educational milestone she and her brother achieved, Raj robotically chomped through the degrees like Pac Man devouring any adversary in his quest to learn.

Outside, Raj worked for some 20 minutes until Aruna appeared. "Raj, I'm sorry . . ." she began.

Raj stood to face her and said, "Don't be. You have a life. I do, too, at least I'm starting to." He nodded in the direction of the church.

Aruna smiled, and said, "She's very nice. You have good taste."

Raj laughed. "She chose me."

"Oh, I feel sorry for her," Aruna laughed in turn, relieved to be back in her brother's good graces.

Raj said, "Amen to that. She's a waitress in her family's restaurant business and so far she seems to be a sensitive and wise woman. She's not exactly your reader of Plato, but she is a good person, which counts for more than the other factors. We've shared a lot of feelings about our lives."

Changing the subject he said, "We still have

close to a ton of 2 mm pellets left. Based on what we've used so far we have the ability to produce 500 of these homes with that ton. Remember we paid $3000 and change for it?"

"Do I remember?" she said, with not-so-distant memories of their hard work and sore butt muscles to earn the money.

Raj said, "Simple math tells us each home costs only six dollars. If we buy ten tons, I'll bet the price might drop by a third or more, so we can make thousands of houses like this at three or four dollars a house. Add a little cost for some other materials, but it's still doable. I ran the calculations in my head. I want the supports to cant inward some 20 degrees. This will cause any wind to hit one side and roll down the other without hitting the side flat-on. At a later date we'll make stackable hollow collapsible cones for the corners with the hole in them pre-set to the proper angle. A round home will be better yet. We'll stick with what we have for now, you know, improve on our design."

"Darn, Raj, that's crazy cheap. Labor and shipping will be the killer, though" Aruna conceded.

"Unless we don't have to pay for labor and only ship once, or maybe not at all," Raj suggested.

"Where in the world are you going to get free labor?" Aruna inquired.

Raj stared her and grinned broadly. Aruna hit

him in the shoulder and said, "You are a sneaky one?"

Sue emerged from the church into the bright sunlight. Shielding her eyes she walked the length of the porch to the side where she heard conversation. Playing it neutral, she declared, "There you are. To me it all looks to be mixing well, but what do I know?"

Raj said, "Why don't you guys help me figure out the best way to attach the tiles to the posts while we wait another hour. Three brains are better than one."

Sue felt somewhat relieved. Raj's off-the-cuff comment made her feel better. At least she had a brain.

16

At the end of the workday, Aruna left for home. She had a date to go to the movies with Marie. Raj saw Sue preparing to leave, as well, and asked, "Why don't you stay for a while. There's a truck-stop diner down the highway where we can have a leisurely dinner. Afterward, I want to show you something special."

Sue looked at him somewhat askance, cautious, yet curious, taking him up on the offer, not knowing what to believe, after learning more about this strange man. Neither spoke during the ten minute drive to the truck stop, nor were they overly hungry. Sue was in no mood to eat and ordered a small chef's salad, which turned out to be more then she was prepared to eat. Raj checked the buffet to select two chicken drumsticks labeled HOT and sides of rice and beans. When he got settled in at the table, Sue confronted him.

"Why didn't you tell me about your education?" she asked.

"What's to tell?" he replied, glibly.

"Don't play with words. You know what I'm talking about. Aruna told me about both of you," Sue shot, instantly regretting her aggressive approach. This was the first time she'd felt anger toward him. Disappointment, yes; anger, no.

About to cut into his chicken, Raj paused and looked up at her, knife in hand. A sudden darkness swept through him. He set down the knife, not trusting himself and explained, "Maybe I liked you and I didn't want to lose you. I knew you'd find out eventually. So what? At least I'd have gained traction by then. If I'd told you at the start, you might have walked. What am I supposed to say, 'Gee, top dogs say I'm really smart' and I have a whole bunch of degrees. It would have made you feel small, not having gone to college.

"Don't get me wrong. I am attracted to you, and screw your lack of education. Education is meaningless unless it's applied. Integrity of the person is topmost. You have that. It's what I appreciate most in you. I get my degrees because I like to learn. If you like people so much, go read about psychology. Each of us has his or her strengths and weaknesses. The question is, can we get along?"

Just because he was in love, or thought he was in love, didn't mean he had to cow tow to her. Still, he hadn't intended to go off on a rant. He meant his words to be statements of fact, until Sue began to cry. He couldn't remember when he'd said so much at one time. He had a lot to let out. Standard stuff. But it did apply. He felt a flush of embarrassment at having to defend himself, while desperately trying to understand what he had said to make her cry.

Sue gently wiped a tear from one eye with the back of a forefinger, smiled slightly, and responded, "Maybe I was being a little motherly. Maybe I felt disappointed in that I wanted to know everything about you and only got a piece of the story. It's my fault for having expectations. Maybe I'm too nosy. No, I am too nosy."

"Sue, there is nothing to beat yourself up about."

Sue felt as though she were listening to a robot that was attracted to her. She had seen the human in that body, albeit one that comes and goes. "Is there anything else I should know about you?"

Raj stared hard at this woman, like she was asking a car dealer about a used car.

"Yes, and everybody is allowed to have some secrets." He'd be damned if he was going to tell her he and Aruna would be multi-millionaires soon enough. Muddy the waters it's called. "If you don't mind, let's eat so I can show you something special," he told her, curtly, having no desire to get into his medical conditions, another factor in the mix. She'd find out soon enough, if she stayed around. He returned to eating his dinner, cold as it was.

Darkness had fallen when they returned to the old church. With the minor exception of 400 billion stars, the moonless sky was almost pitch black. Almost imperceptible head and tail lights in the distance on the interstate looked like the dim glow of fireflies moving back and forth horizontally.

Raj didn't stop at the church. He continued on past it using only his parking lights to guide the slow moving vehicle.

"Where are we going?" his date asked, very concerned.

"Right here," Raj said, and stopped the car. He got out and walked to the rear and opened the tailgate to remove two reclining lawn chairs and two blankets. He set up the chairs, motioning for her to join him.

"That's it? I thought you wanted to show me something," she said, reclining the chair to a 45 degree angle.

"Stop talking, relax, and look up," he bade, gently.

She did, and gasped. In the absence of house lights or buildings to obscure the view, on a moonless night, in the crystal clear air of the desert, she saw the galaxy as she had never seen it before. This was different than the many pictures she had seen. This was real life. Huge and monstrous, uncountable suns filled the entire sky from horizon to horizon from dwarf stars to red supergiants.

The evening breeze sprung up, a living creature sent to remind them they were still on Earth. Overwhelmed beyond words, Sue reached out to grasp Raj's hand and gave it a squeeze in appreciation for sharing this gift, at the same time dispelling any doubts she'd had about him.

"I'll tell you something else my father, well, Tony, told me. He said the very first picture taken by the James Webb Space Telescope was of an area out there in total blackness just to see if it could pick up anything. The field of view was the size of the eye of a needle held at arm's length, or about the size of a grain of sand. He asked me if I knew how many grains of sand it would take to cover our entire sky around the globe. I said probably a lot. He said, "According to NASA, it is something like 30 million. In that single picture alone, tens of thousands of galaxies were counted—galaxies, not stars.

"The interesting part of the story is that it doesn't matter if any other intelligent life exists, because you will never communicate with it. It would take countless years for any signal we sent to reach anybody out there, let alone receive a return signal. The same holds true if we receive a signal from a life form in a star system, say, ten thousand lights years away. Do they even exist anymore? We're stuck in our own morass."

"Which means each of us has to do our best to ensure life on this planet survives, with or without humans," Sue summarized, reading his mind.

"My sister is the ecology expert. She says we're on a road to self-destruction. We're in-bred to eat and use what we can when we can, like a dog eating everything from its bowl until it is satiated. There will always be a correction factor, one or more events, each of which will be our own internal meteorite as big as the one that killed the dinosaurs and most of the life on the planet. It will rearrange the world at some point. It could be a lot of things. Over-population will be the foremost key factor. Our own technology will be both directly and indirectly responsible.

"Maybe 10 thousand products are made from or contain silicon ranging from glass to micro-chips. What do we do when the sand is all gone? I want to delay that shift as long as possible."

After a moment of silence, still absorbed by the majesty of infinity and of his thinking, Sue said, passionately, "Raj, I want to go on that journey with you. Will you let me?"

He turned his head toward her in the darkness and said, "Yes, I will, under the condition that you watch a few videos of mine. I want you to see what you're getting into."

"All right, but let's stay here a little while longer. I need to absorb this."

"It's not going anywhere," Raj said.

After some time she got up and began to fold the blanket as a hint she was ready to go. She followed him back to his apartment and within minutes, the couple sat in front Raj's TV. Raj had seen it before. She hadn't. The first CNN episode began, highlighting him and his sister and their growing up in the depths of poverty, followed by all the other episodes.

When Melanie Brown finally signed off, Sue did her best to overcome the sensory overload of what she had walked into this day; first meeting Aruna, working on their special world-changing project, finding out about his intelligence and their educations, the night out looking at the heavens, the doomsday lecture, and the CNN series she had just watched. Her mind had numbed. She wouldn't sleep tonight.

Granted Raj was not the type of person who would find bliss at an all-night frat party. His qualities lay in other areas. Life's experiences dictated that complete faith in one's mission can be a powerful force, one that easily cut through virtually any resistance. What really frightened Susan was that Raj had the whole package; complete faith in himself, high intelligence, and practical application of his great talents. Hopefully, the couple would find compatibility on a more normal level.

"Raj, I have to go. I need to sleep. I'll call you tomorrow. Thank you for everything," she said. Kissing him lightly on the lips, a blasted and dazed Susan Gardner slowly ambled out the door closing it quietly behind her.

17

Megan wore a pink turban (part of her collection) over her shaved head as she joyfully served dinner to her house guests. Another two weeks off and she could return to work, about which she had serious misgivings. The more she thought about going back into formal teaching, the worse she felt. She didn't think she could take the come-down. It was letting the air out of a fully inflated balloon. She half made up her mind to ask her husband if he need any help in the office.

"Maybe I'll start by taking a slice out of Susan's lemon meringue pie." Tony said.

Seated next to Aruna, Marie offered, "I'm going for the apple." This was Marie's first meeting with any member of Aruna's family and she did her best to follow her friend's advice. *Relax, this is only another family having guests over for dinner.* Yeah, right.

Megan had supplemented the pot roast and potatoes dinner with numerous vegetarian dishes, some of which Sue had helped her prepare earlier, which gave Sue a chance to exhibit her culinary skills. The conversation remained light for some time until Tony couldn't resist. He finally threw out the inevitable question, "So how's the project going?"

Eyes turned toward Raj. Seated next to Susan. He offered, "The attachment points of the sides to the posts are worked out. They're simple and use minimal materials. We have two sizes, a four-foot and six-foot. The six-footer is the luxury suite. They both are luxury suites for their intended target audience. Ample light and ample opacity; you can't see out clearly and nobody can see in clearly. Total weight of the entire structure is from four-to-six pounds and can be carried in one or two bags for travel purposes. This includes telescoping posts, poly top, and poly bottom. The top has easy attachment points to the sides so it can be lifted and tightened easily. The entry is a simple flap opening.

"One last thing. Aruna and I are going to spend some nights in the two we constructed out of sight behind the church. We'll block the vision of curious drivers by parking our cars on either side of the two we have set up, one on each side."

As Raj objectively told of physical constructs, a chord struck his heart. Here he was declaring they would move into a little container meant for a family to live in. For them, it was not about living together for a couple of weeks in a tent because they decided to camp out, it was about the possible mental torture each would have to endure on the road to their goal. Nobody besides himself and Aruna needed to know his entire game plan.

"You told me you were going to do that, Raj. I want to be there with you," Sue said.

Others seated at the table, not in the know, watched the drama unfold like a soap opera, or the daily news, setting up for the next episode.

Raj didn't feel he needed to tell everything to everybody. People are permitted to have secrets. "Sue, we need to live there to find the flaws in our design. It has to be us. Radar tells us a minor hurricane is moving up from the Gulf of Mexico. This will create perfect situation for us to test our models. They will be well monitored to give us lots of data." He spoke like a true talking head scientist speaking to the masses.

Raj's family saw the coming storm as a two-edge sword. His headaches would soon begin in earnest, whether he stayed at home, or stayed overnight an hour south of home. What did concern Raj the most was that Aruna's mental wall was more fragile than his.

He had heard it said that no matter where you live, it always feels good to come home again. There were caveats to the statement. Aside from being abused by a bad parent, which was not his situation, he had misgivings about his and his sister committing themselves to spending any time at all in the new habitats; about how they might react psychologically. Their initial discussion centered on each person spending time by themselves and decided that naysayers would find something wrong no matter what their decision. This led them to conclude there was more to gain by living together, for a variety of reasons, all positive.

Watching the conversation unfold, Tony asked the next logical question. “You already have enough data to show the superiority of your plastic house compared with the other models, now what?”

Raj answered, “Improve what we have. The top panels will have to be cut more than the middle ones because the structure is tilted inward somewhat. When it works, we market.”

Only Sue and Marie gave a short laugh, stopping when they saw none of the others smile. Tony nodded, “I think we can help you with your efforts.” He didn’t define the “we” part.

Spending any time at all within the makeshift homes required serious deliberations, especially when it came to promotion of the product, if it ever got that far. When Raj mentioned he was going to bring his cell phone and tablet in with him, Aruna claimed it wasn’t authentic. “We never had those,” she declared.

Raj asked, “So what? When others had a

phone going, we'd all crowd around to watch it, didn't we? We also played with other kids after we ate dinner. Didn't we hang around somebody's campfire at night? We had a tight-knit community. Nothing is the same. The main idea is to test the integrity of the structure, not whether we can survive."

"I'll give you that," Aruna admitted.

"Don't you have to cook inside to make it authentic?" Sue asserted.

Raj nodded, "Yes. In fact, for that I purchased a single burner propane stove."

"Beats using cow chips for fuel," Aruna admitted.

`"You used cow chips?" Sue asked, shocked.

"Do you think we plugged in electric stoves?" Aruna joked.

"If you have sensors, why do you have to live inside?" Sue said.

"Because humans are better sensors than machines are," Raj answered.

"Remember when bapu brought home a Bollywood poster for the floor?" Aruna laughed.

"Yeah, till the monsoon rains flooded out everybody," Raj added, failing in his attempt to be jovial.

"I always looked forward to picking up trash in ankle-deep slop during monsoons. What a delight," Aruna threw in, almost cruelly, milking the cow, enjoying the look on the faces of Sue and Marie.

Raj said, “Yeah, another day at the office. The good news is that we don’t have to work 12-14 hour days anymore. We’ll still need to stay 6-8 hours a night in our shelter to keep it honest.”

Sue watched the interchange with shocked amusement. The two laughed off the most disgusting aspects of life. Well, she’d better get a report in the morning from Raj. If not, he would get a call from her.

Marie asked, “Is your house supposed to be weather proof?”

The engineer replied, “Not for anything more than a drizzle or a very windy day. About 5 miles per hour is average for Delhi.”

Aruna cooked three cups of rice and reheated the lentil soup she had brought from home. Darkness had long since fallen. The hour now approached 8:00 pm, the time when dinner had been prepared back in the old days. A slight glow came from the Plasti-Brik frame, as it reflected moonlight. If a neighbor were present and had a campfire going, the interior of their home would be well lit.

The couple ate in silence, each concerned about how they would sleep when the flame went out; when the time came to say goodnight and what dreams might assail them.

Aruna drifted off and went into REM sleep almost immediately. In her dream, everyone was picking up trash with her: Raj and Sue, Marie, umma and bapu, Megan and Tony, Melanie Brown and the cameraman, Gunta-Rao, and Vishaswami, Christina, and even Arthur, the prick. Everyone had a trash bag into which they deposited their treasures. Other unidentifiable vague forms came and went. It was a feel-good dream, although everyone was jealous of Aruna because she possessed the powerful magnet.

The scene morphed into another in which everyone was seated inside the small trash-bag-constructed home of hers all trying to watch a movie on a cell phone she had recovered. In an instant, she awoke in the darkness in full panic mode, sweating, waiting for the bite of a rattlesnake so common in the area, or for the sting of a desert scorpion, each of which could easily crawl underneath the frame to seek warmth. She had decided not to mention the two creatures to Raj lest his night be spoiled in worry.

Raj had a similar dream except he was the one with the magnet. The first portion of the dream morphed into one in which everyone was on the airplane with him coming back to America. In a short while, the plane began to fly erratically until it nosed dived into the ground and Raj woke up with a start.

He looked around in the pitch blackness of the night totally disoriented. The moon had set and the stars were not visible through the top cover over the dwelling. Not knowing where he was, he reached for a flashlight, fumbled for the on-switch, and played the light around to immediately get his bearings.

Aruna, who had wakened earlier, had returned to sleep, lying on her side, head to the south, like she always did.

Raj preferred to sleep on his back. The only sound he heard was that of his own breathing; no racing motorcycles, distant fire engines, barking dogs, or cicadas. He had never experienced such quiet, as if all life had ceased to exist.

He turned off the flashlight to settle back down onto the hard floor, which, somehow, felt comfortable and reassuring. Pulling the single sheet over him to the shoulders he tried to quell random thoughts, giving tacit permission for the electrical sparks in his mind to randomly traverse nonsensical circuits until they, too, went to sleep.

Like automatic machines, the two awoke at sunrise. Raj had been dealing with a headache for the past couple of days and this morning it dominated his life. He double-dosed his headache pills, something he hated to do, and helped Aruna clean up their cooking efforts from the evening before.

Long-haul and short-haul truckers rolled in to hit the breakfast buffet, both men and women, greeting each other, trading war stories about their adventures on the road, exaggerating stories they had heard, adding life to the building. Kitchen staff brought out fresh pans of scrambled eggs, hash browns, sausages, bacon, biscuits, and gravy.

Working on his first cup of coffee, Raj checked the weather app and said, "It should be interesting tonight. Let's move the cars away from the structures so we don't block the wind. I want to get an accurate reading of its speed. The good news is we're not going to sleep inside tonight. We're going to monitor from my car. We don't want to be inside and get hit with a wall of Plasti-Brik, when he structure blows in on us."

Lost in memory, Aruna smiled and, said "That never happened when our walls were made of bags filled with trash."

"Which gives me an idea . . . "

"Oh, shut up," Aruna jibed, elbowing him.

Raj checked his phone app to note a drop in barometric pressure and took a pill. His headache had begun hours earlier. The wind sign in the monitor appeared next to the temperature for the day. It could be breezy for the week. If so, conditions would be perfect for the experiment. The day turned out to be a long one, waiting for night. The project today entailed the identification of numerous agencies that worked on programs created by the governmental and private concerns to assist ragpickers.

Evening slowly crawled forward. Back at the church, Raj went outdoors to check the sensors attached to numerous points in both structures to find them fully functional in the silent night, except for the whispering of the breeze that had sprung up out of the darkness carrying a scent of damp earth. The recorders measured every environmental parameter from sensors established inside and outside the two small dwellings and the velometer measuring wind speed.

A cloud layer moved in from the west. The taller 6' home was the first to buckle, the windward side first, pulling down the two support poles followed by the collapse of the entire structure. When it did, Raj checked the remote in his hand and announced, "Six miles per hour."

The wind backed off, gusted again, and short moments later the smaller 4' home collapsed. "Eight miles per hour," he said. "That's it for tonight. We're good. The improved design works. Let's dismantle the houses and take them inside."

"How are you going to redesign? Do you know yet?" Aruna inquired. She hoped this would be the end of it for her.

"Yes, I do. I want to run computer simulations to see if I got the angle of cant right. I'm going to contact Dr. Richards. He's my old professor of materials sciences. I want to go over everything with him and make use of their computers. While I'm doing that, I'd like you to draft a letter to some of the agencies that serve the pickers and tell them we are in the final stages of preparation for our idea."

"Final stages?" Aruna questioned.

"Okay, it's a stretch. At least it will get their attention," Raj said. "I want to get all this done before we get dad involved."

The hour was 2:13 am and rain was imminent. Working quickly, the houses were quickly folded and loaded into the back of Raj's vehicle. Both were wide awake and decided to return to their apartments at this early hour, an hour's drive north, rather than sleep in their cars or in the church to finish out the night.

Raj appreciated that Sue had left him to do his work. The man had a mission. On the drive home he dismissed the impulse to call her to report the results. It wouldn't gain him any brownie points.

He did call when he got up at mid-morning to explain in a few words what had happened.

She sounded delighted to hear that the projected stint had come to a temporary impasse. She was also delighted to hear from him under any circumstance. "I missed you," she lamented over her cell, while turning her back on a table of customers to take the call.

The time spent with Professor Richards yielded excellent results: The angle of deflection was modified slightly thanks to higher math and wind tunnel tests. Three different-size mold frames were created to accommodate the different angles of the end panels. The time had come to sleep inside the homes again, with one major modification. Aruna had suddenly walked out on the project.

As for Sue, she knew with certainty what she was getting into when she chased after a driven man who was in love with goals. Unfortunately for her, she couldn't stop herself.

PART FOUR

1

When Aruna approached the tip of Cape Cod, Massachusetts, she flashed back. It is said that the sense of smell retains the longest memory of all the senses. When she smelled the ocean breeze, she flew back in time to when she was two or three years old, when she and Raj had lived close to the Arabian Sea, which she had never seen, when her parents worked the trash heaps before taking the train ride to New Delhi. The smell was the same. Now she saw the vastness of a real ocean for the first time and it far exceeded her imagination.

The Woods Hole Oceanographic Institution (WHOI) on the cape accepted Aruna Rossi into their doctoral program on a full scholarship, although their classes were conducted at MIT. Her vast knowledge of ocean currents, sea life, and especially the prevalence of plastics in various areas placed her in a coveted position. Her post-doctoral studies found her, at the age of 21, aboard the Atlantis.

Owned by the U.S. Navy and operated by WHOI, the highly sophisticated research vessel is specifically dedicated to servicing and occupying the Alvan submersible, not exactly what the young scientist had in mind.

The Atlantis boasted six science labs along with advanced navigation and satellite communication systems. It had a machine shop, cranes and winches, along with two-score crew members and highly trained scientists from around the world. Once she was on-board, these same persons became attracted to her.

In this rare instance, the real person exceeded the hype. Charming and beautiful, the aspiring oceanographer wanted to collect microplastics from the sea floor and further track the migration of the substance, if nothing else but to collect and recycle the damn stuff that was killing sea life by ways not yet measured.

For that, she would have to join another vessel. In a rare show of accommodation, WHOI accepted the non-qualified, woman. According to administrative staff, it had nothing to do with her fame or money. For now, the trainee needed to learn how this boat surveyed the ocean floor, (a boat which was armed with side-scan sonar detectors keyed to looking for unwanted submarines).

As the only one aboard the vessel with no seagoing experience, she soon found herself seasick and spent two weeks of the first voyage enjoying the benefits of a rocking boat. The decision to temporarily change careers introduced the possibility of working with the vast library that belonging to WHOI, a library covering every aspect of the oceans, correlating data, presenting requested reports and spend virtually all her time at a desk. She opted out of the offer.

Instead, Aruna made the decision to take a leave of absence from her short stint at the coast to return to her roots. She joined her brother and his wife near a mountain of trash heap outside of Old Delhi. She had been pulled out of the muck for some reason to grow into an educated woman, only to return to do . . . what?"

After Sue had encouraged Raj to pace himself, he paired with Dr. Roberts. The men had produced three home models. The first two were the 4' and 6' varieties Raj had initially designed, except that now, with patient computer and exciting wind-tunnel work, the researchers established precise angles of wind deflection for the pair that were more trapezoidal in shape.

The third mini-home was a 7' diameter circular model based on yurt and Mongolian Ger designs with a floor space almost exactly the same as the square models. This design proved to be even more wind stable than its square brethren and able to withstand gusts of some 10 miles per hour. Raj and Roberts filed for U.S. and international patents under the Plasti-Brik corporate name. Encouraged by what he saw, Tony put serious money into attorneys and politicians. Soon, ReCyclo built a manufacturing plant and within two years, had gone international. In addition to serving India, requests for the plastic shelters began to come in from other continents.

Tony and Megan Rossi's wealth had grown considerably, despite providing each of their children with some $10 million, thanks to wise investments by Hans Hobert, who also fared well out of the deal.

Raj delved more deeply into human anatomy and physiology, which led him to pharmacokinetics, the science of how drugs, antibiotics, and foreign chemicals affect the human body. Why hadn't he studied the science sooner after all these years on medications, he frequently asked himself in the dark hours of the night.

Except for brief periods, his mind never stopped creating. He could not get what others called a good night's sleep. Instead, he became enamored with the idea of self-monitoring watches and clothing, already a developing field.

With great amusement, Sue evaluated her present circumstance. She came to the conclusion that somebody had to add a measure of sanity to her husband's mentally retarded and financially destitute family, so she did a normal thing. She joined a culinary school to earn her own degree. Her parents were endlessly proud of her accomplishment. This pride had nothing to do with her marriage to a multi-millionaire who provided for her occasional whims and the additional monies they received from their financially secure daughter.

She also found herself an occasional nurse, taking care of an injured man, namely, Raj Rossi, who absolutely needed to stay up on his medications and to pay attention to weather reports in order to keep his bipolar behavior at bay. She soon found herself in a second career as an amateur meteorologist wondering if any change in weather might be having an effect on her cooking skills. At least she could blame a bad meal on an external force.

Negotiations had been ongoing for some time between Tony and his newly hired Phoenix-based attorney familiar with Indian land law and the country's political system. The greater Phoenix metro area was rife with attorneys of every ilk, some even specializing in obscure legal challenges surrounding helicopter crashes and amusement park accidents.

Earlier, under Raj's direction, ReCyclo constructed a plastic recycling/production facility at the northernmost mega-dump site at Old Delhi, the same site where the Singh/Rossi twins had been discovered. At a shared cost to the central government, the plant would convert plastics from bottles recovered from the dump site(s) into housing for the local ragpickers at an average cost of $6.00 per home.

Tony and his children wanted the pickers to be paid twice the wages they had received on the "street" when they turned in their plastic bottles. When the pickers had saved enough, a home could be purchased. Employees at the plant had to be 14 years or older, the minimum age at which children (legally) can work at hazardous jobs in a country that has the highest number of child laborers in the world.

Eyeing the higher prices the company paid per kilo, the infiltration of pickers from other areas near and distant from the site was a given. The profit came from the test-market sale of plastic shoes in New Delhi designed by Raj and Roberts. The 2 mm plastic beads had been combined with spandex in a mold for flexibility. An enzyme catalyst served to contract the shoe to foot size once the foot was placed in it.

ReCyclo requested Aruna to be the spokesperson for the sale of the shoes on Indian TV, initially to the Delhi audience. Everybody knew her. Their own daughter had returned home.

For better or worse, Bollywood discovered her. A producer on a business trip from Mumbai saw her on Delhi TV, connected the dots, and flew her down to Mumbai for an audition. The public speaking classes she had taken with Marie paid off in acting school where she began dating the most famous of all male actors. The news went viral in a country that produced more films than did the United States.

When Sue arrived home she found the house darkened with Raj in bed. The curtains had been drawn and he appeared to be sleeping. On the floor next to the bed lay an opened envelope with a loose some page atop it. She presumed something in the letter had caused him to have an instant migraine. As quietly as possible, she retrieved the papers and retreated to the living room where she examined them.

The letter was addressed to Dr. Raj Singh Rossi and was from Lucrecius Solari, Minister of Water Resources, New Delhi.

Solari was a true Greek. He had worked for the government of Greece as a geologist until his country had found itself in deep economic woes. Suspecting he would soon to be laid off, he read about the need for a geologist in India in a trade magazine. The country desperately needed someone skilled in the location of trace minerals such as lithium and cadmium for their effort to build up their electronics sector and space efforts. Solari applied for the job and was hired. Shortly, he found himself moving some 5000 km or 3100 miles to the east with his wife and three year old son.

The letter read:

Dear Dr. Singh, I have followed your interest in assisting us with the "relocation" of our dump sites, i.e., your strident proposal to bury them. It is with deep regret that I inform you your proposal is, for the most part, untenable. Permit me to be honest with you and elaborate further.

Much of the central portion of India is underlaid by hard rock; thus, water is not replenished by rainfall. It is only a matter of time when the remaining water is used up. The water table in these areas is quite variable, but in general, is continually falling. Our agriculture is seriously threatened and much of the water is already contaminated by toxic pollution from industry and human mismanagement. Mining activities, for example, are notorious for releasing unwanted heavy metals into the water table (e.g., mercury from coal mines), and virtually all mines typically flood. Unfortunately, there is little we can do about either of those situations. As you know, industry is a self-driving force.

Therefore, your suggestion to bury the refuse has a major problem: The water table throughout the remainder of our country is relatively too close to the surface for deep digging. If deep digging occurs, such as you propose for burial of waste, the water tables will be contaminated by heavy metals, pesticides, refuse, microbial growth and a myriad of other contaminants. Preparing a hole with a lining to prevent that leakage is theoretical and irreversible. In short, once leakage occurs, it cannot be stopped.

Finally, even if the water table were not an

issue, proceeding with your proposal to bury the dump sites is beyond budgetary allowances and is not practical in our country from several standpoints when money can be spent elsewhere to accomplish greater good.

If you have any questions regarding this letter, please feel free to contact me and I will be happy to engage you and invite my engineers and groundwater specialists to share their expertise with you.

Sincerely, Lucrecius Solari, Minister of Water Resources

Xc: Hari Mohammad, Minister of Finance; Rahul Mehta, Interior Minister

Sue set the letter down on her lap. Raj hadn't even gotten to first base; not even a slam-bam, thank you, mam. She had a lot to think about. At least Solari was honest and straightforward in his stab to her husband's heart. He could have written, "I'm surprised a man of your expertise hadn't researched this matter prior to making this proposal."

Tony had warned Raj he could expect to get skewered along the way. So much for saving the planet. Negative thoughts aside, she knew her husband. He would say something like, "Well, damn it, if I can save the world, then maybe I can save humanity."

Which is exactly what Raj planned to do.

After he recovered from his shock of having

one of his life's ambitions shattered and somehow managing to escape without health repercussions, Raj decided he was bored without a project to work on, which helped his attitude a lot. He also got tired of living in Delhi, one of the three most polluted cities on the planet. So did his wife. After making a few phone calls, he grabbed her and took the one hour flight southward to Mohali in the State of Punjab.

On the trip down, Raj explained, "The Plasti-Brik project was my sole goal for many years along with the trash issue, and now one is gone and the other is beginning to take off, I find myself consumed by another passion called nanotechnology."

Sue said, "Where you make medicines on a miniature scale, right? I saw it in a movie about little robots swimming in the blood going to different places in the body to make repairs."

Raj smiled, "Yes and no. It's more than medications. On the small scale we are talking about, the basic laws of physics we live by don't apply, because we are talking about atomic size particles that are used in many areas of study—probably even in cooking," he added to pique her interest, completely uncertain of what he was talking about.

"It is the medical aspect I'm interested in. These particles are ten-thousand times smaller than those BB-size beads we use for the panels and shoes. Lets' put it another way. A nanometer is so small that it is to a meter as a marble is to the size of the earth."

Sue made an obvious show of scratching her neck, as she tried to wrap her head around the size difference. She found herself following this man around, chasing his dreams, trying to make due, wanting to start a family, and trying to get her own sleep in a bed where her husband was up and down half the night, reading, figuring, on the computer. For that reason, for a long time she had considered they sleep in two bedrooms, or at least two beds, but lacked the courage to mention it to him.

Raj continued, now in his zone, "We're talking about fabrication, energy transfer, semi-conductors, antimicrobials, engineering, agriculture, as well as medications and sensors. We're talking about injecting or swallowing a pill that will send the tiniest particles you can imagine to an injured area."

Sue let him do his thing. She was especially happy to get away from the smell of the dump-site that always permeated the ReCyclo plant, especially in the damp morning hours or whenever it rained. Her visits to her husband's place of work had become less frequent over the months for that reason.

A black Cadillac Escalade picked up the couple at the Mohali airport and within minutes, delivered them to the sprawling 35-acre complex that constituted the famed Institute of Nano Science and Technology.

"Is this where you want to work?" Sue inquired, as the couple was led inside to take a seat in the glass-fronted waiting room. Their driver checked in at a central desk where a receptionist made a phone call. Short minutes later, a tall, turbaned, fully bearded man, sharply dressed in a dark suit greeted the couple. To Raj, it was déjà vu, like seeing Vishaswami from their old orphanage.

As did Vishaswasmi and native Indians in general, the man spoke with a British accent, "Dr. Rossi, it is my great pleasure to meet you. I took the liberty of researching your background. It is quite impressive. I am Ajeet Agarwal, the director here. We spoke on the phone. And I take it this is your lovely wife. I hear she is quite the great chef."

Sue blushed at the compliment. The man was full of it, but she'd take the compliment. She could only smile and shake his hand, lady-like.

"You said you wanted a tour of our facility. Please join me for some tea in my office while we talk."

Ajeet nodded to the receptionist, who nodded to a dark-skinned man wearing khaki shorts and shirt, who stood in waiting. He immediately departed and would reappear in moments with the requisite drinks.

Ajeet bade his guests be seated in an unremarkable room where dark foam chairs replaced leather. He began, "You're interested in the medical aspects of nano, you told me."

"Yes, along the pharmacological lines, specifically," Raj agreed. "I wanted a tour to get an idea of ongoing research in the field in general. Perhaps that could help me blend them into useful products."

The servant brought in the teapot on a silver tray with three cups, ample sugar, cream, and small stirring spoons, then he departed. The parties took a moment to pour their cups and settled back to continue the conversation.

Somehow, Sue knew what was coming. She often wondered about her husband, this *wunderkind* of hers. She had once asked him why he walked the halls of the college library when anything he wanted to know could be found online. "I go to the sections I'm interested in and read the titles," he had told her.

"That's all?" she asked, curious about this strange behavior.

"That's all I want. Titles add up, blend to stimulate my imagination. They rumble through my brain at night like sheep, but instead of jumping over the proverbial fence, they flock. I like to touch the books too, especially the well-worn ones. Once in a while I'll read the book and skip over a bunch of stuff at the same time. Do you understand?"

"Completely," Sue said, feeling confident that no matter what she replied, it wouldn't matter when he got in this state of mind. That part concerned her. In her own regard, she tried her best to follow the twins' recommendations to read Descartes and the great philosophers. None of it grabbed her. Neither did the great poets. Her mother saw her struggle trying to follow the suggestions of others, until she followed her own mother's advice to do what felt comfortable. From then on, she became enamored with the subtleties of cooking foreign foods and began to accumulate books on the subject.

When she had first been invited to the Rossi family dinner and assisted Megan in the preparation of dishes, Megan had leaned in to her and asked, "I hope you know what you're getting into."

Sue thought, *Here we go,* and replied, "What *am* I getting into? Are you afraid of losing your son? We're only dating, Megan."

"No, no, don't take offense. I didn't mean it the way it sounded. Not long after we brought the twins home, Tony and I took him to a psychiatrist . . ."

"Psychiatrist?"

"He was having behavioral problems in excess of what we expected, that's all." Megan replied.

"And?"

"We were told he was pretty smart and that Raj doesn't see the world the way the rest of us see things. Maybe he sees more colors, or sees motion in terms of numbers, he wasn't certain."

"Come on, Megan, don't tease me," Sue said. She felt the warmth of love in this family. It gave her comfort. She also needed to stand her ground.

Megan said, "Okay, Nobody knows how smart he is."

Sue was surprised at Megan's choice of words. How do you measure 'smart'? She's very smart. He's not too smart. Somebody is a 3 out of 10 on the smart scale. Is it different from a sting that smarts? The word smart sounded like it could the name of a fish, or the sound a handful of clay makes when it hits the wall. SMART!

Sue got the idea and saw the truth. Megan was being cautious in her wording. She took a glance around to see others engaged in their own conversations and replied, "So what?"

In her simplistic answer, she had wanted Megan to know smarts had nothing to do with affection and other qualities inherent in a good relationship. In truth, she saw a man who could live by himself on the moon. The same man required loving affection, weak though he might be in expressing it. She wanted to be both to him. She wondered, *Whatever am I going to do with you, sweetheart? Wrong. Whatever are you going to do with me?*

Sue combined Megan's statement with Raj's comments about reading book titles in the library, along with his mental lapses. She considered what he told her on the roof back in the day, something she failed to understand then, but what she understood now: He had quoted Van Gogh, who had said: I dream of painting and then I paint the dream."

In the next moment, the library came to Raj.

2

Ajeet began, "Before we get to your expressed topic, let me begin by saying the medical field relating to nano is quite broad. It is like the first laser, when people said, 'Well, that's nice. What do we do with a narrow beam of light'? Look at where it is today.

"Nano tech is 1000 times the laser in that regard. Nano tech is a seedling swiftly growing into a giant tree. Already on the market, or soon to be, are wearables other than smart watches. These include shirts and pants that self-adjust to temperature and which read bodily functions such as blood pressure, sleep patterns, blood sugar, respiration, and hormone levels, that sort of thing. Solar powered collars and long-life batteries will provide energy to the clothing to do what it will, shoes will automatically adjust to different terrains, yoga pants will sense your stretching capabilities, sports science will take a giant leap forward as will sports performances, microfibers in clothing . . . the list is almost endless. You know science, doctor, the more we move forward, the more ways we find to move forward."

Ajeet leaned forward, almost conspiratorially, and said, "My personal interest is in gas monitoring."

He entertained an expected quizzical look from Raj to explain, "Our breath. For a long time alcohol monitors have been available, Labs are developing systems to analyze breath to detect diseases. I know a lot about how those work."

Raj could not hold back his excitement and leaned forward in turn to say, "Ajeet, I know a few things, too. Maybe we can share."

In saying those words, Raj was thrown back years in the past to when his parents had taken him to a restaurant and his mother had made the comment about cell phones being addictive. He didn't know it at the time, but her innocent statement had served as the seed of an idea, soon to be expressed.

For his part, Ajeet sat back in surprise. He had just received an offer to pair with Raj Rossi from the man himself.

From Ajeet's presentation, Sue got another glimpse into her husband's mind. He was gathering disparate puzzle pieces, sorting them, arranging their jagged edges by color and pattern, subconsciously framing a picture. Knowing her husband as she did, she embraced his mental processes, which even they might not yet understand what the full portrait would look like.

Raj's mind leapfrogged over ideas to come up with new concepts. Ajeet had presented him with titles of books. The day had just begun and he couldn't wait to turn his imagination into solid material. "How readily available are these materials?" he asked, expectantly.

Ajeet shrugged, "Some a great deal, others are difficult to find; others have to be made individually, some are only concepts. Why? This is a research facility, we don't produce end product."

"No reason," Raj answered.

Sue read his statement to mean, "Every reason."

"I wouldn't mind it if you could provide me with a list of producers," Raj added.

"I'll make sure you get it before we're finished. By the way, if I may ask, what is your time schedule here in Mohali. I have a reason for asking," said the director, a doctor of engineering from MIT, in his own right.

"No schedule," Sue said quickly, before Raj could say a word. She saw his foot wag in nervousness. It gave her a small thrill to guide him toward what could be some fun, other than mental stimulation. In Raj's case, his mind served as his playground.

Ajeet grinned broadly and offered, "Then why don't you two be my guests for a day or two. I'll take you to dinner tonight—for my bragging rights, of course. We'll even have a photo together. After that, I will take you to our absolutely magnificent Mohali Mall in case you want to find trinkets to take home. Also, and most importantly, as a very minor aside, there is a must see cricket match between India and England being played right here in our newly remodeled cricket stadium tomorrow. I'm already booked. Tickets are impossible to get, but I'll see what I can do if you give the word."

"We don't know anything about the sport, at least I don't," Raj confessed, feeling foolish to the point of shame. Like die-hard American baseball or football fans, every good Indian knew every statistic about every player on every cricket team. Cricket and soccer were their national sports. Why couldn't he have just said he'd love to and be done with it?

Ajeet nodded in understanding, recalling Raj's history and feeling sympathetic for his guest. Courtesy must prevail. He offered, gently, "Then I will explain it to you. I will make a call and we will all have the best seats. Say 'yes' and it is done."

Sue said "yes" before Raj could come up with an excuse. Ajeet picked up the phone and, speaking in Punjabi, made a lengthy, forceful statement, listened a moment, made another forceful statement, set down the phone and, with a toothy grin, stated, "There, it is done. We will be seated alongside the governor of Punjab who is anxious to meet you. Your sister wouldn't be available by any chance, would she?"

"Sorry, Ajeet, rumor has it she's in Bollywood," Raj replied.

Ajeet's eyebrows went up at the information, then checked his watch and said, "Our mall will be open for some hours yet. That is a must see along with our skyscrapers. After I show you our facilities here, I will have my driver take us on a tour."

Ajeet led his guest from room to room, most occupied with white-coated workers peering through microscopes, rooms decorated with reflux condensers, retorts, Erlenmeyer flasks, machines humming and buzzing, the scent oil and drilled metal, punch presses, exhaust fans, safety hoods, electron microscopes, atomic microscopes, pulverizers, ceramics galore, high-end computers, wall charts everywhere, storage rooms with rolls of a dozen materials.

Raj glared, walked around, spoke to technicians like a starving man being fed the foods of his choice, like a dry sponge in a tub of warm water. He stared at the charts, memorizing. One room could not be entered. Through the window set in the door he saw masked characters wearing space suits pulling samples from unseen objects floating in vats of liquids—Raj absorbed it all, intoxicated. His eye missed nothing, each new scene another data point. The aura of invested research enveloped him like a cloak.

He once turned to look at Ajeet who stood at a doorway to see the man smiling, Sue standing next to him also wearing a smile, perhaps seeing herself visiting a kitchen run by master chefs.

Raj was silent for the first half-hour of the flight to New Delhi two days later, deep in thought. Sue left him alone while she read a cookbook on Punjabi cooking she had picked up at the airport, her mind reeling with the events of the past two days. The cricket match was insane. The fans were insane. She got insane. Raj got caught up in the complexity of the game's scoring system with penalty runs, overs, wickets, getting bowled, or stumped; it was all so complex in a fun way, mostly because she gave up trying to grasp the rules. The mall was gorgeous. The dinner was sumptuous. The company top tier.

At last Sue said, "You had a good time, didn't you?"

Raj said, "There was so much. My mind filled with new things at the facility."

"You always told me to let it sort of its own accord, not to force anything. You should do the same," she offered.

"Yes, I will."

She went on, "When you were staring at some wall charts, Ajeet pulled me aside and asked if you were always like this."

"Like what?"

"Like a kid in a candy store."

Raj asked, "What did you tell him?"

"I said 'not always, when he gets focused on a project he leaves the world behind'."

She had the urge to tell him more, about how she'd heard the occasional person in her restaurant talk with complete sincerity about some adventure in their life, but she had the sense their story was a total fabrication, a fantasy they totally believed was true; or perhaps it was something they did or said that wasn't them at all and later they wondered how the hell they could have done such a thing, and here was Raj living his entire life in some kind of netherworld. He wasn't a narcissist, who absolutely believed he could do no wrong. He was a man who believed in a vision.

Raj admitted "Oh, I guess I do."

"Ajeet said his wife tells him he's the same way. In his case, he has children at home to take his mind off work."

"Oh."

"He said he knows Dr. Roberts because they presented papers at the same conventions. Maybe you could do the same someday," she threw out, knowing it would get his attention.

Raj turned to her and said sharply, "He didn't mention it to me."

"In my opinion, he said it as a teaser, knowing I'd mention it to you without being too direct, or too showy on your first meeting."

"So he knows Roberts . . ." his words trailed off. Raj reached into the side pouch of small briefcase he had taken along with his carry-on. He pulled out a sheaf of papers Ajeet had given him listing suppliers of various nano-related materials. A letter fell to the floor of the plane between them. Sue saw the letter drop, picked it up, read the envelope, and announced, "Raj, it's from your parents. It's dated ten days ago and it's unopened."

"Oh, boy, I wondered what had happened to it," he muttered. He took the letter from her and tore it open. He had maintained regular communications with his parents, although he hadn't spoken with his sister in a couple of months. Reading the letter, he exclaimed, "What's today's date?"

She told him and he said, "They're coming to Delhi day after tomorrow to see the plant. My dad put a lot of money into it. I have to call over there to warn them visitors will be coming. After the tour, they want us to go with them to Mumbai to see Aruna."

"So?"

"It would have been nice to have had some warning, that's all," Raj replied, grimly.

Sue shook he head, leaned over and kissed him on the cheek. Which of them had changed the most since the days on the roof when they shared the simplicity of a cool breeze; Raj telling her of his life, she feeling a yearning to be alongside the boy-man? She had made it happen to what end, to sit beside him in another part of the world, always trailing in his wake and feeling like Aruna must have felt?

She took the letter from him and pointed at the date, without saying a word. What she knew he wanted to say, but was too afraid to say, was that he had fixated on an idea—a laser beam focus to the exclusion of all else, and all of a sudden he had to shelve the idea relating the burial of trash. Now, of a sudden, he was off and running again. Was there ever a good time to capture his attention in its entirety?

She had her own focused idea that would express itself starting when they went to bed tonight; an idea, in her turn, she would have to shelve because her husband would be too self-immersed for the kind of fun she had in mind.

Raj grunted, closed his eyes, and said, "I think I feel a headache coming on."

"Me, too," Sue said, in all seriousness.

Megan insisted the four take the half-mile walk from the ReCyclo plant to the side of the mountain to where their children first lived, "that is, unless you don't want to," she offered her son.

"No worries, mom, it's in my head all the time anyway," Raj replied.

In the 14 years since he had left, the mountain

had grown considerably in height and breadth. The number of scavengers had also increased, considering the higher wages paid by the company. The landscape had also changed. A good thousand small square and circular white homes dotted the area. Creative minds had blended many of the homes such that their entries adjoined one another to enable family members or neighbors to come and go. In one would-be palace, three six-foot homes adjoined. Raj did not rejoice when he saw he had given only a few of his people a chance at happiness. A thousand was not a million. With considerable discomfort, he evaluated where he was compared with they were.

Otherwise, human activity in the neighborhood remained the same. Fire pits burned, trash dotted the flat ground like cacti in a desert, arguments ensued, and the occasional musician played some small instrument.

The four walked some distance into the encampment until Megan stopped and asked, "Where was your little home?"

Raj shook his head, "I can't tell anymore. Somewhere on that side, I think." He pointed.

Megan looked where he pointed and saw more of the same. She saw several areas where piles of trash-filled bags were used as walls, but none with Raj and Aruna's name written on them. She turned to look at the mountain and finally had to admit the smell was too annoying.

She glanced at Sue, who had only seen it from afar until that point. Sue was slowly shaking her head in wonderment, looking at her husband, trying to match the two, wondering what other minds might be in waiting among the children.

Megan took a deep breath and began walking back. "All right, I saw it. Let's go. Aruna will be expecting us." She got no argument from the others.

Tony pulled out his cell and made a call. Thirty seconds later, a black taxi left the plant and pulled up to them under the watchful eye of the residents, none of whom knew of those who had walked among them. The four got in and 20 minutes later were at the airport, the smog so thick it was a wonder that pilots could see to land or take off.

The guide led the four down a long hallway of the movie studio. People came and went, with and without makeup, some hurrying, some pushing equipment. They walked past two sound stages, glancing at the characters in the posters on both walls; close-ups of handsome men, beautiful women, dancing, singing, one holding a gun, another playing a sitar, names highlighted, exuding life energy and excitement.

Finally, the dressing rooms. The guide knocked. The door opened. Aruna stood in front of her family wearing a blue sari; 18 feet of gold and silver brocade, golden earrings dangling, red dot in her forehead, the buttu, red lipstick, hair cut shorter and styled. It had been worth the journey across the ocean to see her.

Raj began to video. When Tony asked him what he was doing, he said it was for grandma.

Megan and Aruna cried together, everybody hugged Aruna, who blurted, "This is so not me. Everybody in India sings; they love to sing in private and especially in the movies. I can't sing. I didn't even know how to put on a sari. I can't speak Hindi, my Marathi is almost gone, I have to take acting lessons, but nobody cares. They want photo shoots because somebody wants me to be a movie star. Worse, my English is American, not British. After I leave here, I get to go to the TV station and sell shoes because that's my job. Go figure."

"Then why are you wearing a sari?" Sue asked.

"I'm trying to get used to it. It's hell when you have to go pee. I'll go change in a minute."

"What good are you to them with all those negatives, honey?" Megan said.

"Somebody here thinks I'm good looking and wants me to play an American. At least I can remember my lines," Aruna grunted with facetiousness.

Everybody laughed at her honesty. Megan perceived something was wrong with her daughter. She understood this girl intimately. The undercurrent was inescapable.

"Come on in and I'll change. You've all seen it before," Aruna directed.

She changed into designer blue jeans and designer sandals and a white blouse tucked in the front of her belt. She put on a gold necklace and tied a red scarf around her neck. She warned, "We won't be going to any fancy French restaurant, but I do know a nice little European place nearby where we can have some wine and various treats. Since all of us are terribly poor, I have a studio credit card we'll use to let them pay for it. Give me a sec to call the limo."

And so, like Dorothy and her wizardly friends, the group marched down the long hallway, past the guard, eyeing the poster shouting out an army man with a cigarette in one hand and a submachine in the other, past colorful glorious stars of the day, into the glitter of Mumbai. A white limousine waited at the curb, the doors of which were opened for them, all directed by Aruna Rossi.

Only fifteen minutes later, the group entered the restaurant with Aruna leading the way. She waived at a white coated man, who saw her, bowed slightly, and came over. He led them to a corner table with a Reserved sign on it. Menus and water were delivered along with a bottle of white wine in a bucket of ice.

After several more minutes, Raj stopped the video and pushed the proper icons to send the somewhat intermittent recording. The electronic signal comprising the video bounced off a couple of satellites and seconds later, in time-warp fashion, equal to 12 hours earlier in the morning, Christina's phone in Phoenix chirped. She glanced at the screen, saw it came from her grandson, and very carefully tapped the phone in the proper place, to ensure she would have a very delightful next several days.

After dinner and before entering the limo for the trip to the hotel, Megan took her daughter's arm and pulled her aside into the shadows. Passersby streamed around them like water flowing around two rocks stuck against an embankment. Her daughter still had sadness in her eyes. "Baby, talk to me, please. We have always been best friends. I know something is wrong. Share it with me."

Megan threw he arms around her mother and sobbed, "Oh, mom, I'm pregnant."

3

"Well, you certainly know how to get attention," Megan chirped, happily. "How far along are you?"

"About six weeks. The tests are a definite positive."

Who's the lucky man?"

Surprised by her mother's response, Aruna said "Samba Patel. He's the biggest film star in the country, that's all."

"Then he must be handsome," Megan deduced.

Aruna smiled, and said, "Very."

"Does he know?" Megan asked.

"Yes."

"And?"

"He doesn't like it," Aruna said. She added, "He's actually a nice person."

"That counts for a lot. The question is, is he a good person?"

"I don't know."

"What's the word on the street?"

"He's a womanizer."

"Is he smart? No, is he intelligent?" Megan corrected herself.

"He doesn't have a lot of depth, but we only went out a few times. Again, I don't know him. Maybe, shit, mom, I don't know."

"What are you going to do?" Megan asked.

Aruna glanced at the limo. Megan saw her look and said, "They can wait."

"Mom, I'm keeping the baby."

"Good for you. Do you love him?"

"How can you love somebody you've only known a few weeks?"

"I guess it's time for you and your friend to become an item," Megan said.

Aruna grunted.

Megan took a deep breath and said, "We want this to be a happy affair. So lighten up. We don't want it to turn into a big stink, which means we have to strategize. Come on, honey, we'll work it out together. That's what families do." She took Aruna by the arm and led her to the waiting car.

The family talked of superficialities until reaching the hotel. Limo drivers have ears. Aruna released the driver and said she'd take a cab back to her place. She joined her parents to walk into their unit. "Something's up," Raj whispered to Sue.

Megan closed the door and directed the other four to take a seat. The picture window in the living room of their 10th floor unit dominated the room.

Tony said, "All right, Meg, what are you and Aruna cooking up?"

Aruna made the announcement to a stunned audience, which began the usual round of questions. No value judgments were made. This family issue needed the sober attention of everyone, like learning about a cancer diagnosis, only this time; it would be about a birth.

Sue offered, "Mr. Patel is going to be tied to the baby whether he likes it or not. I'm sure your dating him made big news, which means he's going to have to admit the child is his. If he doesn't, that puts you in the hot seat, because the public will want to know who the real father is, if it isn't him. And there is no reason for you to lie."

Even as she said those words, Sue wondered why Aruna was the lucky one and if there ever would be a good time to pressure Raj into becoming a father willingly, although the word "willingly" has some flexibility in its interpretation.

Tony said, "I agree. Be yourself without pretenses. You'll be appreciated for your honesty."

Raj said, "The question is, how do we deal with Mr. Patel?"

Tony chuckled and threw in, "One thing is for certain. His options are limited. He won't be able to buy you off."

Sue said, “The way these things work, his popularity at the box office will increase.”

“You’re sure it’s his,” Megan stated.

“Yes, positive,” Aruna returned with certainty.

Raj asked, “Can the guy add and subtract?”

Aruna said, “Mom already asked me the same question. Believe it or not, he does have a college degree in theater arts, but they still have to cover core courses—and yes, he’s pretty sharp. He’s a humble person beneath to glitz of the business.”

“You have his number, right? Why don’t you give him a call,” Tony suggested.

“Now?” Aruna replied.

Tony nodded, “Yes, now. It’s not that late. Who knows? He could be out on a date. There is no need for rancor. Tell him politely that his family would love to meet the famous actor either tonight, or within the next couple of days.”

Megan said, “Don’t you think the two of them should work this out in private first?”

Addressing Aruna, “Megan asked, “What do you think, honey?”

Aruna looked from mother to father and answered, “Let’s do both. I’ll call and meet with him first. I need to see where he stands, because denial is not an option. During the conversation, I’ll tell him what dad suggested. If he’s any kind of a man, he’ll agree to the meeting.”

Tony said, “You could casually mention your

brother is working for *The Times of India.*"

"The biggest newspaper in the country?" Sue asked.

"Just saying," Tony shrugged.

Megan chastised him. "Tony, don't be an idiot. It's too early to start the pressure cooker."

Aruna made the call.

Patel had just entered his home with another woman who carried a thick sheaf of papers with post-it notes demarking several pages. He picked up and said, "Samba here."

"Samba, this is Aruna. I would like to speak with you. I think you know why,"

Patel held up his hand and walked into the bedroom, closing the door behind him and said, "I am preparing to go over script with my costar. Can it wait?"

"What's her name?" Aruna asked.

"Priya Krishnamurty," he replied.

"Oh, yes, I saw her name and face on some posters at the studio," Aruna said, calmly, trying to ease into a position of control.

"Samba, I know you're a good person. I also know we need to talk. I prefer we meet sooner, before I begin to show."

Patel blanched and said, "Yes, you remember where I live?"

"I remember very well, especially the bedroom. I'll be over shortly," Aruna concluded.

Aruna looked at the others and exhaled audibly to be greeted by thumbs-up signs and congratulatory nods. Megan said, "Guess you better get going. Give us his address just in case, and keep in touch. Call no matter what the hour."

On a whim, Aruna changed into her blue sari before calling for a cab. When she arrived at Patel's home, a servant opened the door and led her inside. The servant disappeared, ostensibly to his quarters. Patel appeared, took her hand, and invited her to take a seat at the kitchen table while he played the dutiful host, bringing a fresh pot of tea and cookies to set on the table.

"What kind of tea are we drinking, Samba," Aruna asked, with such openness one might have thought the two were relatives.

"It's our own Darjeeling," Patel responded.

Aruna fixed her cup, took a sip, and said, "I like it. And I like you, Samba. Look, as Americans like to say, this isn't a shakedown. Do you know what that is?"

"Uh, no," he replied, warily, as though he did know the term, which sent Aruna's alarm bells ringing.

Aruna explained, patiently. "It is a term used by somebody who wants money from somebody because they want to file a false claim, like a poor woman pretending to be pregnant to get money from a rich man she slept with. Well, that's not me. I probably have more money than you do. What I want is you. Neither of us is married, you're 25 and should get married. As for the baby, we can wait until I can have a DNA test done to prove it's yours. Once the press finds out, it will be too late for you. I'll be fine. I'd rather share with you. Samba, I don't want the press to eat you alive. I am her to protect you and to marry you. By the way, do you have any other children I should know about?"

Patel looked shocked. Almost angrily, he replied, "God, no."

He looked at this woman who had garnered the world's attention over the years. She and her brother were ten times smarter than he was. She expressed sincerity and word had it her family was solid, although the father could be a problem, if the situation got ugly.

Aruna watched him carefully. The black haired beauty of a man was incredibly handsome and would remain so the rest of his life. No wonder women swooned over him. And the bastard could sing, too. She saw him caught in the web of fame, rolling with the punches, eating up the glory. In her estimation, they both needed to make personal adjustments.

She reached across the table to place one hand on his. A beautiful woman trying to find a purpose in life, feeling at home and feeling distant at the same time, trying to merge the two. She said softly, enticingly, "Samba, we can make a good team. Think about marriage, reorganizing your life. You know more about mine than I know about yours. I want you to meet my family tomorrow. They're here in Mumbai at the

Intercontinental. Say 'yes'. You'll like them." She wanted Sue to be present when Patel made his appearance because Sue could read people better than most. She should have taken up a career as a police interrogatory obviating the need for a lie detector.

Patel ran the flip-cards of his life from the beginning to the present, like a flip-book with each picture slightly different that the one before it leading to either an uncertain or a certain future. The moment to take a path in the crossroads was now. Only one path looked good, the one she was offering—a way out. The others promised embarrassing disaster of epoch proportions, possibly career ending. He had not come from riches, but his looks and years spent in small theaters, while working his way through school, led to his discovery by agents who trolled such theater houses.

A "pregnant" pause ensued, each evaluating, calculating. Both lives were in the balance. Aruna expected the man to hem and haw, to wait until he thought it over, to delay until he could consult his lawyer; but to her utter shock, he replied in that deliciously velvety voice of his, "Yes, I would like to meet them."

To Aruna, it seemed as though he had already thought it through and didn't need any help making up his mind, which spoke to his strength of character. Was it possible she would marry the right man?

In the end, Sue made the evaluation. Samba Patel loved his life of fame and glory, but felt diminutive in the presence of Raj, and he was lonely. His education in the theater arts gave him a shallow perspective on life. Like a career politician, he needed a part time job working at a Mumbai ship dismantling yard, or scavenging for trash at a dump site, or do a photo op in the middle of a war zone. Yet beneath it lay a good person willing to learn and importantly, willing to accept reality to begin a family with Aruna.

A similar meeting occurred at the Patel household when Samba met with his parents where family discussions were commonplace. The father was in the import-export business, although exactly what he imported and exported was open to question; the mother was a former beauty queen. Suspecting their only son had a problem, based on the tone of his voice in the call, the parents made adjustments to their schedule to accommodate his visit.

Seated at the end of a long mahogany table that frequently sat 16, the three family members were served coffee and biscuits along with an ample supply of sugar and cream.

The mother said, “Well, Samba, tell us what is on your mind. It must be serious.”

Samba nodded, “It is. A woman says I got her pregnant.”

The father scratched his beard and asked, “Is it true?”

"I believe it is," Samba replied.

"Did she say how much money she wants to go away?" asked the mother.

"It is not a problem. She has many millions already," Samba said.

"Who is she, another actress?" asked the father.

"Aruna Rossi," Samba stated.

"Aruna Rossi!" the parents chimed in unison.

The father began to laugh. "My, my, you do like to fly high don't you?"

The mother scratched her own chin, absent the beard. "It could be a good thing, my son. You're 25 and you should get married. It won't hurt your career to start a family, especially with her. If you treat her right, it's a no lose situation."

Samba sighed, "I am forced to come to the same conclusion. I met with her family, Megan and Tony, and Raj too, although Raj appears to be in his own world. They seem to be good people with good hearts. They want to keep us both safe from trouble, you know, keep this quiet."

The mother said, "You are certain it is your child?"

"Mom, I don't want to wait months for a DNA test. By then, it will be too late. And yes, it is mine."

The father said, "Then it is settled. Put me in touch with the parents so we can all meet and discuss the particulars."

The father stood. The conversation had ended.

Four days later, the Times of India published the following headline:

SAMBA PATEL TO WED ARUNA ROSSI

In what many are calling the wedding of the century, our two idols are joining forces in marriage. Samba said he has been in love with Aruna the moment he saw her and will dedicate his life to making her happy. Although she is an American citizen, Aruna intends to apply to our government for citizenship and belong to both countries. She said her love for Samba has nothing to do with his fame, but for who he is as a man.

The wedding is going to be limited to select friends and will be held in Agra in front of the Taj Mahal.

A movement is afoot to hang an emblazoned red-on-white banner at the entrance to the site that will read WELCOME TO THE RAJ MAHAL. (Reportedly, Raj himself, would not take part in festivities if the banner were present.)

Aruna insisted Melanie Brown of CNN be present and wouldn't take no for an answer. Samba announced that he and his bride want to start a family as soon as possible to begin their long lives of bliss.

Aruna has graced our airways with her brand

of shoes and her roles in a number of Samba's movies. She announced a new and improved model of shoe will soon become available, once her brother completes the retooling of the manufacturing plant.

Note: For a variety of our colorful postcards, pictures, and poster reprints soon to be available after the wedding, contact us at TimesIndiawedding/subscribe@TI.com. Pre-orders are accepted. Please reserve your selection early, as supplies may run out. Our price schedule is presented below.

4

Tony offered to take charge of enlarging the new plant to accommodate increased production of the plastic houses and the shoes until the wedding, while Raj insisted he be left to his own devices to work on his new projects. His mind held the blueprints. He needed to hook up with Roberts and Ajeet to put his plan into high gear. Ajeet would provide the materials, Raj and Roberts would work on the prototypes and the partnerships would be made with iPhone. Ajeet would make appropriate calls to ensure the device was manufactured entirely in India, probably in Mumbai, the financial capital of the country. Nothing would need to be imported.

Raj's idea was as complex as it was simple: meld existing technologies into one unit that would cover the bases. Improvement in technology over time would take care of the rest, like the model T-Ford to today's cars, like the biplane to the spaceship, like the first cell phone to the RAJ. Raj held the view that most of the hormones and enzymes identified in the blood can also be detected either through the skin or through breath analysis. His concept was to develop a wrist band with a slide opening like a roll-top desk to protect the phone screen and the search buttons. Thus it would combine a phone, TV, radio, eBooks, search engine, and blood monitors, which could be interchanged, as technology developed. A breath analyzer would be included for alcohol consumption purposes. The data would be absolute and also compared with the norms. The device could be voice activated.

The wearable would be approximately four inches across with a base of Spandex microfibers interlaced with sensors that would read for a variety of potential diseases such as cancer, blood sugar, estrogen, testosterone, serotonin, oxygen, carbon dioxide, diabetes, asthma, even autism, and whatever else came down the pipeline.

The real beauty was that, when in use, because it is inconvenient to turn the wrist in either direction in order to do extensive reading, the unit could easily slide down over a palm held flat for ease of reading, attributed to the Spandex component. Plus, it was hands free. No fingers were tied up holding a phone. And it was the ultimate wearable.

The couple moved back to Phoenix to enable Raj to work more closely with Roberts. Sue found herself almost a non-entity, used as a sounding board for her husband's monologues on data points. She'd had her fill. One evening at home she confronted him, lecturing him to find herself lapsing into a rant. She didn't care anymore and made it clear she loved him for what he was, not what he had become.

"And don't you dare tell me you're doing all this for me," she managed to throw in for good measure. She had a lot more to say if it came down to it. She was not going to lose this fight.

"I want children. I want a family. I want you to care about both of us as much as you do about your ideas. They will always be there, I . . . I may not be."

"What does that mean?" he asked, staring hard at her, with great concern.

"It means you taught me what it is to feel lonely" she shot. Tears began to stream. Crying was not in the game plan. Her words weren't true at all. She had plenty to do in her own fashion, but she had to make a statement strong enough to penetrate his thick self-absorbed skull. At least she had gained his full undivided attention. She was in the relationship for the long haul. She would prefer it to be a shared life, not each person for themselves.

Raj had been seated on the sofa confronted by an angry standing woman. He had never been reamed out so thoroughly. Even his parents kept it short when he overstepped his bounds. He stared at his wife, emotions changing from anger, to shocked disbelief, to guilt, to acceptance of the truth, and finally, to a deep feeling of compassion and true love. The robot had temporarily become human again.

Raj stood and put his arms around Sue, towering a full eleven inches over her. "You're right. Thank you for bringing me back to you," he confessed.

"I want children, Raj," Sue repeated.

"Yes, so do I," he whispered, caught up in the moment.

She led him by the hand, this time both of them willingly making an honest effort to create a new life.

Aruna did not find herself in such an endearing situation. After the shine had worn off, she found herself without a husband. His hours of work and his travels of the country kept him away from their mansion. Depending on the movie—which are cranked out at an amazing speed—he could be in any one of a number of terrains, of which India had an ample supply.

He could be gone for weeks at a time. When the scene required the local sound stage only, he would be home evenings for weeks at a time. Like Sue, the resourceful Aruna found many ways to entertain herself amid an endless array of servants who washed, cleaned, fed, and clothed her. Others drove, sanitized, repaired and gardened, as was their wont. The most populated country in the world hosted three times as many citizens in a land mass 40% that of the United States. Some 1.1 billion required employment.

She found herself living among wealthy people of multi-ethnicities from numerous nations, many quite educated in their own right who owned numerous homes spread around the world. She was host to them, while the baby inside her grew. Tapped into it all, she attended lavish parties, her presence enriched by the occasional appearance of her husband. At the insistence of Samba's marketing agent, Aruna played small parts in his movies, yet enough so that both could be featured together in the billing.

Yet she was alone. Finally, in the middle of a sleepless night, she paused to make a critical evaluation of her life. In a sense, she evaluated her present circumstance to be a shallow wallow in the realm of mediocrity. This is not to decry the intellectuals who surrounded her every turn; it is to evaluate her own goals in life.

She evaluated the amount of food she was served, the amount available to her at any given instant, and weighed the present reality against where she had come from. She felt uncomfortable. She evaluated the splendor and felt guilt. In a word, Aruna was unhappy. Samba Patel tried to be a good husband, yet his shallowness overrode his superficial efforts to keep up with his wife's intellect.

Living only a short distance from the west coast, the breeze constantly blew into her home, which she demanded remain open in order to capture the smell and to renew the vigor of her old romance with the sea. She yearned to take control of her life and swore to become familiar with what she saw as her future only minutes away.

When she arose, she called the family physician to reinforce what she knew about Dramamine. She found the old-time drug was commonly used by pregnant women to quell nausea. She then sent one her servants to go to a local pharmacy and obtain a number of tablets of the medication, after which she asked the family driver to take her to the Mumbai marina.

She told him to leave and await her call, which would be within two hours. He opted to wait curbside.

Aruna walked the marina looking for a craft, the size of which she had in mind. Among those she saw, several were being serviced by low-salaried workers; with one particular boat being detailed by a middle-age man dressed smartly. She took him to be the possible owner.

She saw the boat's brand as a Chris Craft. At 24' in length with a beam of 8', it had twin Evenrude outboards at 150 hp each. The name on the side of the boat said Dhoop, which meant Sunshine in Hindi. Not surprised to find the man spoke English, Aruna found the boat to be available by this man named Harsha, who, indeed, was the owner. Reportedly, he also owned a car dealership and was presently on vacation. He sold the standard black 4-door Tata Motors sedan and would she like to purchase one at a discounted price.

Aruna declined the one time offer, explaining that they already had one in the family. She offered him a better deal—$50 an hour to take her out. When she saw him pay particular note of her swollen belly, which gave him pause, she upped the offer to $100 an hour in American cash, pulling out five twenties and handed Harsha the bills.

Harsha could not hide his pleasure. To him, he would get far more on the black market exchanging the money than he would by exchanging it at the bank. His wife would be pleased to receive a portion of the windfall (relative percentage undisclosed).

Within twenty minutes, the boat had left the harbor and cruised northward up the coast making the round trip in the allotted time. Harsha showed her the operation of the radio and the GPS, letting her guide the dual outboard craft once they were well out of the marina.

She felt absolute exhilaration while doing so, at one point throttling the boat to a speed in excess of 30 knots. She felt alive as the wind whipped away her concerns. Feeling the surge in hormones, the baby inside her began to kick, wanting to get out so it could be part of the fun rather than being cooped up inside a warm body.

Harsha turned out to a long-time sailor with a great knowledge of the coastal tides and sea life. On the journey, he happily pointed out that the boat had a galley, a small bath, and sleeping accommodations, should she like to enjoy an extended journey. When Aruna told him she would pay him by check next at the same rate, she made a steadfast friend. The two exchanged cell numbers and a deal was struck.

Aruna's immediate goal was to gain her sea legs without the use of medication to quell her nausea. She had no desire to load her bloodstream with unnecessary drugs. She struck a compromise with herself in that she would go out with Harsha two to three times weekly for longer and longer periods while gradually cutting down on the pills, unless real life dictated she change the schedule. She did have civic functions, neighbors calling, and a husband to entertain.

She was in her third trimester and the worst of the morning sickness was over. She counted herself fortunate in that she wasn't one of those who suffered throughout the entire pregnancy.

She took advantage of that variable by going out for longer and longer periods each journey. Over the next six weeks she was able to spend most of the day aboard the vessel going out into rougher seas each time. That is, until the time came to slow down. Each day she found it more and more difficult to do anything out of the house, with staff and neighbors admonishing her not to bring bad luck into the household by doing things a pregnant woman should never do, of which a long list of no-nos was offered.

She needed to talk things over with Marie and especially her mother. She could be certain Samba would be chasing his career forevermore. There was nothing wrong with staying put to be a dutiful mother who gave up a career to raise a family. People did it all the time. Did she want join some oceanographic institute somewhere else in the world? There were a score she could choose from. If so, how would the child work into the change? Sonograms had identified the baby as a daughter, which is considered a negative because a dowry had to be given to the suitor's family upon marriage—that is, if she remained in India.

Samba's publicist reported that the baby would be some six weeks premature. No photos would be permitted for some time. The mother was coping. She wanted to raise her own child. If so, should she follow her heart? How to talk to Samba about it? Would he care one way or the other? Her head swam. One thing she couldn't do was to talk to well-meaning neighbors. If there was even a hint of trouble in paradise, the gossip would spread faster than a plague. If that happened, both of them would be in the middle of a scandal.

Megan suggested, "Honey, take care of the baby first. Stay home, be a good mother, bond with her. At the same time, you can continue your research. Download good journal articles on microplastics. Didn't you tell me there is a National Institute of Oceanography in your city? After a few months you can go out again. Whatever you do, Christina will be spoiled rotten by all the attention she'll get at home with or without your presence. Give it time. Other solutions may present themselves."

Reluctant at first to make the call to her mom, scratching at solutions like a chicken pecking for grains to eat, she now found herself looking at the mother lode. Her mom had rolled her concerns into one package and from the way it looked right now, it *should* work.

She wanted to share with her husband her vision of their future here in Mumbai, until she remembered he had left for an adventure movie to be shot in the state of Andhra Pradesh, the jungles of which were home to cobras, kraits, and 4"-8" red and black scorpions, all in abundance.

5

Test marketing of The RAJ to a thousand subjects provided a richness of feedback, primarily in terms of sensitivity of readouts. Even so, while retooling was in progress, The RAJs began to appear like "official" Rolexes sold on street corners in Mexico. It didn't take the three entrepreneurs, Raj, Roberts, and Ajeet, to re-strategize. Their product couldn't be publicized as introductory; it had to be reinvented using state-of-art technology so advanced their competitors would spend years trying to emulate. By the time that occurred, The RAJ would have established itself as the gold standard and would have been a publicly traded company.

The iPhone had brought in nearly 700 billion dollars. The potential for the RAJ was significantly greater. It could change the human landscape. Unfortunately, at the present time, the three, and their investors, were bleeding money. Raj understood the solution lay in the most simplistic manner. It had nothing to do with the nanos themselves, or little to do with the electronics on the wearer's device. It had to do with the receptors. It had to do with resistance/sensitivity of the skin to receive the signals sent by the nanos in the body to the receivers in the band. It had to do with vaporous chemicals leaching through skin to activate the receptors in the band.

In other words, the natural resistance of the skin impeded the signals. If a proper skin lotion could be applied beneath the wrist band, or alternatively, incorporated into the Spandex of the band itself, more information would be received and more disease-related compounds could be detected.

He also understood the role probiotics had played in his life since the early years. A huge percentage of the immune system is located in the gut, which is inhabited by a wide variety of life forms that shift their population through age. These life forms include bacteria, fungi, protozoa and viruses trigger signals for human-generated hormones to be produced leading to proper or improper mental and physical health. These affect mood, behavior, and sleep patterns. The proper balance of gut microbes is affected by diet. The old saw "you are what you eat" becomes truer the more we learn.

Nano bots were added to a new health-related sports drink in diluted form, the concentrations of which had been trial tested. The number of added bots was in dilution form lest the consumer try to overdose for unspecified reasons. These additives attached themselves to the lining of the gut and would send signals to the RAJ, alerting the wearer of a malfunction in the diet and would subsequently recommend an improvement, i.e., less red meat, more vegetables, nuts, and fruits, less processed food, more Vitamin C or B complex vitamins, and so forth.

While Roberts and his people concentrated on the design and Ajeet's team concentrated on the finer aspects of data collection, it was Raj who saw the grand vision. Because the device had a memory equivalent of a 512 gig thumb drive, it would open new vistas in medical research. In addition to serving the average man and woman for their daily needs, it would monitor before, during, and after episodes of people who had seizures; predict potential criminal behavior by signaling a rise in hormonal activity and could set off an alarm via noise, vibration, or flashing red light. It could provide new data bases in terms of averages within population groups.

These ruminations led Raj to a truth he had been avoiding. For him to be confident in his own product, he would have to use himself as a guinea pig. He would have to go off his daily meds, begin tracking before he did so, find a nice incoming storm system, not take any pink pills to suppress the body's responses, and see; no feel, the effects, while reading and recording the data. If that were to be the case, he decided it might be a good idea to discuss the matter with his wife; otherwise, she might contribute to a worse headache than he could imagine.

"You're going to do what without medication?" Sue challenged, wiping her hands on her chef's apron.

"Come on, we'll learn so much. You know we need the data," Raj responded. He hated confrontations. He walked over to the stew pot, dipped in a spoon, and took a taste. He turned to her and said, I've been monitoring myself for the past few days, ever since I stopped taking any meds."

Sue threw up her hands and said, "You did what? Say, is that your new gadget on your left wrist?"

"I wouldn't call it a gadget," Raj replied, shyly, defensively.

Sue glared at him. The man could be so straightforward at times and such a wimp other times. "Here's an idea," Sue returned, in a sarcastic tone, "why don't you get any one often million people to do the tests instead of you sacrificing yourself? If you're looking for me to take care of you, count me out. I am beginning to see you as a glutton for punishment."

Sue instantly regretted the words. What a terrible thing to say. It wasn't as though he was feeding himself to the lions. He had good altruistic reasons for what he was doing. She was about to apologize when Raj said, "Okay, just like the houses we built, I have to test my own product. If I personally don't do it for better or worse, how can I know what to tell people when I sell to them? Yes, I can pay a subject group to do it for me, but that's not the way I approach problems."

Giving up, Sue pulled out her phone and checked a couple of apps. With a smile, she said, "It looks like you're out of luck, my dear. No weather is expected in the Desert Southwest for the foreseeable future."

"I know. Check the east coast or the Pacific Northwest and tell me what you find out," he replied, objectively, without trying to be cute.

She did and shook her head sadly. This man was going to do his thing with or without her. Best she go along to keep an eye on him. She reported, "There is a storm system crawling up the coast of California and may not be a problem for several days yet. I'm going with you. If we go now to Washington State, we'll have enough time to prepare. Let's straighten up and start packing."

"I was hoping you'd say you would go with me. I want you to wear one. We need comparative data." He disappeared for a moment, dug into his briefcase, and pulled out another unit.

Sue dried her hands again and let him explain. "Wrap it around your wrist. It works better with the screen on the inside because the skin is thinner and the sensors can pick up more. Use the Velcro to attach it. You can slide it down onto your palm if you want. Now roll back the cover. See how it lights up the flex screen. It's as big as the one on your phone. You can set it for Apple or any android.

"This yellow button is for settings. You will be asked for age, height, weight, race and language preference. The latter two are so the device can match your data with that of others like you. It takes into account your ethnicity, which can pertain to diet and liquid intake preferences. In the future, we plan to include a listing of medications taken and amount of alcohol consumed. For now, experts warn us about using too many variables at first. The mini-camera lens is located at the top here. By the way, it is quite water resistant.

"The green button activates the hormonal sensors. Scroll down the list; it's alphabetical. Stop at the one you want to look at, give it 10 seconds to measure, and read the absolute and how it compares with norms for you and for everybody else in your category. By the way, as long as you wear it, your body is being continuously monitored.

"Sue, this thing can identify any disease you have from AIDS, to the common flu, chicken pox, malaria, cholera, a staph infection, or a bladder infection. It checks the function of your heart, liver, spleen, thyroid, kidneys, and prostate. Here's your download port."

Sue held up a hand to halt the presentation. She pushed buttons, went from a TV program, to average serotonin levels, to finally stop on a function that told what time it was. "Raj, can the average person navigate through all this?"

"It's no different than learning how to use a phone. There are billions out there who do it already. Think of all the medical advances coming out of this," he said.

"I hate to say it. I can see possible detriments," she told him.

Raj chuckled and said, "Of course. Initially, there will a lot of false positives and false negatives, especially when diseases are concerned, until we get it fine-tuned. This means doctors' offices will get flooded with calls. For that reason, we'll ensure the purchaser understands the RAJ is in its early stages.

"Also, data hackers will try to sell you ads to fix your specific problem, the pharmaceutical companies and health food stores will do quite nicely, some people will make a mountain out of a molehill, and vice versa.

"The worst outcome is that people will become addicted to it like the phone. They read it in the gym, or walking it across the street in traffic. Let them worry about that aspect. However, I believe our advancement in knowledge gleaned from this will add many years to our lives.

He concluded by saying. "We presently have translators who are creating a small startup manual for this in a number of languages. These translations will come with purchase of the device and will be in the form of a small booklet called, *Use of the Raj for Dummies.* Details of operation are stored in the memory. The one you are wearing runs a general scan and stops when there is unusual . . ." Raj hit the pause button and showed her the readout.

"What?" she said.

"It looks like your blood alcohol level is up a bit," he noted, teasingly.

Sue flushed, "You were here when I drank the wine, dear."

Raj continued reading the scan. He reread the data to query, "Hold on, you're pregnant?"

"It's a joke, right? I mean, how do you know?" she stuttered, leaning toward the screen. Raj said, "When the fertilized ovum attaches itself to the uterine wall, the signature HCG hormone is released into the blood stream. The most sensitive tests will detect the hormone 7-10 days after implantation. Obviously, most women won't discover they're pregnant until well after this time frame. This device is way more sensitive than a standard test."

"HCG?"

"Human Chorionic Gonadotropin."

"Could it be a false positive?" she asked, stunned and elated at the same time.

Raj said, "I doubt if anything can mimic HCG. We'll track it daily if you want. "

"If I want?" she threw out.

"Uh, we'll track it for *us*," he stammered.

Duly impressed by his presentation and the instrument, Sue unwrapped the device from her wrist and handed it back to her husband, thinking she might need to be one taking a stress pill if he didn't calm down soon. She grabbed him by the arm and said with great merriment, "Like I said before, let's get packing."

As he was being pulled along, Raj said, concernedly, "Let's do this right. I don't want to have to go through it twice."

On the three-hour flight from Phoenix to Seattle, Raj schooled Sue on the use of this multipurpose device each wore on their wrist, until she became thoroughly familiar with shifting from one mode to another. Both set their RAJs to Long-Term-Memory good for 30 days. He guessed a week should give them the information he sought.

Sue was deeply concerned from a number of standpoints. Megan had given her details about Raj's condition, more so than he had. Since the early days, his migraines were not as severe as they once were thanks to improvement in medications. This time he wanted to go the whole route, from start to finish, a full seven days, without any assistance at all because her cute husband wanted to record a bunch of numbers, including blood pressure changes. As he had explained, numerous chemicals were involved in the genesis of migraines (he didn't know which ones they were) however, one common denominator was the presence of serotonin, which causes vasoconstriction. The meds he took reduced the serotonin level and therefore vasoconstriction and concomitant rise in blood pressure. He wanted a closer look at this relationship.

Twenty minutes after unpacking in their hotel near the water front, the couple took a casual stroll along the Alaskan Way waterfront, selected a restaurant at random, and relaxed for an excellent meal of lobster and salmon. He tried to stay away from any food or drink that might act as a stimulant to affect any but very temporary readouts.

Data checking: blood pressure going up last 36 hours. barometric pressure beginning to drop, serotonin increasing, headache already beginning for Raj, no effect on Sue, the slow moving storm now hitting San Francisco, 800 miles down the coast, moving north at 15 miles per hour, more than two days until it makes landfall, an irrelevant fact.

Too early to hole up. Time to visit the space needle, take a tour, get back by dinner, stay in the lobby for maximum effect, read a book. Sue stays in lobby monitoring the rate of baro drop and other chemical functions, checks on Raj every couple of hours, then stays with him, pulls the blinds and turns off the lights.

Raj knew what to expect when the headache began in earnest. Sue fed him numbers until he couldn't process them any longer. It hurt too hard to think. Instead of fighting the vibrant colors floating among the numbers, he tried to relax and let them play out. This time he heard sounds above and below the normal frequency of hearing—harmonic overtone whistling sounds produced by lightning itself and by discords associated with the crack of thunder; sounds of the earth itself sighing, of the sun's outgassing, of the cosmos expanding, all expressing themselves in terms of colors.

At some point, he fell asleep. He awoke to see a dim light coming from a corner lamp. Sue sat in a chair reading. He must have moaned because she looked up and poured a glass of water from a frosty pitcher on a nightstand next to her. She sat on the edge of the bed, pulled his head up, and let him drink. "Do you want a cool compress?" she asked, gently.

He made a slight up and down motion with his head. The sound of the pouring rain came through the windows. She found a wash cloth, wet it thoroughly with cool tap water, wrung it out and placed it on his forehead.

"Thanks," he muttered and relaxed. She

knew better than to offer him any pill. He wanted this to play out. The way he was laying, she couldn't read data from his RAJ, so she returned to reading. Two days later, head still hurting, Raj worked on a cup of soup in the hotel restaurant scanning the data on his device and comparing it with the data on Sue's. Shooing away another waiter, he said, "Look, baby, you are more pregnant than you were before."

Sue feigned surprise, exclaiming, "Wow, let me write that down." She feigned scribing on an imaginary piece of paper.

Lost in his numbers, Raj gave a quick twist of his mouth in recognition of what she said and offered, "Blood pressure went up long before serotonin. Other chemicals are involved. These chemicals affect serotonin. Medication should be directed toward them specifically. Something associated with the storm activated them; lightning, negative ions, something. They are our targets. Once they are shut down with the proper meds, you're good to go. All you have to do is to follow your monitor."

"To do what?"

"I'm thinking one or more of these chemicals may precede all headaches. If so, there is a possibility the entire headache process can be shut down altogether for everyone," he told her.

6

Raj laid out his drawings on Ajeet's desk and proceeded to explain his idea in detail. The men spoke of electrons, microcapacitors and impedances for several minutes until Ajeet asked his guest to take his seat again.

He said, "While we were talking I am thinking. My friend, I am one step ahead of you. India is the second largest producer of cell phones in the world. We have six companies making phones. Our biggest one is called Metro. The plant is located in Jaipur, not far from here; less than an hour flying time. They employ 50 thousand workers. My best friend owns the company. In order to produce, say, a thousand of these, we'd have to pay a considerable amount because part of their operation would have to retool."

"We could upgrade their existing high end Metro. The sensory wrist band with the Spandex and the sliding cover would be the big addition," Raj offered.

Ajeet said, "If we gave him a million dollars

for his expenses, he'd turn it down. A million dollars comes to some 80 million rupees, which amounts to a few grains of rice in this game. We'll both have to save what we can to buy all the stock we can. As always, don't invest what you can't afford to lose."

Unperturbed by Ajeet's cautions, Raj suggested, "I'll see if my parents want to get involved. I want to keep this low key, maybe have your friend's own employees try out the prototype. Once we get feedback and make our upgrades, we could strike a deal with him to be the exclusive manufacturer. I'm sure he wouldn't mind."

"I like it." Ajeet beamed, delightedly. "What's your schedule for the next day or so? Want to see a cell phone manufacturing plant? Maybe have a conversation with the man himself?"

He'd heard Raj always played for high stakes. His inner voice flashed red, cautioning him the pendulum could swing either way on this deal.

This time it was Raj who beamed when Ajeet pulled out his cell to make the call.

Three years passed before the RAJ hit the market with a mega advertising blitz. Celebrities demonstrated the endless features of the devices.

The world was unprepared for the explosion of human behavioral changes poets would later say, "Rocked the planet to its molten core."

When tens, soon to be hundreds of millions knew virtually everything medical about themselves, it magnified an element of human behavior to such an extent societies changed overnight. This was immeasurably different from a thousand subjects testing a device to determine whether the electronics worked properly.

Suicides increased when many found, or perceived, a terminal disease was eminent. Thus, the funeral parlor business flourished along with that of attorneys who specialized in the drawing up of wills and estate management.

Everyone became a self-proclaimed expert in linguistics. In addition to the commonly used words serotonin, melatonin, melanin, progesterone. testosterone, estrogen, and diabetes, newer, harder to pronounce words associated with plastic became part of the vocabulary.

When ketchup was used with fries, the public became paranoid about the amount of sugar, onion powder, and saturated fat that flooded their bloodstream. When a can of soup was consumed, paranoia took hold pointing the finger at added salt; when farmed fish was consumed, the mycotoxin level of the blood increased from the contaminated grains fed to the fish.

And so it went product after product. The canning and bottling industries were set back on their heels. Sugar and salt industries took a major hit and jobs were lost in trade for better public health. Natural tuna was found to have more mercury than suspected; the farmed fish businesses from a number of Asian countries went bankrupt for similar reasons.

Elements detected included sodium, magnesium, manganese, lithium, cobalt, cadmium, lead, zinc, silver, gold, copper, aluminum, uranium, nickel, and a dozen others.

Litigation became more commonplace because more people were getting hit while walking across the street and suing the drivers, both of whom were reading their RAJs at the time of the accident.

Ads everywhere were rife with self-proclaimed experts, all of whom corresponded to the endless number of mom and pop stores claiming they had every herb to cure whatever ails you. Chinese herbal sales skyrocketed. Now everything ailed everyone. Business boomed. The names of new diseases couldn't be made up fast enough. OTC medications flew off the shelves. Permutations and combinations of good and bad factors were infinite.

7

For all of this, Raj could care less, because the human race could finally monitor the level of plastic in their bodies for the reason that micro-plastics already present in the blood and tissue from hard plastics would degrade into measurable chemicals. The studies he had read calculated the number of plastic particles inhaled by a human over a lifetime to be in the tens of millions.

Among many other points of contention, Raj added fuel to the issue of the bisphenol or Bis A firestorm. In particular, Bis A is used in food wraps, packaging, kitchenware, toys, dental materials, healthcare equipment, and even auto parts when he sided with researchers who conflicted with the U.S. government. It was and is used in plasticizers found in hair spray aerosols. Scientists from the FDA and the U.S. National Toxicology Program conducted extensive research and reported hard plastics were and are safe to use. Studies conducted independent from the government in the U.S., Scandinavia, and Europe, however, found it to be absorbed by the skin and inhaled to be subsequently metabolized by the liver. The resultant compounds interact with estrogen receptors to cause endocrine disorders, resulting in infertility in men and women and possibly exacerbating precancerous conditions. Researchers found the chemical to cause early puberty and contribute to a variety of cancers.

At one point, Raj wanted to redesign the RAJ to specifically detect the number of airborne nano plastic particles each person inhaled at any given moment. Unfortunately, he lacked enough clinical data to drive home the issue, as is usually the case in a nascent science. And to what end? The unfamiliar feeling of self-doubt slithered in. What plastics already existed had only begun the degradation process. It represented a minuscule percentage of the total number of particles life would have to endure forevermore. For a person to track the increase in numbers would result in more paranoia. He gave up on the idea.

The public was not told that each device had been encoded and the data were sent to a super-computer located the basement of the Metro production facility. If they had known, chances were good that few would care. The public had been aware for some time they were being spied on. Order a movie and the next day your TV is loaded with similar movies. Go online and everything is transmitted to the "Cloud" data base, accessible by "authorities" when a crime is committed, and so forth.

The collection of data was not done for nefarious purposes. The stats were correlated to determine the best health options for citizens that might fall in any one of many categories with the hopes of creating an easily accessible master chart that could be accessed via their personal RAJ. At least, these were the original intentions. Hackers thought otherwise.

As is the human condition, the public disbelieved the government's reports about no harm from exposure to hard plastics. Right vs. Wrong became an irrelevant issue. Get the damn stuff out our bodies, cried the public. Stop using it for manufacturing. But hundreds of thousands of jobs will be affected, cried the industry. They were right. Panic spread. Had we reached a tipping point the experts wondered?

The next generation, RAJ-2, would have an injection port to determine the level of lead in water, commonly used pesticides and chemicals associated with plastics in drinking water and streams, and a breathalyzer for diabetes, alcohol, asthma functions, Alzheimer's, and cancer precursors.

Self-monitoring became such a craze that congress was prompted to pass legislation, but elected representatives couldn't come up with anything to legislate for or against, since most members wore the device and happened to be in love with it.

By the age of 24, Raj had earned his first of many billions. This, while the Indian economy boomed. Raj, Ajeet, and Roberts obtained scores of patents, locking up their new technologies tighter than a miser's fist.

Coincidentally, in the same city from where the RAJ was shipped overseas, Aruna Rossi Patel got hired by the Oceanographic Institute of Mumbai to travel the length of the western coastal Indian waters to quantify the level of microplastics along the sea floor. She and her actor husband resided there with their daughter.

Aruna had not spoken to her brother in some time, taking a break from the intensity of his driven personality to seek a normal career and family life. She understood most couples were not in an idyllic marriage. Welcome to real life. So far, no crash and burn with Samba. No gossip to prove her otherwise. She did not watch television, preferring to spend her time with baby Christina and reading, or shopping at the Old Delhi marketplace and visiting with neighbors.

Wealthy as she was, she absolutely refused to be extravagant. With a certainty, she knew with only pennies to live on, she could be healthier than she was now because she would only purchase small quantities of foods containing the highest nutritional value. She had always appreciated the poorest of the poor for what they didn't have.

For her part, Sue Gardner Rossi had accepted her fate. She had given birth to a son, Tony Junior, to whom she devoted the majority of her time. She served as a sounding board for her husband, providing for his occasional ministrations, fearing he might seek culinary excellence for his next project in life. Her vast wealth meant little to her, but not so her husband. He coveted money to cover huge expenses required to navigate the shark-infested waters of higher business. For him, billions worked better than millions, if there were to be any chance of affecting change.

Aruna had just arrived home from a short trip up the coast to one of the great ship-dismantling facilities where cruise ships lay in all stages of dismemberment and where oil covered the water and the shore. Various parts were sorted by type and size over many acres. Workers climbed to the heights of the once great vessels risking their lives at every moment. Health or injury insurance was unheard of. From her hired boat, she had collected sea bed samples to be analyzed and data logged to determine the concentration of plastic in the sample and how far it had spread.

Seeing a number of people around her, each wearing a RAJ, she was prompted to touch base with Sue, rather than her brother. Knowing how persuasive he could be, she wasn't in the mood to get pulled back into his orb. He could be similar to three timeshare negotiators, skilled in the art of countering arguments, dedicated to selling you their product, oblivious to the fact that the client would kick himself, or herself afterward.

She made it a point to call Marie, who had her own married life. The last time they had spoken, her friend had told her that Stephan's appeal was denied. It went unsaid that each felt terrible about that fateful night. Marie's father had spent a fortune on legal fees trying to get his 20-year sentence reduced, but to no avail. Their family savings were gone.

"How much is a fortune?" Aruna asked.

"Hundreds of thousands," Marie told her.

Aruna could hear the ache in her voice.

After closing the call with Marie, Aruna changed her seagoing togs for more land worthy fashion wear. She called Sue, who was walking a toddler around a local mall. Sue paused to answer the surprise call. The two women hadn't spoken for several months, each lost in their own lives. The two chatted lightly for a few minutes until Aruna had the sudden impulse to invite her old friend over to her house. Surely, the two little cousins must meet.

Sue's driver stopped in front of the mansion. Once he assisted his charge and her toddler to the front door, he returned to the vehicle to await her return, quite happy to entertain himself with the latest soap opera, all streamed by the new RAJ he had purchased. He paused occasionally to check his vital signs. The data were streamed to the central Metro computer and relayed to the production company, who found great use in the feedback they received about particular scenes in the drama.

Fifteen minutes later, a tour of the home completed, the two women sat in comfortable lounge chairs on the second story balcony, while servants tended the children. Down below, a lap pool graced the back yard. In the distance, two cruise ships had pulled into port. Only a few miles distance separated the two behemoths brimming with vitality only miles from death by dismantling. The women drank Aruna's favorite Darjeeling tea, from an eternally ready pot.

"So this is what you have become," teased Sue.

"I'm sure you live in a shack too," Aruna teased in return.

"How's Samba treating you?" Sue asked.

"He's turning out to be a pretty good husband, certainly a lot better than those of a lot of married women I hang with," Aruna confessed.

Sue said, "Sure, when he's home. What about when he's away?"

Aruna grinned sheepishly, "He knows I have eyes on him. That helps. By the way, speaking of abject poverty, where is my brother these days?"

Sue snorted, "He's back over in Mohali

meeting with an Indian guy named Ajeet we met in Punjab a while back. He heads a major nano research facility. From all the data they're getting in from this RAJ, they're cooking up a new scheme," Sue said.

"Like what?" Aruna queried, mystified.

"All I know is, in addition to making big upgrades to his current best seller, he wants to develop a more sensitive model to fit on the forehead," Sue reported.

"The head? What the hell?" Aruna declared, trying not to spill her tea.

"One can only imagine," Sue replied. She finished her own cup of tea, set down the empty, and, smiling sweetly, added, "Trust me, by the time I get finished with him, he'll see the error of his ways."

Aruna scoffed, "Hah, good luck with that."

Adverting blitzes jump-started the RAJ. Some investors were wary of yet another flash startup, promising everything, yet delivering nothing, until sales skyrocketed. The damned gadget seemed to deliver as promised. Like the cell phone, it served to accelerate the near elimination of the knowledge base and ability to reason. Why do math in your head when you can look up the answer? Although families occasionally sat together for meals, members talked less and looked at screens more.

If the cell phone blazed the trail, the RAJ

paved the super highway. Of the nearly 1.8 billion smartphones sold worldwide each year for the past ten years, the RAJ raced to take over some 40 percent of the market share, and was growing explosively year after year. China, the US, and India, accounted for over 700 million of those sales followed by Indonesia, Russia, and Brazil. Another 14 countries made up the bulk of the remainder.

The devices couldn't be sold fast enough. In some instances, national infrastructures were improved to ensure delivery of the new instruments. Discounts were offered for trade-ins and India reaped the harvest, now with enough capital to pour into other elements of its technology sector.

Inevitable knockoffs soon appeared. One brand contained an added feature. Music apps from around the world could be played by anyone without the presence of an earphone jack. Voluminous annoying sounds soon permeated every airway to the extent that governments had to outlaw the production of the knockoff devices. This action had profound effects on the public's right to continue use of their existing knockoffs and listen to whatever music they chose.

The Notifications App constituted another annoying and socially disruptive factor. This App gave the user free rein to receive a signal (sound to be chosen) when various wanted or unwanted criteria were reached. For example, when trans fat, potassium, and blood glucose levels were stabilized, or unstabilized (according to "norms"), the alarm would sound. Or, when testosterone, serotonin, and any other variable were maximized, the signal would be given. Each individual could choose any number of variables he or she thought might be helpful for their knowledge base. Alarms or chimes were going off annoyingly at all hours and in all venues. Updates were installed on a monthly basis; a feature as much anticipated as an exciting episode of a favorite TV series.

With so many improved nano sensors in operation the NCAA found that virtually everybody used *something,* or was suspected of using something, whether it be steroidal or non-steroidal athletic enhancers and was on the verge of going out of business as it banned athletes. Soon, the following organizations found many, if not most, athletes to be ineligible to participate in their respective sports: IOC, FIFA, NCAA, NBA, WNBA, MLB, NFL, WBA, UFC, and WWE, to name but a few.

Sports nearly disappeared altogether, until an enraged public forced the NCAA to finally say, "To hell with it." In a surprise twist, which many suspected might be related to a loss of cash flow to the organization and its staff, the NCAA finally passed a bylaw permitting anybody to use anything anytime they wanted. Curiously, only a relatively few decried this proclamation. It quickly filtered sideways and upward to the topmost level until the clarion reached the International Olympic Committee. Done deal.

The public now could enjoy new record-breaking performances, as athletes at every level of competition tried to test the limits of the human body. Sports became to the go-to most discussed topic of the public at large; that is, after accounting for individual nuances relating to daily health. None of which harmed the sale of a new generation of OTC medications directed toward the sports-minded consumer at large.

When set to present large size readouts, joggers and serious runners could pace themselves and skiers could check their speed in either miles or kilometers per hour and distance traveled. GPS could prevent becoming lost and enable one to be found, or could direct one to any location. The RAJ was the perfect present for birthdays and holidays.

Loss of connection with the world (read nature) had profound effects on humans who were, until recently, a social species. If ignorance was bliss, then the world could not have been a happier place. Instead of social interaction, entire populations became introverted, communicated less, divorced more, lost more jobs, became less educated, and backslid to new lows. School grades were further adjusted to accommodate the lowest performers to avoid hurting feelings, a practice already well in place. Work production lessened and entire economies faltered—the average human mind was in lockdown. All this, while technology plodded onward, as is the nature of man.

The super-computer provided constant updates, so much so that each category and sub-category provided the average consumer, now awash in data, the latest in data inputs minute-by-minute. This compelled him or her to constantly follow their wellness status. In short, everybody became an expert in everything relating to health, nutrition, food additives and preservatives, biological functions, life expectancy, death expectancy, and whatever else the human mind could conjure up. This sum of this information overwhelmed the mind, which soon morphed into a variety of psychological illnesses.

The end result was the creation of a state of super-hypochondria in the fragile human psyche, significantly worse than that which occurred during the Covid-19 pandemic. The term "Hyper-Involvement" or HI became the term of choice by clinicians and talking heads, who themselves, waved about the devices as they spoke.

To make matters worse, because the RAJ was classified as a wearable, it became the norm to wear it to bed just in case one wanted to check their vital signs should they awaken during the night. And if awake, why not watch a movie or a recorded sports event? Thus, sleep deprivation and it attendant symptoms overtook the workforce. Road rage and traffic accidents increased, as did insurance rates and lawsuits.

Metronomics introduced a bluetooth connection between the wrist band and small TV monitors to be posted on every device in gymnasiums to enable wannabe athletes to have something about which notes could be compared. The athletic centers soon overflowed with clientele. Others, more astute, decried any personal electronic device within their establishment which resulted in members who were more fit and robust than their counterparts.

If the "ordinary" cell phone were left behind, one felt naked. If the RAJ were left at home, a person felt useless, without purpose, without knowing their body's chemistry, or note being able to compare notes with anybody, especially spouses. There was nothing to talk about otherwise. Their soulmate had momentarily disappeared; that organism whose single function was to provide life-giving information. Survival through the day might be up to question. A pale area on the forearm demarked the location of the absent device, like a wedding band gone missing. Pens, pencils, note paper and even the printed word were becoming obsolete.

With the exceptions of death by pestilence and wild beasts, early man was better off than his modern counterpart. Ancient man knew threats, felt the sunlight, cherished the bonded family, fought for food, and protected his territory. Modern man had no family, had food provided for him, sacrificed his well-being for the vagrant, sought no sunlight and in his quest for knowledge, became more ignorant while doing so.

8

The wealthiest family in the world sat at an elongated dinner table in the old house in Phoenix. The kitchen had been extended to accommodate an add-on room constructed over the old swimming pool to accommodate the table. The residence was now walled in with security cameras and alarms serving as hidden outdoor decor. Police cruisers frequented the neighborhood.

Sue and Megan had prepared dinner. At the table sat Tony and Megan, Raj, Sue, and their two children, Christina, Hans and Klara, along with Aruna and Samba and their three children. No cell phones or RAJs were permitted at meal time, no chance to check health updates or the latest violence somewhere in the world. No gossip. No he-said she-said. No ring chimes or vibrations going off. The topics centered on the physical and educational health of the children.

Samba had ridden his fame to further fame. The actor had visited with kings and queens, yet he felt dwarfed in the presence of the entire Rossi clan. He knew when to direct and when to act. At the moment he did neither.

Aruna said, "Dad, I've been thinking a lot about what Cragmore wrote way back. He was wrong in his condemnation of God. He was confusing God with a fundamental human need for spirituality in our search for the meaning of it all. There is nothing wrong with that. It binds us to nature, to our planet, to art, it sparks our creativity, it eases the pain of death, it helps us live with suffering and the unexplainable, it gives us a purpose and it has nothing to do with how smart you are."

Raj began to laugh. He held up a hand to Aruna as an indication his response wasn't about her, and offered, "She's absolutely right. How often do we encounter a group of people who, for a short time at least, isolate themselves from outside influences, laughing, enjoying the moment? I call this spirituality." He swept his arm outward to include the entire group.

Tony set down his soup spoon and asked, bemusedly, "What do you think about your trade off now, Raj, Aruna?"

Aruna responded first by saying, in her philosophical note, "I'd say we saved the individual and lost humanity."

Raj shrugged, saying, "I'm quite certain we lost them both. And, by the way, I've decided on my next project."

All eyes turned to the world's richest man to

see what words of wisdom might be written into posterity. He proclaimed, "I've decided to start a community where no WiFi or Internet exists, except for surgical rooms and the like. We go back to landlines for communication and libraries for learning; no social media permitted."

Sue leaned into Aruna and whispered, "Where would the countries be today without the RAJ?"

Aruna replied, delicately, "We'd have half a planet full of zombies."

Sue grunted and threw in, rhetorically, "What do you think we have now?"

Klara said, "I know everybody has investments and we've all donated well to our causes. It seems to me, though, with all your money, Raj, you could buy an entire country, not simply develop a community."

Raj frowned. He knew he had screwed up royally. It continually ate at him. Typically impetuous, his fatal flaw was not projecting ahead to envision consequences of what his endeavors might entail.

How could anybody so smart be so stupid? Sue had once told him he was penny wise and pound foolish. Aruna wasn't vocal enough to say the same words. Sue was right. He had always refused to accept his flaws; he might acknowledge them briefly, then vacate the painful feelings in light of the greater picture. It was earlier to rationalize his actions by priding himself in creating plastic houses to affect a lot of lives for the better. He saw that as a shallow enterprise, noble but shallow.

Now that a few years had passed, he could finally admit that the RAJ had sped up the inevitable decline of civilization. Like the atomic bomb, others were well on their way to creating a variation of the same outcome in their effort to create the same disastrous results. Whatever, Raj's fingerprints were all over the decline.

His father had once told him that there is usually a vast difference between what one expects and reality.

Like the creation of more trash overtaking that which was recycled, so would man's effort to support the advent of technology advance the decline of his intellect. Man was still the same animal as he was 50 thousand years ago. The addition of a lot of toys made up the only difference. To his mind, all else remained equal.

There was no going back, isolated community, or not. He fantasized the creation of a community like the one described in Ray Bradbury's *Fahrenheit 451*, where people recited memorized books after all others had been burned, in an effort to reverse their mistakes. Too little too late, or was it. *"Sometimes, when you try to do the right thing, you only make the situation worse.* More words of wisdom from his father.

There was another slight problem. His engineers had told him to expect the super-computer to crash at any given time. Millions of jobs would be lost, jobs associated with the manufacture, sales, and distribution of the RAJ; jobs dependent on the data provided; people who depended on the accuracy of the data to give their lives meaning. Chaos would ensue. Raj would have to find a way out.

Because data calculations were based on factual input by the consumer, at least two insurmountable hurdles were confounding the machine's ability to process data. These included false input by more than half the users regarding the true amount of alcohol they consumed, and the illicit drug usage injected, ingested, consumed, or inhaled. The ibuprophen, acetominophen, oxycodone, aspirin, and all occasional pills taken must be logged. Each and every one caused some change by itself or in combination with something else.

The failure to input these data was attributed to an inherent human suspicion of over-watch by authorities, which made them reluctant to tell the entire truth about their lives. The computer saw unknown variables it could not process, especially as the number of users increased, which pointed to meltdown as the only option. Once that happened, Raj would be a marked man; indeed the entire family would feel the wrath, when a large percentage of the world's population screamed bloody murder at the failure of their device, attracting international class-action attorneys galore, unless Raj came up with a true game changer. Even so, could it be trusted?

Raj had a sudden perverse thought in that in a strange twist of fate, at level 10, the computer would actually win the game by abdicating.

Wondering how many could read the pain in his eyes, Raj tried to inject levity into the conversation by saying, "I don't know how to go about finding a country to buy let alone how to make it work. As dad would say, 'I'm just a simple guy trying to make it from one day to the next."

He was unperturbed by the ensuing round of laughter. At least they were laughing with him. Raj had to go on. Gathering himself in a desperate attempt to redeem himself, he asked, "Do you know what the greatest killer is of mankind?"

"Cancer," offered Hans.

"No."

"Respiratory infections," contributed Megan.

"No."

"Heart attacks," chimed Aruna.

"No, it's poverty," remarked the scientist, with great knowledge. "It kills more people than all the others combined. I have a few ideas toward that end. What is not renewable is sand, petroleum, glass, coal, and metals. What is renewable is ordinary tree mulch.

"Question: If nobody rakes up leaf debris in our forests, which have incredibly rich soil, why do we rake up leaf fall in our yards. Leaves are a natural fertilizer. In the US alone, 10 million tons of leaves fill 700 million large plastic bags, all of which go into landfills. That's delusional. We're doing exactly the opposite of what should be done.

"So, instead of dumping the leaves and their bags in our landfills, we resuse the bags and use natures' fertilizer in new industries I have in mind. One is directed toward creating a whole line of durable inexpensive products from their cellulose, of which 15% is present. Their nutrients will also be applied toward farming. No more importing fertilizer from foreign nations. The leaves will be brought to local centers for their new applications and I'm looking for investors."

Eyeballs around the table to meet other eyeballs. To Raj's chagrin, no hands were raised. The only gesture came from Sue, who slapped a palm to her forehead and audibly moaned, "I do believe I feel another headache coming on."

This time nobody laughed.

Other Books by Mark R. Sneller

Greener Cleaner Indoor Air – 2nd Edition

"This book may save your life" *Doris J. Rapp, MD*. Written for the layman, GCIA2 is acclaimed as the best indoor air quality book ever written for the layman. With 120 chapters, it covers such topics as the basics of allergy and asthma, allergens in schools, pets, air filtration, fragranced products, pesticides, mold, which products to purchase, chemicals in the house, vacuuming, proper housecleaning, the worst rooms of the home, health tips on buying and selling the home, pesticides, and much more.

The Mars Virus

In Lincoln, Nebraska, cancer researcher Jason Randolph and his geologist friend, Don Jennings, decide to search for life in a meteorite the geologist found in Antarctica years before.

What's the worst that can happen? Everybody tried it, from NASA to the Russians, *and nobody found a thing,* until Randolph discovers the virus and it gets loose.

Unwilling to admit the truth, Randolph is reluctant to tell the world a simple fact: He had inadvertently released a living nightmare threatening not only mankind and all life on Earth, but the stability of the planet itself.

Once the genetic mutations begin, Randolph and Jennings try to make hay before the sun stops shining.

The Persian Connection

Mad-Cap research scientist and adventurer, Jeffrey Shenero, finds himself caught up in a terrible plague sweeping across a large portion of the nation, as countless evaporative coolers begin exuding a green slime that smells like dead fish. A dark cloud of disease-causing insects in astronomical numbers surround every affected home, driving the residents to the streets, filling the hospitals with diseases, some originating from the African continent. Tent cities crop up everywhere.

His pending fatherhood leaves Shenero reluctant to become engaged in solving the problem, while his alluring doctor wife, Carmen, tries to counsel him. Assisted by their Swedish researcher, Ingrid, the three find themselves in constant disbelief as new developments occur almost daily.

Mike Sutton, a tortured war hero with PTSD, who services the coolers involved in the epidemic, is reluctant to assist them and is thought to be behind a suspected plot. Unbeknownst to anyone, the plot turns out to be much deeper than any of them thought. International forces are at play to bring down the United States, while Jeff and his crew chase false leads, until Jeff is forced to play hard ball, with the assistance of the Department of Homeland Security.

Miners' Revenge

At the age of 16, Draco Harwood killed a man. Frightened and not wanting to return to school, he followed the advice of his mining father and joined the profession. Over time, he grew to have great physical and inner strength, all the while trying to redirect an underlying anger.

Wronged on a mining job in New Zealand, he vowed vengeance, but knew it would take time to bring his plans to fruition. He learned that revenge takes patience. With his close friend Josh Alday, the two work various mines in a several countries, preferring mobility to growing roots. Suddenly, they find themselves embroiled in an international conspiracy with themselves and their loved ones in peril, as attempts are made on their lives.

Gaining money through their poker-playing skills, the two hardened men earn enough to plunge deeper into the conspiracy now threatening the safety of the entire world.

The Mongolian

Sequel to Miners' Revenge

Considered wealthy by some, Anna Chan, an American born Chinese woman, is freshly out of college. On a whim, she signs up to teach English overseas. Hoping to get sent to the glitter of Hong Kong or Beijing, where she can speak Cantonese and enjoy the trappings of the life she is accustomed to living, she finds herself being sent to Mongolia, the birthplace of the famous Genghis Khan.

Trying to come to grips with her emotions, she finds her appearance blends well with the native citizens in Ulan Bator, their capital city, the coldest and most polluted city in the world.

Unexpectedly, she meets David Alday, a foreign chemist with a mining background who was sent to Mongolia to stop a Chinese takeover of a new project that will save the lives of countless Mongolians. The couple bond, until Anna is transferred northward to the edge of Russia and into the cold Russian wind to further her teaching, separating the couple.

From the windswept plains of Siberia to the Gobi desert, the two struggle to maintain contact in an upside-down world filled with romance and personal challenges, in a third-world country that is secretly hiding the city of the future. There, the couple must play a vital role to save an entire country.

Strange Adventures

Tales of fantasy and science fiction including:

The Fight at the Poker Game
A world traveler gets more than he bargained for

New Colony
Invading another planet doesn't always go well, even for aliens

The Magical Powers of Laszlo Pearce
A boy discovers he has magical powers. The problem becomes, what to do with them

Entity
A young camper is introduced to a being from the outer universe

Split Times
Where the past and the future collide head-on

Telepathy School
Sometimes telepathy is not all it's cracked up to be

Time Zone
A married couple crash-land on a bizarre time-warped planet

The Mushroom Caves of Palau

Jammed in a flooding tunnel, a scientist is surrounded by psychedelic mushrooms

Soap Opera

A galactic news agency broadcasts the latest scandals, even those that occur on Earth

About the Author

Mark Sneller, PhD, is a former professor of microbiology and medical mycology. He lives in Tucson, Arizona, where he operates Aero Allergen Research, a company specializing in indoor air quality and the identification of mold in contaminated buildings. He is the author of several health-related books, as well as the Jeffrey Shenero series of adventure novels.

www.ingramcontent.com/pod-product-compliance
Lightning Source LLC
LaVergne TN
LVHW021219080526
838199LV00084B/4266
* 9 7 9 8 9 8 8 1 5 8 8 4 4 *